I0819113

Praise for

the EPIC STORY of EVERY LIVING THING

A *Kirkus Reviews* Best Young Adult Book of the Year
A *BookPage* Best Young Adult Book of the Year
A *Booklist* Editors' Choice
A Chicago Public Library Best Book of the Year
A Bank Street College of Education Best Children's Book of the Year

★ "This **gorgeous coming-of-age novel thoughtfully examines questions of identity, family, kindness, and a longing for connection.** . . . Also deftly and empathetically engages head-on with anxiety."
—*Kirkus Reviews,* starred review

★ "Caletti's bighearted novel, which endorses the wonders of being present . . . uses two seemingly perpendicular voyages to **expertly navigate themes of belonging, connection, family, and identity.**"
—*Publishers Weekly,* starred review

★ "Through this novel about overcoming fear and expectations, **Caletti examines what makes a person**—is it their DNA, their lived experiences, or the family who raised them?"
—*School Library Journal,* starred review

★ "[A] heartwarming and authentic story that's packed with a collage of well-researched detail, people, and themes. . . . **Will find itself right at home in collections with strong contemporary YA.**"
—*Booklist,* starred review

★ "Caletti's **sophisticated, intricate storytelling** brings complexity and richness. . . . Both deeply introspective and profoundly engaged with the world." —*BookPage,* starred review

"**A rich, contemplative story** about looking beneath the (literal and figurative) surface to find love, purpose, and joy."
—*The Horn Book*

Praise for

PLAN A

A *School Library Journal* Best Young Adult Book of the Year
A *Kirkus Reviews* Best Young Adult Book of the Year
A YALSA Top Ten Best Fiction for Young Adults Title

★ "Extraordinary. . . . Offers **a powerful argument for choice,** bolstered by an exploration of women's oppression and strength, told through a personal lens: It's an individual story through which many readers will find universal commonalities. . . . **Brilliant and multilayered; an absolute must-read.**"
—*Kirkus Reviews,* starred review

★ "Through Ivy's frank first-person narration, Caletti offers a matter-of-fact exploration of abortion and its use cases, **interweaving myriad perspectives on pregnancy and body agency with a deft and nonjudgmental approach.**"
—*Publishers Weekly,* starred review

★ "*Plan A* nails several elements, from the true-to-life and engaging voice to the tight handle on the nuance in the people who hold contrasting opinions. . . . **Dynamically painted with detail, as well as Ivy's sharp observations.**"
—*Booklist,* starred review

★ "What really makes this story shine are the main characters. They are relatable and multifaceted, and the ways in which they love and support one another feel deep and meaningful. **An accessible, powerful portrayal of the importance of choice. A must-read.**"
—*School Library Journal*, starred review

"Caletti **approaches a provocative subject with humanity, nuance, and compassion**; here, Ivy's story is deeply personal but also contextualized within women's stories throughout history."
—*The Horn Book*

Praise for

True LIFE *in* UNCANNY *Valley*

★ "Caletti **combines a coming-of-age narrative with a buoyant summer romance and a technological mystery** to craft an intriguing novel about figuring out one's place in the world."
—*Publishers Weekly*, starred review

"Caletti compellingly explores big questions about class, the ethics of AI, and the price people pay for depicting perfect lives online. But Eleanor's **poignant vulnerability** with those around her as she yearns for a family that will truly accept her is the real focus, easily bringing readers into her corner. . . . **An at times heartbreaking but ultimately hopeful story about chosen family.**"
—*Kirkus Reviews*

"Caletti's latest offering builds into **a fast, complex read that feels both classic and topical** as Eleanor discovers her own sense of self, separating the imperfections of her parents from her own identity, and comes of age in **a thoroughly enjoyable summer read.**"
—*The Bulletin*

"From the first lines, Caletti continues to share her gift of dropping her reader seamlessly into the scene. . . . This story asks **timely and important questions about the origin and nature of AI.**"
—*Booklist*

"**Her questions are likely to prompt readers' own** about how to know what to believe, and about what makes AI (or anything else) go 'from cool and interesting to creepy and disturbing.'"
—*The Horn Book*

ALSO BY DEB CALETTI

True Life in Uncanny Valley

Plan A

The Epic Story of Every Living Thing

One Great Lie

Girl, Unframed

A Heart in a Body in the World

Essential Maps for the Lost

The Last Forever

The Story of Us

Stay

The Six Rules of Maybe

The Secret Life of Prince Charming

The Fortunes of Indigo Skye

The Nature of Jade

Wild Roses

Honey, Baby, Sweetheart

The Queen of Everything

You, Me, and Infinity

DEB CALETTI

 Labyrinth Road | New York

Labyrinth Road
An imprint of Random House Children's Books
A division of Penguin Random House LLC
1745 Broadway, New York, NY 10019
penguinrandomhouse.com
getunderlined.com

Editor: Liesa Abrams
Cover Designer: Ray Shappell
Interior Designer: Michelle Gengaro-Kokmen
Copy Editor: Clare Perret
Managing Editor: Rebecca Vitkus
Production Manager: Natalia Dextre

Library of Congress Cataloging-in-Publication Data is available upon request.
ISBN 978-0-593-70865-1 (hardcover)—ISBN 978-0-593-70868-2 (trade pbk.)—
ISBN 978-0-593-70867-5 (ebook)

The text of this book is set in 11.25-point Adobe Garamond Pro Regular.

Manufactured in the United States of America
1st Printing

The authorized representative in the EU for product safety and compliance is
Penguin Random House Ireland, Morrison Chambers, 32 Nassau Street, Dublin D02 YH68,
Ireland, https://eu-contact.penguin.ie.

To Oliver Paul

Chapter One

"Hello from the children of planet Earth."
–Greeting from Nick Sagan, age six

People don't usually talk in there, or even make eye contact, so right away I knew you were special. You were sort of slouched down in the chair when I came in. Wearing your old classic Levi's and your bright yellow sweatshirt, the shade a kid would pick for drawing the sun. It really set off your hair, your black curls springing in every direction. You could pat those curls and they'd bounce right back up, but of course I didn't know that yet.

I slipped my backpack off my shoulder and took my usual place by the table of magazines. You looked up and gave me a half grin. "You celebrating?" you asked.

It was a strange question, given where we were. Not a lot of celebrating happened in there, I was pretty certain.

I squinched one eye. I worried I'd find myself on the bad end of a joke. The end where someone's making fun of you. At times, I was prickly and on guard, which was partly why I was there, probably. When people looked at me—quiet, smiling—they thought they were getting a flower. Something you could approach or even pick to bring home and stick in a vase. I was supposed to be a flower—then, surprise, a cactus. Don't come close.

"National Depression and Anxiety Week," you said.

"I thought that was every day," I replied.

You smiled all the way then. A big smile that went all the way to your eyes. Why that's so rare, I'll never know. Those things are supposed to go together, but sometimes there's no twinkle.

It got a little embarrassing for a second. Awkward. We both were awkward in general. Me more than you, okay, for sure. I looked at the clock on my phone. I was early. I was always early. Being only on time made me nervous, since it wasn't early enough. On time was practically late. But mostly I looked at my phone because your cuteness was filling up the whole room, and so was my embarrassment. Everything cringeworthy about myself had sort of busted my seams and was rising, like those films about the *Titanic*, the ocean surging into the rooms.

You got up, went to the watercooler. You pulled one cup from the stack, and, like, ten tumbled out and fell away from each other, rolling on the floor. Haha! It was wonderful; it made me like you right away, but still, I blushed in empathy. There was some frantic clutching and crawling as you gathered the cups, including one that had escaped under the nearby love seat. I watched your adorable Levi's butt scoot around. Then you rose again, in a moment of *now what*. You held the unruly cups in your hands, wearing the expression of a baffled dad with a newborn. You glanced at me, and I looked down again quickly, as if I didn't even notice the whole hilarious show. I punched at my phone to appear completely immersed and accidentally tapped some game I'd installed but never used. Suddenly, there was a blare of excitable cartoon music. A very loud blast of inappropriate, circus-like mania.

So, we were a pair.

I peeked. Well, anyone would. Your energy, you know. You crumpled up the extra cups and dropped them in the trash like a criminal hiding the bags of cash. The kind of criminal who's too guilty and full of remorse to be very good at being a criminal.

You pulled the little blue lever, and the water flowed into the tiny cup. I prayed that this went well. No more humiliations. The watercooler sent up a big, burping bubble.

"Glug," you said.

I quietly snort-laughed. You laughed, too. My phone—so pretend-riveting—changed to 2:59.

Dr. Quentin Baleaf, the other guy, opened his door and came out. I had Winnifred Evans, MSW. I don't think she was an actual doctor, and she was always late, but I liked her. She had a big, cushy bosom, as comforting as an old sofa, and an aquarium that didn't smell the best, and those plants called spider plants that can give you the creeps, as they are indeed spidery. But she was nice. Dr. Quentin had a gray beard and round glasses, and always wore a cardigan, even when it was summer, and that's about all I knew.

"Mars?" he said.

Mars.

You.

You raised a hand in my direction, a *later* gesture that seemed supremely confident. I could tell even then that it was uncharacteristic. You looked slightly embarrassed that you'd done it. Mars, with the heartbreaker hair and the sexy jeans—you were, above all else, a dweeb, a one-hundred-percent, rare and beautiful, dweeb.

You followed Dr. Quentin Baleaf. The door shut.

All at once, I felt something in my chest, like a landmass shifting.

I typed *National Depression and Anxiety Week* into my phone. It actually *was* National Depression and Anxiety Week. Well, more accurately, National Depression and Anxiety *Awareness* Week. I wondered which one of those you had, or if it was something else entirely. I wanted to know more. Like, the whole story. Twinkling eyes are like stars, aren't they? With the possibility of a million more, a whole universe.

I made note of the day and time, you better believe it. It was my usual appointment day, but I already had a plan. I would come exactly that early for my next appointment. I never saw you there again, though.

Still, I already had the odd feeling that I'd never forget you. Winnifred Evans said a lot of things about feelings—that they weren't facts, and that they didn't last. That you had to hang on through them sometimes, because they'd change. Disappear, even.

She never mentioned, though, that some feelings *do* last. A feeling like love could. It seems unbelievable that, against all odds, against all circumstance, against all possible distance, unimaginable distance from the Earth and the sun, it could remain. No matter where either of you were in the great galactic sea, and no matter if it was 2:59, or forty-five years, or timeless time, love could be the same thing as infinity.

Chapter Two

Footsteps, Heartbeat, Laughter: *Sounds of Earth*

I was in the room with you a whole six or seven minutes, but I couldn't shake that encounter. It was as if something moved in that wasn't going to move out. I told myself that this was ridiculous, because of course it would leave me. With enough time, I'd forget it ever happened. How much of your life do you really remember anyway? Not much. And what you hold on to—even those memories are unreliable. I always went on about how much I loved my second-grade teacher, Mrs. Carterett, until Addison, my best friend and some years my only friend, reminded me about the time I raised my hand to say that only the *worker* honeybee died after stinging. After she was corrected like that, Mrs. Carterett said, *You're a little stinker, aren't you?* and grabbed my arm hard enough to leave fleeting marks, like indentations in rising bread. You have to be careful about embarrassing certain people. *And you didn't tell your parents*, Addison said, and then it all came back. How I was sure that this would only lead to two equally drastic outcomes: my mother suggesting it would have been better to be quiet, my father going to school and making a scene. My only option was to just be so good, it never happened again.

The point is, stuff faded, good and bad. I was being silly, carrying around some sense that I was on the alert after meeting you, as if something was about to change in a major way. I don't even like change, but I felt a quiet excitement. It wasn't exactly love at first sight; it was more future at first sight. Like I discovered a book of my life, already written, and opened it to find that, there you were, a main character. I didn't love you the moment I saw you, but I had a sense that I could, or would.

I looked for you as I drove around the city in my (well, Papa Angelo's) old Chevy Spark painted red-and-green, and green-and-white, with the giant triangle of smiling pizza with its little waving arm on top. I rang doorbells with new hope. I also typed *Mars* and *Seattle* into the search bar of the family computer, netting varied results: a vegan cocktail bar called Life on Mars; the Mars Society, dedicated to furthering the goal of life on that planet; and a spooky-looking carnival ride called Flight to Mars, from the 1962 Seattle World's Fair.

No dweeby boy in sexy jeans, of course. I wasn't really expecting to find you. It was just a way of staying in contact, same as playing our meeting over and over again in my mind. Winnifred Evans said that retreating into a fantasy life is a way of avoiding real connection and escaping the overwhelming stress of real life, an understandable safe place, but a *hiding* place, and okay, okay. Still . . . Why turn the best stuff into a shaky coping mechanism for some dark psychological need? Daydreams, reading books, staring off into space, wishes, and imagination—why not let it just be the magic it is?

I didn't tell her about the guy in her waiting room, and the space he was taking up in my head. I already knew what she would say. This was hard to explain, even to you, but it was easier to have relationships and experiences in my imagination. I wanted them badly, I did. I wanted to be one of those people with lots of friends around them, lots of activities they loved and were interested in, but that seemed so immense. Scary-immense. Winnifred Evans would remind me that staying safe to the degree I required was a small, small room, while being in the world, trying new things, *loving* people, was a risk, but it was freedom. Who needed freedom when you had your pj's and some books?

Whatever, you know. *Leave my coping mechanisms alone*, I always wanted to say to her, but never did. This, though. You—it was more than a relationship in my imagination. I knew it. I just did. A once-in-a-lifetime alignment, same as they said about the Voyager mission. Calculations done way back in the summer of 1965 predicted that a spacecraft launched in the late 1970s could visit all four of the major outer planets—Saturn, Jupiter, Neptune, and Uranus—the rarest of possibilities, occurring only once every 176 years. It was facts merging with fate.

After a few weeks of regular life, doubt crept in. I *did* have an overactive imagination. Anyone with anxiety does. It's one of our finest and most problematic qualities. No, it's a *skill*, honed to an art form, and not just at the usual worrying hour of two a.m., either. All hours. Each of us could be a writer or something, the way we make up stories and believe them. Winnifred Evans was right that I was hiding from scary things by imagining great things, and imagining scary things so they couldn't take me by surprise. Hiding from people, maybe, most of all. Plus, when you have three older brothers, you develop a good imagination after all those hours in the farthest corner of the back seat, staring out the window and dreaming, just to remove yourself from their elbows and fighting and farting.

Finals were coming up, too. I needed the brain space you were taking up. I had three AP classes (English, biology, calculus), plus US history, third-year Spanish, and ceramics (thank God), so my head was exploding. I seriously didn't even know what this was all for, if I was only going to get my AA degree like my brothers before working at Papa Angelo's full-time. My youngest brother, Maurice, who I was closest to, once told my father he wanted to be a musician, and things were thrown. Now he was the front-of-house manager, even if I still occasionally saw him drumming with a set of knives or just his index fingers.

Besides finals, we were getting our yearbooks, another stressful end-of-school event. It always felt awkward, those days of carrying it around, everyone hunched over each other's pages, writing missives of love and importance. I was too shy to ask anyone to sign mine, and it was hard to know what to write about a person I sat next to in history and barely talked to, but who still wanted my love and memories of stuff we'd already forgotten. There was the end-of-year picnic, too, which had the same strain, only with hot dogs.

And then there was the junior prom. Me and Addison and Priya were going to go together. We had our dresses and everything, but then Liam asked Addison, and Maddie asked Priya, and I decided not to go. My dress was green satin, short but not too, so my dad wouldn't freak out. Now it hung like a broken promise in my closet, tauntingly shiny.

I wanted them to have fun, but maybe not without me. The dance part, not going—it was a relief in some ways. I didn't like Liam, but maybe I was just jealous. Addison was acting all silly, and she wasn't a silly person. Fun, yeah, really fun, but not silly.

Prom was on my mind, is all. It started working its way into my body, causing an alarm that something was wrong. My stomach started to ache again, and my chest had that feeling like my heart was being wrung out, same as a wet washrag. Maurice said he was going to take me to do something special on prom night instead, but the stuff Maurice liked . . . I should prepare myself for a Mars Society meeting, you know. His idea of special wasn't necessarily the same as other people's. I was grateful, though. Maurice, with his glasses always knocked off-kilter. The best.

Probably, my head was just full of the same thing it always was. Overwhelming loneliness. A problem I was too afraid to fix.

What I'm saying is, I hadn't forgotten about you so much as you were shoved out of my mind by what was required in the moment: enduring, mostly. Maurice told me, *One day your life will start*, and I was still waiting. It wouldn't happen in high school, not for people like me, he said, which also meant people like him. I wanted to ask him if his life had started, but I was maybe worried about the answer.

Well, then, you know what happened.

I parked on the gravel strip in front of the dock. I opened the Velcro tab of the carrier and slid out the pizza. I double-checked the sales slip. Extra-large Roma. The bottom of the box was still warm, the steam softening the cardboard ever so slightly. The Chevy Spark was a shit car, but I should have paid more attention—Eastlake was getting pretty strange lately. I thought I'd be one minute, at the most.

I pushed through the wooden gates. Jogged down the steps. Hunted for houseboat number . . . I checked the slip again. Four. It was the tiny one that was second from the end. I always felt a little nervous going onto the houseboat docks. *Residents only!* the signs warned. I'd been invited (well, Papa Angelo's had), but still. I was one of those annoying rule-followers. I'd better be, you know, with my dad. I annoyed even myself about it, though.

The houses—and that's what they actually are, floating homes, not boats one would drive—bobbed and swayed a bit, even the large two-story ones. It was evening, and the wind had picked up, the waters of the lake choppy. Overhead, strings of lights arced charmingly. At number six, a family jumped aboard a sailboat and headed away, the bow slapped by waves. Number four looked a bit tired and worn. The paint was fading, and the plants in the flower boxes overflowed with a mix of weeds. Still, from the scratchy welcome mat (also worn—*elco*, it read) I could see across Lake Union, where the Space Needle rose in retro intergalactic dignity.

The windows of number four were flung open. The residents weren't too considerate of their neighbors—that's what I thought, I'm sorry—because music boomed out. Some honky-tonk blues thing. Maurice would know, but not me. I heard the words *Rub me raw*, oh my God. It was always a hazard, right? To wait for the door to open. It was my one brave thing. Well, against my parents' wishes and dire warnings, I'd gotten myself into this, the right to deliver pizzas like my brothers had, and now I had to face the music—literally, that day. Doing deliveries took courage, my second-oldest brother, George, told me whenever he was trying to build up my confidence. *See? You've got guts.* I *couldn't do it.* George had a bit of swagger, too, a mini Dad minus the rage, and even he only delivered for a few weeks before quitting. He'd rather run the kitchen, which could be brutal, hot, and intense. During one delivery, he told me, a woman answered in a towel, and then dropped it when she reached for the box.

I rang the doorbell. A dog barked his head off, but still, no one answered. How could they even hear with that music? I pounded with my fist. I couldn't stand around there forever. I had two more deliveries and then my biology test tomorrow.

I heard some negotiating with the dog. Firm talk turning to pleading, then the drag of toenails against the floor. A clang. The volume of the music lowered, still spewing blues guitar. Finally, the door opened.

I dropped the box.

"The fall of Roma?" you said.

"I'm so sorry." Seriously, that box slipped right from my fingers when I saw you. I knew it, see? I just knew it, that we'd see each other again. It *was* something. And yet, I was shocked. You were there. I'd spent so much time with the Mars of my imagination that it was almost too intimate, immediately both less and more. Oh,

God, my hands had already been on you in my mind. We'd spent time together in my head, you telling things to me and me telling things back, honest things. Jesus. This was so embarrassing. And yet, it was you, and you looked just like I remembered, not diminished at all, which seemed like a miracle, given the way a person can build things up. Your eyes were just so sweet. So open. And your curly hair had actual ringlets, a word from a Victorian novel. You wore a faded T-shirt with a comic book–like vintage rocket on it, and crumply chino shorts. Bare feet, which I saw up close when I picked up that box.

"Hey. I know you," you said.

"Green Lake Psychiatric Services waiting room," I said. Way to kill a mood.

"Tangerine skirt." You remembered what I wore. I blushed.

"Extra-large Roma." I handed you the box. Over your shoulder, I saw the dog, medium brown, undetermined origin, peering with interest from a metal baby gate barring his exit from the kitchen. I'd spent time with you in my mind, so it was like I knew you, and yet, of course I didn't. There was so much to find out. A dog, for one. This house, which seemed like a suitcase you had to sit on to close. Too much stuffed inside, and bad planning, maybe.

You stared down at the box, with that circle and the triangles. Papa Angelo's logo. "Are you an Angelo?"

"A Vittorio. Angelo's his first name. He's my dad."

You didn't respond at all. People usually loved this. They got all excited, but you didn't. "Vittorio? No kidding. Is he related to Roberto?"

"Roberto?"

"The astronaut."

I folded my eyebrows down. I had no idea what you were talking about. "I don't think so. It's just us. Arthur, George, Maurice?"

You shrugged an apology. You must have just moved here, I realized, if that didn't ring some sort of bell. Papa Angelo's was famous around here. Only ten dine-in tables, and a small patio in summer, and we were booked into the next year. Best Pizza in every poll in every year since forever. An Italian family with a pizza place is a cliché, but we were an Italian family with a pizza place, okay? It was what it was, whether it was convenient for breaking stereotypes or not. No one needed to know that it was my mother's sauce recipe and that she was Norwegian and hated pizza, hated all food, pretty much.

"The Arturo, all meat? The Giorgio, sausage with peppers? The Maurizio, a pizza bianca, with a white cream sauce . . ."

"Oh, right! The menu! Is the Roma a someone?"

"A some*where*. My dad's dad came from a town nearby. Anguillara Sabazia?"

You looked baffled. Of course you wouldn't know where that was. No one did, but you better not tell my father that. It was the center of the world, in his mind. "And you are . . ." You waited.

"Margaret."

"The Margherita!"

"Right. But my name . . . It actually means daisy? In Italian?" Ugh! Who cared? But I didn't want you to think I was named for a tomato. And that song that was playing. God, it was the longest bluesy guitar solo ever.

"Great to meet you. For the second time! I'm Mars."

Like I could have forgotten *that*, your name being called out by Dr. Quentin Baleaf, a name that had been in my head for the last few weeks. I had to pretend like it was new. "Oh, wow," I said, which covered it all.

I thought you were holding out your hand, and oh, man, I almost took it. I almost slipped mine right into yours, but thankfully some infrequently generous part of me came to the rescue. You wanted the receipt. I handed it over, and our fingers touched. My skin met your skin, and it could have been our whole bodies.

And then the music changed.

It changed so drastically that it was startling. A tender, tender voice began to sing: gravelly, heartbreaking, and beautiful. Just the singer and his guitar, a ballad from the soul, you could tell that. *Keep me in your heart*, he sang. Your eyes met mine. They stayed there, too long, and there was meaning between us. Undeniable meaning. It was like our eyes held our own space and the space held our own truths, all of them. That moment was a promise. I'd never tell Addison or Maurice or Winnifred Evans that. They'd think it was too much, that I was living in the safe and glorious gardens of my head again, but they'd be wrong.

The song—well, I thought it was about love, but I later learned it was about leaving. It was about loss. Which is also about love. At least when loss breaks you, you've loved and loved deeply.

And then the moment was gone. Your mom appeared. She wasn't what I expected at all. The idea of your mother or father or even a family hadn't really occurred to me, but if it had, it wouldn't have been this particular woman who hurried from your hallway. A mom with long blond hair, in a tank top with both bra straps showing, waving a single flip-flop. “Have you seen my shoe? Oh, is the pizza here, *finally*?”

I turned and fled. I don’t know what came over me. I think I waved goodbye, though maybe I added that part in later to make myself feel better. Fleeing is embarrassing. It’s a confession. My whole body was filled with emotion, and it was more than I could hold. Already, I was replaying it: the eyes, the eyes, the eyes.

When I got to the top of the dock, I saw the damage. My car door had been flung open, and the extra-large Maurizio and the extra-large Giorgio were both gone. My father was going to kill me. The smiling pizza with the waving hand was also now wearing a condom for a hat. It was maybe an omen.

I hadn’t locked the doors, so it was my fault. I hadn’t been careful enough. Maybe that was an omen, too.

Chapter Three

Wind, Rain, Surf: *Sounds of Earth*

They sent a driver out with the other two orders as soon as they could, but they were late enough for the customers to be pissed. When you're waiting for a pizza, it seems like the most important thing in the world, but it never is. When I got back to Papa Angelo's, my father yelled at me in front of everyone in the kitchen. His eyes blazed, and his voice was loud enough to rattle the metal utensils hanging on the wall hooks, while the cooks layered pepperoni and shoved the peels through the arches of the brick oven without looking up. My father wasn't a big man. He was only as tall as George, the shortest of my brothers, but he always seemed enormous. *How many times have I told you to lock the damn door? One thing I'm not gonna tolerate, being irresponsible!* But there were a lot of things he wouldn't tolerate. Some you could guess and some that were a surprise until you did them.

Maurice was in charge of front-of-house, which basically meant he did everything for everyone, including being extra nice to his sister after she fucked up. "I'm sorry, Margaret!" he called across the parking lot as I left.

I waved and blew him a kiss of thanks. When I drove off, I could still see his dark hair and the glint of his glasses shining under the streetlight.

With all my brothers now living on their own, our hundred-year-old Craftsman near Green Lake was too big. It felt echoey, even with Mom banging pans around as she made dinner. That night, my father came home shortly after I did, a rarity, and with the three of us at the table, I braced for it, the verbal lashing, or more, about the theft. I had my apologies ready, my comebacks. My body was ready, too. I'd laced up my spirit, like you do a shoe. Tight and secure, so it doesn't trip you or fall off entirely. But nothing happened. Nothing at all. Not a word. Maybe Mom or one of my brothers set it up for me so I'd be okay, or maybe my father just had other things on his mind. He ate like he had a job to do, and Mom just heaped more food onto his plate and moved the little bits of vegetables around hers as I lined up my French fries in order of height before eating them. It seemed like when I was ready for it, the storm never came, and when I wasn't, it did, which made me feel like I had to be ready all the time.

After I did the dishes, I studied for my biology final like it was dinner, and dessert was coming. Dessert was looking up your address to find out your last name. It was trickier than you'd think. Your mom's name was Janite, I discovered, and I wondered if she'd tried to make Janet fancier, the way you paint your toenails but they still look like toes. But under the *People associated with this address* heading, there was a Janite Johnson and a Janite Rivers and a Janite Martinez and a Janite Abadias. Either you guys were living with four other Janites, or your mom had been married a few times. You had a long-ago address in New Mexico, I saw, three previous addresses in California, and one in North Bend, associated with an entirely different person, Gwen Laurent, and other Laurents. There was a disappointing lack of social media. Like, zero.

I tried *Mars* with each of the last names. Bingo. One hit. One single hit. Mars Zevon Rivers, the third baseman for the JV team in the North Bend High winning game against Issaquah last spring, 14–0, a skunking that was big enough news to make the *North Bend Herald*. You. I squinted at the photo. I couldn't say for sure it was you, but it had to be. I couldn't tell how old you were, either, what grade you were in, but if you hadn't graduated yet, it was a long drive to your school from that houseboat.

Zevon. It sounded familiar. Maurice-familiar. I typed it into my search bar. And, boom, just like that, it was there. That song that was playing. "Keep Me in Your Heart" by Warren Zevon. *Your mom must be a big fan*, I guessed correctly. After seeing the musician's face, I remembered a CD—Maurice had a player in his old truck—with his photo on the front, a kind, shy face, round glasses. I sat back in my chair, satisfied. I felt like I'd solved the crime, found the essential piece of evidence. I played the song on YouTube, waited through the annoying, vibe-killing ad about invisible braces until the magical time machine of music zoomed me back to the moment. Again, again. Your eyes, the song, my heart. God.

My mom knocked on the door, popped her head in to say good

night. "Studying going well?" She glanced at my screen with a raised eyebrow. Addison sometimes called her mom her best friend, but my mom always seemed somewhere else, in a place too distant for either love or hatred. Occasionally she sent a postcard, and you saw where she was. Mostly, though, she was busy, you know, with her other relationship, the one with food. They were in deep, those two.

I nodded, and she was gone. I played the song again and let myself feel everything.

The night of prom, Maurice honked the horn of his truck from the driveway. He didn't want to come in. I didn't know where we were going. It was a surprise. I'd just gotten back from Addison's, where I'd helped her and Priya with their hair. I couldn't do a French braid to save my life, but I wanted them to have a great time. They both looked beautiful. I felt like a proud mom or something, and I kissed their cheeks and told them they were gorgeous, and to be careful and have fun. I left before Liam came, so I didn't ruin it by hating him. George, the executive chef at Papa Angelo's (*kitchen manager*, he called it, second-in-command to Arthur, general manager, who was second-in-command to Dad, owner), had given me the day off weeks ago, when I was supposed to go with them. It was extra time for mixed feelings, but most of all, I loved those two.

By then, it had been a few weeks since I delivered that pizza to your house. I thought that maybe you'd order from us again, or come by the restaurant, or call. You knew who I was, and where I was. I was being ridiculous again, probably, I decided. Feeling all these things by myself, in my head, alone. A person could do that, create a whole story that wasn't even real. Like, you probably just went in and ate dinner, the end. Maybe you went around making meaningful eye contact with lots of people just to spin them off their axis; how did I know? You didn't seem like that kind of guy, but I had zero idea about what kind of guy you were. We had, like, twenty minutes of interaction, tops.

I knew *your* name, and where *you* were, too. But me reaching out, making the first move, didn't seem like an option. We girls, women, were supposed to be past these things, but it didn't seem like we were past them. There were still all these traditions or customs or habits, outdated rules, like guys getting on their knees to propose, and engagement rings, and waiting for him to call first, or say *I love you* first, all that stuff. Essentially, you were supposed to be chosen and not choosing. There should be some big display about being chosen, too. Splashy evidence of it: the ring, the videos of how he'd asked you (to prom, to a whole life together) in a special way. Some women were disappointed about the ring, too, how big it was, all that, and it seemed so sad for the guy. I pictured one of those nature videos where the male bird is showing off all his feathers and doing his special dance, and the female bird just says, *Meh*.

It was confusing, because *chosen* was supposed to be amazing but, when you thought about it, wasn't all that great. It involved waiting, and being judged worthy. It involved being chosen by someone you maybe didn't even want to be chosen by. It was hard to be clear about it. Last year, when Asher Allen sent me all those notes and started flirting and stuff, and asked me out, it was exciting. We were a couple for a few months. He broke up with me after that, said I didn't make him feel special. I guess the unspoken agreement was, they do a little special stuff in the beginning, so you'll make them feel special forever after that. I felt bad about it. I failed at some job. But then I realized I'd never liked him all that much, and I'd never really thought to ask myself if I did. I'd have never gone out of my way to choose *him*. I'd just been swept along by some unseen force that maybe we should be seeing by now.

Choosing, being chosen, the whole mess of it: It seemed like another reason to stay comfy in my tiny world, with the people I knew for sure loved me.

Like Maurice. I hopped into his truck. He peered up through the windshield toward the sky. "I hope it doesn't rain," he said.

"So we're doing something outside," I guessed. What I appreciated—he didn't make a big deal out of what was happening, or not happening. The whole non-prom thing. He didn't ask me if I was okay and jam himself right into my personal feelings. Which made it okay for me to feel my personal feelings in his company. My voice got all wobbly. "Hey, thanks for doing this tonight. For me, you know."

"What do you mean, for you? You're doing this for me. No one else I know would want to come along to this."

"Oh, God. Don't tell me it's bowling. Or roller-skating."

"I said *would want*. You'd hate those things."

Those tiny moments where someone got you—they just made

you want to bawl your eyes out. "Remember when Arthur and his girlfriend took us ice-skating?"

We cracked up.

Arthur and, what was her name? Lia? Ava? Something with an *A*. Our oldest brother, Arthur, so handsome, smart, and kind, was always popular with girls, so it was hard to keep track. Anyway, the two of them wanted to use us to show each other how great they were with younger kids, but it was a disaster. My ankles kept folding together, and I could only inch my way around the railing, holding on, near tears, and Maurice barfed up the ton of snacks they bought us. Arthur learned a lesson, apparently, because he and Maeve never let Maya, Max, and Baby Millie eat crap. All those *M*s—I sometimes felt bad for Arthur, but he didn't seem to mind. He didn't mind much of anything—he was even-keeled and capable to the degree I was fumbling and anxious, like we were the two bookends of the Spectrum of Dad Management.

Maurice got on the freeway. Hmm. The mystery deepened. "Where're we going?"

He ignored me. He was trying to keep the secret, or maybe he was in his own head. He popped in a CD instead, turned it up loud. He liked music from all eras, and it could be hard to tell if a song was current or not. When it was good, it was just good.

We were on I-90, and we crossed the bridge over Lake Washington. We passed Mercer Island, and then Bellevue. He took an Issaquah exit. Out that way, things got a little blurry, what was familiar or not. I grew up in Seattle, and everything on the other side of the lake was a foreign country, and this was far enough out that there were bears and stuff. I was here for one of Priya's soccer games before, but that was about it.

"Where the hell are we?" Now we were on some remote country road. Well, it probably wasn't a remote country road to the people who lived there, but it was to me. "It's getting dark. Like, way dark."

"That's the idea." The clue made me nervous. I liked surprises until they started being too surprising. He turned off onto a gravel road then. His tires crunched. The nose of his truck slanted upward.

"Is this a *mountain*?"

"Technically."

"What does *that* mean?"

"A small mountain."

"Are we going hiking? Night hiking?"

He snorted. "Is there such a thing as night hiking? Did you just make that up?"

"Are we going *camping*?" It was hard to hide the horror in my voice. I couldn't imagine ever going to sleep with only a sheet of canvas between you and what might eat you.

He laughed. Put his hand to his forehead and rubbed, like I was hard to take.

"Watch the road."

All I could think was that we were going to die out there and no one would ever find us. But he pulled into a little circular area, where there were a handful of other cars. It was unexpected, and I got excited again. Other people seemed safer than just us alone, so this might turn out okay. We got out of the truck and followed a little trail, a very, very dark trail, but I could hear voices in the distance. My mind scrolled through every night-gathering possibility, which took less than a second. Addison's mom took her and her sister to this goddess thing once, where they sang songs around a campfire, haha.

But it wasn't a goddess thing, thank goddess. It was a bunch of people and their telescopes. Cool, cool, cool. I loved it. All sizes of telescopes, all different ages of people. I always wanted to look through a telescope and actually see a planet or something. Like Saturn's rings, something unimaginable. My mother got my dad a telescope for Christmas when we were kids, but you could tell he didn't really like it. He loved the set of weights she got him one year, which he and George both used to pump up their stocky selves, but he only set up the telescope once, in the backyard. Maybe it was too complicated. I thought I saw something, but it was only my own eyeball staring back at me. A few years later, the telescope sat with a bunch of other stuff we were donating. Or rather, stood, waiting for the truck to pick it up, like a lonely traveler heading for the next chapter in its life.

"Perspective," Maurice said, and that was all, because he was deep like that. A quiet, deep, music-loving best guy.

Quickly, I realized it was more than *perspective*, though. A girl, a young woman, raised her hand across the hill, waving us over. She must have been watching and waiting for us specifically, because it was really dark up there.

"Who's that?" It sounded accusing.

"My friend Sandrine?"

"What's wrong with your voice?" I asked. It had gotten high-pitched, like he was about to break out into giggles. His mouth was pinched in the corners, I could see, even in the dark, that kind of look where you just can't suppress how pleased you are.

Oh my God. Maurice was giddy. Maurice was never giddy. He was the kind of guy who always carried a paperback, whose wilder side only came out when he was playing drums. He was quietly pleased, sure. Giddy—no.

She was coming our way.

"Hey," Sandrine said. She had a cute nose piercing (oh, God, I could already hear my father's opinions on that), and torn denim shorts, and hair that looked like she took some scissors to it herself, and the warmest smile you could imagine.

"Hey," Maurice said. He twined his fingers with hers. "Seeing anything?"

"Everything."

Oh my God again. She said it while looking in his eyes.

There were introductions. Turns out, Sandrine had a band, Solar Flare. She sang and played guitar. Wrote their songs, too.

"My cousin's got his scope trained on some black patch in the sky, so forget him," Sandrine said. "But this dude over here"—she motioned to an older guy with a woolly gray beard and a Harley-Davidson shirt, bent over a large elaborate telescope—"has got Saturn."

I suddenly didn't care about Saturn.

I cared about the cousin.

"No fucking way," you said, after I excused myself from Maurice and Sandrine and tapped you on the shoulder.

I shrugged. I mean, what else was there to do? Something was going on, something like fate. "What are you doing here?" I asked, like this was my place. You were the one with the telescope, after all, not me.

"What are *you* doing here?"

"My brother brought me." I gestured.

"Maurice is your brother?"

"You know him?"

"The new drummer."

"The new *drummer*?" Oh, shit. Maurice had secrets.

"Wait. No way. Is he *the* Maurizio? All meat?"

"Bianca. White cream sauce." It was easy to get them confused.

And so, it turned out that your mom, Janite, and Sandrine's mom were sisters. That you and Janite lived with their family when you moved from California. Their house was in North Bend, just a few miles from where we stood on Tiger Mountain. It might seem like another country over here, but this mountain and their house were only a few miles away. Maybe this wasn't fate after all. Or else, it was Sandrine and Maurice's fate.

"This is so weird," I said.

"I'm here every week, basically?" Now *you* shrugged. "But, man, I'm feeling mighty embarrassed at the moment." You were the kind of guy to use the word *mighty*, and you were the kind of guy to plunge forward to address super-awkward things that were about to shock me. "I mean, I'm sorry if I made you uncomfortable with all those pizzas."

Huh? "All what pizzas?"

"Wait. You didn't know?"

"Didn't know what?"

You let out a noisy exhale. "Oh, God! I feel so much better!

I thought I was being such a . . ." You groaned. "I, uh . . . After, uh . . . *That day?*"

Oh, wow. It *was* a *that day*. It was a *that day* to you, too. "Fall of Roma?"

"Right. You ran off . . ."

I smack my hand to my eyes to cover them.

"I didn't get your number. I . . . uh, called? Papa Angelo's? I asked if Margaret usually delivered to Eastlake, the houseboats? I tried to explain, so they'd know I wasn't some freaky old dude or something. The guy on the phone said, *Yeah? Depends on the day?* And so I ordered a Margherita. On a Wednesday, the day I saw you. But nope. You didn't show. I tried Thursday. Friday. This is humiliating."

I started to smile. I was trying hard not to burst with joy. I'm sure I had that same face as Maurice.

"It started to seem, uh, like a bad idea. Not, uh, fun, you know, like I imagined? I've never done anything like that before. Have you ever noticed that rom-com moves sit right at the edge of stalker-y ones? I was sure you weren't coming on purpose."

I thought I'd been rerouted after the car theft, but now I understood. Dad. This wasn't a bad omen, exactly, but it sure didn't mean good things were coming. My father likely answered the phone the day you called Papa Angelo's. He had ideas about me and boys, ones that were different from the ideas he had about my brothers and girls. Ideas that people, men-people, were supposed to be done with by now, but weren't done with. The sad and horrible thing was, it didn't seem like they ever would be done with those ideas.

How weird, this emphasis on our breasts and lower halves. Just leave us alone, you know. What are you so afraid of? Our real power is a lot higher up.

When my father met Asher, he got all pretend-threatening. All that *You better look after my daughter* kind of stuff. *You better treat her right, or you'll be dealing with me*, that sort of thing. It was supposed to be a joke, but it didn't seem like one, not really. It was hard to understand why I suddenly belonged to my father, when I usually wasn't all that interesting to him, compared to my brothers. It was about sex, at the end of the day. Like everything throughout history was. Basically, making sure girls didn't have it, but boys did have it. And since the boys had to have it with someone, I guess it meant only certain girls, the wrong girls, the bad ones. People still thought like this. My father did. He got all ownership-y about me, my body. Like what I wore or didn't wear, what I showed too much of. It was hard to understand, it really was. The way we had computers and the internet and AI and were still doing stuff from the Middle Ages. The whole thing was embarrassing. The idea of bringing a guy around was. It made me feel guilty and wrong, like I was still a little girl, so I guess it worked.

"My route changed, is all," I told you. "But seriously, I'm changing it back now. I can't believe you ordered those pizzas. That is so sweet. That is just the sweetest thing." My heart was overflowing. Everything seemed unimaginable but possible, universe-huge, a gift. I hadn't even looked up at the sky yet, even though there we were, surrounded by people who never forgot to do that, who made a point of doing that. So, that's what I did next, and I couldn't believe it. Even with my own eyes, the stars were astonishing, a glow-in-the-dark mural of magic, a twinkling carpet above us. How could we not take them in every single night? Just how? But we didn't. Don't.

I try to now. When something unimaginable happens, something tragic, it helps me remember.

"Wow," I said.

"Yeah," you answered. "The best, right? This is my regular meetup group? Me and Sandrine's. That's Chester, and Santiago and his son, Norton, and Lily, and Ben, and Rainey . . ." You pointed around to the Harley guy, and another man and his little kid, and an old lady, and a college-aged guy, and another woman a little older than Sandrine, all bent over their telescopes or adjusting things. They were chatting, laughing, calling little bits of advice or information to one another, and I could tell there was some teasing going on. They really liked each other, is the point.

"Whoa. All these people that you know," I said. It seemed astonishing. I mean, I couldn't imagine this for myself, even if that was what I both longed for and stayed far away from. So many *relationships*. My own world had my family and my two best friends, and even that could feel like a lot. Too much on some days.

"The more people, the more . . . connection?" It was the most *you* thing to say, ever. Your defining quality, really. Immediately, I understood we were opposites, at least in that way. You for sure were going to think I was an alien, hard to understand, ugh. "It keeps the visits to Dr. QB to a minimum, you know? Plus, look at them!" You flung your arm around to indicate your friends. "These people are awesome. Each one of them has their own particular astronomy obsession, too. The one thing they're interested in more than anything else. I love that about them."

"Sandrine said you were only looking at some dark patch of sky."

You snorted. "She's full of shit."

"Can I see?"

You stepped aside, made a grand, game-show-hostess gesture. I leaned forward, looked into the eyepiece. I couldn't tell what I was seeing, honestly. It's wrong to say *just stars*, but just stars.

"Don't hate me," I said.

"If you say, 'I only see a dark patch of sky . . .' "

"I only see a dark patch of sky." Mostly, I just said it to see what would happen. Teasing, like these people were doing with each other, even—it could be so great. My family was pretty serious. My friends were, too. It often seemed like we lived in serious and worrying times, compared to lots of the other ones.

You made a monster face and monster hands and let out a long "Aaargh!" of protest.

"Okay, so tell me what I'm looking at. What's your obsession?"

"The object farthest away from Earth. Human-made object, that is. The first spacecraft to make it into interstellar space—"

"Interstellar?"

But you were one step ahead of me. Another omen, God. "The space beyond the sun. Where the sun's rays, its magnetism, its forces, no longer have an effect."

I was trying to pay attention. "Whoa. But, what's the farthest-away object?"

"Voyager 1. A NASA space probe launched in 1977, to explore the outer solar system, where nothing from our planet has flown before. Along with its sister craft, Voyager 2, which was actually launched *first*, due to— Stop me. I could go on and on, and I haven't even gotten to the best part."

"Wait. You can see it right now? The thing launched in 1977?" I put my eye on the scope again, but I couldn't find anything resembling a space probe.

"Well, not exactly. It's over fifteen billion miles from Earth, so . . . we're looking in the piece of sky it's in."

"The dark patch of sky, but it's not so dark, really." There was so much light in that dark. Pinpricks everywhere. I popped my head up again.

"You're watching Ophiuchus." You pointed upward. "Serpent-Bearer. Basically, a guy holding a snake?"

"Wow," I said, but I didn't really see it.

Lily, the older lady wearing a flowered sundress and Birkenstocks, lifted her white pouf of head and shouted to you. "Barnard's, and M-fourteen," she said. "I got a few resolved stars in my two hundred fifty millimeter."

"On to the Oort!" you shouted back, raising your fist in the air and waving it around.

Chester snorted loudly, but Lily raised a fist in return. "On to the Oort!"

It was clearly your thing. Some private phrase of yours and Lily's, same as how Addison and I always shouted, "Choco block!" when we saw yet another one of those new town houses popping up everywhere, since Addison said they look liked bars of chocolate. A new person was another world to discover, but that whole night was like a world within a world. You were. All these people, all these connections. A universe within a world. I knew better than to even ask a person to explain those private jokes, but you actually jumped in and did it anyway.

"The probe is headed for the Oort Cloud. It won't get there for three hundred years, though. Lily was actually an engineer on Voyager." Your voice filled with quiet respect. Awe. Lily gave a little wave, and I waved back.

"Huh. Oort Cloud, though?" I still thought the phrase was part of the joke.

"It's this . . . what scientists think might be a thick shell, a bubble, surrounding our solar system, made up of trillions of ice objects. It's named in honor of the Dutch astronomer Jan Oort."

"I was sure it was a made-up word. I don't know any of this stuff," I confessed.

"I can't even believe you're here," you said. "It's making me so nervous that I'm babbling."

"You're not babbling. This is all so cool." It was. Is. An everlasting is.

"It's just so wild." You shook your head. "You and your brother? Here? It's like a *present*. Like, *how*?"

"Like, *why*?"

"I know, I know," you marveled. We stood around awkwardly, in the presence of each other and a miracle. Wonder seemed everywhere, suddenly.

"Wait. Your name," I said finally. "Is that part of why you got interested in this stuff?"

"Nah. Mars stands for Marsden. Not the planet. My dad's name. I'm a Junior. He died a few years ago, so maybe I'm a Senior now? You don't need to say you're sorry and look all sad and stuff, because he lived in New Mexico and I didn't know him very well, and I'm doing okay about it. Are our relatives kissing?"

Jesus.

"Don't look," you said while looking.

"How can you not?"

It was true. Everybody was.

"Whoa, chemistry," you said. It was making *me* want to kiss you, as if I didn't already. Then you looked at me, too long again. It was dark, but even in starlight, I could see that we had it, too.

Our gaze broke when I felt a poke on my leg. "Who are you?" It was a little kid, Norton. He looked like he was about five. At least, somewhere between my little three-and-a-half-year-old nephew, Max, and my six-year-old niece, Maya. Norton's T-shirt featured a shark riding a bike.

"Norty! Get back here! Leave Marsy and his friend alone," his dad, Santiago, called.

"Marsy?" I asked as he ran back to his dad.

"Norton thinks everyone here has a *y* at the end of their name, with Daddy, and Lily, and Rainey, and Norty. Right, Chesty?" you yelled to the Harley guy, who beat his chest like a gorilla and gave an *ooh, ooh, ooh* to go along.

"Hope that's not a mating cry," Lily called.

"Hey," you said, looking only at me now. "You know what I would love?" *Me*, I thought. I did. I'm not sure if I ever told you that. "Your number!"

"Oh, definitely." I handed you my phone, and you handed me yours. After you typed it in, my phone felt so happy, I swear.

"Now *this* is a present, too," you said, shaking your phone. We just stood there smiling at each other, as if we'd just accomplished something great, and we had.

"Hate to break this up," said Ben. "But I just felt rain."

"Me too." Rainey wiped her cheek.

"One drop, big deal," Lily said. She undid the flap of her pack at her feet. In seconds, she was unfurling an origami of rain ponchos, one for her, and one for her scope. She peered out from a little hood with a crescent-moon visor.

There was a long, low roll of thunder. A crack and crash in the distance.

"Fuck!" Chester said as he rapidly packed up his gear. "Let's not be the tallest thing on the mountain."

"We weren't supposed to get rain for another hour," Santiago said. He handed Norton his sweatshirt just before the pit-pats started up, splattering on my forehead.

"We've got to get out of here," Maurice said. Sandrine was already folding up her abandoned scope. As we raced across the trail to the lot, Maurice and Sandrine ran together, holding hands. You carried the heaviest of Lily's bags. Santiago ran with Norton on his hip as the rain pummeled down and drenched us all.

"Wait!" I called to you across the lot, where you and Sandrine were packing up an old VW. Everyone had scuttled to their own cars. I saw a bolt slash down the sky. "The best part! You said we hadn't gotten to the best part yet." Well, we hadn't, in so many ways. So much was coming.

"The Golden Record!" you shouted back. "Unforgettable." I didn't know if you meant that record or that night.

Maurice flung open the doors of the truck. "Jesus Christ, Margaret. Get in before we're hit by lightning."

It was pretty clear, though. Both of us had already been struck.

Chapter Four

Fire, Speech: *Sounds of Earth*

I didn't text you or anything. And you didn't text me. That was totally okay, and kind of nice, actually, since the waiting before the having can be almost as good as the having itself. After that night, I was happy, carrying my smug anticipation around, because I was sure I was going to see you again. Fate three times—in that office, the pizza, the mountain—it meant . . . Well, it meant meaning. Like the Voyager spacecraft, launching at a specific time to travel at a specific distance to catch certain planets in a certain alignment, all in order to reveal previously hidden grandeurs of life . . . I'm sorry, but how can you not see the parallels to two strangers falling in love? The smallest human experiences and the largest natural truths just seemed to do that, reflect each other, offering metaphors. Tornadoes, earthquakes, flowers blooming, leaves dying. But maybe I was just feeling so much.

Going back to school was strange after a big event like prom. Everyone who was there had experienced something together, and the rest of us hadn't. Or rather, Addison and Priya had, but I hadn't. Maddie started eating lunch with us a few months ago, snitching Priya's grapes as Priya pilfered her Goldfish crackers, but now Liam was at our table, too. He made some gross comment about being the only guy, using the word *harem*. Priya and I looked at each other, our eyes saying, *Gross*, but Addison ignored it. She was already ignoring things, and I could feel him sticking his foot in a door and wedging it open wider and wider with bad behavior he'd probably get away with his whole life. It was how things felt in general in the world—the big foot, the bad behavior. But you could tell Addison was trying hard to keep some guy not worth keeping, tale as old as time. She was better than him by miles, but she kept trying to prove herself worthy as he made comments about her talking too loud.

"How was your weekend, Margaret?" Addison asked. It sounded hesitant, and I understood why. What a knot. Do you *not* ask me and make everything seem like it's all about you, or *do* you ask and risk hearing an answer that makes you feel like shit?

"Good," I said, but nothing more. We talked about this, Winifred Evans and me. Feeling sad about being closed off from people, but then acting closed off. "Really good."

"Oh my God! You met someone!" Addison knew me so well. "Look at your face! What happened? Tell us!"

I wiggled my eyebrows as if I had a secret, but then I jetted my glance quickly toward Liam, as if to say, *I'll tell you later*. Faces can say all that. Faces can say much more and barely move, too. My mom's, for example.

“Marga*ret*.” Addison gave a dramatic, exasperated sigh.

“Is this all you guys talk about? *Relationships?*” Liam swirled a plastic spoon in a pudding cup.

It was a ridiculous thing to say. Priya played every sport imaginable and kept beehives in her backyard, and Addison had organized a whole Get Out the Vote campaign at our school, and I was in DECA and generally loved books and music, and we talked about all of those things and more: Our fears and hopes, our families and friends. Other people. Lots of talking about other people, especially the popular kids who ignored us to the point of borderline cruelty, like Severin Gyles and Gwynyth James and their friends. Addy also loved to tell us about stuff she baked, and Priya drew comics, and you shouldn’t even get her started on Marvel, her dog, one of those big kinds with the hair like ropes. But, too—

“What’s wrong with relationships?” Maddie asked. Well, plenty, but she was right. Liam could fuck right off.

I looked down at my lunch. My mom had packed it, even though I’d told her a thousand times that I could do it myself. There was a thick bagel sandwich piled with turkey and cheese and mayonnaise, a baggie of chips, cut-up fruit. She’d never eat those things herself. She barely ate anything. It’s a weird thing to say, because the not-eating was sad, and a torment (for her *and* her family), but it had a self-righteous quality, too. Like she was somehow higher up than the rest of us mere mortals, mere mortals like me, who wanted this sandwich. When I thought of my dad and his comments about girls and guys and sex, and my mom, with her feelings about women and food, it seemed like a lot of life was about wanting and not having, control and lack of control. Keeping things that were too large and unmanageable at bay. I took a big bite of that sandwich. It was delicious. I could have scarfed the whole thing, but I didn't.

"If you're not going to eat that, can I have it?" Liam asked.

I usually went to work around four-thirty, just before the dinner rush. At Papa Angelo's, drivers helped the prep cook chop vegetables and stuff, and, depending how busy we were, we sometimes made pizzas, too. We did lots of other jobs, as well—cleaning, dishes, answering phones, taking out the trash, scraping pizza dough off of basically everywhere. Delivery is harder work than you think. People assume you drive around listening to music and getting tips, ha.

That day, I got there early, though. It was our last week of school, so I didn't really have any homework, and I wanted to catch George before the orders started coming in. Mostly, I wanted to talk to him before he organized our routes.

When I parked behind the restaurant, I saw George there with one of our cooks, Marv, wrangling the giant produce order we got from our wholesaler once a week or so: crates of mushrooms; peppers; wispy, bound stalks of fennel for a seasonal special; and bushels of onions. Whoever ended up dicing onions . . . The worst job. There were so many that your eyes burned, your throat, too, like being sprayed by mace by the time you were done.

"Hey," George said. He held a bundle of fennel near his face, pretended it was a fringy mustache.

"Nice! Très seventies," I said. He handed me a crate and picked one up himself as we headed inside. That time period, the seventies,

1977 to be exact, was already on my mind after that night on the mountain. I looked it up as soon as I got home: Voyager, the Golden Record. It was an *actual record*, gold-plated, placed aboard the Voyager capsules, a message to any alien life-form that might find it as it traveled to the outer edges of the universe. Everything on that record was meant to convey life on our planet, and so it was filled with sounds and images and even greetings in every language. A *Hey, friends! This is who we are!* to whoever might find it. Wow—I'd never even heard of it. Just wow. I loved that you loved stuff like that. It conveyed *your* life on this planet. What you cared about. Big stuff, you know. The biggest. That goofy guy with the deep, warm eyes and the springy hair, *you*—you were a curious person.

George put the fennel back in the crate. "That's the only mustache I'll ever grow after . . ." George trailed off, and I snickered at the memory: George, in junior high, with the speckle of longish hairs on his upper lip that we all very fairly gave him shit about. Now George and I hauled the crates to the cooler, where we kept the perishables.

"Why is our order coming in this late in the day?" I asked.

"They're getting later and later. If it's not one thing, it's another." George looked tired, and the rush hadn't even started yet.

"Hey, I was meaning to ask you . . ." I called this to George's back, because he was ahead of me now, hurrying, working hard. "I haven't been delivering to Eastlake for a while? Since my car got broken into, but also maybe because I have a friend out there, and Dad changed the—"

He looked at me over his shoulder, and winked. "Got it. No problem. If you want to go that direction, we'll fix it." And he would.

George managed delivery logistics, too, making sure all the phone orders were registered before they went into the make-line, routed long before we shouted our out-the-door times and rushed to our cars. Papa Angelo's prided itself in its exceptional quality, fresh ingredients, and thirty-minute arrivals, so we were a well-run machine, unless some irresponsible delivery driver left her car doors unlocked in a sketchy neighborhood.

I plunked down my crate and wound through the kitchen, where the already-prepped dough, made a day ahead, was in the proofer, and the sauce—endless cans of tomatoes, tomato paste, and fistfuls of herbs and spices that we were supposed to keep secret—was mixed in those twenty-gallon tubs. I could hear Maurice whistling in the dining area, and so I headed there. The tables were set and ready, napkin holders filled, red pepper containers, too, but Maurice was on all fours, his rear end sticking out from underneath a table.

"Are you finally fixing that crap linoleum square?" I asked.

Maurice emerged, bonking his head on the table and holding a glue gun. "What do you mean, 'finally'? It only chipped last week. You sound like Dad."

I made a face, peered. "Looks great." Honestly, I didn't care about the linoleum. I wished we'd start talking about the night on the mountain, about you and Sandrine. It was all I wanted to talk about.

Maybe Maurice felt the same. "I'm so glad you're here!" Usually, his eyes seemed like he was contemplating sad things from the past or worries from the future, but now they were more like two kids on a trampoline. He reached into the back pocket of his jeans, handed me a folded-up piece of paper. "I, uh, was wondering . . ."

"What?" I took the paper, suddenly nervous about what I might find. Generally, I worried about anything I didn't know the end result of, which was . . . everything. Everything, including the contents of this mysterious document I began to unfold.

"Don't look so concerned. It's good! I think it's good." Now *he* looked concerned, honestly.

It was a flyer. "Solar Flare at Neumos?"

"Underage club, so you and the cousin can get in." He lifted one eyebrow, a nifty trick I always wished I could do.

I smiled. "You're playing?"

"I'm a Solar Flare, aren't I?"

I wasn't going to ruin the moment by asking if our dad knew about this yet. "Heck yeah, you are," I said. "I can't wait." I *could* wait. I'd never been to an underage club. Clearly, it would involve lots of people and dancing in public and many things I couldn't envision. I had no idea what I should even be anxious about, so tons of undetermined stuff could go wrong without me seeing it coming. But . . . I might see *you*. "Did Sandrine already ask Mars?"

"Not sure," Maurice said.

A week. It seemed like a long way away.

Maybe it was that sandwich, the way Liam just took it and bit in. Or maybe it was Maurice, quietly but firmly being himself. Or maybe I'd already decided something this morning, or even before that—the night the rain poured down as we drove home, Maurice playing some song on his old CD player that talked about a fast car, and a ticket to anywhere.

But suddenly, or at least since that day I saw you in the doctors' office, I wanted things. *I* did. I didn't want to be superior through my superior denial, or wait while others determined what I was allowed. I was going to act: I'd place my own pizza order. A Roma, heading for houseboat number four.

"It's going to be great," I told Maurice. "See you later? I've got a few things to do before my route." One thing to do. One order to place.

On a hunch, though, I headed to the kitchen. On some days, I was sick of the smell of it, the way it clung to my clothes and to my life. Garlic, tomatoes, oregano; the sour-cold odor of our mozzarella-and-Monterey-Jack mix; warm dough, slightly singed from high heat. I was in DECA because I was supposed to do as my brothers had—join the business. But sometimes I dreamed of doing something else entirely, something I was passionate about but hadn't discovered yet. Right then, though, I was generous about the smell. It was home, the good parts. It wasn't a ticket to anywhere, but it was a ticket to here, a place I liked most of the time. It was a ticket to houseboat number four, too. I scrolled down the list of orders on the computer screen.

There it was.

Oh my God, there it was.

You placed an order, too. A medium Roma, for six p.m. delivery, the same time I'd seen you before. My insides danced, all balloons and confetti. This wasn't about what one person wanted. We *both* wanted. That's how it should be, right? Two people choosing.

This wasn't like me at all, because I *wanted* to let you in. It was as if some secret part of me that wanted more, more love, more connection, was plotting and scheming behind my back. I was giddy. I was seriously impressing myself with my bravery, I've got to say.

I found George again in the walk-in fridge. "Remember that friend I told you about? He called in an order, so, I was wondering if you could—"

"I got you covered. Executive decision, you're off early tonight. We'll make it your last stop." He smiled. My brothers were good guys. They were kind. Arthur could be a hard-ass sometimes, but only when it was required, as a boss. George had his moments where he acted full of himself, but he was always trying to boost me up, never down. When he wasn't working, George did dude stuff like lift weights, but he and his girlfriend, Cora, also liked to paddle kayaks, and hike, and take photos of sunsets. *Nature stuff. Outdoorsy crap*, my dad said, as if it were slightly suspect. I hated when people said bad stuff about all men, because I was surrounded by so many great ones. I hated when people said bad stuff about all anyones.

"Thanks," I said. I felt suddenly shy for some reason. Maybe because George really saw me right then.

"No problem. Have fun. Just lock that car up, huh?"

Your mother would be there, I kept reminding myself. I might not even go inside your houseboat. We might get to talk for five minutes. Maybe I'd have gotten the night off, driven over there in my car with the waving pizza on top, locked the door with shaking hands for no real reason. It didn't matter. I just wanted to see you so bad.

I walked down that dock.

Your dog began to bark the minute I stepped onto the float. I had my finger on the bell and hadn't even pressed it when you opened the door.

You grinned and I grinned back. Tell me a person can't feel big, forever things at our age. Tell me, too, that you can't feel love, or at least the imminent future of it, when you first meet someone. I know what I felt.

You took the box and put it on the couch. Kind of flung it there, really, pizza Frisbee. Look at me, I stepped over the threshold. Your dog—I didn't know his name yet—stared from the kitchen. All those facts would come later.

What came right at that moment was this: We took each other's hands, entwined our fingers. We were just smiling so hard. I almost wanted to cry. I'd always felt so anxious and out of place, my mind a clicking whirl of what might happen next, worried about all the ways I'd wreck things or hurt people or not give someone what they needed. Trying to keep my world small, because there was less to keep in control that way. Too large, and who knows what might happen. My mind was so mean to me sometimes. But right then, I just wanted to be where I was, doing what I was doing. Smiling at you while you smiled back. Like, what a perfect thing. So simple, but perfect. Just, *all.*

You put your arms around me, and we hugged. It was you, sort of skinny, in your denim shorts and T-shirt—God, what color, what was on it? I forget. And me in my denim shorts, too, frayed cuffs, tank top with the octopus graphic down one side, my hair in braids. I might have summer love, I realized. That magical best thing I'd heard about—sun, songs, hope. The coconut smell of lotion on your skin, or maybe mine. Even right then, the houseboat bobbed slightly, and there was the sound of a speedboat in the distance, music drifting over water, the shouts of people having fun on the lake.

From where I stood pressed against you, I saw your house, the actual place you lived: a crocheted blanket flung over the back of a couch, a coffee table messy with magazines promising travel to foreign places. I want to remember all the details, but mostly I remember my head against your chest. One ear on your heart, listening to it for the first time. I heard it beating, your heart, that traitor. That horrible, horrible traitor.

Chapter Five

"We wish you everything good from our planet."
–Serbian greeting

"Come on," you said when we separated again. "Let me show you around. It'll take all of five minutes." You didn't have to even move to show me, the place was so small. "Living room." You gestured to where we were standing, to that blue couch that had seen better days, and a rocking chair, and a kilim rug on the wood floor. "Dining room." A table by a window, piled with mail and a plant and a pair of place mats. "Kitchen." You pointed. "Let's not go there. Frank will get all wild to see you."

"That's okay. I love dogs. Hi, Frank." I waved.

"He'd wave back if he could. He's been totally depressed and not himself since our other dog, Jesse James, died."

"Jesse James? He was some kind of outlaw, right?"

"It's from a song? 'Frank and Jesse James'? My mom's a big Warren Zevon fan."

"Got it." I remembered. The same guy from that other song that was playing before: "Keep Me in Your Heart."

"I like him, too, honestly. I think it'd be cool if Solar Flare did their own version of some of his stuff. Okay. Onward! Follow me." You actually lifted your arm when you said *Onward*, a finger in the air, haha. It made me want to grab your butt, that cute one going down the hall in those denim shorts. I realized that Asher hadn't been my type at all. You were my type—a combo of dweeby and messy adorable.

"Okay!" I said with an overabundance of enthusiasm. My happiness was spilling like a fountain.

"Mom's room," you said. We only poked our heads in oh so briefly to be respectful. There was a mattress on the floor, and a tornado of clothes everywhere. A tall basket of laundry stood in one corner, clean or dirty, hard to tell. An array of undies was scattered around it, like fallen flower petals. Janite had either gone hunting for her favorites, or aimed and missed. A large purple crystal, slightly swinging like a pendulum, hung in the window. A clock on a nightstand had stopped at nine-fifteen.

"Nice," I said, to be polite.

"And mine."

We stepped into your room. For a minute, I felt a nervous energy, us there alone. The bed was this large, shouting thing, because I was suddenly thinking of what we might do in it. I mean, we could do it anywhere, but *bed* was somehow the big forbidden object. The specter of my dad appeared. Just, you know, how pissed he'd be at me for even being here. How his pissed-ness and control might *really* make me want to do everything he'd be furious about. But also, as I stood there, I realized with terror, and whatever is the opposite of terror, that I wanted it on my own. There was *that* energy, too. We barely knew each other, but I felt it, desire, like an electric current. It was a cliché, but how else to describe it? You couldn't see it, but it was so obviously there, crackling and zinging, and you knew it could potentially start a fire or maybe destroy you.

And you . . . You seemed a little nervous, too. About us being in there. You jammed your hands in your pockets and took them out again, and your forehead got a little sweaty, and you knelt on the bed to open the window above it. When you got up again, you smoothed the covers back in place. You weren't planning on us having wild sex there or anything, were you? Not *yet*, haha. I mean, you didn't bring me in there for that purpose like some guys might. Like Severin Gyles might. Severin, the most popular guy in my class, stereotypical bad boy, super good-looking but a streak of cruelty, like a line of fat in meat. His whole body was a sneer, and there were rumors of him drinking a lot, all that, girls doing whatever because he wanted it. This is the wrong way to explain it, good/bad, no sex/sex, you know. I just mean, I never understood liking bad boys. They seemed like those gross kids in the third grade who drilled holes in the desk with their scissors and shoved girls and tried to look up their dresses, only larger. *I* liked guys like *this*. Like you. Sweet and smart and curious. Friendly and kind and open. Who maybe didn't get stuff right all the time and wouldn't expect me to, either.

But then . . . I stopped thinking about us being alone, and

sex, and liking, really liking, you already, because a stark realization slammed me. Your room—it was the exact opposite of the one we'd just seen, your mom's. The *exact* opposite. Like, my own room was somewhere in the middle, with my vintage travel posters and *Be Kind to Your Mind* wall art that Maurice gave me, with the girl watering her head made of flowers. With my messily made bed, and stuff on my dresser, earrings, lotion, school binders, and yesterday's outfit over my desk chair. Your room was pure order, as your mom's was pure chaos. Everything was in place, the bed tightly made, the drawers crisply shut. On your shelves, the books had their spines aligned, and the framed photos were placed at purposeful angles. No disarray anywhere.

It told me a story right away. A story that maybe involved Dr. Quentin Baleaf. I mean, I could see the tornado right next door, and the way, in that room, you were fighting the tornado. Instead of boarded-up windows and sandbags, candles and matches, you stockpiled calculated order. It probably told many stories. Someone once warned me—I can't remember who, someone who I believed, anyway—that it was the edges you had to worry about. The extremes. One end or the other. Not much happened in the middle. The middles were fine. The middles were mostly safe and okay, but the edges . . . If you're over there about anything, something's going on. It's either too much, or, in my mom's case, too little.

It didn't make me worry about you or us or what was coming. It made me sad. Like, my heart ached. I could already see how hard you tried, and what you were up against.

The edges cause trouble, though. Big trouble.

"Voyager!" Now I noticed the poster that covered the whole side wall of your room. I moved in front of it to examine it more closely. It was purple and titled *Voyager: The Grand Tour and Beyond*, and it featured the timeline of the space probes and the planets they'd pass. I could tell you'd had that poster for a long time, and that it had been in lots of places. One corner was ripped off, and there were lots of tiny pinholes in the others, as if it had been put up and taken down again multiple times.

"Yeah," you said. "And look what Sandrine gave me a while back."

It was a framed album. A gold record. It looked like the kind you'd see in the fancy houses of famous musicians. Only, it had mysterious etchings on it. A starburst, a circle that looked like a toy train track, another that resembled a tiny keyboard. Two that could have been the heartbeats on a hospital machine: one too fast, the other too slow. It took me a minute. I don't know why. I could sometimes be a bit behind everyone else, the last to catch on to the joke; but there were also a lot of distractions, namely you. "The Golden Record," I realized. A replica. "I read up about it."

"You did?" You seemed shocked. You even scrunched your face in disbelief. But I could see how pleased you were, too. "That is *so* cool."

"I didn't see a picture. This is what it looks like, huh?"

"All of the images on it . . . They're basically directions. They tell the alien life-forms how to play it."

"Huh." No idea.

"See this?" Without touching the glass, you pointed to the circle that looked like a train track. I could tell that this record was very precious to you. "This represents the record, and shows where they should place the stylus. The symbols communicate in the universal language of math? Any civilization intelligent enough to find this should be able to decipher it."

"I don't know. If I stumbled upon it in a space thrift store, I'd probably make it into one of those clocks you see on Etsy and totally miss the major discovery. You and Sandrine are close, huh?"

"We've lived with her and my aunt when my mom has been, uh, between things. Once when I was little, then around twelve or thirteen? And then again last year. Sandrine's like a sister to me. My aunt Gwen is like a mom to me, too."

It was a funny thing to say when you had a mom of your own, I thought, and tucked it away in my more-info-needed brain file. I strolled in your room like it was a Mars Museum, examined your bookshelf and the stuff on it: astronomy books, a few shells and rocks, a photo of baby you in your mom's arms, a ticket that read *Santa Cruz Boardwalk*, which had been laminated and made into a key chain. Also, a greeting card with an image of those Sky Glider rides, legs of the riders hanging down. There was lots of writing in it. Girl writing. It went on and on. In the framed photos, I spotted you with groups of friends, tubing at a lake, sitting on bleachers, sprawled out on a beach. So many friends! Huh—the same girl was in all of them. I felt a little flare of jealousy. I wondered if all that handwriting belonged to her, too. Maybe this was a red flag. Or not a red flag exactly, but a maroon one. Meaning, a reason I might be marooned.

"Friends from my old school," you told me. And then you

pointed right to her, the girl. "This is Ella. She was my closest friend. Is? Was? After we moved, we stayed in touch, but not much anymore. We tried to date a little, but it didn't really work out."

"Oh," I said. It made me feel terrible, but also great at the same time, because you just said it, you know. Right out there, right away. Supposedly, I didn't make Asher feel special, but the whole time we'd been together, his old girlfriend had been texting him and stuff, and I'd had zero clue she even existed.

You picked up the key chain and smiled down. "I went on a trip here with her and her family. They were really great."

I wondered if you'd say that about mine. There were reasons, parent reasons, why that might be unlikely. It was perhaps another maroon flag.

"Whoa," I said. I'd just noticed your top shelf, which was full of trophies—little gold people kicking balls and throwing balls and hitting balls. A medal or two, also. I started to worry about the ways we seemed very different. The friends, the sports. "You must be a really good athlete."

You snorted. "I suck."

"They give trophies for sucking?"

"Look closer. Participation. But, hey, one or two *Most Improved*. And my pride and joy, *Most Inspirational*, for track in my freshman year. Long jump and high jump?"

"That's a lot of jumping."

"Look at these babies." You waggled a skinny leg. I smiled. I liked those legs a lot, but they didn't scream *athlete*. "Actually, my long was short, and I never made it over the bar once. When it clatters down and you land on it . . . Fuck, it hurts."

"Ooh. Your pride, too?"

You shrugged. "Don't care much about that. Like I said before, the more people, the more connection, right? That's what matters to me most."

It seemed even more brave than facing that high bar. Oh, we were different, all right. Opposites, those unnerving ends of the spectrum again, maybe. I moved on from the bookshelf, continued my Mars Museum visit. I stopped at another framed photo—one on your bedside table, the most important spot. It was the only thing on it, aside from your clock. The surface was clean, no messy tubes of ChapStick or water bottles. No stray pen caps or candy wrappers. Just this photo of a man. He was wearing a tan turtleneck with a blazer over the top. His hair was parted on the side like a newsman, and his chin was resting thoughtfully on his hand.

"Is this your dad?" Man, he had the kindest eyes ever.

You started laughing, you butt. You laughed so hard, you had to raise up one hand, like *please forgive me*. I felt kind of embarrassed, but glad at the same time. I mean, your laugh was just so nice. You wiped your eyes, like *whew*. "It's Carl Sagan," you said. "The astrophysicist? He played a leading role in Voyager and oversaw the creation of the Golden Record. Lily actually got to work with him."

"Wow. How cool. He looks so nice."

"Right? His face is just calming. Mr. Rogers of the cosmos."

I laughed. "I can see why you'd want it by your bed."

"You can?" You couldn't believe it.

"A hundred percent." It didn't seem weird to me at all. And maybe we were more alike than it first seemed. I sometimes watched the video of Mr. Rogers singing "You Are Special" when I felt like I sucked. It was such a comfort. I believed him. I liked how Mr. Rogers always fed his fish before his show started, too, like even they were his friends that deserved respect. Maybe that's what you felt when you looked at that photo. A kindness toward all humanity, including your own messed-up self.

"So, change of subject," you said. "Because I can only think of one thing right now."

If you were Severin Gyles, or even Asher Allen, I knew what would have happened next, but you were not Severin Gyles or Asher Allen. Not by a long shot.

"I give up," I said, though I hadn't even tried to guess.

"There's a pizza in the other room we're totally ignoring. I've eaten plenty of them, and they're incredible. And it's sitting on the couch like it's nothing, when it's something. Something special."

"Well, come on. Let's have some, then."

Honestly, it was true. That pizza was special. I could be so sick of it sometimes, but I wasn't right then. I was suddenly starving.

Chapter Six

Dolphins, photograph by Thomas Nebbia:
Pictures of Earth

Frank wasn't really all that wild. It was mostly the door-bell and cats and the arrival of the mail, an understandable thrill. And yeah, he jumped up for a minute on my knees when we went to the kitchen, but you just needed to notice him, and he was fine after that. He just needed to be seen, like any reasonable person.

You cracked a few bubbly waters, and we took our pizza on paper plates out to the deck. Frank sat up like a gentleman beside us, on his best behavior in hopes of a dropped crust. It was so fun out there. I'd delivered to the houseboats before, but I never got to hang out. It was like a busy little village, all charming shingled shacks and odd-shaped houses mixed with elegant, modern two-stories, all jammed together on that dock that swayed and creaked. You called out a *Hi!* to a woman watering her plants, and you waved to another guy coming home with groceries. You gave a thumbs-up to another man climbing into a kayak, and he gave one back.

Another woman opened her front door for air, propping it ajar with a flowerpot.

"Hey, Mars!" she called. "Hey, Mars's friend!"

"Hey, Adelaide!" you answered, and I just smiled. "Beautiful day!"

"This is so great out here," I said.

"I love it." You took a drink from your can. "It's my favorite place we've lived so far. We've actually only been in this place for a few months."

"You've moved around a lot, right?"

"Every two years or so? Lots of places in California, and back here again, where my mom's from. She, uh, tends to meet some guy? And then our plans are his plans. But hey. I can pack a truck like a pro so shit doesn't fall out the back."

Oh, God. That sounded like a maroon flag for sure. "Wow. Is that hard? We've *always* lived in the same house. Near Green Lake. How do you keep changing schools and stuff? I can't imagine. I've been going to school with the same people for as long as I can remember." It was a way to find out how old you were, I admit. Aside from a vague idea from that photo in the *North Bend Herald*, I had no clue. I knew so little about you, but I kept having the strange feeling that I'd known you forever. Or even way past forever. Going back in time or something. It's hard to explain.

"I just . . . try to be open, you know. Meet people. See what might happen. If it's horrible, I won't be there long, right? But I'm done with all that now."

"You graduated?"

"Nah. I'll be a senior next year, but I'm at Seattle Central

College? I've been doing my AP classes over there this year, and next year, too. When we first moved back and lived with Sandrine and Aunt Gwen, I went to North Bend High. But now that we're here, it takes, like, an hour to get to school." You shook your pizza slice to make a definite point. "There's *no way* I'm moving again. UW has a great astrophysics and astronomy program I'm applying to. Okay, major confession, my biggest dream would be to blast off into space, but astronomy is a lot more practical. Lily is a professor emeritus at UW? She still teaches occasionally. Usually in the area of interstellar, intergalactic, and circumgalactic medium."

"I have no idea what that is, but it's so great that you have a plan. I'm going to apply to UW, too, but I have no idea what major. I wish I had a thing like you have a thing."

A confession: I worried for a second that you might start to explain interstellar galactic-whatever. I already liked you a lot, but that could shift, you know, if you insisted on instructing me, the way Arthur did whenever we got on the subject of car engines, or the way my dad did whenever we got on the subject of pretty much anything. I loved the wonder of all that stuff, planets and the universe and all, but I didn't need to know the factual details. You didn't do that, though. Instead, you just tilted your head in a question. "You're not studying business?"

I made a face.

"Well, you've got all of senior year, too. You never know what might just spark some passion," you said. And then you blushed.

There was a lot to blush about. Not just the *spark some passion* line, but the fact that you knew how old I was. You looked me up! Haha, you did. You probably saw that DECA competition we did last year, the Virtual Business Challenge-Entrepreneurship, where me and my partner, Hannah Chen, simulated opening a new restaurant.

"We're the exact same age, hmm," I said.

"It seems like . . . we're the exact same a lot of things." You looked into my eyes again. We weren't, in a lot of ways. I mean, beyond your friends and the sports, there was your whole hardcore astronomy interest, your single mom, where you lived, how you guys moved around, pretty much everything I learned about you so far. I would never, not in a million years, want to blast off into space. Still, I knew what you meant. There was some sense that we *were* the same, or at least really, really similar, down deep where it mattered. This might sound weird, but . . . like a twin or something. Not in a biological way, but like someone who was once a part of me who I was reconnecting with.

I looked into *your* eyes, too. And Frank stared at both of us, still wanting pizza, or maybe just watching Human TV. Your eyes and mine—it was like falling into something, a world or a universe, a cosmos where only the two of us walked around. It was intense. Too intense, really. I mean, that universe might have a beautiful sea to swim in, but it might also have volcanoes and earthquakes, deserts and mirages. Maybe that's what love always felt like. I never experienced it before, so who knew, but it seemed suddenly very dangerous. I was crossing over into some vast and unsafe space, and all at once I felt the way I did when I thought about getting drunk or having sex or driving a car. Or going to college or moving out or traveling, or a hundred other things. Only worse, because it was big, scary stuff *plus* my heart.

I was the one who broke it, the gaze. I was overwhelmed. I'd never been that close to anybody.

"Moving so much and all . . . Is that part of why you go to Dr. Quentin Baleaf?" Nothing like a little mental-health talk to kill a romantic vibe. It's like I did it intentionally.

When my eyes broke from yours, you looked out toward the lake and shrugged. "Yeah, no." I wasn't sure which of those was the answer. "I saw him back when I was, like, ten? Aunt Gwen made me go. She thought it'd be a good idea to see him again now. Just preventative, like? I got really, really depressed back then."

"When you were only ten?"

"My mom was getting divorced from Leon, her third husband. There was my dad, then Oscar Maltez, then Leon Johnson. He was a real creep. I hated him. He was always demeaning her, and she cried all the time, but when they broke up, she, uh, made an attempt. To, uh . . ."

"Oh, man." It was okay. You didn't have to say it.

"Right. And I uh, had to call, you know."

"Oh, God." You didn't have to say anything you didn't want to.

"Right. And we ended up at Aunt Gwen's, and I was just sad all the time. I felt like I weighed a thousand pounds. My aunt dragged me in there, and Dr. QB really helped. Him, plus Sandrine, and . . . This is going to sound silly, and we don't have to talk about it every second, but that's when I learned about Voyager and the Golden Record. Sandrine already had her first telescope. Telescope and a guitar, the coolest person ever. But . . . thinking of this thing out there, this record of humanity that would last beyond all of us, just so far *out* there . . . It was comforting. It was, like, uplifting.

Connection. The hope of it—it seemed like a clue to survival, almost. So when my mom and Alan broke up—he was the last guy, in Palo Alto?—Aunt Gwen thought I should go back to counseling. What about you?"

"Winnifred Evans? I started getting all . . ." I put my hand against my chest. "Anxious and stuff, before I started my job? All of my brothers did delivery first, too, but way younger than me. My dad and mom said it was too dangerous for me, a girl, driving in traffic and ringing strangers' doorbells and stuff. They wouldn't allow it. So I fought for my right to be treated equally, but when they finally gave in, when I won . . . Panic."

"That makes sense."

"It does?" Now I was the one who was full of disbelief. "I don't even know why I fought for it. Just because it was unfair, I guess. Anyway, I was scared, *am* scared, to do a lot of things. Like that. And that. And that." I pointed to a woman kayaking. To a sailboat. To an airplane. If I told you I was anxious to even say hi to the neighbors, you might flee, and I wouldn't blame you.

"Sure, but now you deliver pizzas like a boss."

I laughed. "I got used to it after a while. Oh! Poor Frank. He's given up." Frank was lying on the dock, chin on paws. His ear twitched at his name.

"I love him, but I'm not sharing my pizza." You peeked under the lid of the box. Whoa. It was a small, but we polished it off.

"He looks so sad."

"He's not the same since Jesse James died."

"I'm sorry for your loss, Frank," I said, and meant it.

"His grief was real. Did you know that lots of animals grieve?

Dogs and elephants and crows and monkeys and giraffes and dolphins . . ." You knew a lot about a lot of things.

"That's amazing."

"It's . . . universal."

"An elephant would use a lot of Kleenex. Wait. What time is it, even?" I checked my phone. Only George knew where I was, and it was getting late. Mom or Dad might worry, and worried people are always making sure no one else has to go through that. "I better go."

"Noooo," you groaned. "I haven't even kissed you yet."

I loved the way you just said stuff straight-out. No games. If the universe of love was risky, maybe you were a good planet. I took your hand. Our fingers intertwined, and electricity zipped through my body.

"MARSDEN ZEVON RIVERS!" a woman shouted. "I could use some *help*, please."

It was your mom. She was carrying a large . . . No idea. It was purple, glittery. A giant rock of some kind.

"Just a sec!" Mars dropped my fingers, pushed his chair back. "My mom," you said to me. "She's been working at this woo-woo metaphysics shop, with crystals and stuff. Sacred Stones or something? Why do I always forget the name?"

"Oh! Mystic Minerals. Right off Green Lake Way, probably." Crystals, incense, classes on finding your inner goddess.

"That's it! When she gets involved in something, it's a hundred percent."

You hurried over to help. "This fucker is heavy," your mom said. "Put it right there." She indicated the little table where we sat.

I stood and removed the pizza box so you could set the enormous rock down. It took over the whole thing.

"Wow," I said.

"It's a half-raw ametrine tower." That day, your mom's blond hair was in braids, same as mine. Her eyes were a startling blue shade. Piercing and beautiful. "It's supposed to be a shield from negative energy, while bringing serenity, and enhancing the ability to take control over your own life, and . . . I forget the rest. Protective."

"Mom, this is Margaret. Margaret, my mom, Janet."

"Jan*ite*. Glad to meet you," she said.

But I'd never seen anyone less glad to meet me in all my life.

"Can you get the groceries out of the car?" she said to you.

When we walked back up the dock, I felt a horrible shame crawl up my spine, like I'd done something terribly wrong. I wondered if this, she, was a maroon flag. In her car, an old Ford Taurus, there was a single grocery bag on the passenger seat.

We stood next to my car. Someone had put an old athletic sock on the smiling pizza's head, and I yanked it off and tossed it into the dock's dumpster. You didn't seem bothered by what had just happened back there. I couldn't even really describe it myself. How would I explain it to Addison? Nothing *had* happened. I was being all weird.

The groceries waited in the car. You hugged me again. You looked at me, blinking with what seemed like happiness.

"I just can't believe . . ." You shook your head.

I couldn't believe it, either. You and me.

"I feel like . . ."

"What?"

"Okay, I'm going to bring it up again," you warned.

"Do it."

"On the Golden Record, there's this image. Number 54. Three dolphins, leaping in the air. It's retro-looking, right? Well, it wasn't in 1977, but it is now. I mean, think of it: It seemed important to show alien life this other weird alien life in our oceans. Sagan said he thought it would be *courteous* to show the dolphins, after including the whale songs. But the dolphins are all leaping in air, and water droplets are pouring down, and they're set against this beautiful beach backdrop. An 'exuberant creature,' Sagan said, and it's just joy, right? Like, look, our planet has *joy.* And, right now . . ." You tapped your chest.

Okay, you . . . No one, absolutely no guy in my entire school, would talk like this. Their eyes wouldn't shine like this. And I felt it, too, the leaping dolphins. I raised my two hands, arced them in the air, a goofy dance move, a joy hand-rainbow.

"Yep," you said. "Yes, yes." Like you loved it. Just loved it.

We didn't say goodbye. You just moved toward the groceries, and I got in my car, and you still hadn't kissed me.

But this is what I really remember: My hands, arcing in the air. You, beaming. You, all light.

Chapter Seven

Kiss: *Sounds of Earth*

"Are you sure about this?" I asked Maurice as he pulled into the Neumos parking lot. "You haven't played anywhere in, what, a couple of years?"

"I've played."

"You've played?"

"Been playing. Never stopped."

My jaw drops. "Honestly?" We didn't know. We had no clue. He didn't live at home, but still.

"Everyone doesn't need to know everything about you." He turned his engine off.

"What's your long-term plan here?" We both understood what I meant. I meant Dad.

"No idea yet. You don't need to know everything about yourself every minute, either," he said. "Come on."

There were already a lot of cars in the parking lot. There was a jazzed feeling all around, excitement. Maybe those people were really looking forward to seeing Solar Flare, or maybe this was how it always was before a performance at a club. I had no idea. I'd never even been to many concerts at all, let alone to a club. I'd gone with my parents to see the Cars Reunion Band when I was, like, twelve, and I saw Maurice play in his old band, Irv and the Irks, once, with my brothers at a brewery, and I&I at Marymoor Park another time, but that was about it. Concerts were not the kind of thing Addison and Priya and I did. We'd maybe watch movies at Priya's, or bake cookies at Addison's house, or go shopping for craft supplies at Ben Franklin and then come back to my house to make T-shirts or something, like those unfortunate red-and-yellow tie-dyed ones that looked like we'd survived a Civil War battle.

Places like Neumos—my dad wouldn't approve. Priya's parents might not, either, actually. It was an underage club, so there wasn't supposed to be alcohol or anything, but he would have been uneasy at all of the . . . What? Possibilities for meeting guys? The music-equals-sex vibe? The danger of me not at home making cookies? That night, I'd lied and told my parents that Addison and I were going to the Grand Illusion to watch some French film Addison wanted to see, and then I walked over to Maurice's apartment, pretty much around the corner from us.

Now I started to get excited, too. I hoped I looked cute. I spent a lot of time trying on outfits, when I didn't ordinarily. When Mom popped her head in my room that afternoon and saw all the discarded options piled up on my bed, she raised one eyebrow. It probably didn't look like I was meeting Addison, and I probably wasn't all that great of a liar.

"Do you like this?" I asked about my outfit. I mostly did it to throw her off—I never asked her about clothes. We never talked a lot in general. She wasn't what you'd call *open*. I had on my orange skirt from last year, pink-green-and-white-striped tank. I wore the skirt maybe twice. My father had commented on the length, and then I felt bad about wearing it. Even now, I kept pulling at the hem, up, down, like it was a decision.

"*I* do." Of course, we both understood what she was saying. It'd been a year since I wore it, and she hadn't forgotten, either. "You look so pretty."

I took another look. The colors were so cheerful. They made me happy. My mom and I smiled at each other. It was almost like she was giving her approval without saying a word. Maybe it was the only way she *could* give it, without facing the giant force of opposition. I remembered her stories about her first real boyfriend, Ned Shepherd, how sweet he was. It made you wonder why people made certain decisions and not others, because my dad wasn't sweet, not at all. She was, though. At least, I thought so. It's hard to tell for sure, when you don't know what someone's thinking. Her not eating—it was silent, too, even if it could sometimes seem like the most hostile message imaginable. Pure anger, you know. Pure *I'll show you*. Dad's noisy, messy force didn't stand a chance against her icy will. Her sweetness could look like powerlessness, but maybe if you ripped off the mask, you'd see fury and determination. No idea, but right then, I could tell she saw my outfit and remembered that love could just be . . . great. She didn't call me out on my French-film lie. It felt really nice. It felt like support.

In the Neumos parking lot, Maurice and I moved toward the graffiti wall and the black double-door entrance. My heart began to thrum, and I had to nervous-pee when I already went ten minutes ago. The excitement, the nerves, the bamming heart: I was about to see you. We'd texted a few times that week, remember? Nothing major. A *hey*, and a *hey*. A *how're you doing*, and a *Great, you?* Some silly emojis for fun. A whale and a smile. An otter and hearts. The friendliest ones. A *See you Saturday?* And a *Can't wait*. I wanted to read paragraphs about you and write paragraphs to you. I wanted to read the whole book of you. But the texts reminded me of what happens when I finally get an *actual* book I've wanted for a long time. I wait to read it, gaze at it on my stack where it nearly glows with all its promise. My book of you felt like that—the happy anticipation of something great.

When we went inside, I took it all in, the kids milling around in the near darkness lit with blue-purple light, the sticky floor, the band kit set up at the front of the small space, shining with a brighter blue-purple. Mostly, though, I looked around for you. I couldn't see you anywhere, and then Maurice took off, headed for the stage where Sandrine was. She was leaning down to adjust some mic cords or something, the bare skin of her back glowing in that otherworldly hue.

"Wait!" I called to Maurice. I sounded like a little sister, but I suddenly felt little, in that place that seemed to be grown up in ways I wasn't. It smelled like years of beer in there, with back-notes of heartache and vomit, and people were filling in all around like in a crowded elevator, something that makes me panic for sure. I spotted Severin Gyles and his friend Ramone in the drink line as I stood there, alone.

Maurice couldn't hear me. I followed him like a baby duckling. Even in the strange light of the room, I could see his eyes, focused on Sandrine, zooming toward her with the singular focus of Voyager on its way to Jupiter. He put his hands on her hips, startling her.

"Hey!" she said, pissed off, until she stood and whirled around and saw it was Maurice. Her *Hey!* turned into a *Heyyy*. Her face got all shy-smiley, and I thought they were going to kiss. Instead, she gave him some command I couldn't hear.

Maurice noticed me again. I wondered if that was Sandrine's command. He reached into his wallet and handed me his credit card, money I didn't need. I made my own, thanks. My mother always said, *Never be dependent on a man*, while always being dependent on a man. Still, it seemed like solid advice, and already I was piling my money away. It felt like a kind of power. It felt like choices. Maybe those were the same thing.

"Go get yourself—" I couldn't hear the rest of what he said. It was getting loud in there.

I took his card, even if I didn't need it. It was for him as much as it was for me, because it allowed him to cut me loose without feeling too guilty. And I was definitely cut loose, all right, in that blue-lit world I suddenly felt super awkward in. Like, what was I doing here when I could be in Addison's basement where I belonged? Safe, watching some movie and eating Red Vines, like we always did. I got in the drinks line. Severin Gyles actually looked over his shoulder at me and smiled. I couldn't believe it. But I could also tell he didn't recognize me. I was just some girl, maybe a cute or pretty girl, not even from his school. I mean, I'd sat behind him in world history for a whole semester.

I got my Diet Pepsi. We never drank non-diet soda in my house. Something terrible would happen, obviously, if we did. Like, we'd gain a few pounds and destroy our lives. Someday, I'd go wild and have one.

Where were you? More and more people arrived, and it was getting hot in there. I could tell my hair was drooping, and I'd already licked off most of my lip gloss. The rest was on my cup, smiling creepily at me. I felt so weirdly by-myself that I had to find a pole to lean against, a pal. I tried to look like I did this kind of thing all the time, even if no one noticed or cared. I took out my phone, punched stuff as if I were doing important business.

That night, no one introduced Solar Flare or anything. They just started playing. I was getting nervous because you were late. I always got nervous about lateness, mine or anyone else's, but this was worse, because maybe it meant you weren't coming. When Sandrine stepped up to the mic, the crowd shrieked and applauded. Severin Gyles had his hands over his head, clapping so hard. Somehow, he felt my eyes on him, from where I was over there, smooshed against that pole, and he grinned at me. He nodded, all certain, like *Caught you checking me out!* when I really was just shocked that Solar Flare had actual fans. I mean, look. They were losing their shit at that first song; Severin Gyles was. A song that the crowd absolutely recognized. Oh my God, it was called "Seeing You, Seeing Me." Severin Gyles's nod had a whole new meaning.

And wait. Sandrine, and Sandrine's voice . . . Oh my God. She was just . . . You couldn't take your eyes off her. I could see, so easily right there, why Maurice fell so hard. I was falling for her myself, you know, the whole crowd was. She was tough and sexy and vulnerable and just . . . *honest.* Her voice was. She held us all in the palm of her hand. Her hair flung around her face when she played guitar, too, a force. Another guy, Dre, played keyboard, and there was Maurice on drums. Maurice—when did he get so cute? His hair had grown longer, shaggier, and I hadn't even noticed. His eyes were sweet, and you could feel his and Sandrine's chemistry when they played. She'd look back at him when she sang, and whoa. Just whoa—whatever they had, you wanted it.

They played another song, and another. No you. No you anywhere. If she wrote all these herself, they were incredible. It got easier to stand there alone in my crushing disappointment, because I got wrapped up in the music, same as everyone else. The crowd was one big person. I was kind of dancing a little on my own, even. But I was so bummed, you know, that you weren't there. You weren't coming. *Face it,* I told myself. The band took a break. I wanted to go see Maurice and tell him how awesome he was, how awesome *they* were, but I was in a human traffic jam.

And then . . . Oh, shit! Severin Gyles was weaving and pushing and maneuvering his way toward me. He still didn't know I was that dweeby girl who sat behind him in world history, the one who always finished her tests before everyone else; I was sure. I turned my back on him. I didn't want to talk to him. And then I felt hands on my hips, same as Maurice put his hands on Sandrine, and I whirled around same as she did.

"Hey!" I growled. But it was you! *"Heyyyy."* I could probably learn a lot from Sandrine.

"Hey." You hugged me. It was so good to see you. So good. I suddenly had a place, instead of being there all alone. You felt like an actual place where I had landed.

From a few feet away, Severin glared. You'd cut him off before he got to me, not that you knew it. "Tease," he mouthed, like an asshole. His story, starring himself, had taken an unexpected turn.

"Who's that guy?" you asked. Shouted, actually. It was so loud in there, with the crowd all talking during the break.

"Jerk from school," I shouted back.

"I'm sorry I'm so late!"

"I'm so glad you found me in here!" It seemed like a miracle. Another miracle. "What happened?"

"I got a job! Remember I told you I was looking?"

"Of course." It felt good, to know things, to remember things. To have a storyline that continued.

"And remember Chester? From the astronomy meetup?"

"Absolutely." Harley guy.

"He's in charge down at the Center for Wooden Boats?" So maybe not a Harley guy. A boat guy. "I get to work the booth for rentals, and manage the sailing checkouts. It was wild down there! So busy. And then we had to check the boats back in, clean them, get them all ready for tomorrow. Chester started talking . . . It seemed rude to just bolt, after he gave me the job. And then I had to go home and change. What a day!"

"That place seems really cool." I'd never been to the Center for Wooden Boats. It'd been there forever, but I never had.

"It is! I love it. How are you?"

"So great. So great." My heart was lifting. I felt so excited again.

About everything, life in general. I almost felt like I could do stuff, you know, new and scary things, even. Like I wanted to experience as many things as possible, which would probably last as long as I was standing there. Still, I guess I felt happy. If this was what falling in love was like, I could see why there were all those songs and movies and books about it. "Sandrine is incredible. The whole band is."

"Right? She's been singing since she was, like, five."

"Maurice has been drumming see *he* was, like, five. Chopsticks on the table. My dad finally let him have a drum set after Maurice bought one and brought it home and begged and cried."

"Whoa. It took all that?"

I made a face, like *You don't know my dad*. "My dad likes people to follow his plans for them." There was another word for that, but I didn't say it.

"Here they come."

Sandrine walked out again, and the crowd began to cheer. She gave a little wave and picked up her guitar. Maurice and Dre took their spots. She played a few chords, and everyone shrieked and got all wild. "They love her," I said.

"It's like this everywhere they play."

"What happened to their old drummer?"

"Sad story." You really had to shout now.

"Oh, no."

You nodded. "Gave up playing to study programming. Sandrine didn't think she could go on. But she could. I'm so glad she could."

I was, too. For Maurice, for all of us. Her voice was still here, telling us the truth. Now she was singing a ballad called "Infinity."

The people in the crowd had made circles with the thumb and forefinger of each hand, linked them together, and were waving them over their heads. I looked at you questioningly.

"The infinity sign," you answered. You made one, too. So did I. We swayed. The song was so beautiful, it made me want to cry. Sandrine closed her eyes when she sang it, chin tilted up, as if she were sending a personal message skyward.

When the song ended, the crowd clapped and hooted, and then the beat picked up. We danced our butts off. God, it was fun, surrounded by all those people and that energy, just in it there with you.

When the show was over, my shirt was practically stuck to my skin with sweat, and so was yours, and it didn't matter. In fact, it was great. It was proof of the experience. Outside, the cool air was like water. We drank it up, waved our shirts in and out, saying, *Whew*. My whole spirit, my whole soul, if you believed in that, the deepest parts, you know, were soaring. It was you, and you, and the music, and the energy, and a feeling of triumph, too—doing this new thing and having a blast. The crowd swarmed to their cars, and *everyone* seemed so happy that I wondered if Solar Flare was going to be famous. Oh, man, Maurice was headed for trouble.

In the parking lot, you were dancing in place, all sexy-goofy, and I was shimmying my shoulders and getting the words wrong. You laughed, and pulled me to you, and—I was going to say you kissed me, but no—we kissed each other. There was your mouth finally pressing against mine, and your breath and my breath merging into *ours*. You grabbed the back of my head to bring me closer, closer. Oh, God, Mars. I'd been imagining some quiet moment, somewhere we were all alone, but it happened there, surrounded by people. In a way, we were still alone, just us. Maybe even more alone, in our private starship, with all the other starships buzzing around us. Plus, who could wait. All that music, all that feeling, all that energy—it made us want, and want bad.

"Wow," you said.

"Wow," I said.

Now I did want to be alone. At least, what I wanted next couldn't be done in a crowd of people.

We kissed some more as we waited for Sandrine and Maurice. The crowd thinned. You waved to a guy. You knew someone there, too. You knew people everywhere. The parking lot quieted. When Sandrine and Maurice emerged, holding hands, we clapped. Dre was still inside with the sound guy, making sure all the equipment was packed up. Maurice suddenly looked shy.

"You guys were incredible," I said.

"Yeah?"

"So much yeah."

There were a few awkward minutes as everyone said goodbye. What had happened between you and me with that kiss—I thought we hid it. We probably didn't hide it very well, because when I finally got into Maurice's familiar truck again, he said, "You had a good night, huh?" and laughed. It wasn't mean at all, the opposite. He was glad. It was like he'd played a part in giving me a key that sprang me from prison.

"What?" I pulled down the visor and looked in the mirror. Holy shit. If the rest of me looked as messed up as what I saw in the tiny little rectangle, I'd better pray hard that no one was awake when I got home.

"Us and the cousins." Maurice started to giggle. Seriously, giggle. I started to giggle. It was really late. We were in hysterics territory.

"Hot cousins," I said.

He licked his forefinger and made a sizzling sound, set it on the steering wheel like it was a hot pan. It was so silly that we cracked up. We were cracking up so hard, he didn't notice that the red light had changed.

"It's green." I smacked his arm.

"Let's fucking *go*," he said.

When he dropped me off at home, I said, "You're the best drummer I ever saw." It helped that maybe I'd only seen the Cars Reunion Band and him, but still.

He smiled. He looked so happy. It was a night I'd never forget. "Night, MG." His nickname for me.

I tried to shut the truck door really quietly. And open our front door really quietly. I wiggled the key in, but it was unlocked.

Inside, only one light was on. My dad sat in the living room recliner, looking at his phone. He set it down when I walked in.

Shit.

Shit, shit, shit.

"Do you have any idea what time it is?" His voice was calm, but I knew better. His cheek muscle was all tight. One time, I heard an expression, *His face looked like a fist.* I'm not sure where, but then I saw it again shortly afterward somewhere else. I told Winnifred

Evans about this. How it can seem like a sign when you "stumble" on things in books or in the world. It was the perfect description of my dad when he was angry.

And, the thing was, I actually *didn't* have any idea what time it was. The clock in Maurice's truck probably stopped working in the late 1990s, and I hadn't looked at my phone in hours. Like, who cared about phones when you were having such an amazing time. I shook my head.

"Two-fifteen." He showed me his phone. He was still reclining. This is hard to explain, but that was maybe more nerve-racking than towering over me. A person who reclined didn't doubt their power.

"I'm going to bed." I hadn't done anything wrong. I didn't have a curfew. I never went out late enough to need one.

I was walking toward the light, anyway. Literally, I mean. Going past the lamp in the living room. He could see me now. How disheveled I was. The whole me, beyond the tiny mirror in Maurice's car. Even I didn't know what he saw entirely. "What the fuck?" he said. "Where have you been?"

"Addison's. We went to see—"

"Don't lie to me."

"A French film, and then—"

"Was that Maurice's car I heard?"

"No!" And then I added a "God!" to up the ante on my outraged protest.

Bam! The recliner folded upright, and he stood. "What have you been doing?" His nostrils flared, maybe sniffing for alcohol or something. Maurice had a period where he drank a lot and got in trouble at school, but he stopped when he started playing with I&I. It was the opposite of what you'd think with musicians. His dedication to playing drums straightened him out, not the other way around, but Dad never gave up the idea of him being a screwup. Maurice was so *not* a screwup.

But the thing was . . . This might sound weird, but I swear, I smelled like I'd been kissing someone. I smelled different to me, like I'd brought you home with me. Your air and my air, our together air. Plus sweat, plus music, plus night, plus want. It all came home.

My dad was looking straight at it. Everything his little girl might become. But I wasn't a little girl, and I wasn't his.

"Nello!" my mom called from upstairs. It was her nickname for him. She didn't even come down or show herself. "Let it go. Stop. Just stop."

It was enough to let me pass. I went upstairs. Closed myself in the bathroom and witnessed my destruction. Oh, wow, my mascara was smeared and my hair was flat in spots and zinging up in others, and my cheeks were flushed, and my eyes looked bright. So bright. Starlight bright. What a mess. What a glorious mess.

I heard my parents talking in the other room. My mother had said, *Stop*, but she didn't sound very convincing. It did the trick for the moment, but it didn't sound like she meant it. How passive she was against him—it made me feel furious, as if I were feeling all her rage for her, because *come on*! The way she didn't do anything to defend us . . . She left us on our own. She left *herself* on her own, staying in her all-consuming world of herself and food—the teeny-tiny pieces of cut-up morsels, the endless cups of tea and coffee and water, the meals of two grapes and a few spoons of nonfat yogurt, the crackers hidden in dresser drawers, the excuses of new allergies and *I just ate*, plus the occasional illnesses, like migraines and mystery pains.

She'd said, *Stop*, but Maurice had said, *Let's fucking* go, and I knew what team I was on. Team Solar Flare, let's go and go and go. To the moon, to the stars, past. To infinity. We might burn up, but oh, how we'd shine.

Chapter Eight

Javanese gamelan performing "Kinds of Flowers":
Music of Earth

It was summer in Seattle, the best season. There was blue everywhere—the sky above, the water below. The clouds were fluffy white confection, the evergreen trees a proud, deep green. The beaches were crowded, and little dots of swimmers sprinkled the lakes, and in the sound, triangles of white sailboats everywhere, too. All around were the zips of bicycles and speedboats.

And it was too hot for pizza. This weather meant watermelon and sandwiches. Hot dogs and potato salad, peaches and Popsicles. I had a lighter work schedule, but you sure didn't. The Center for Wooden Boats, a tucked-away treasure in South Lake Union where people could rent historic wooden boats to take out on the lake, was always busy.

"Come, please?" you asked for the hundredth time.

"Are you sure? I mean, your workplace? Your boss and all?"

"It's Chester. You know Chester."

I did know Chester. At least, I was beginning to. And Santiago and Norty, Lily, and Rainey, too. Ben was pretty shy. I'd gone with you to the top of Tiger Mountain three more times already, and he hadn't said a lot more than *hello*. But Chester, who seemed to know a lot about a lot of things, showed me how to ward off a bear if I ever saw one in the wild, and taught me how to tell when the sun would set, and always said I reminded him of his niece. Norty shared his fruit gummies with me, and showed me how he could zip up his jacket and walk backward, and Rainey asked me lots of questions about college and my future. She'd studied business at UW, like I was supposed to, but changed her mind midway and recently became a librarian instead.

Lily, though. She was the one who was closest to you. You two had a thing, a grandmother-grandson thing, not that I had any great experience with those. My dad's parents died when I was little, and so did my mom's dad, and I only knew my grandmother through the checks she'd send in the mail and the phone conversations that always upset my mom. But Lily was the kind of grandma most people hoped for. She wasn't anything like your real grandma, your dad's mom, who lived in New Mexico and was fussy and prim and the sort of religious that's actually just a cover for racism and more. Lily was smart and funny, with so many interesting experiences, and I could tell she loved you. With her playful eyes, she taught me telescope basics. How, yeah, they magnified things, but their larger purpose was to collect light. She told me that Galileo said that telescopes revealed the invisible, and that, to her, telescopes proved that invisible things, unseen things, could be *as real and true as that tree over there*.

We'd been a couple for a little over a month, so I knew a lot of things. All the petals that made up one flower. I knew that you bought your old VW by selling a vintage record collection, which was hard, but necessary. Hard, because you loved music, and all old records reminded you of *the* old record, the golden one, that beautiful and somehow inexplicable record on a record, a record of us—a holy relic time capsule of outreach to the future and to *other*. Necessary, because you had to leave, you know. Home. As often and in as many ways as you could. Leaving was breathing.

I knew, too, that you thought dandelions were the underdog of flowers, and that you'd scoop a spider onto a paper towel instead of killing it, and that you pretty much only judged people who judged. You didn't like to talk about your dad, not because his death was some big, traumatic thing, but because you had little to say about a guy who felt like a stranger after only a handful of visits to New Mexico over the years. You worried about your mom, a lot, and didn't drink alcohol because she *did* drink alcohol. You could fix almost anything, from cars to kitchen sinks, because you and your mom had plenty of everything that had broken down. Your pants were always slipping down your hips, and you used your milkshake straw as a spoon, and you believed in always taking your shoes off at the beach and looking at sunsets and staying up as late as you needed to in order to see a meteor shower. You were a collector of people; you had friends of all ages. That kept coming up again and again, didn't it? How different we were that way? Because over and over I saw it, how friendly and open you were in ways I sure wasn't. People saw my hesitancy first, an uncertainty that they sometimes thought was aloofness. But your kindness and curiosity were the first things anyone noticed about you.

Most of all, what I knew was that *you* were golden.

We saw each other as often as we could, at night after work, and on our days off. We went to Shilshole Beach, and on a hike up Mount Si, and we talked on the phone late at night, you in your room, and me outside, sitting behind the big tree in the backyard so I couldn't be heard. Because, in terms of knowing things: Your mom knew about me, but my parents didn't know you existed. Sure, she barely tolerated my presence the handful of times I saw her, treating me the way a kid might treat the peas on his plate, eating a few because you had to, for now. But I hadn't given my mother or father the chance to do even that. I hiked with Addison and went to the beach with Addison and was on the phone with Addison.

I'm so sorry. You hated that. You tried to understand, but didn't really. It was a maroon flag! I didn't want my dad to destroy things with his blustering control. You were like a precious ruin he could bulldoze, or a beautiful historic building he'd smash with a wrecking ball.

Okay, well. I was wrong about what would destroy us.

I also maybe liked the secret; I admit it. I understood Maurice, the way none of us were aware that he'd still been playing drums, performing for months with Sandrine in Solar Flare. No one's boots could stomp your flowers if the flowers were in a secret garden. It could flourish or not on its own. It could do what it needed to do and be what it needed to be. But the garden was just so sweet, too, you know, so deliciously hidden, so much *mine*, when no one else knew about it. I wouldn't say that I loved the secret more than I loved you, but I did love it. It was so great, honestly. Secrets get such a bad reputation, but when you're used to people in every corner of your life, taking it, taking you, smooshing their selves over your breathing face, a secret is a place to be alive.

I told Addison and Priya about us, though. Addison seemed relieved, like she didn't have to worry about me anymore, now that she had Liam and Priya had Maddie. She wanted us all to get together, meet you, at least, but I kept making excuses. I was still protective of my garden. You were the kind of guy who'd have gotten bullied in our middle school. Sorry to say that, but it was true. I couldn't even imagine you and Liam in the same row at a movie theater. See, I was someone who thought dandelions were underrated, too.

And I did tell Winnifred Evans. Weirdly (I thought weirdly), she didn't even give me a hard time about keeping us a secret from my parents. Instead, she said, *I notice how you always use the word* alive *when you talk about him*. I got the idea that she approved of the way that my life was suddenly larger. *Trying new things*, she said. *A real relationship, not in your head. Taking risks*, she said. *Being out in the world*, she said. *Kind*, she said. *Pfft*, she said about my maroon flags. But she was wrong about that.

You and me—our emojis had gone from whales and otters to comets and fire. Starbursts and lightning. After that kiss at the concert, there were so many more, in your car and at the beach and in your room, and everywhere. We didn't have sex or anything. Maybe I'd be ready when you'd be ready, but maybe you'd be ready when I was; it was hard to tell. But I did also know how your skin felt. I knew what it was like to be in your room, to slide my hands up your shirt after we'd heard "Music of the Spheres," *Sounds of Earth* on the Golden Record, haunting tones meant to correspond to a century of planetary motion. And what it was like to loosen the drawstring of your shorts, too, after the Chinese ch'in "Flowing Streams" on the record ends and the raga "Jaat Kahan Ho" begins, kissing you silent after you started to explain that *raga* meant color, mood, passion.

Do you remember when Janite came home once unexpectedly and caught us all intertwined on the couch? Oh my God. Your shirt was off, and mine was all hunched up. We flung ourselves upright. I'd never been more embarrassed in my life. She was pissed, but silently. I hurried out of there. She didn't seem to like me anyway, even if you kept trying to tell me otherwise, something you said to make me or you or us both feel better. The next night, we were supposed to go to Seattle's Outdoor Cinema with Maurice and Sandrine to see *Asteroid City*, out on Lake Union Park, but you canceled. Janite was sick, you said, and you needed to stay around. Maurice insisted I go with them anyway, and I loved being with Sandrine. She made all this great food, because she could cook, too, but it was awkward. I kept thinking they'd rather be alone.

I had learned *all* of these things about you. And, well, you knew things about me now, too.

"If this is about the boat and the water, you don't have to be afraid," you said.

Saying *You don't have to be afraid* to someone who's afraid is about as pointless as saying *You don't have to bark* to your dog when the delivery guy is on the porch.

"I'm not afraid," I lied.

"It's okay to be afraid. But you don't have to get stuck there."

See? You'd already found out so much about me, but you still thought I was golden, too.

"Okay, okay," I said.

I met you after work that day. The little boats had all been brought in—the Whitehall, the Knockabout, the Peapod. Lots of others. I didn't want to get in one. The water was choppy, and they looked about as sturdy as Curious George's newspaper boat.

"Hey, Margaret!" Chester called.

"Hey!"

"Your guy's inside."

I smiled. *My guy.* And there you were, inside the shingled shack that was the rental booth. "Can I help you?" you said when I leaned over the counter.

I kissed you.

"This is going to be a *blast*. And you get to pick our boat!"

"How about that one?" I pointed at one of the giant yachts moored nearby. We wouldn't fall out of one of those and drown.

"Perfect. I'll ask Chester for a raise."

You buckled me in the life jacket like I was a little kid, snapping the buckles under my chin and across my chest. "Life jackets make me feel like a seal."

"Like, all snug in a skin?"

"Or a sausage." We walked down the dock. "A sausage about to be dropped in a soup." The lake was so busy. It always looked charming from a distance, ringed with houseboats, sailboats gliding around picturesquely, party boats bobbing with their music blasting, seaplanes landing. But up close, the waves were large and rough, and the boats seemed to miss each other by inches as they tacked or turned or whatever it's called. That's when I remembered that the lake was an actual airport runway. The tiny boats seemed like leaves on rapids.

You showed me my options. Admittedly, all the little wooden boats were adorable. I chose *Pelican*, a small sailboat with a super-colorful sail. Might as well fall out of the most stylish one.

You held out a hand and I got in, sort of. "Oh, shit!" One foot in, and the thing started rocking. I sat down immediately, on the floor of it, not even on the bench.

"Totally fine, if you feel safer down there."

"I *know* it's totally fine."

Oh, jeez. It was maybe the first time I'd snapped at you. Fear isn't friendly, you know. I felt instantly horrible. Your eyebrows folded down in concern. "I shouldn't have forced this," you said. "Want to just get out and get a burger or something?"

"No!" I suddenly wanted to cry. You were seeing why I went to Winnifred Evans, and I didn't want you to. I was scared to ride this little boat that hundreds of people got into all the time, no problem. I'd told you about my anxiety, lots of times, but it felt different, you witnessing my sucky self with your own eyes. "Let's just *go*."

You looked totally baffled as to what to do. Mixed messages have that impact on people. "Okay. I'm going to push off, all right? See this little—" I don't remember what it was called. The steering thing. "And then we're going to—" Blah, blah, blah. You were treating me like a baby, but then again, I was acting like one. We were rocking and slopping around, and I gripped the sides of the boat as I sat on the bottom, as you sat high up on the opposite bench. It was pretty embarrassing down there. Super sloshy, too.

"Uh-huh," I managed.

"See? We're doing it!"

Shit. The dock was getting farther and farther away.

"Look at you!" you said. "See, when I—" Something-something about the sail and turning it and whatever.

"Stop mansplaining," I said. I was wrecking this.

"I'm . . . uh, boat-splaining?"

I smiled.

"I'm a boat-splainer." You grinned. You saw your opening and tried to widen it.

I snort-laughed. A guy driving a boat taxi honked his horn at us, friendly, and waved, and you waved back.

"That's Yves, from the water taxi place. He used to run a surf shop in Maui."

I realized we weren't going to die after all. We probably wouldn't. I mean, you already had friends out there, too. It was a sunny evening, and when I really looked around, I realized it was gorgeous on the lake. The light was turning that magical yellow. I slipped off my shoes. You smiled, gazed up at our rainbow sail billowing out.

We started really zipping along. The wind felt good on my

face, and wisps of my hair escaped my ponytail. Okay, okay. It was glorious.

I inched up until I was on the bench. I was still fine. I was great.

"You love it?" you asked.

"I love it. Don't rub it in."

You didn't. You didn't say *I told you so*, or even try to tell me that I'd conquered something. You left it alone. You let it just be happy.

I could practically eat the way that air smelled. A seaplane was—oh my God—right above our heads, close enough that the pilot waved, too. But hey, that pilot knew what he was doing, and so did you. I could forget that people were competent and that I could maybe relax. And, wow. I'd lived in the city all my life, and I'd never done this. I was having the best time.

And then your phone rang.

I thought you were going to ignore it. I mean, that would be the sensible thing, just safety-wise. You were in charge of that whole little boat, zooming along on the busy lake. But instead, you reached toward your pocket. You had to stretch your leg out to even get your fingers inside, rocking our little boat unnervingly. "I'd better—"

"Mars!" It was like someone using their phone while they were driving, if it also made your car rock violently back and forth. There, just like that, my trust in anyone being competent enough to relax was gone.

You groaned when you saw the screen. "I've got to get this." And then, "Hey, what's up?"

I gestured to the steering thing, mouthed, "Should I do something?" with wide eyes. We sat there sloshing, the small sail going from full to flapping.

You shook your head vigorously. "Is it still like that when you lie down?" you asked. "Uh-huh. Oh, man. Uh-huh. Okay."

Now I made a concerned face. I *was* concerned. I knew it was your mom. She called a lot when we were out together—a sickness, an emergency. I kept seeing that particular maroon flag in the distance. You probably shouldn't allow that, you know, the distance. You should walk right up to it if you see one out there.

"I'll be there as soon as I can," you said, and hung up. "I've got to get back. I'm really sorry. My mom . . ."

"Is she okay?" I thought she was maybe actually sick. It was hard to tell already. These things were tricky. Needy people who do a lot of dramatic things to get attention were. What if they really were sick and you ignored it? What if they truly needed help and you were just being a selfish bitch about it because you wanted to keep sailing in *Pelican* on a glorious summer night? I saw this with my mom sometimes. With her, dramatic wasn't even necessarily dramatic—it was as quiet as a stomachache, a grimace, a silent limp that appeared out of nowhere. There wasn't usually anything wrong, and after she saw the doctor, the mystery issue would vanish. The thing is, you can't see someone else's pain, but sometimes they need you to. They need you to see it really badly, even if it leaves you, *especially* if it leaves you, helpless and guilty.

"She's been feeling weird? Ever since she hit her head . . . Did I tell you she hit her head?" You were steering the boat. Concentrating on turning it to fill that sail again, to get us in the right direction. It looked like a lot of work. You looked tired.

You didn't wait for an answer, either.

"She doesn't want to be alone, you know, in case . . ."

"Yeah, of course," I said, but I was suddenly feeling all kinds of things at once. Disappointed, for sure. The air had left my own sail, and the fun new confidence of conquering this fear was gone. We were heading back with hurried determination. I felt some ugly, hard thing at the center of me, as well, like the gross, poisonous pit at the center of a beautiful nectarine. I didn't know what it was then, only that it felt bad. I couldn't understand why I felt competitive with her, why I was in a competition at all. I didn't have these words for it there, in the boat, but that ugly feeling included anger, too. I was part of something not of my own choosing, inside a dark issue that was yours and hers, where I didn't even belong. I had a role to play, but it wasn't the essential one. I just got to hold up a corner of a triangle so it could be a triangle. I wanted to go home.

I also felt like a brat. Maybe something was really wrong with her, I kept telling myself. But I rode back to the dock silently. You weren't talking anyway—you had a look of concentration and preoccupation, like you were alone in the boat, like I wasn't even there. This sounds horrible, and I'm sorry, but I could tell right then that if me and your mom were both drowning, it wouldn't be me you saved.

I guess we were having our first fight, whether you were aware of it or not.

You docked the boat. That knot you made to tie it up didn't even look very secure. You flung off your life jacket. Held your hand out for mine.

"Hey, sorry," you said.

"No, I understand." My voice betrayed me. It said that maybe I didn't.

You made a face. "Are you *mad*?" Like it was incomprehensible. What a monster, to be mad under such circumstances. But you looked guilty, too. You did. Yeah, you'd been there before. I thought about Ella from your old school and wondered if we'd have a lot to talk about.

"No!" I lied. "Go! You better get going."

You dashed off. Headed to your car in the parking lot. Before you reached it, you turned back to me. You made two circles with your index fingers and thumbs and linked them, the infinity sign. It had become our thing. We hadn't said *I love you* to each other. I'd been wanting to tell you that forever, but I didn't know if it was too soon or too much or if it was real. But this seemed even bigger. It said, *You are a forever person to me*. It said, *Maybe we existed in the past, and will exist in the future*, if you believe in that kind of thing. I didn't necessarily believe in that kind of thing before, but maybe I did now.

But when you held up your hands right then, *infinity*, I wondered. I doubted. I smiled a not-really-a-smile face. It was unkind, but we were arguing without arguing. It was putting you in the middle, but honestly, you and your mom put me there first. That evening on the lake, you'd witnessed why I went to Winnifred Evans, but maybe I witnessed why you went to Dr. Quentin Baleaf.

As I left the parking lot in my old car with the smiling, waving pizza on top, I hit the accelerator hard. The poor pizza was probably like, *What the hell?* But as I drove home with my windows down, the sky was pink and yellow, and I began to feel a bit generous again. How could I not, with the smell of blackberries ripening and night coming. As I approached our house, I thought of the Golden Record. On it, there were the dolphins and the snow-covered sequoias, and waves crashing on a shore, showing that on our planet there was water and ice and rock, and there was wind. Showing that there were objects of beauty and joy. But there were also the images of the wasp, and the hunters, and the rush-hour traffic. And there was a fertilized ovum, too, a baby being born, and the silhouette of a family. You weren't one thing, just some perfect image I was falling for. You were real. I was. What it meant to be human, a human in the world—it was all of it: wasps and sequoias, a woman walking in leaves, a face visible in a train window. Rock and wind, birth and survival, pink sky and a ride home. What it meant to love—it was all of it, too.

Chapter Nine

Demonstration of Eating, Licking and Drinking,
by staff photographer Herman Eckelmann:
Pictures of Earth

There were regulars that summer. The Gandolfo family, with their usual order of two extra-large Arturos. The dry yellow grass of their front yard was littered with every outdoor toy imaginable: plastic slide, playhouse, water table, trike; T-ball stand, half-inflated kiddie pool filled with a murky soup of Barbies and pine needles and floating insects. "Pizza!" one of their boys would yell before I even rang the bell, and they'd all come press their faces against the screen door. There was also Mrs. Lee, one extra-large Giorgio. Her TV blared the Hallmark Channel whenever I came, families rejoicing in Christmas miracles or romance, snowy trees and jingly sleigh bells when it was eighty degrees in the middle of summer. She always forced a crinkly five-dollar bill into my hand. There were Bud and Greg, a medium Giorgio and a medium Maurizio. When I arrived, the table on their front patio, with its rows of string lights, was already set for two with a bottle of wine.

And there was my favorite regular. I always went there last, though lately you only ordered when your mom worked late at Mystic Minerals.

"One Roma, sir," I said that night.

"The Roma. A classic. Though the Margherita is my real favorite."

"You know you don't have to keep ordering just to see me, right?"

You grabbed the box. "Are you kidding? I'm totally hooked. I love this pizza." But you set it down. "And I love you," you said.

Okay, it wasn't what I expected, or rather, it wasn't *when* I expected it, you telling me you loved me when I still smelled of onions and peppers from prep, wearing my shorts and my Papa Angelo's T-shirt, the Roma sending out an aroma—whiffs of garlic and oregano right through the box. But I was so happy.

It was real. "I love you, too," I said.

"I love you," you said again. You were grinning. "I've almost told you that, like, five thousand times."

"Same."

"Why didn't we just . . . ?"

"Not sure. Too s—"

You kissed me. "I woo oo," you said, your lips stuck on mine.

"I woo oo, too. Oh mch."

We were such goofs. We laughed. Your laugh went right inside my mouth, and mine yours. It was weird, but great. I was just a balloon, lifting skyward. You stepped back. "Now that I started, I can't stop."

"Don't stop."

"Oh my God, Frank!" you groaned. "Don't look so sad. This is a celebration."

"He feels left out!"

"Come here, boy." You lifted Frank up. Took one of his paws and danced with him. " 'Keep on riding, riding, riding,' " you sang as Frank's tongue lolled. By now, I knew that this was the "Frank and Jesse James" song, the one Frank was named for. I had learned pieces of *all* your lives. How you guys always had about two squares left on a toilet-paper roll whenever I went to pee, and how Janite splurged on DOGTV for Frank to watch when you were both gone, and how she taught you to drive in Palo Alto with her old stick-shift car you had to push down a hill and pop the clutch in order to start.

You kissed Frank's cheek. *You* were so happy, too. *You* were a balloon going skyward. Frank squirmed free, but once he was on the floor again, he kept jumping up on us, catching our mood, his toenails scratching my knees.

I changed into my bathing suit, and we went out to the end of the dock. We brought the pizza and a bottle of A&W that was sort of flat, but it was as romantic a picnic as Bud and Greg's.

"I love you," you said, and we cheersed our red, plastic cups of root beer.

"I love *you*," I said. My eyes were stars, I know it.

We jumped in and swam around, and we kissed with my legs wrapped around your waist. We'd be having sex soon. We'd better. I couldn't stand it much longer. "I love you," you said and I said and you said. Ducks paddled in the distance. Kayakers passed and waved.

"Oh my God, you guys are so adorable you're making me sick," said Mrs. Fosmire, who lived in the houseboat at the end of the dock. I used to think she was mean until we started spending time out there. She once even brought out cookies and lemonade for us. Maybe her face just appeared mad after whatever the years had done to her. Maybe meanness and loneliness could look a lot alike.

"We also love *you*, Mrs. Fosmire," you called. You never thought she was mean. You two were friends. We had climbed out of the lake, and you hadn't toweled off yet. Water drops glistened on your skin. You squeezed the excess moisture from one swimsuit leg.

Mrs. Fosmire waved her hand, like *Stop*. "Cut the crap, kid," she called back with her permanent scowl. She said that a lot to you. I'd have never believed it before, but *Cut the crap, kid* could also sound a lot like *I love you, too*.

"You're sure there are no tigers out here?"

"Do you seriously think there are tigers out here?"

"Well, we haven't seen any before." I was huffing and puffing. It was a tough trail. Straight up, with vicious switchbacks, to the top of Tiger Mountain.

"There's nothing to be afraid of," you said.

You were wrong about that.

"I think I like it better when we just drive up," I said. I meant on the astronomy meetup nights, which we'd been going to every week. At least, I liked driving better right at that moment, even if

I knew that the end result would be worth it. We'd hiked the trail once before, and every bit of my cranky exhaustion vanished when we'd finally made it to the top, a large grassy area where the paragliders ran toward the ledge and lifted off. If you persevered and made it to the pinnacle, you were treated to a sky full of rainbow chutes, arcing and soaring over the evergreen-treed foothills. Tiger Mountain—it was becoming our place.

"Well, maybe we don't have to go all the way," you said. And then you laughed nervously and shook your head, as if you'd made a joke to yourself. We'd reached a part of the trail where a lesser-traveled option veered off. "Um."

"What?"

You blushed. Or maybe it was just the exertion that was turning your face and neck so red. "I was thinking . . ."

I stared at the alternate route, which disappeared into the trees in a tangle of camouflage. "You were thinking we'd take some shortcut and have to be rescued by rangers after walking in circles for days and drinking our own saliva to survive?"

"No . . ." Your eyes glittered. "I just . . . might know a spot."

"Oh!" I finally got it. I suddenly liked this hike a lot better. "So that's why you brought those blankets." I'd thought, I don't know . . . we were having an extra-large picnic, maybe.

You smiled. "Yeah?" One word held a hundred questions.

"Yeah." Yes, to all of them. Just yes, yes, yes. It was all so thrilling and happy. At least, the thrill and the happiness were so much louder than any fear. They shouted it right out. It was funny how that worked. How I could almost forget about my anxiety when we were together.

I followed you down that trail, keeping my eyes fixed on your khaki shorts and the heather blue of your T-shirt as brambles scraped my ankles. I plucked a blackberry vine from my tank top, where it tried to cling. You moved purposefully, detecting the route from where the ground was most trodden. I wasn't so sure, to be honest. Your right turns could have been left turns, if you asked me. But I was willing to see where we'd end up.

It wasn't my dream idea, you know, to finally have sex in a forest, with bugs and sticks and dirt, but we'd had a lot of near misses at the houseboat: Janite coming home early a few times from Mystic Minerals; us leaping up in heart-pounding panic, trying to get my bra back on in a flurry, my face flushed and my hair all smooshed up; you stammering a casual, guilty *Hey, Mom!* My own house was out of the question. My mom—who still didn't know about you but seemed to suspect *someone* was in the picture—was usually there, and so what were our options? Where could we even go? I was already getting worried about fall and winter, since we'd spent so much time outside these past weeks. Where would we get together, even just to hang out? When the rain started to pour and it got dark by four, you'd have to come to my house eventually.

You straddled a giant fallen tree and held out your hand to help me over. Your pack slid down your arm, and stuff fell out: your water bottle, a couple of protein bars, bags of snacks, a few foil-wrapped condoms. My confidence was slipping, too. It seemed important not to show you that, though. This is hard to explain, but sometimes I could see how much your capability mattered to you. When you were in charge, your mistakes could make your mood drop.

I wondered if this was a bad idea but kept my mouth shut. I swatted away a mosquito making a meal of my neck.

But then the trail widened. We were at a clearing, a private, mossy glade surrounded by ferns and huckleberries. It was sun-dappled and cool, and I felt relief. Relief from the heat, but also from the weight of your plan going well, because it was. Look, it was going perfectly.

"This is so pretty!"

Your eyes danced, pleased at making me pleased. You laid out the blanket. "Come over."

"It's something out of Disney. Bambi's forest," I said. Maybe not entirely. I saw a couple of beer bottles near a log. The stub of something that might have been a joint. Kids probably came here to get high.

I wished I wasn't so sweaty, and had worn cuter underwear. I felt suddenly nervous as I sat beside you and unlaced my boots and took off my socks, my bare feet ecstatic to be free again. "How did you know about this place?"

"I asked Sandrine where she used to go to make out with her old boyfriend Marco in high school. She wasn't sure it was still here, or if it had gotten overgrown."

"You took your chances." It was one of your things, your life mottos. Number one was your belief in connection, and number two was your belief in taking a chance, in *why not*, in *you never know*. There was that quote from a Carl Sagan article that you loved, how somewhere, something incredible was waiting to be known. I loved the idea of that, but it was the opposite of what anxiety told a person. *Why not? You never know* . . . Well, there were distinct and logical reasons why not (danger, and you might die). So you'd *better* know. The never knowing was precisely the problem.

Both of your life mottos, the connection, the *why not*—they came from that guy in the turtleneck on your nightstand, and from the makers of the Golden Record, you told me. They took their chances with a *huge* why not. They had no real evidence that extraterrestrial life even existed, let alone that anyone might actually one day find that record. It was hope, that's all. Hope and goodwill, the hope and goodwill of every single individual involved, from Carl Sagan himself to the scientists and engineers and producers and each individual voice giving each individual greeting. Enough to create an everlasting outreach, an object that will last a billion years, one of the most enduring things ever created.

"We took our chances," you said. "And here we are."

A crow stared down. A fern tickled my bare ankle, and I jumped and swatted it away. A woodpecker fired his bird nail gun, *da-da-da-da*. In the deeper part of those woods, there weren't tigers, but there were cougars and bobcats and bears.

You kissed me, and I forgot about those. And why not? In space, there were super-voids and gamma-ray bursts, black holes and white dwarfs. And still, a pair of gold records sailed on a tiny spacecraft, ready with greetings of peace and good wishes.

I let go of all of it—the worries of thorns and bugs and not-cute underwear, of being found by other hikers. You'd almost had sex with Ella, but you hadn't, and so we were two virgins in a forest, like humans from the beginning of time. That only occurred to me later. Right then, I was just thinking about bodies, yours and mine, where things went, a rock under my hip bone, smells and sweat, and how fast that was. How I wanted to try that again, slower. With more experience the next time, so I could not think instead of think so much, and when we did just that, it was better.

Afterward, when we just lay beside each other, my head on your chest, your arms looped around me, it was like waking up. Like we'd both been on some storm planet together and had now suddenly landed back on Earth.

"I'll never forget this," you said. Not in a sappy, momentous way, but just happy, a happy fact. Your eyes gazed upward through the limbs of the trees toward the sky. "No tigers, just us."

"I'll never forget this, either. This head." A kiss landed on it. "Or this shoulder." There, too. "Or this." I poked his chest.

"Check out those abs."

We laughed. You didn't really have any.

"Or this." Your penis.

"Flubber blub," you said.

Now we really cracked up. Haha, the perfect name, as it slumped there all squishy and tired. My head rode up and down on your chest as we laughed.

"Oh my God, what time is it?" I'd forgotten where we were, almost. When I opened my eyes, the forest was a surprise. I was in a world of your limbs and my limbs, stickiness, the heat of our breath, and when I untwined, a shocking coolness hit. The real world, and the afternoon air of . . . three-thirty, shit! I had to get to work.

"Oh, jeez!" You scrambled, gathered up our stuff. We were

disoriented, not ready for this place. We'd been on our own new planet, the two of us. Back at our old one, it now seemed inhospitable, too sudden and glaring.

We had to run. We reached your car and drove back, stuffing our faces with snacks. I was so, so hungry. It seemed completely inexplicable that someone could ever deprive themself of something as essential as food. God, I wanted a burger and a milkshake and just more of everything. I was worried about getting back in time, walking into Papa Angelo's with this confession all over my face, but I could feel something else rumbling underneath there, too. A sense of . . . *Whatever.* Not rebellion, exactly. More that nothing could matter that much, nothing could really touch me now that you had.

Something had shifted. Not just from having sex, but sex and love together, and you and me . . . Well, I remembered how, when I was a little kid, I couldn't imagine ever leaving home. How I thought I could live there forever. And even more recently, as much as they got on my nerves sometimes, a life apart from them, my family, seemed terrifying. But now—I could suddenly see it, I could truly understand, the way we grow up and have a partner and even create a new family together, away from our childhood one. The way we make our own life on our own little planet. I missed you already, in the car heading back, and we hadn't even left each other yet. When we said goodbye, I felt a wrenching. We were two travelers now, buckled into the same ship. Even when you drove off and I stood there watching you go, we were.

Chapter Ten

DNA structure magnified, light hit:
Pictures of Earth

Maurice was already at his drum set when Sandrine emerged from the wings and picked up her guitar. We screamed along with the crowd, and suddenly, there was a blaze of strobe lights, pink and green and orange, as everyone began to dance. Began—like a bursting. The room filled with heat, a solar flare.

You lifted me off my feet. We nearly fell. You weren't much taller than me, so we wobbled, but then you jammed your face on mine, and we kissed to "Baby, You Got Me." We were at Chop Suey that night, but we'd also watched Solar Flare perform at another all-ages club, El Corazón. They'd been playing at bars we couldn't get into, too—the Tractor, Darrell's, Sunset Tavern. Maurice was looking exhausted, to be honest. They were getting so many gigs, and he was also working at Papa Angelo's. We both had our secrets, but not from each other.

I could feel something imminent, forces pressing on two sides.

There was that audience and their need, but I understood very well how hard my father could press, as well. He'd run those same Papa Angelo's ads for years, the photos of him and Arthur and George and Maurice, all lined up in front of that brick wall, wearing those vintage caps and looking like a family of charming gangsters. The group mattered, the whole group, four men. I guess Maurice himself, the pressure inside of him, his own need, would have to be the one who broke the stalemate. What a position to be in, disappointing people either way. Sometimes, your own disappointment doesn't feel all that important against someone else's, though. At least, you try to trick yourself by saying so. But your own disappointment has a power of its own.

Of course, I had it, too, the forces pressing on both sides. My own need versus some idea of who I was supposed to be. My father didn't require my loyalty to Papa Angelo's; he just required my loyalty to him, Angelo, to some idea of young womanhood that had a long history going back to Catholic roots and male dominance, even if no Vittorio had been Catholic for years, aside from maybe on Christmas. I knew you'd be a problem, in other words. A big problem.

My dad and mom *still* didn't know about you yet. The press, press, pressing of my worrying and hiding—how long could it go on? We were spending so much time together that I could feel Mom's suspicion turning into an investigation. She'd been asking more and more questions about "Addison." Her voice even had the air quotes. The only thing saving me was that my mother hated a confrontation. She couldn't do that thing where you stood up and forcibly used your voice, making a demand. Her worst quality was working in my favor for once.

Meanwhile, Addison herself kept complaining about how the summer was almost over and we'd barely done anything. How we only went to Shilshole once, Green Lake, too. We went to see a movie with Priya and Maddie the day it was, like, a hundred degrees out, too hot to be outside, but that was all. I was being one of those sucky people who ditched their best friends when a guy was in the picture, and Addison would have protested louder if she hadn't been spending so much time herself with Liam and his friends. They all went camping together in the Cascades, even, she and Liam cracking up over how they pitched their tent next to that old RV with the license plate that read *Captain Ed*, belonging to an old couple who rocked it all night long to the beat of sixties hippie music. If Dad knew that Addison and Liam were alone in a tent for a weekend, he would have been shocked. The few times Asher came over, we had to keep my door open, and he patrolled back and forth, like we were going to do it right there in my room.

Same as Maurice, I was getting tired, too. Of not being out in my world with you. I wanted to just tell my parents about us. I wanted to talk about you all the time, really—if *NOVA* was on, I wanted to say that it was your favorite, and when Mom offered me a Popsicle (she was always trying to feed people, even if she wouldn't have one herself), I fought the urge to tell her that you liked ice cream sandwiches best. Just, I wanted your name to fall out of my mouth all the time, whenever I wasn't with you. It was time to face the wrath and get it over with.

Then again, the wrath, you know. It might mean the end. I couldn't even imagine you and my dad in the same room. In some ways, a lot of ways, my dad would appreciate a guy like Asher more. Alpha gorilla and mini alpha gorilla, versus you, a quirky, intergalactic light, not an animal. I was sure my dad never really saw me, even when I was right in front of him, but maybe I was wrong, because he was suspicious, too. One time, in the middle of August, he'd gotten home early. I was on the phone, lying on my bed, chatting. He barged in and grabbed it. *What are you doing? Who is this? Hello?* But that time, it really *was* Addison. What the hell? Can you imagine? Addison was like, *God, Margaret! You poor thing!* But my father was right. He could feel it: I was moving away, from him, from them. In my mind and heart. My body, too. If I had a fast car, and a ticket to anywhere, I might have taken it, if you were with me.

I didn't tell you about that, my dad and the phone call. One, you were starting to complain, rightly, about being a secret. But also, I couldn't tell the whole truth about *him*, my father. Sometimes, it's hard to understand why you protect a person's reputation. It's complicated.

At Chop Suey that night, Sandrine put down her guitar and sang "Infinity." You and I kissed during the whole thing. Things were hot between us, after we'd had sex and gotten better at it, those times at the houseboat when your mom was at work. We had to tell each other, we had to promise, that when we were together, we'd just talk sometimes. Remember that? We could forget to talk, because we'd get so wrapped up in kissing and stuff, and we wanted to make sure we kept finding out stuff about each other. I even made you sit across the room that time, so I could concentrate on your story about that ER visit with your mom after what-was-his-name Abadias took off. I think it was Mr. Abadias. I kept getting the boyfriends and husbands mixed up, but I never could've forgotten what you said about finding her in the bathroom, the blood on the bathtub edge and on the mirror. You were ten. Ten, and she called you the man of the house. A nurse gave you a tiny *Despicable Me* Minion to play with while you waited in the hospital. It was still there, on your bookcase, next to the rocks and shells. You said you couldn't get rid of it, even if it had bad memories attached. It was a silly little yellow toy, but it was important to you. You told me that it reminded you how people are still there for you, always, even when you feel alone.

That night, during "Infinity," though, we kissed away, pressed together in that jam of people. After "Infinity," they did two fast songs—"Speed of Light," which Maurice actually wrote, and "Radio Signals," one of Sandrine's. Maybe the crowd didn't love Maurice's as much as Sandrine's, but it was so cool that he was starting to write his own stuff. And then came "Loved and Missed," another ballad.

When Sandrine sang, you could feel her *soul.* I still didn't know her all that well, even though we'd seen her a bunch of times, either at the concerts, or with Maurice, or that day I went to your aunt Gwen's house in North Bend to pick up an old microwave of theirs after Janite's broke. Sandrine made us her signature chicken salad–and–avocado sandwiches, set on paper-towel plates with a side of chips, as Aunt Gwen made sure the old cheese was scraped off the inside of the oven. I still felt shy with Sandrine, the way you do when someone is just so awesome, you don't want to look foolish around them. But I was proud of her up there, too, playing her guitar and giving the crowd her heart. She was so brave, just showing her real self in front of all those people. I couldn't even show myself in front of my own family.

Sandrine caught Maurice's eye, and he nodded to tell her he understood what she wanted him to do next. She plucked her T-shirt and fanned it, mouthing, "Whew." When he grinned back at her, I could tell how proud he was, too, of her success.

Love wasn't just the gossip and breakups and drama I saw at school. Love was private and powerful, generating heat from inside, like stars. Lily, at the astronomy meetup, explained the color of stars to me, blue being hottest, then white, then yellow, orange, and red, exactly the opposite of what you'd think. The bluest, she told me, are hotter than the sun, and larger, too. Hotter yet are the violet stars. That night, we were bathed in violet light. Maurice and Sandrine and Dre were, up on that stage, but so was your ecstatic face as we danced.

If I had a fast car, and a ticket to anywhere, I might have taken it, if you were with me. But what was even more dangerous . . . You might have, too.

In the middle of "Loved and Missed," your phone vibrated. Your hips were locked onto mine, and I actually felt it. We were so into the song, and into each other, and then the mood broke. You reached into your pocket and looked. Honestly, we didn't have to look to know who it was. You always got calls from your mom when we were together. She couldn't stand for anyone else to be first in your mind; that was just the truth.

You shoved it back in your pocket, ignored. "I'm tired of this bullshit," you shouted.

Already, I felt a sense of a clock ticking, even before you did that. Like something was going to be either over or starting, and soon.

But first, that song was. "Loved and Missed" ended with Dre's heartbreaking keyboard solo, and then Solar Flare began the last song of the evening, "Greetings in Fifty-Five Languages." Wow, that one was pure wild energy, showing off Maurice's playing, drumming like a man possessed, sweat rolling from his face, his T-shirt clinging to his chest.

That summer, everything was music. All of the concerts, yeah. The way you and I danced our butts off right then, yeah. Warren Zevon at the houseboat, "Keep Me in Your Heart," swaying to your mom's old LPs, yeah and yeah and yeah. And the Golden Record itself. A phonograph disc ready to spin on some intergalactic player, hovering in the heavens above us as we moved together at Chop Suey, bathed in violet light. The Golden Record was full of music, and so were we. The only handwriting on the records was a secret message snuck between its grooves: *To the makers of music—all worlds, all times.*

It might as well have just said: *To life.*

Driving home that night, Maurice and me, we were both giddy. I used to be the person who always carried a paperback and who was usually only quietly pleased, too, but we had both been transformed. Two cousins loved us, and we would never be the same.

Maurice was dropping me off before heading around the corner to his place, where Sandrine would meet him. It was logistically convenient, but, too, I couldn't chance you driving me home late at night.

I wondered when Sandrine was just going to move in with Maurice. That's how serious it was getting. Or maybe her staying with him was also logistically convenient, instead of her trekking back and forth to North Bend. It was hard to know where you were exactly when you were dating, when things weren't permanent. There was a lot of guessing. Even *you* were guessing, feeling insecure about not meeting the rest of my family yet. Why was I hiding you? you asked. Why couldn't I trust you to handle my dad? Well, trust *me*, I didn't want you to meet my parents like *that*, showing up at my house at almost three a.m.

Maurice and me—we were all hyped up that night. It's how we all felt after one of those concerts. Tired in the best way, exhausted, so it looped around on itself and became energy again. The success of the night poured fuel into Maurice, into the usually half-empty vessel of his confidence, and he was playing me a new song of his, "Baby Blue." On the recording, he sang, and he wasn't a singer, and wouldn't be singing this, so it was distracting. But he was playing it loud, and it boomed out of the truck, and I could tell how good he felt about what he'd made.

"I love it!" I said.

"Yeah?" His eyes shined. He smelled pretty sweaty after that night, to be honest, though maybe it was me.

"Yeah!" I didn't know if I loved it. Maybe not yet. Not before it got a little better, but I was sure it would. I had to picture Sandrine singing.

We were totally forgetting the thin, old-days metal of the truck, the way that, well, if we could hear and feel every sound and rumble that happened outside, it worked in reverse, too. We sounded like thunder on wheels, probably, and at three a.m. on our silent street, everyone was sleeping except the particular neighborhood cats who liked trouble. When Maurice pulled up to the curb, I could see the green, glowing eyes of Mrs. Thiebold's tabby peeking underneath her Camry. The cat was innocently named Ginger, but she weighed a good fifteen pounds, hissed whenever you got close, and clearly had a chip on her shoulder.

We were talking really loud, too, I'm sure. In our joy, we'd forgotten to be careful. When Maurice yanked the parking brake, he treated me to a drum solo on his steering wheel, the end of the new song. I applauded, and he bowed, and then the door of our house flung open.

"Oh, shit," I said.

"Let me handle it," Maurice said.

He couldn't handle it any better than I could, but okay. Mom couldn't even handle it.

My heart started to pound. Dad was wearing that plaid flannel robe from some past Christmas, though we were still deep in summer. Even at this hour, you could feel the warmth in the asphalt, trying to release into the cooler night air. My father's feet were bare. Under the streetlights, I saw that his hair was threaded with silver, something I hadn't noticed before. It was like it happened overnight, or just my realization had. That he was older, you know. That Maurice looked young and strong beside me.

I, uh, forgot to mention that our windows were down. That old truck didn't have air-conditioning. Or if it did, it stopped working a long time ago. The noise, you know. What were we thinking? We weren't. We were just *in* life, one hundred percent. The way two cousins had shown us.

My father put his face right in the window. "What the hell are you guys doing? I could hear you from inside. Your mother is trying to *sleep*."

As if he always put her first, ha. And he was being way louder now than we'd been. But he could totally lose the thread of logic once he got rage-y. His anger was a pot of soup where the water boiled, and everything got thrown in.

"Sorry, Dad," I said. "We were having fun and just forgot." It was always my first instinct—to explain, to show all the reasons why something might make sense—but understanding was never his goal. Silly me, I thought that understanding was *always* the goal, but it just wasn't true.

"I don't want your excuses! It's sorry and only sorry!"

"I'm not excusing, I'm just trying to expl—"

"YOU'RE DOING IT *AGAIN*!"

"Okay! I'm sorry about the sorry."

Maurice got out of the truck. There was no need for him to get out. He should have just dropped me off and driven home. So, of course, I felt the temperature go up. It was all in Maurice's silence, the way I could see the tightening in his jaw. Give me the tiniest facial movement, and I'll predict what might happen next.

Maurice—he never talked back to Dad; none of us did. Or else, we tried it once or twice and learned our lesson. Rage is pretty effective at silencing you. Efficient. But it sure looked like Maurice was about to talk back now.

He walked around the truck to the sidewalk where our father stood. Now I got out. My body readied itself to prevent something. Right. Like it could. I was also silent, but panic shot through me, a sense of things going out of control. But I remembered that one time George told Dad he should be nicer to Mom, and how the pan of lasagna went sliding across the table like a heavy cheese toboggan, crashing against the kitchen cupboard and creating an instant murder scene. I remember, too, when Maurice bought that motorcycle. *What are you, crazy? You trying to kill yourself?* The fight rattled the windows. *He's just worried about you*, our mother had told Maurice, but it seemed like worry would look different. *I'm sorry, all right?* Dad had said later, his voice raised, his eyes intense. It seemed like an apology would look different, too. It seemed like love would.

The motorcycle went back to the shop.

I'm not sure what we thought might happen if we disobeyed him. It seemed like we'd be annihilated. Maybe none of us wanted to risk finding out. He was scary, but . . . How to explain? There was a sense that we'd be destroying him, too, if we stood up to him. A sense that telling him the truth about himself would wither him. He couldn't control himself, we said. But that was a lie. We'd all seen him with customers, or with his longtime friends, Mortimer and Jack and Terry. He never lost his shit with those guys. They would sometimes tease him in a mean-true way, and you could see the flicker of fury, but he always managed to keep his mouth shut. He felt free to be a shit to the people who tried hardest to love him. It was difficult to understand. Certain people under your own roof . . . Well, if everyone saw what we saw, let's just say that maybe Papa Angelo's wouldn't be so crowded.

"Come on. Back off," Maurice said.

Oh, God.

"What'd you say to me?" The *me*—that was the important part.

"We were just having fun. Lay off."

For the briefest of seconds, it seemed like he might. Like maybe this was the way all this time, standing up to the bully. But the bully was always bigger. Bullies have power because they're willing to use it in ways other people aren't.

"And what kind of fun were you having? It's three in the morning. Don't you have friends your own age to play with, Maurice? What exactly can you do at this hour with a sixteen-year-old?" I swear to God, he sniffed us. Like, wondering if we were somewhere smoking weed or drinking alcohol, which was a joke. Maybe Maurice did those things, but never with me. I was too scared to try either one. I didn't like the idea of being out of control, in some altered state of mind where I couldn't be aware of what might happen.

"I'm *seventeen*, Dad. Fuck!"

The *fuck* popped right out, in an exhale of frustration. The funny thing is, I don't even really swear, either. Even that's a risk. You might offend someone. You might actually feel the anger of the word, and who knows where that might lead.

Oh, man. Maurice sucked in his breath when I said it. My father's face—it transformed, like those Hulk movies.

"What did you just say?"

"Dad!" Maurice intervened.

"I said *fuck*, okay? So what! Plus, I'm *seventeen*. You don't even know how old I am." Stuff was just pouring out of my mouth in a stream of *who cares*. Maurice was standing right there, making me brave, but the music had made me brave, too. Sandrine had, up on that stage. And so had loving you, and you loving me.

"Don't you *dare* use that kind of language with me. You little *shit*."

"Come on, Dad, stop. It's late." Maurice had zoomed into peacekeeper mode now. Two antagonists against one father was entirely too dangerous. Our neighbors, the Guptas—their porch light went on. I worried they might call the police.

Now my father faced Maurice. "What have you done with my girl? Huh? She used to be so sweet, and now look. Sneaking around at all hours, with a foul mouth."

He was blaming Maurice for my downfall, and I wanted to be blamed for my own downfall. My downfall was mine, thank you. I was too sweet to even get to own it, I guess. Sweet—you know what that means. You do what other people want, without complaining. You go along. Sweet and scared can look a lot alike. I wish people understood that. I wondered it, not then, but later, if every sweet person had a lot of experience with a bully. But here's a truth about sweet people: No one really knows them, and it's a secret power.

"Go inside, Margaret," Maurice said.

"No."

"Go inside."

Fine. I went. I could hear the rumble and rise of their voices, the sharp tones. I heard *It's your job to protect her, not lead her down—* I couldn't make out the rest. I would never understand it, how girls were treated like dangerously sexy adult women one minute, and little babies the next.

"What's going on?" Mom was halfway down the stairs, hovering. The thing is, she didn't look sleepy, not at all. She looked like she'd been up for a long time, and now we both hovered there. She had stayed inside when Maurice and I were out there. And now here we both were. Passive. Sweet. A couple of cowards. No power at all, who was I kidding. Poor Maurice. I hoped he ran away with Solar Flare and became a famous musician.

There was the slam of Maurice's truck door and the screech of him driving off. He wasn't the type to screech. He drove safely. I felt embarrassed already, that the neighbors heard all that. They knew we were a mess. That things were going on under our roof that were abnormal, that I doubt went on under theirs. At least I'd never heard Mr. and Mrs. Gupta yelling at each other at three a.m. Now I'd have to hide my face every time I got the mail or dragged in the garbage cans. Or, at least, feel the shame crawling up my spine.

I was trying to avoid him, but I ran into Dad right when I was coming out of the bathroom. His eyes had grown cold, and he looked at me like I was air. No, something less consequential, but more disappointing. Spoiled meat. Something you'd better toss.

But he also looked tired. Very tired. Big bags swelled under his eyes, and I hadn't realized it, either, but his ears had gotten larger, his nose, too, the way they do when they're on their way to becoming an old man's nose and ears. It must be exhausting being that mad all the time.

He was losing us.

Too bad we belonged to ourselves.

Chapter Eleven

Morse code message reading *"ad astra per aspera"* – *"through struggle to the stars"*: *Sounds of Earth*

We were in the part of August where, in the Northwest, there was heat and wildfire smoke. It didn't used to be this way, Mom said as she looked at the sun, which had turned into an eerie red sphere on the horizon. Flakes of ash could be seen on windshields and skylights. I tied a bandanna around my face to do the deliveries, and at the end of the day, my hair smelled like smoke, my clothes, too. We had to keep the windows shut tight, sweltering inside, a claustrophobic doom descending, seeing the apocalyptic air out there. The Center for Wooden Boats stayed open, but when I went to see you there, *Peapod*, *Whitehall*, *Sid Skiff*, and *Lightning* were oddly still tied up to the dock, and only *Pelican* could be seen bobbing on Lake Union. Alone on the lake, it looked so odd, so vulnerable, with that colored sail in that strange orange-gray smoke-sky, a hopeful little voyager on the inhospitable Sea of Tranquility.

We went to the houseboat after your shift, remember? When we walked in, we were both surprised to see the shiny foil gift bag on the coffee table, with a note that just read *For Margaret*. It was from your mom. It was from your mom! That's how I felt—the hope of the exclamation point. I fished around the crumpled tissue paper and pulled out the candle. It was purple, and smelled . . . purple? It had a Mystic Minerals price tag on the bottom, and a label that read *Season of Serenity*.

"Wow," I said. "That's so nice!" I felt happy. I kept sniffing it, thinking it was a message, the *Season of Serenity* thing, like she was telling me we were entering a new phase. So silly. That's what we do, when we badly want something, don't we? We pile on the other person's intentions, when they sometimes don't have any or have entirely different ones. You, though . . . Your face was unreadable. You shrugged, as if you'd seen this before. I put the candle back in the bag. Maybe it didn't mean what I thought.

You took my hand, and we went into your room. In that small space with the windows shut, even kissing felt too close and sticky. You turned your fan on, and there was one whirling in the living room and kitchen, too, but they just shifted the stifling air around.

"I'm dying," you said.

"Too hot," I agreed. "Poor Carl, in that turtleneck." In that frame, Carl Sagan really did look hot as he stared at our half-naked selves with his kind eyes.

"Did I ever tell you? About the photo NASA wouldn't allow on the record? A naked couple, just standing there holding hands. Carl and the team tried to pick the most inoffensive one possible, to show what human bodies look like. They're just standing there, calm, smiling at each other. The dude has a tan line; that's my favorite part."

"But NASA wouldn't let them include it?"

"They were worried about public outcry or something. They decided to keep the silhouette of them anyway, because, how do you show what it's like to be human without showing humans, you know?"

"Let's just play it and hang out in front of the fan. You've only shared pieces. I want to hear the whole thing." The record, I meant. We'd never actually just listened to it beginning to end, which suddenly seemed like a strange empty space in our history.

"Really? The whole-whole thing? It's ninety minutes. You're probably going to think some parts are boring. Or just odd. The UN guy talking with whale songs in the background . . ."

"That's totally not boring. Can you get us something to drink?" It was a scorching desert planet in there.

"Yeah! Of course!" You hopped up. This made you so happy, I could tell. That I wanted to hear something that you loved this much. "You don't think I'm weird about all this?"

"Of course I think you're weird."

You swatted my butt. "You're weird."

"I love weird," I called. You were already in the kitchen, clanking ice into glasses.

So, we did just that—sat on the floor in front of the fan in the living room, listening to the Golden Record over your mom's old speakers, the giant kind people used to have before we learned that bigger wasn't always better. We listened to the mesmerizing greetings in fifty-five languages, cheerful and somehow sweet, ending with the tender "Hello from the children of planet Earth," spoken by Carl Sagan's little boy Nick. We smiled at each other. I felt surprisingly choked up. That child made me want to cry and rejoice at the same time. His voice, you know, it was spinning above us a jillion miles away. He was a grown man now.

Then came the UN guy with the eerie whale songs in the background, just like you warned me.

"Will the aliens think whales are singing behind us all the time?" I asked you.

"I wish they were," you said. "But the whale songs were there to show that we aren't the only intelligent creatures on Earth. Right, Frank?" In the kitchen, Frank's ear twitched. He was lying on the cool tile in front of the refrigerator. He knew a compliment when he heard one.

After the UN guy, the eerie, unsettling *Sounds of Earth* began: volcanoes, crickets, hyenas, storms; so much scary howling wind, and the drilling of tools and helicopters, footsteps, laughter, a kiss. A baby crying, a mom soothing, the *rat-a-tat* fire of brain waves. There were no introductions or explanations between them. It was like being lost and alone in a capsule of our planet, awash and disoriented with noise. Transported from a frightening jungle in the deepest, darkest night to a harsh, frenzied city, to the warring clatter from the depths of a body, sounds that vibrated in my own body, the heartbeat becoming my heartbeat.

You poked me. I realized I'd been transfixed, concentrating so hard to decipher the sounds and staring at that blue crystal your mom had brought home, set on your television. I hadn't expected *Sounds of Earth* to be so unnerving. They were scary, honestly—a swirling reminder of all we were up against. When you took my hand, I was glad for it. I realized something huge then: *That* wasn't on the record, you know. How a hand could make our world feel more bearable. A hand was silent. Companionship and love were.

It was a relief to move on to the music. The music brought a reprieve from all that was scary in the whirl of gurgling pots and shrieking chimpanzees, the crumbling rocks and wild, howling dogs. I understood why we needed it so bad, music, how it brought joy to what was overwhelming, and a rhythm to what was chaotic. *Sounds of Earth*—it was the Earth and the people on it *being*, but the music conveyed what it *felt like* to be. We listened to the mystical "Kinds of Flowers," and the lively Senegal percussion "Tchenhoukoumen." But when we got to "El Cascabel," the mariachi song, you stood, pulling me up with you. You started dancing, shirtless, and I joined you. How could anyone not dance to that song? Even the aliens would, I thought, and we shimmied and bobbed and moved our hips. Sweat dripped down my face as the strange red sun sat in the gray sky, and ash fell down like snow around us.

"Sharpies for the win," I said, plunking two packages into the cart, which was parked in the school supplies aisle of Fred Meyer. "I love Sharpies."

"They always make a bold statement," Addison said as she perused the notebooks.

"You could write *fart* and it would seem important," Liam said.

I snort-laughed, and it *was* funny, but I wished he weren't with us. Addison had said we'd go alone, but when she came to pick me up, he was in the front seat, and I had to sit in the back. Her eyes beamed an apology, and I shrugged an *It's fine*, but I was annoyed. They held hands in the store, which made it hard to even navigate the aisles, and now we wouldn't try on clothes like we planned.

"He asked if he could come, too, and I couldn't say no!" Addison whispered as Liam lingered in front of the non-graphing calculators.

"You've been saying we haven't been doing stuff, just us. And this is our tradition." Well, honestly, our tradition for only the past two years before, when we could get our school supplies ourselves. And, too—I still hadn't introduced her to you. It wasn't fair, to keep people away and then be mad at them for being away.

"Mars could have come." Her voice was icy. She got that raised-eyebrow look she always had when she knew she was right. We'd been in the store for a solid forty-five minutes already, but I hadn't really *seen* her. I hadn't really taken her in, but now I did. Her hair had grown longer, and there were these beautiful coppery tints in her blond that I'd never noticed before. Her body seemed different, too. I couldn't exactly describe how, only, maybe more mature. Like, I could think of her more like a young woman in front of me in a line at Starbucks, instead of Addison who hid with me behind the school during field day. We both hated field day, with the relay races that involved running in tires like we were in the army instead of in sixth grade.

Liam plunked a calculator in the cart. He rested his hand on

Addison's back, the bare part where her shirt rode up. We weren't the type of friends who talked about stuff like sex. It didn't mean we weren't close. We were really close. She knew everything about the real me and my real family, Mom and the restricting, Dad and the rage, how I felt so alone a lot of the time, and anxious, sometimes so much that I couldn't even look at social media. Sometimes so much that regular daily tasks seemed like climbing a mountain, not because I was too sad to do them, but too small against them. And I knew her—her feelings about her dad, gone for work almost all the time; her mom, relying on her to be her "best friend." The stress she felt to get good grades and seem perfect to everyone. But we didn't talk about that—sex, her boyfriend Mason, the one before Liam. What either of us might have done or not done with guys. It was private, I guess, even from each other.

I could see it now, though. Her and Liam. Addison and I had grown up together, with field day, and her mom's radiation that year in middle school, tormenting PE classes, and her and me and Priya making that film together when Priya briefly decided to be a film director. There were the three years of Señora Rubio, and painful arguments, and pretending to forget that the sweatshirt was originally mine and the hoodie was hers. Learning to bake, pans and batter drops and wooden spoons, fallen cakes, rising cakes, ugly frosting to *not so bad, huh*? And we were still growing up together, it seemed.

"I got the TI-X304060," Liam said. I may have gotten those numbers wrong. But that's how he described it, numbers, blah, blah, blah. "That'll be the best one for you, Add. Easy for you to use and a good price."

I folded my eyebrows down in the direction of the spiral note-pads so Addison wouldn't catch my expression. Right there, I just couldn't envision you with us. I couldn't see you there in Fred Meyer with Liam. You'd never calculator-splain. Sure, you boat-splained that day, but you knew more about boats than I did. Addison had been in practically every AP math course there was by then, and Liam hadn't. And Addison hated being called Add. She didn't mind Addy, but not Add. The strange thing was, I couldn't imagine you there with her, either, or with Priya. I don't know why exactly. Just picturing you in Fred Meyer with us, with your wild hair and thin body and Voyager obsession, I felt worried. You seemed vulnerable. From a different planet, one they might not understand.

"She already has one," I said. I tried to sound like I was on her side, but it just came out all unfriendly.

"It's not working anymore?" Addison said.

"Add said that *you're* so good at math, you barely even need a calculator," Liam said.

"She did?"

"She said that you're so good at everything. And so *sweet*, haha." Like he doubted that part. Still. It made my heart fill, and I felt bad, too, that I was acting like such a shit.

"Sorry," I said when we walked out to Addison's car with our bulging plastic bags.

"Me too," she said.

Best friends could go through stuff, but when it was real, it stayed.

"How'd you get this?" I asked Liam when we were in the car again. I poked his big arm muscle. Addison was driving, but I could see her smile. "Impressive." I did it for her, but he went on and on about certain reps or whatever. Some powdered stuff he drank. You and me—we made fun of those giant tubs of powder whenever we saw them in a store. *Power powder*, we said, cracking up.

When Addison dropped me off, we seemed okay again. I'd made him happy, so she was happy. I wondered if it would work the other way around.

"I'm beginning to think . . ." You looked worried. No, you looked *sad*. We had the first good day of no-smoke skies in a while, maybe because it was almost September and things were cooling off. I could *feel* fall approaching. I could practically smell the first changing leaves, I swear.

We sat on a blanket at Shilshole Beach. To our left was the marina, the boats all lined up in their spots, masts so diligently straight, and in front of us was the sound. The horizon still looked odd, that hazy pink-gray, but we could breathe at least. We could go outside without getting ash in our hair. Little kids were playing in the surf. A few gathered to look at something in the water before a mom shouted and ran, shooing them away, flinging the jellyfish far into the water.

"What?"

"Are you embarrassed of me, Margaret?"

Oh, no. "Are you kidding? Of course not! Why would you say that?"

You made a face, like, *you* know *why*. I did know why. We'd talked about this before, of course. Enough that I understood I was running out of time, or already had. "We're always at *my* house. You've been around my mom tons. I haven't even seen your room, let alone your family."

I *had* been around his mom tons. Enough to see maroon flags and more maroon flags. There was that brief period where she seemed to want to be my best friend, texting me about our plans, cornering me on the dock to ask me how you *really* were, after she gave me that serenity candle from Mystic Minerals. But that had lasted about a week. Now she was cool toward me again, calling you in to dinner when she was home but not inviting me to stay. Telling me you were going to be busy on a Saturday, helping her with various errands or home repairs. But the thing was . . . if you came to my house, the flags wouldn't be maroon, with the possibility of being marooned. They'd be red, with the certainty of being burned.

"You *have* been around my family."

"Maurice doesn't count."

"Maurice counts the most."

"But you've also hung out with Sandrine, and Aunt Gwen, and my friends." Chester, and Santiago and his son, Norton, and Lily, and Ben, and Rainey, and your other friends at the Center for Wooden Boats—Bao, who went to Roosevelt High, and Amelia, a junior who was homeschooled.

I'd told you already, again and again, that I was worried my people would wreck it. Wreck us. All at once, though, I remembered something—what Mom and Dad used to say about me doing the deliveries. That it wasn't me they were worried about, it was the other people, the drivers, the customers, the everyone else. It made me feel like they didn't trust me, among other things, and right then I realized, really realized, how you'd been feeling.

"Okay, okay. Come over tomorrow night for dinner."

My stomach twisted just saying it. Dread just filled me. I dug my toes deep into the warm sand. I watched people playing and having fun and wished I could just do that, too, without worrying all the time. How do you not worry all the time, just tell me, you know? You didn't know the rules, the rules of my father, and the first rule was to know the rules. The outside world didn't know them, so it was always a risk to bring people in. I couldn't really explain the rules, either. You just had to know what might set him off. You had to understand that you couldn't disagree with him in any way, that to disagree meant he was being criticized, and criticism was the ultimate sin. It was tricky, because criticism was a field of land mines you couldn't see. Not loving chicken when he loved chicken could be one. Speaking up about not loving chicken after he'd just said he did—definitely. Agreeing with everything was important, but some people understandably didn't want to do that. Who would? But I needed you to do that. To play by the rules of our family. Like, maybe I should play you a record. It wouldn't be golden, but it would tell you what we were like.

"Really? Okay?"

I was already regretting it. But you were right; it was getting silly, just hiding. We had to live in the real world at some point, if we were going to stay together. *Stay together*—it was part of this conversation, I was sure. Because, how did you do it? We were starting school the next week—you at Seattle Central College, and me at Roosevelt. How would this change us? The real world was coming at us, and we both knew it.

"Yes."

"And it's really going to happen?"

This made me irritated. But you weren't wrong to accuse me. I'd promised it again and again but didn't follow through. "Look. I'm texting now." I was. Mom. I said something like, *There's someone I want you to meet. Dinner tomorrow?* It took her seconds, I swear, to reply. She'd been waiting, I'm sure. *OF COURSE.* Smiley face, smiley face, smiley face. "There, see?" I showed you my phone. "Done."

"Don't sound so happy about it," you said.

I kissed you so we wouldn't fight. It made me think it was happening already, my family coming between us, even if I was the one doing it. "I just love you so much," I said, and then you said, "I just love *you* so much," and the kiss was good. Good, turning to great. It was beautiful out, too, and the sun was a nice warm and not a terrible warm, the kind that makes want more wanting.

"Is your mom home?" I asked you. Her work schedule changed all the time, like, daily. I wanted to go back to your room. You wanted to, too; that was obvious. Us, now—it felt deep. People might make fun of me for saying this, our age, I mean, and that we'd only been together a few months, I get it. But it felt permanent. Us in love did. Us together. Say what you want; I know what

I felt. It was how it *should* go. We belonged. How it was to be loved by you—it wasn't usual, and I might never find that again.

"Uh-uh. Let's go." You were already standing, and I rose, too, and you shook out the blanket, and I gathered our stuff.

We'd never make it to that dinner.

Chapter Twelve

"Hello to everyone. We are happy here and you be happy there."
–Rajasthani greeting

I knew immediately that Janite had come home early– you could feel it when someone stepped onto the houseboat dock. It was as if your personal continent tipped ever so slightly, and there was a slight groaning noise, too, as the floats and chains that kept you anchored shifted. We were deep in our own planet, us exploring its wonder and beauty. Everything felt deep, feelings of love, declarations of love, skin against skin, and my body was speaking, right then. It was saying words without saying words, ones it didn't ever ordinarily use, words like *exquisite*, and then—

"Oh, shit!" you cried. You heard our continent shift, too.

"Oh my God!" My heart started to pound in pure panic. It was all the disasters that go along with abrupt changes involving the body—rising too fast to the surface of the sea, dropping into the Earth's atmosphere too quickly. My brain wasn't working. I could barely breathe. My legs got tangled in the blue sheet of your bed, and I half fell and then stumbled, trying to get my clothes. You were hopping on one foot, trying to get your shorts on. It would have been comical, if it weren't terrifying.

We were so guilty. Your face was flushed. My hair was smooshed, and my cheeks all red. The air in the room was pure sex perfume, unmistakable. How can we have a record of humanity without smells? Smells were instant information, present and past, inextricably linked to memory, too. Ask any dog. But there was no waft of peaches or skin or cow manure or pine trees on the Golden Record. No cut lawns or new books. No clean sheets or sweaty, twisted ones.

"What. The. Hell." Janite's voice was surprisingly calm. But her eyes blazed. They were fixed on me, two lasers of fury. "What are you doing here?"

"Mom, Mom, Mom," you said. You were a *broken* record, a malfunctioning player, stuck on repeat.

"What have you done to him? He never used to be like this! He used to be *good*. Look what you've done! Get out of here. Go. Go!"

"Mom, no—"

"I'm sorry. I'm so sorry," I said. I couldn't find my other flip-flop. I was wearing only one. So powerless, one flip-flop, as you stand there being yelled at. My mind spun with calculations, whether I should just leave or search under the bed for it, turning my back on my aggressor, never a good idea.

I abandoned it. On my way to the door, Frank gave me an apologetic stare, and I gave one back. He didn't deserve this. He'd been through a lot already. He was someone who worried, too. You could see it every time we swam in the lake, the way he'd stand there at the edge of the dock and watch over us.

I hobbled out of there. Well, not a hobble exactly, but with one flip-flop flapping the back of my heel, and the other foot silent. Finally, I just took it off and went barefoot. I couldn't take it, the way I was half finished, half not. Half of anything seemed like chaos. I wasn't so proud of my downfall then.

I reached my car. The triangle pizza was wearing a mostly empty yogurt cup for a hat and looked happy about it. I flung it off. Stupid pizza, always looking so cheerful while being unknowingly tormented. I cried on the way home, driving through a blur of tears. When I arrived, I wiped my eyes and tried to get myself together before I went inside, but my skin was all blotchy.

I took a shower. I was supposed to go to work in an hour anyway. But I didn't usually take a shower at this hour, and my mom knocked on the bathroom door.

"Honey? Is everything okay?"

"Yep. Fine. Just hot."

"Super excited about tomorrow!" She waited.

"Me too. Thanks for that!"

"Absolutely! Can't wait." I could feel her lingering there, her concern, but then she decided to walk away. In some ways, I wished she'd pressed, been more decidedly there for me, but it must have been hard, you know. To tell when you should be there and when you shouldn't. Either way could be wrong. I had no way of knowing what it was like to be in her mind, working so hard all the time trying to get things right.

"Bye!" I called when I was leaving. I attempted to sound cheerful, normal. I felt sick with grief and embarrassment, though. Grief—I already knew that was the right feeling. I'd sent you, like, four texts to see if you were okay, but there'd only been silence. Some horrible dread had filled me. As if we'd gone too far to the edge of the Earth, and we weren't supposed to enter our own land like that.

"Have a great night, sweetie!" Mom called back. It seemed impossible that she herself might have ever gone through stuff like this. It was frustrating, how perfect some people needed to seem. We heard about sweet Ned Shepherd, and her and Dad meeting at that wedding, and that was it. We didn't hear about the bad stuff, the mistakes.

When I got to work, Dad was there. Sometimes he worked the front counter, seating people or handing customers their pickup orders. Denise, who'd worked at Papa Angelo's forever, had it handled, but he just *liked* to do it. People knew he was Angelo, *the* Angelo, and they chatted and joked and complimented and asked questions, and it felt great, I'm sure. Being back there in the kitchen with the heat and the noise, the big crates of tomatoes and produce, the stack of boxes needing to be folded, the heat of the oven, George telling the cooks for the thousandth time not to go so heavy with the salsiccia—you could probably forget the whole point. You could forget that pizza could make people happy, or, at least, allow them to forget their problems for a slice or two.

"Hey, Bella!" he called, even though I was right there. "What are you looking so happy about?"

Talk about a misread. Then again, I had pasted a big smile on my face, a disguise. "Being here at work with you!" He loved it. We had an audience. The scene we'd had with Maurice and me that other night—it went the way of most things. A tension in the air between us until a gesture of peace was made, some offering of a ride somewhere, or a candy bar, whatever. You knew it was okay, on his side, anyway. You breathed a little. You leaned into it, because it was easier than fighting. You felt so relieved, even if you'd been bought off by a Reese's.

"Get your butt in there," he joked. "My daughter," he told the couple waiting for their table. The pride in his voice cinched up my throat. I could cry my eyes out, right there, walking through the doors to the kitchen, the scent of cold cheese and oregano and singed crust, the scent of this particular home, welcoming me in.

"Hey, Momo," George said.

"Hey, Gogo." Our nicknames, back from when I was learning to talk and couldn't say George. *Everyone* in my family had nicknames. Nicknames were love names.

"You're all set," he said. I sometimes wondered, you know, if we didn't see each other so regularly, whether we'd know each other better. If we actually talked instead of him pointing to my stack of orders as I whisked them away, waving my hand in a goodbye.

It wasn't until I got back in my car, the windows steaming slightly from warm pizza and my own breath, that her words, Janite's, began to haunt me. *What have you done to him? He never used to be like this! He used to be* good. The way they made what happened my fault. Him changing, him growing—it was an accusation. It struck me, of course it did, how those words echoed my dad's that late night after the concert. I was sweet and Mars was good, no longer.

I wondered if *good* and *scared* could look a lot alike, too. If every good person also had a lot of experience with a bully. It struck me, you know, that bullies didn't just look one way, the way you think, guys like my dad, or the ones you see in the movies, some big dude with his posse, pushing the smaller guy. A bully could maybe be weak and vulnerable and sick all the time to get attention. It didn't matter how it was achieved—bullies made sure they got their way. The truth about sweet people was maybe the same for good ones: that no one really knows them, either, and that it's a secret power.

By the time I got to my first house, a tiny cottage two blocks from Green Lake, I didn't feel sweet, or good. I felt angry.

"Have a great night!" I sang anyway. Only bullies took their shit out on other people.

After work, when I got back, the restaurant was packed, and the kitchen was in full swing. "Momo!" George shouted. "Dad is on a rampage, watch out. He went home. He got some call—" George didn't have time to explain, but he didn't have to.

A kitchen drawer was slammed, a towel tossed down, that was the extent of physical harm—to objects. But there was yelling. Rage, as my mother stood by, looking down at her hands. The words were weapons: *whoring around*, also *betray* and *trust* and *how could you* and *if you ever*. There was *Get out of my sight!* But I was already gone.

Not gone-gone—I wish I were, but I had nowhere to go. I wouldn't want to get Maurice in trouble, or drag my brothers into my mess. I felt too ashamed to face Addison's mom and dad, or

Priya's. So I went to my room. I sat on the floor with my back against the door, and I sobbed. I wished I could have done the thing you see in the horror movies when the girl or woman, always a girl or woman, is being chased—they put the dresser against the door. I just put my body there instead, the thing that was causing all this trouble. I hated myself, but I hated him more.

Can you imagine getting a call from some stranger telling you your daughter is fucking her son in her own house? he'd yelled.

Shame filled every millimeter of my body. It pressed outward to the point that I wanted to vomit. I cried, and tears flowed, and my nose ran, but the shame was the thing that pressed and pressed.

Anger and injustice boiled inside me, too. I maybe hated Janite. In some ways I understood—she was being a parent, right? Telling my father something she thought he needed to know? But it also seemed like she was just trying to wreck us. It was the maroon flag that had shouted from the beginning.

I checked my phone. No text from you.

It was late. I went to bed, but couldn't sleep.

There was a light knock on my door. It's hard to explain, but my heart filled with relief and hope, like maybe I wasn't banished after all, or banished forever. "Margaret?" It was Mom, not Dad.

This is also hard to explain, but I almost didn't answer. Finally, though, I gave her a reluctant "What?"

"Can I come in?"

"I guess."

There she was. She looked like she'd been crying. Her face—I don't know. I just saw a coward's face. I was judging things I didn't understand, probably, but all I knew was the way she'd looked down at her hands and kept her mouth shut while he railed. It was easy to speak now, wasn't it? Just to me?

"Are you okay?"

I shrugged.

"I'm sorry," she said. "The stuff he said—it wasn't right. I hope . . ." Her eye caught the round, bright moon visible through my window, and she gazed at it, as if she wished she could travel there, and maybe stay. "I hope you could come to me and talk about these things."

It was the last thing I thought I could do, honestly. "Okay," I said. But only because I felt exhausted.

We sat there in an uncomfortable silence until she sighed and said, "Okay. Good night." I wasn't sure she knew what to do with me. Now, or maybe ever.

In the morning, there it was. Your text, finally.

We should talk.

We decided to meet on the steps of Denny Hall on the UW campus, where we both hoped to go after we graduated. It was the oldest structure there, built in 1895 to house the entire campus then, an old mini palace with turrets, if a palace had chipped tile floors and nondescript classrooms and a bell tower that only played recorded chimes. It was a beautiful spot, though. A long walkway spilled from the steps like a bridal veil, surrounded by huge, old maple trees that had seen some things, plenty of breakups, likely, and the ancient stone benches that lined either side likely did, too. How many conversations were they a part of? How much gossip, and hope, and heartache, over almost a hundred and fifty years?

You were already there when I arrived. You sat on a step, spinning a leaf by its stem.

"Hey," you said.

"Hey." My stomach felt sick. I was trying not to panic.

"Look at this." You held out the leaf.

"It's enormous."

I took it. I realized they were all around me, and I looked up at the trees changing. It always seemed weird that people celebrated this season, that they drove for miles sometimes, to see something dying. That's what those leaves were doing. It was beautiful, though, for sure.

"Are you doing okay?" you asked. But your voice wobbled.

I shrugged. I couldn't speak.

"My mom thinks . . ."

I tightened my jaw. My teeth actually gritted together. I didn't care what your mom thought. A bunch of words, arguments, arguments for us, burbled to the surface, but I kept quiet.

"That things are getting too intense between us, you know. That we should maybe cool it down. Like, take a break, or whatever."

"You mean break up."

"Or whatever." You stared down at your hands. It reminded me of Mom. I felt furious all of a sudden. It would be nice, you know, if someone fought for me for once.

"What do *you* think?"

"I think only about you, and how much I love you, and want to be with you, and so maybe she's right. Especially with school starting and stuff. Like, maybe we should put the focus back on what we should be focusing on. Our priorities right now."

I could see that you'd made up your mind. I was shocked, mostly. And I didn't want to make some argument for myself. I started to cry. You started to cry. We held each other on the steps, and I could feel your sobs against my body, as you likely felt mine, one body of grief and goodbye.

"I love you," you said, intensely.

"I love you," I said, intensely.

We stared into each other's eyes, intensely. This is what you looked like when you were devastated. There was still so much to find out about you.

It seemed ridiculous, really, to break up, when there was so much feeling between us. To break up *because* there was so much feeling. When the Fates had put us together like that, too, over and over again. When our story had barely begun. When we weren't finished yet. I could feel how we weren't done, no way.

"I can't . . ." You trailed off. "I'm just going to say goodbye now. Fast. Okay? I'm just going to—"

"Go," I said.

It felt all dramatic. But also, it *was* all dramatic. We weren't ready for this. We didn't want it, either, so why do it? We understood that it was required, but why? In some ways, I didn't even believe it would stick, that this was it, forever. At the same time, my insides were collapsing, because this *was* it. You started walking down those steps, away. When you got to the bottom, you held your hands up, linked your fingers over your shoulder.

Infinity.

I did it back, but you didn't turn around.

You walked in the direction of the Jacobsen Observatory, the second oldest building on campus, the sandstone tower that held your future. Or so I thought. I walked—well, nowhere. I didn't know where or what *my* future was, aside from home. Loneliness and anger were my future there.

I still held that leaf. I looked down at its impossible, shocking beauty. Its veins, you know, echoing ours. I felt stunned. I sat on one of the ancient stone benches. When I realized I didn't even get to say goodbye to Frank, I began to cry again.

What had been mine the day before—it was yanked away. Gone. Breaking up—it was grief for the past, sure, but grief for the future even more.

My heart ached. It was a novice ache. Beginner angst. I thought I was at the end point of grief, maximum capacity, a red zone. But I knew nothing about grief, not really.

Chapter Thirteen

"Melancholy Blues," performed by Louis Armstrong and his Hot Seven: *Music of Earth*

I was so sad. My whole body felt heavy, cement boots, cement clothes, a head of cement. My mind was a cement cellblock, no escape for the thoughts banging around it. Some part of me still had the will to escape, though, because I texted Addy. She and Priya and Maddie came over to break me out of my sorrowful, heavy prison. They forced me up and out, made me go shopping, even though I usually don't like to do it much anyway. I needed a new outfit, they insisted. Even though I had some new school clothes ready for next week, a breakup outfit was essential. Addy and Priya chipped in and got me a flowered top at H&M, and Maddie bought me some scented lotion. It was so sweet. There seemed to be a whole protocol of breaking up, which included new outfits and ice cream and shit-talking the guy, even if you'd never met him. It was his loss, and he'd regret it, and he clearly didn't deserve me. These were the things people said. I wondered how long these particular rituals had been going on, if cavewomen brought each other an ice-cream equivalent back in the day, a heartbreak remedy. I wasn't sure that clothes or words could cure you, but the fact that people tried—maybe that did. Not *cure*, okay, but the medicine was offered, and I saw I was still loved.

It was another thing that couldn't be recorded. Those offerings. Care and compassion.

Breaking up seemed to fix things for my father. I did my deliveries wearing my cement shoes, trying so hard to drive the ever-smiling pizza around. It all seemed to take hours, every street a hill, every porch step a climb. But Dad had started talking to me again. First with a cold voice, and then a very slightly warmer one, even if he wouldn't joke with me yet, even if I wasn't Bella, or any name of love. I was Margaret still, punished by my given name, but there were glimmers that he might one day love me again. And Mom—I'd catch her sitting in the chair of their bedroom, flipping through her *100 Bakery Treats* book, or one of the many cooking magazines that came to our house, and later, a plate of cream cheese brownies would be sitting on the counter with a note: *Love you, MM.*

Her love name for me. She never even licked the spoon when she made those.

Maurice—being with him was the one place where I felt okay and relieved because he was kind and he knew me, and he knew you, and with him there was hope. I might hear him say something about Sandrine, or I might even see Sandrine, which was almost like seeing you. She might say your name. I might hear a tiny detail about you. The first time I saw her after, she was over at his place, and she hugged me, and said she was sorry. I wanted to ask her a hundred questions, and I wanted to cry and tell her my side of things, and hear her say that you couldn't live without me. But I didn't and she didn't. She mentioned that she'd taken you out for burgers, and that you were having a hard time, and I rolled that detail around in my brain for days. What did that look like? How hard of a time? Hard enough to change your mind?

Why, oh, why weren't you active on social media? Your pages sat unchanged from several years before we met. The silence was killing me. The not knowing anything. A hundred times a day, I fought the urge to text or call. I didn't, though. You were the one who wanted this, so there.

I saw Winnifred Evans. I hoped so hard I might see you in the waiting room, but I never did. I cried in her office, using more than my fair share of the Kleenex box. She went through a lot of those. I always kept track, remembering what color the box was the last time I was there. I wanted her to say reassuring things, but she only reflected my feelings back to me. Those were not reassuring. Me telling her things felt hard, and her telling me things felt hard and wasn't moving me from where I was. Feelings were temporary, she said. Constantly changing, evolving. I wondered if she'd ever felt what I had, that kind of love, the sort that just spun you, you know. But I shook away that thought, because she had a speckled neck from too much sun, and a wrinkled cleavage, and sometimes wore socks with sandals, and just because you realized that every single human being likely experienced passion at some point, you didn't necessarily want to picture it. When our fifty minutes were up, my pocket stuffed with Kleenex, I lingered in the waiting room. I sipped two little paper cups of water, perused the magazines on the table, marveling that *Popular Mechanics* was a thing. I was hoping for fate again, but it had done its job already. The rest had been up to us, and we'd ruined it.

School started.

I wore my new skirt, and the flowered blouse from Addy and Priya. They'd been kind of right; feeling cute helped. Cute was tiny power, but whatever worked. I met a new girl in AP Lit, Sujia, who'd moved from Oregon and was hilarious, and the photography elective I thought I'd gotten stuck with was turning out to be really cool, and Addy and Liam had my same lunch, so we got to sit together, at least. Even if we now ate with Liam's friends at the largest, most crowded table, with people like Severin Gyles and Ramone and Gwynyth James, who never really talked to us, or even noticed we were there, way down at the end of the table.

I ate my Tater Tots and thought of you—you loved those. I chose the blue cheese dressing, because it was your favorite. It made me feel less lonely and more lonely at the same time. I had so much homework again that I jammed my mind with AP Government and AP Physics and AP Statistics until there was no room for you, except at two a.m., when you'd sneak in. There was your skin on mine, or your laugh, or your eyelashes when they got wet, or the sweet way you said my name, or how you'd crack yourself up with a joke, which was so much funnier than the joke. But I'd think about that day with your mom, too. And that afternoon when you gave me the leaf. The infinity sign over your shoulder. Meaningless now, right? *Right?*

When I checked in with my body, though, as Winnifred Evans suggested I do, concentrated on where my heart was, I actually felt an ache. Why right there? Why in that exact spot of my chest?

It had a long history, I understood. Heartbreak. I mean, going back to the time when the word was first invented. People back then felt this exact thing; people had been feeling this forever. A broken heart should be on the Golden Record, too.

"Neumos again, huh?" I said to Maurice. "Maybe I'll come." Solar Flare had a website now, and an account on Snapshot, their favorite photo-sharing app, that I followed. A growing number of fans did, too. A number big enough that it seemed both impressive and surprising. I mean, they had no idea that Maurice was a quiet dork, basically. Our quiet dork, who happened to play drums really well. But fans. Wow. It was weird. I wanted to tell them that he sometimes wore the same shirt, like, for a week. He ate ketchup with his eggs, which I'm convinced is a crime against humanity, or against food, at least.

We were hanging out at his place. It was getting more and more rare, for it to be just us two, or having time together at all like this. School, work, and Maurice with work and the band and Sandrine. He was zooming Baby Luigi around in an airplane, and

I was zooming Baby Rosalina, from Arthur's old Mario Kart from a hundred years ago. We didn't really play video games, aside from this one. George used to be Mario. Arthur, being the oldest, didn't even play with us very much, but when he did, he was Bowser. The paper wrappings from our Subway sandwiches lay open, splattered with lettuce bits and discarded pickles, the wavy kind. Maurice lifted his eyebrows all suspicious in answer.

"What?" I tried to sound innocent, but he knew me too well.

"He probably won't be there."

"Why?" The information door opened a crack, and I intended to kick it down.

"There's no why. He probably just won't."

Oh. "Maybe I just want to come see you play," I said. Maurice was beating me, bad. Baby Luigi was so far ahead that there was no hope for Baby Rosalina.

"Right."

"I do!"

"Well, come, then." Winner. "Ha! Kicked your ass!" Maurice did an uncharacteristic victory shimmy, fists up.

"Fine," I said.

I'd debated about asking Addy and Liam, or Priya and Maddie, or even my new friend Sujia, but I went alone. What if Maurice was wrong, and you did come? I wanted to be free to fully embarrass myself.

"Are you sure you're going to be okay?" Maurice asked. He didn't believe I'd really show up and just hang out on my own, and now he was worried that I had.

"I'll be great! Are you kidding?" I was already watching the doors, hoping so hard for your beautiful curly hair on your beautiful head to appear.

"MG . . ."

"What?"

"Don't get your hopes up. Come on."

"My hopes aren't up. They're not even hopes."

They opened with "Seeing You, Seeing Me," and the crowd shrieked and whistled and clapped. When they moved on to "Infinity," someone shouted, "We love you, Sandrine!" And she smiled, all shy. But she wasn't shy, not at all. She was quiet power, a firelight, in that shimmery orange dress, her hair in two braids. The room hushed, and the words washed over me and squeezed my heart. Maybe going there was a bad idea. A really bad idea. Emotion rose up, threatening to drown me.

But then they started doing "Baby Blue." Maurice's new song! It sounded so different from when he'd played it in the car. It sounded full. It sounded . . . I don't know, *real.* A real song from a real band. It still seemed funny, coming from my doofy brother who ordered the pickle on the Subway sandwich, then took out the pickle. Okay, I did the same thing, but you know what I mean. I was so proud of him that I took out my phone and snapped some photos. In my photography class, Ms. Costa wanted us to take shots of things that were personally meaningful to us, and not just sunsets and stuff, to try to see how the mattering *mattered* in the art. And, well, Maurice mattered. His new song did. The photos weren't great, with all the heads in front of me, but they made me happy to look at anyway.

When Solar Flare played "Greetings in Fifty-Five Languages," that oh-so-wild frenetic energy song, I put away my phone. I didn't even care anymore that I was there alone, with only my familiar post for company. I just danced—how could I not? Everyone danced. My partner was the whole room.

You weren't coming.

But Severin Gyles was. He was coming right then. Heading over. I hadn't noticed him in the crowd, and when I looked behind him, at his group of friends, I saw that it wasn't Ramone this time. It was other kids, from another school. Imagine that—being popular at your own school, and another one, too. My body took me on a wild amusement park ride—from the euphoria of dancing to the dread of him winding his way toward me to something unexpected: a curiosity. A *Why not?* You had dumped me, after all.

I smiled. I tried to be cute. Tried to channel Sandrine's shy fire, haha, no such luck. I was aware of how sweaty I was. Some sour body odor was coming off me in waves, maybe, or else the whole room just smelled like that.

"I've seen you here before," he shouted.

"Yeah," I said. I could shock myself with how witty I could be. But the weird thing was, he seemed to have forgotten entirely what happened last time. How you had arrived, and how he'd turned around all pissed, accusing me of being a tease, making any rejection he felt my fault.

"Don't you go to my school?"

He seriously wasn't sure. It was insulting beyond belief. I mean,

I'd been sitting right at his lunch table since school started. Plus, we'd been in world history together for a whole semester. It was pretty clear that people could be invisible to Severin Gyles until he beamed them into existence with his gaze. And I didn't miss it, either. The way he'd said *my school.* He wasn't exactly wrong. In lots of ways, it did belong to him, way more than it did to me.

"Yeah," I shouted. I was such a sparkling conversationalist with the amazing Severin Gyles right in front of me, wow. Some people could just freeze you right up, while others somehow let the real you just walk on out, ready to be yourself.

"I thought so. You like these guys?" He arced his thumb toward the band.

"Love. The drummer's my brother."

"No shit!"

"Shit," I said. I could never be with someone like Severin Gyles, clearly. Or rather, I could never be me with him. My insides were clumsily bashing around, trying hard not to mess up, which pretty much guaranteed that I'd mess up.

"I like this." He took a pinch of my top. The flowered one that Addy and Priya had bought me.

"And I like *this.*" I swirled my finger up, down, and around Severin Gyles. I had no idea what came over me. The amusement park ride was on its wild zooming descent, and my arms were up in the air. Who was this girl? That's what I wanted to know, but it was a question for another day, not right then, when there was energy in that room, energy that might bring me to some new and interesting place.

The compliment did its job. Severin leaned his whole body toward mine. He kissed me. No, that implies one kiss, when this one might not be ending anytime soon. It was hard to concentrate, or rather, hard to not concentrate, because my mind was giving a running commentary, crafting a kiss documentary, with film footage and a me-interview with observations. His tongue seemed so big and thick, so much thicker than yours—sorry for these details. It had a serpent quality, and it was, like, overtaking my mouth, and I couldn't quite get over the fact that I was kissing Severin Gyles enough to actually kiss Severin Gyles. Me, the girl with, like, three friends, and him, who everyone thought was so awesome. Everyone, which meant, uh, that tongue had been in lots of mouths, not the nicest thought, for sure. Still, what would Addy or Priya or, even more, Severin's ex-girlfriend Gwynyth James, who'd never even said hi to me or Priya, like, *ever*, think of *this*? *Hey, look*, I wanted to say. *Check it out.* But, too, I hoped Maurice and Sandrine wouldn't see me. Then, wait—I hoped she did. I hoped she'd bring you back some steamy report that might hurt you. I hadn't thought of that when Severin's mouth first clamped onto mine, but it wasn't the worst plan.

Jeez, his hips, and oh, God. I mean, I didn't want more than this, but it seemed like he did. Actually, I wasn't even sure I wanted *this*, to be honest. It was just what happened next.

The crowd was clapping now, song over. The kiss wasn't. It was maybe a world record. It made me think of those dance contests, where you see the last couple slumped in each other's arms and barely on their feet but still trudging on, hours later. I was starting to maybe need air. I gave him a little push back, which seemed to have the opposite effect, weird. Like, now he was really clamped on, and that serpent tongue just got all going again.

Now Sandrine's guitar began to strum. Just her, no drums, no electric anything. The chords sounded familiar. It was hard to concentrate, but the strumming hit some part of me, some real part, connected and alive, not this distant girl with Severin Gyles's tongue jammed in her mouth. Sandrine began to sing, about shadows falling, about running out of breath, and I shoved Severin Gyles hard enough that he almost stumbled.

"Fuck," he said. I couldn't tell if he was mad or frustrated or just interrupted, and I didn't even care to figure it out. Because Sandrine was singing "Keep Me in Your Heart." She was singing *that* song, the Warren Zevon one, our song more than any other, and I realized she must have taken your advice, about the band doing some of his music. It wasn't the band, though—they sat silent. I couldn't think of the word *acoustic* right then. But it was just her, and it wasn't just "his music," either—it was that song. It was you and me.

I looked around. For a minute, I was sure you had to be here. You just had to be, but you weren't. I asked Sandrine later, and she said no. That very minute, though, I was certain of it. You can be so certain and be so wrong.

But Severin Gyles *was* there, and my whole heart and soul just thought, *What?* Like, *Who are you, and what are you doing here, and where is my Mars?* Like I woke up.

And then, maybe it was the song, but I was sad, way sadder than I'd ever been before, because there was only a non-you future from here on out. Even though, right that minute, you were in the world doing who knows what. You could be kissing some other girl, for all I knew.

That kiss served a purpose, is what I'm saying. A horrible purpose. It made me understand, deeply, how many people weren't you, and how many kisses weren't ours. It made me realize that loving you and being loved by you was unique and irreplaceable, so what was I going to do now, huh? Just feel the loss of it forever? Any single person from here on out, it was going to be different. It would be not-you.

"Sorry, sorry," I said to Severin. "I've got to go!" I didn't have to go anywhere, but it seemed like a smarter idea, to make my push away about time, or the clock, or whatever, and not just about him.

"*I've* got to go," he said.

"Oh! Okay! See you."

"See *you*."

He pinched the flowered shirt again, this time on my sleeve. He got a bit of my skin with it, maybe on purpose, a real pinch. I'd have to wash that shirt, in really hot water, so it could be new again, and mine again. I wished you could do that with memories. Just wash them in superhot water so your mind and heart could be new and yours.

"Who was *that*?" Maurice asked later. We were in the truck driving home.

"Just a guy from my school," I said.

"He looked like a douchebag."

This is hard to explain, but he wasn't being critical of me, or giving me some big warning, anything. He was just stating a fact.

"He *is* a douchebag."

Maurice glanced at me. I shrugged.

"The new song sounded amazing," I said.

"The Zevon one?" I could hear the hope in his question.

"Yours, doofus," I said.

There are a lot of breakup musts, I guess. There's the get-a-new-outfit one, and the eat-ice-cream, and the shit-talk-the-ex. But there's also this: The minute, the very minute, you even slightly move on, the breaker-upper will feel it in the airways like a zap of dark matter, the most unknown thing in the universe, the unseen force that draws galaxies together.

The next day, I got a text from you.

I miss you so much I can't stand it.

I looked at it a hundred times. I couldn't stop looking at it. It was real, though.

Chapter Fourteen

Olympic sprinters: *Pictures of Earth*

It was Sunday, and my day off, so we decided to meet when you got off work at the Center for Wooden Boats. I didn't want to tell anyone, but then I realized . . . it should be different this time. I wanted to respect you in every way possible, no matter what. I texted Addison and Priya. After all the bad stuff they'd said about you post-breakup, it was probably tricky to know what to say now. *We're with you, no matter what*, Addy responded, and Priya sent hearts and that little celebratory horn thing. It's hard to tell what it really is, but it looks happy.

I tried to do homework until it was time to leave, and then I cleaned my closet for something to do. I don't know why, but throwing things away always made me feel better, more organized, calm, though Winnifred Evans would likely have answers to that. I tossed old tennis shoes into a garbage bag, and clothes that had bleach splotches or marker stains. It was the longest day of my life, but then, finally, it was time to go. On the porch, Mom was picking off the dead flowers from her hanging basket. Fall didn't just get the leaves—the flowers were shriveling up, too.

"So . . ." I said.

"You going somewhere?"

"I heard from Mars."

She raised her eyebrows.

"I'm going to go meet him."

"Okay, honey. Hey . . ."

"Yeah?" I waited. I was hoping for some reveal, like she might tell me when this exact thing happened to her. Some new bonding moment you might read in a book or see in a film, where something changed. A connection blooming where there's only been dry, empty ground.

"I trust you."

I wasn't sure what that meant. It probably meant *Don't have sex.* It was disappointing. I wished I'd stop having hope for a relationship like Addy and her mom had, or just for some kind of closeness, or whatever the word was. But no. I'd have the hope and lose the hope in a hundred tiny moments, probably forever.

Well, whatever, because my stomach was already a mess of nerves, and my spirit was going to soar regardless. I was going to see you again, oh my God. You wouldn't think you could get so anxious just seeing someone you already loved, but wow. I didn't know what was going to happen. I thought I did, but who could tell for sure. The teensiest little Band-Aid, those really small ones that don't seem to have a true purpose, had been stuck over my heartbreak since your text. It'd be really easy to yank it right off again.

The Center for Wooden Boats was open year-round. You could rent a little sailboat even in early October, that day when all the trees were bursting with orange. Beyond Lake Union, all of Queen Anne had turned orange, and at the north end of the lake, the trees around Gas Works Park had turned orange, and the yellow light of the late afternoon of autumn gave everything a pumpkin-y glow. I rolled down the window of my car and snapped a photo. It was one of the nature shots Ms. Costa was urging us to move away from, but nature mattered to me, too. And this very moment mattered so much, my hands were shaking. The orange trees blurred in the image.

It wasn't truly cold out yet, just crisp. Sweatshirt weather still. I had the happy thought that I'd get to see you in every season. I'd get to see you in a dripping rain jacket, and I'd get to see what you looked like with snowflakes landing soft on your dark hair and on your lashes. We'd get to run through the hard, pelting rain of November, and stroll the city streets at night after the city was blanketed in thick white snow, the evergreen boughs weighted down, the streets transformed into a new and magical place.

Those thoughts made me walk fast from where I parked. *Please*, I begged the smiling triangle of pizza. I don't even know what I meant by it. Maybe, just don't be that happy wrongly. I hurried down the slatted-wood gangway and onto the dock, headed for the charming shingled boat rental shack.

"Margaret!" It was Chester. He gave me a big smile that I read a bunch of stuff into, like, maybe he was so glad to see me, and glad you and I were back together, though maybe he wasn't even aware that we'd broken up. Chester looked changed to me, but I realized it was only his windbreaker, the long sleeves and navy color looking more serious than his array of T-shirts. Time had moved things along.

"Hey!" I called.

Chester arced his thumb over his shoulder, indicating that you were on the dock beyond. And then, yes, there you were. Talking to an older couple in matching REI attire, the guy making a joke as you all laughed. You held a clipboard. You were probably finishing a sailing check, the brief evaluation of sailing skills that was required before anyone rented the boats. I held back and just watched you. It made you seem both new and familiar. Like someone I'd known all my life, but couldn't wait to meet.

When the three of you were done, the couple walked back up the dock holding hands. I loved seeing older couples hold hands. It seemed hopeful. The woman smiled at me as they passed. I wondered if passion just turned into that, something cozy and settled, and it seemed like a nice thing. A good thing, like the hot, hot summer turning to the crisp calm that was happening right then.

I was halfway to you before you looked up and saw me. Your face was so glad, and the muscles in mine already hurt from smiling so hard. It seemed like one of those moments where you do that thing from *The Bachelor*, where the girl runs and jumps and wraps her legs around his waist. But that was never me. I'd probably make it halfway or something, one leg hanging down.

But, what? Whoa. *You* were running. The guy never ran, okay? It was *her* job to run, hers to show her willingness and want, hers to cling with her legs, while he stood there, waiting for it all.

You were running.

God, I loved that. See why I loved you so much? Could you ever, in a million years, imagine a guy like Liam running like that? You were thin and odd and loved Voyager's Golden Record to the point of obsession, and you had a big nose, and those otherworldly sapphire eyes, and you ran. You did.

You flung your arms around me, and you lifted me off the ground. Pretty much. Almost. We stumbled. Good thing we didn't fall off the dock and into the lake. It was a guy-running, couple-stumbling reunion, as imperfect as we were, so full of joy. I couldn't believe your face. That I was looking right at it. God, I missed it, and it was so silly, just ridiculous, that I'd spent a little over a month not seeing it.

We kissed. Not a lengthy, world-record, tongue-jamming kiss, but a regular Mars-and-Margaret one. It was so familiar. As if, *Right, that's what a kiss should be like*. That's the one that was home.

You looked into my eyes like you couldn't believe me, either. I sniffed your shirt. You just smelled so good. I inhaled the you-ness of you, and you gazed at my hands as if they were treasured things, and not just my regular old hands that did stuff.

"Let's not ever do that again," you said.

Chapter Fifteen

Diagram of conception: *Pictures of Earth*

So, we got back together. We avoided your mom as much as we could. She wasn't thrilled that we were a couple again, but she wasn't nearly as pissed as I expected, maybe because she started seeing that guy, Jake Gooligan, who did some kind of work with golf courses. Janite was the last person you'd expect to see on a golf course, but so was he, so who knows. I met him maybe twice, a big bald guy who obviously still smoked cigarettes, from the smell of his clothes and his yellowing fingernails. You saw him more than I did.

And we started to hang out at my house. We never had that "meet the parents" dinner, but I introduced you to my mom one day, just out of the blue. We walked in while she was staring into the fridge and she startled, and stammered, like we'd caught her watching porn. *He's really sweet*, she said later, but I wished she'd said how great you were, and how happy we seemed, and, well, just more. I wanted her to pour down the compliments that you deserved, but I also just wanted her to see you. I wanted her to understand what happened between us, all of it.

Finally, I brought you to Papa Angelo's to meet Dad, too. God, you were nervous, remember? I was. It seemed like a better idea to do it with my brothers around. My dad stuck his hand out to shake, and I could tell he was doing the alpha-male move, squeezing too hard. Your eyes narrowed in a wince. I'm so sorry. I wanted to kick him, my dad in his signature tracksuit with the stripes up the sides, his hairy wrist sticking out, his big hand swallowing yours.

"This is where the magic happens, huh?" you said. "I can't even believe I'm here." It seemed like a kiss-ass thing to say, but you *meant* it. And my dad could tell you meant it. *I can always spot a bullshitter*, he'd say. It was something he prided himself on, a trophy he awarded himself, though that shelf was fairly full, to be honest.

"I'll take you back," my dad said.

Arthur was there. He said a reserved hello and stood back, watching things play out. In my family, when something happened to one of us, everyone knew about it, so Arthur was aware, I was sure, about the blowup after your mom found us. When Dad offered to take you to the kitchen, Arthur looked at me and raised his eyebrows. I thought it was a warning look, and I gave him a horrified *oh my God* face. I started to follow you two to ward off any bloodshed, but Arthur stopped me. It wasn't a warning face after all. It was an astonished one. For a second, I wasn't sure which one of us read the moment more clearly, but Arthur always knew. He'd had seven-plus more years of reading our father than I had.

"Are you sure?" I asked Arthur. I was worried about letting you go with my father without a bodyguard.

"Yup." Arthur was a man of few words, but I trusted every single one of them. It's part of what made him such a good dad.

I paced the black-and-white floor squares of the small dining area of Papa Angelo's. I almost had stopped seeing that room and the restaurant in general, the way you do with the places and things of your daily life. But now I took it in, the handful of tables, the red-checked tablecloths, and napkins in metal holders, the shakers of red pepper. The window covered with the Papa Angelo's red script and the green-and-white triangles. The counter, with its fishbowl of chocolate mints wrapped in green foil.

I texted Addison. You and me—we'd even hung out with her and Liam one time. Priya and Maddie were there, too, thank God. We went to Shilshole, but it was cold and we didn't stay long. Liam kept talking about that protein powder we always joked about, and then challenged us to play volleyball, three against three. The sandpits were empty. Liam kept spiking the ball hard over the net, and Maddie lunged and hurt her knee. It didn't go great. It was as awkward between you and Liam as I'd imagined, but you and Addy and Priya really got along. It was a start.

THEY'RE ALONE, I told Addy in all caps. *HE TOOK MARS TO THE KITCHEN WHERE THERE ARE KNIVES*. I added a knife emoji and a scream face.

It's going to be okay, she texted back, with prayer hands. She'd been my friend for so long that she understood—when you have anxiety, it's all you need to hear sometimes. Someone else having that certainty helped you believe it, even just a little. The little got you through.

I peeked in the rectangular windows of the doors to the kitchen. I couldn't believe it. There you were, behind the long prep counter with Dad. You had plastic gloves, as baggy as anything on your narrow hands. You were spreading sauce on dough with the back of the ladle, until Dad snatched it from you and showed you how to do it right.

"Oh my God!" I said to Arthur. "Look!"

Arthur only smiled. Then he grabbed my shoulders and gave me an affectionate shake-squeeze. *What did I tell you?* he said without saying.

"Did you have something to do with this?" I asked him. My brothers—they'd talked to Dad, I was sure.

"I think *he* did," Arthur said, indicating you.

I watched you pile on the cheese. You and Dad were chatting away. I couldn't hear it, but I saw it—animated conversation. You had all the ingredients in front of you, and, oh, God, you were wrecking it now. Two discs of salami soppressata for eyes, a mushroom-slice nose, anchovies arranged in a smile. Arugula hair.

But my father only scoffed. It was an indulgent scoff, not a pissed-off one. The two of you emerged a few moments later, and you were carrying your finished creation on the long-handled wood pizza peel. You were sporting a Papa Angelo's apron now, too, and had a Papa Angelo's bandanna tied around your head.

"The kid likes anchovies," my dad said proudly. To him, it was a mark of character, for sure. I'd been pretending to love them since age five, at least.

"Gorgeous, huh?" you said about your first pizza. "I've got a long way to go, but she's friendly looking, right?"

"She?"

"He's aiming for a new menu item." Now my father did the exact same thing Arthur had just done to me. He put his big hands on your shoulders and gave them a shake-squeeze.

"A new menu item?" I got a little worried, to be honest. I'm sorry, but I was concerned that the menu might soon be sporting a Janita, with soppressata and anchovies and arugula.

But my dad only winked at you—he winked at you!—and you only winked back. I'd never seen you wink before. And you clearly didn't do much of it—both of your eyes sort of closed, haha. It was honestly adorable. I couldn't wait to tell Addison how great it went. I couldn't wait to tell Maurice, either. Maybe he'd finally bring Sandrine around more, too.

After we left, carrying your pizza in a signature Papa Angelo's box, the bandanna still tied in your hair, I stared at you in disbelief.

"Did you spike his coffee?"

"I kind of loved him."

"You *what*?"

"I was totally freaked out to meet him, but I kind of loved him. Maybe he just felt that? He's one of those old-timey guys, you know? They hide how lost they are with a lot of bluster and hypermasculine shit."

I never thought of my dad as lost before. It was almost making me feel sorry for him. Bad, too, for all the bad thoughts I'd had about him. "It's no excuse for being an asshole, though."

"Of course it isn't. There's never an excuse for that." You'd had plenty of experience with those, I'd forgotten. From what-was-his-name Abadias, and a few other of Janite's boyfriends. She'd told you, her confidant, every gruesome, worrying detail. "Hey, did you know that your dad did a report on Voyager when he was in elementary school?"

"You're kidding."

"He was born the day after the launch of Voyager 2, which would be August twenty-first, 1977?"

"Right."

"His own dad thought that was so cool that he made a big deal about it. He always got a rocket-ship cake on his birthdays. So, when they had to write a report in the fifth grade, that was his topic."

"I never heard this. That's wild."

You just smiled. "I think it was a huge thing to those kids in the seventies."

"What did you . . . *do*? I mean, he's never told us that. And . . ." I gestured to the pizza box and the bandanna. Seriously, I was in shock.

"I didn't do anything. I was just excited to be there and make a pizza. I was interested in his interests, and he was interested in mine. I told him how much you respected him, too. You know, having that place. It being such a success."

"I don't remember ever telling you that."

"You didn't have to," you said. "I heard it, every time you talked about the place."

"Huh," I said. It *was* a huh. I'd learned a bunch of new things, and we hadn't even tried the pizza yet. After we did, there'd be another. Anchovies went really well with soppressata and arugula.

You stuck your nose to the box and inhaled. "Mmm. Man, this is a day I won't be forgetting."

"Wait," I said. I fished my phone out of my bag. "Do what you were doing." You looked so cute, you know, in that bandanna. You pretended to take a bite out of the box, and I snapped it, because you mattered most of all.

You tapped the name written there. *Papa Angelo's*. "Legendary," you said.

A week later, you and I were in my room doing homework. The door was propped wide open, so no one would get weird about us being in there. We barely even kissed at my house, as much as I might want to. The whole idea still made me nervous. It was five-thirty, and dark already. An arc of headlights swerved in our driveway. My dad was home. He wasn't always home for dinner, but he was that night.

I gathered up my papers and stuff. I said, "Okay, great job, us," or something like that. Something to indicate that we should wrap it up, and that maybe you should go home. I was nervous about it, you in my room and Dad home.

"Yeah, I should probably head out," you said.

The front door opened and closed. All at once, I heard my father's heavy footsteps as he climbed the stairs, and in a hurry, too. Shit, you know. Shit, he sounded mad. His feet did.

And then his frame filled my doorway. I was already on my feet. I was bracing myself.

"What do you say?" my father boomed to you.

"Is tonight the night?" you asked.

What?

"Tonight's the night!" He winked at you, and you winked back. The wink had gotten absolutely zero practice since the last time, so you still squinched both eyes.

What the *hell*?

"They'll be here in a half hour."

"Oh, great!" you said.

"I told 'em six on the dot."

"Perfect!" you said.

"Bella, get your butt down there and set the table."

"Okay . . ." It came out *okaaaay*. When we headed down the stairs, I gave you a *Tell me!* look, and you gave me a smug *I'm keeping my secrets* one. A part of me loved it, that you and Dad had some surprise you'd planned together. The *together* was completely unexpected and pretty adorable, honestly. But how could I not be worried. You might get swooped up in my father's largeness, my own maroon flag.

Downstairs, in the kitchen, my mother had a pan in her hand and was turning up the gas on the stovetop. "Oh, Mars! Are you staying for dinner?"

"I guess I am. But you won't be needing that."

"What? *This?*" She held up the pan. It seemed really heavy.

"Not tonight," you said.

"Are *you* cooking?" she asked, puzzled. Well, make that two of us.

"Sort of."

Mom looked my way, her eyes questioning.

"Don't ask me."

The two of you chatted as I set the table. You asked her about her day, and she told you that she'd gone to Bellevue Botanical Garden, where she sometimes liked to get coffee and read, even on a gloomy day like that one. And then you told her that you used to love to go to this garden in Palo Alto, one with tons of roses and herbs and a carriage house you always imagined living in. Two more things I didn't know. Three, because Mom told you that she was thinking about volunteering there. You told her that you'd work for free in a garden anytime, and she smiled, all happy and relaxed.

"What is he *doing*?" Mom asked, meaning my father, because now came the creak of the pull-down stairs to the attic storage. We heard shuffling and booms, as if he was moving boxes or furniture, who knows what. A few minutes later, he was there with us, too.

"Look what I found." He handed you some stapled-together construction paper, faded to a pale blue. I stood beside you, gazed down at *The Mitey Voyager by Angelo Vittorio*, with a crayon drawing of a white circle with legs.

You opened it, so carefully, too. Inside was the cursive *Excellent!*

from my dad's teacher. "'Voyager is a twin space *prob* launched like a slingshot to understand outer space'," you read aloud. "'It is a grand *toor* of the planets. They have visited Jupiter, Saturn, and *Urnus*, and will soon go past Neptune!'"

"I love the exclamation point." Mom laughed.

"You got an excellent, even if your spelling sucks," I said.

"Hey, now," Dad said.

"If they'd have called it Urnus, that planet wouldn't have been bullied," you said, kissing up.

The doorbell rang. I moved to answer it, but you stopped me.

"Sarah, would you get that?" my father said.

You and my dad were grinning at each other like a pair of goofs. Whatever was going on, you were thrilled with yourselves.

"Okay, you guys. I don't know what's happening here . . ." Mom said, but she looked pleased. "Meg?" we heard her say as she answered the door.

Meg was one of our delivery people. This, I had to see.

"Okay, your order of one extra-large Sarafina. And a family salad?" Meg handed over the box and bag.

"A Sarafina? We don't have a Sarafina," I said, as Meg flashed a thumbs-up to Dad, who flashed one back as she headed down our steps.

"A Sarah-fina! Get it?" Dad was downright giddy. "A Sarah-fina!"

"Really?" Mom looked like she might cry. Now I felt like I might, too. My throat was getting all tight with tears. She'd been the only one in the family without a pizza named for her, I realized. It was a sudden realization, too. We never really thought about it.

It never actually even occurred to me. And why *didn't* she have a pizza? The pizzas were my father, I guess. His heritage, his lineage, us. It's just the way things were.

"Open it," Dad said.

Mom set the box on the table and lifted the lid, as if it were precious, a velvet box holding expensive jewelry. This *was* our jewelry, the thing that we held as valuable.

Inside, I saw two discs of salami soppressata for eyes, a mushroom-slice nose, anchovies arranged in a smile. Arugula hair.

Now Mom smiled back at it. She smiled so hard.

"Makes you happy to look at, doesn't it? *You* make me happy," my father said to her.

Tears fell down her cheeks. "Oh, Ang," she said. He handed her one of the paper towels on the table, and she blew her nose. I didn't know what was going on here, what you were doing to us, for us. Just, a person could shift things with their noticing. Just by seeing, you could. Seeing with kindness. And I could tell that Mom saw you now, too. She didn't need to pour on a bunch of compliments after all. I felt it.

It seemed like a miracle.

We sat down, a family circled around a pizza. And she ate two pieces. Two. She didn't even pick off the cheese. Lately, I'd been taking pictures of everything, but I wish I'd gotten a picture of that—her biting the triangle right off the end of that slice, her eyes shining. I'm not saying her eating disorder was solved or anything. Of course not. Things that take a long time to build take a longer time to unbuild; that's something I know for sure. But it was just a normal night, a human family on our spinning planet, and what was normal about it, what was just everyday, felt precious. I gave you the infinity sign across the table, and you gave it back. I was so grateful.

"Oh, this is so good!" my mother said, and it was, it was.

Chapter Sixteen

Diagram of continental drift: *Pictures of Earth*

God, it was cold up there. I wore my puffy parka and hat with the pom-pom. Also my gloves, and a scarf wrapped around my neck and half my face. But I could still feel the frigid night through my pant legs.

"Brr, brr." I couldn't help it. I said it again. I tucked my chin way down into my scarf. But you were ignoring me. You weren't perfect, of course not. I'm sorry to say. You could be entirely self-focused, like right then. Also, though—I'd agreed to go, and that meant agreeing to what going involved, all of it, cold, too. A person didn't get to say yes, then complain the whole time.

It was an important day. December tenth. On December tenth in 1977, Voyager 1 entered the asteroid belt beyond the orbit of Mars. And on December tenth in 2018, NASA announced that Voyager 2 had reached interstellar space, the space between the stars. The whole month of December was significant to Voyager, you told me. On the sixteenth, in 2004, Voyager 1 reached termination shock, where the speed of the solar wind became slower than the speed of sound in a shock wave of heat and compression. It was one of the most important boundaries of space, the outermost point of the sun's influence. The asteroid belt, termination shock, and then the vastness of interstellar space, where no man-made object had gone before . . . Those momentous markers had been reached in the month that I was right then freezing my butt off in.

"Look," you said. You stepped back from your telescope so I could see.

"Is this Rasalhaggle?" I bent down, peered in. "It's superbright tonight."

Chester snort-laughed.

"Rasal*hague*," you said. I could never remember the name. It was the brightest star in the Ophiuchus constellation, the head of the snake-holder guy, the spot where you usually pointed your scope all the times we'd been there before. It was the spot where Voyager was still speeding away from us at thirty-eight thousand miles per hour. It's what we always gazed at—its increasing distance, that explorer traveling farther and farther away. "But no. That's not what we're looking at."

"You can't see it this time of year." Sandrine always cut to the chase, thankfully. Made things simple for me to understand.

"It's in the southern hemisphere now," Maurice said.

"Since when did you become the big expert," I said, and he made a face at me.

"That's *Sirius*," Norton said. He was five, his tone said, and even *he* knew this.

"Serious?" I removed all humor from my face.

"SIRIUS," Norton basically shouted. "The *star*."

"Be nice," Santiago reminded him. "Everyone is learning, all the time."

"The brightest star in Canis Major, aka the Greater Dog," you explained. No one else spoke. It was Astronomy 101. No—it was elementary-school astronomy that I'd somehow missed out on. I was absent that day, my dad would say about any lapses in basic knowledge. "Bigger than the sun and almost twenty-five times as bright."

"But not as bright as Venus, right, Dad?"

"Right. Or Jupiter."

"Totally wild that we can see planets," I said.

"Sirius means 'glowing' or 'lit.'" Sandrine always liked the name origins.

"Lit," Chester chuckled. The word inspired him to take a long swallow of his beer.

"Wait. So, we can't see where Voyager is? Even the general area?" I asked.

"Only from May to October. But best in July and August," you said.

"Then why—" I stopped myself. There were plenty of reasons to be there, besides looking at the piece of sky where the Golden Records were speeding rapidly away from us. Not just all the stars and planets and constellations, but those people. Chester, handing over a box of Chicken in a Biskit crackers for us to share; Ben, announcing the news that he'd finished his twelve weeks of the

Firefighter Recruit Academy; Santiago, asking Sandrine and Maurice to sign the Solar Flare poster he'd gotten at their last concert.

And Lily, just being Lily. "Guys!" She pointed.

I saw it, streaking from the sky—the bright flash, and then another, right after it.

"It never gets old," she said. "Unlike me, unfortunately."

Another flash. Another!

"Mars!" I cried. It was sky magic. *This* was what you wanted me to see. *This* was why we were out there on a mountain on the tenth of December, freezing our butts off. You didn't tell me. You let it be a surprise. The cold was worth it; of course it was. Some people wouldn't go the distance to see the sky, but you always would.

"The Geminid meteor shower." You smiled. "Every December." I kissed you, right there in front of everyone. It was such a present, to witness it. That month was seeming more incredible all the time, more than I ever knew, that's for sure.

"You missed one," Lily said as we kissed. "Oh! Another one." I wished I could get a photo of those, but they zoomed by too fast, and then they were gone.

We watched until everyone was freezing, and until Norty started to whine a little. It was getting so late. We packed up. There were always a few moments at the end of the meetup where everyone gathered in a small huddle by the cars, just BSing until next time, prolonging the goodbye. A prolonged goodbye—that's love. Love you want to stay in for a while. Norty was getting buckled into his car seat, and Chester was giving his congratulations to Ben again, and Rainey and Sandrine were chatting about some film Rainey recently saw, and Maurice was helping Lily load up her truck, when you fished in your pack and brought out an envelope.

"Before you guys go?" you said loudly, gathering everyone's attention. You waved the envelope, and I saw what it was. We'd been waiting. Mine came the week before, and when it did, I revealed to you and only you a tiny new dream. That maybe I wanted to study photography. You grabbed my hands, your eyes all glittery. *A dream should be respected*, you said, as if it were a solemn yet exciting oath, and not a terrifying unknown. We were starting to get worried about your dream, though. You hadn't gotten a letter yet. But here it was, oh my God.

Sandrine let out a little squeal.

"I got in. Early acceptance. Double major, astronomy and physics, and then onward to the graduate program, and then—"

"On to the Oort!" Lily shouted, waving her fist in the air.

"On to the Oort," you shouted back.

Lily wasn't normally all that demonstrative, but she went right over to you and held her palms against your cheeks, staring at you hard with her decisive blue eyes. She just shook her head with that cap of white hair. "Wonderful," she said. "Wonderful."

"Was there any doubt?" Chester clapped you on the back. I could feel your narrow shoulder blades rattling from the force.

"Some doubt," you said. Not really, from my viewpoint, but you'd been worried about your physics grade. You'd gotten a 3.8, not a 4.0. You were a great student. Smart, obviously. But you worked hard. Man, you expected a lot from yourself. It was funny—my parents expected a lot from us, so we did, too. But Janite didn't expect a lot from you, so you did that job, double.

"Way to go, bro." Maurice gave a fist bump, and then Sandrine kissed you on the cheek.

"I told you, you're home now," she said.

When we were driving back, the dark lumps of the mountains on either side of us, the heater blasting, you turned down the volume of the music and said, "I hope it's okay, that I didn't tell you first?"

It had crossed my mind, if I'm being honest. I mean, on the way over, I'd asked if you'd heard anything yet, and you shook your head. It was a half shake, come to think of it. But since we broke up, I was being careful, you know, not to do anything to make it happen again. I was keeping a little more quiet about what I really thought and felt. It's a wrong and disastrous thing to do, to make yourself disappear so someone else won't, but that's where I was.

"Of course," I said. "They're your family."

"The main thing is, we're doing it!" you said.

"We're doing it," I agreed.

" 'Husky fe-ver! I think it's going around!' " you sang, doing a bebop car dance in your seat. It was some oldie fight song or something that your aunt Gwen always sang whenever we talked about the University of Washington.

"Watch where you're going," I said. We were on I-90, and the traffic was picking up, and the road looked icy from where I sat.

"We're fine," you said. "We're perfectly safe."

We weren't. Who is? That's the big trick, going forward with the truth that we mostly are, but not all the way. We have to be okay with that sliver of a chance that things might go disastrously wrong, because the sliver will wreck the good parts if we don't.

I decided to believe you. I turned the volume back up. The next song played. It was Sandrine singing "Infinity." Solar Flare had pooled their resources and recorded a few songs to stream online and to send to demo drop spots at a few labels. But, of all their songs, it was our song. You had thousands of songs on your phone, but that's the one that came up right then. Okay, it was probably on Recently Played or something, but we locked eyes, like, *Look! Here's us, being all fate-and-meaning again!*

But that night . . . What struck me most was Sandrine saying, *You're home now*. It was obviously something you and she had talked about, probably a lot. And you'd talked about it a lot with me, too, how much you wanted to be there, in that city, with those people, including me. How you didn't want to move around anymore.

That's why I got so mad, is what I'm saying. That's why I wrecked things in the end. And why I'll never forgive myself. Never. Not entirely.

Chapter Seventeen

Leaf, photo by Arthur Herrick: *Pictures of Earth*

It was just after Christmas. Four days, to be exact. Our tree was still up. We were still on break from school. We were watching a movie, an older one, super charming, about a Scottish village that saves a sea creature they were sure would destroy them. It was supposed to be cute and uplifting, but the mood in the house was stressed. Sometimes I wondered why I'd kept you from my family those first months we were together, because you and my dad and my mom got along so great. But then I'd remember. That night I sure did. We were alone in the family room, and you were in your socks. You had your feet up on the table, your flannel shirt untucked, free access, you know, for my hand against your skin. This would have been enough ammunition for a fatherly freak-out normally, evidence that we were having sex right there on the Angelo family couch, when, honestly, we always waited until we were sure-sure-sure we'd be alone at the houseboat. But my dad didn't even notice. He and Mom were in the kitchen with Maurice.

A rep reached out to Sandrine from Sub Pop Records. It didn't even happen from that demo they spent all that money making. The rep—she'd gone to one of their shows at Neumos. She'd experienced what we had, too. She'd seen it—the wild lift of music and emotion, the way it made you want to dance, and kiss, and live.

A record deal.

The rep called just before Christmas. Best present ever, only Maurice just couldn't tell Dad he was quitting Papa Angelo's. A week later, he still hadn't told him. I maybe could imagine what that secret was doing to him, that needing to tell but not being able to tell. Mom and Dad didn't know he and Sandrine were living together now, either, and Sandrine was getting fed up. She didn't understand what Maurice was so afraid of. You couldn't, either, until that night. Multiply that by every day we'd ever lived. Once you experience it, the possibility of rage never leaves you.

Some pie-in-the-sky dream! Some stupid lark! You fool, you idiot! Gonna throw away everything I've given you? Everything me and your brothers built together? Well, there was more. The words written down don't even sound that bad. Also, *pie-in-the-sky* sounds delightful. But the shouting—the tone, the guilt, the fury—it froze us to that couch, as we stared at the charming Scottish villagers in the glow of the colored lights of the Christmas tree, peace on Earth. Maurice must have been frozen, too, because he was silent. We wanted to get out of there, but it meant crossing the kitchen. It was like a swamp of crocodiles in some adventure movie. Like, if we could get past it, we might have a chance to survive, but it didn't look good.

You were frozen, too. I could see by your whole body, even your feet in those socks, that you understood some things now that you hadn't before. *Now do you see?* I wanted to say, but didn't. You barely ever saw your own father, but I'm pretty sure it never looked like *this*.

Your whole body seemed to be holding tension, balancing something fragile. There was a sense of breath-holding. You squeezed my hand, or maybe I squeezed yours. I was wearing the silver bracelet you gave me for Christmas. We'd decided not to give each other gifts, but we both broke the deal. The bracelet was a silver band with two conjoined circles, an elongated figure eight that sat at the center of my wrist—our symbol, infinity. And I'd given you *Murmurs of Earth*, the Carl Sagan book about the making of the Golden Record. You'd read it, of course, but you didn't have it. We both teared up. We were both glad we broke our no-gift vow.

When the shouting died down, we fled. We reached the night air like we'd crossed into our homeland after a hair-raising time in enemy territory. I breathed deeply, but you looked shaken.

"Are you okay?" I asked.

"Are you?"

"I've done this before."

"I'm . . ."

"What?"

I worried that it was coming. You'd seen what things were really like, what my family was really like, and now you had some things to think over. Like me, and how you felt about me. No one outside my family had seen this before, okay? I never let anyone see. No one, not even Addy, who I'd been friends with forever. You saw, and it was maybe a test of acceptance, and you were standing there looking all horrified, and stammering, and, well, that's what I thought was happening.

I was wrong.

"I have something to tell you. And this just seems like awful timing after . . . that. Like, the worst. But then again, that was terrible, so, let's just do all the terrible and get it over with. I can't not tell you for another minute. I've been not telling you for a week."

Wait, what? There was another *need to tell but can't tell* going on? That whole night, I thought your tense discomfort was because of my dad and Maurice, but something else had been going on. It was shocking, the way a person can misread things. Dread filled me. Instantly. It was a tsunami of dread. I suddenly felt like I might throw up. I just stood there by your car in front of our house. I folded my arms, already mad. I glared. Like, what, for God's sake? Just tell me, just get it over with, but I didn't speak. I was afraid to.

"My, uh . . ." Your voice cracked. You looked like you were about to cry. One of your shoes was untied. We'd hurried out of there the minute my dad left the kitchen.

"What?" My voice was still angry. If you cried, I couldn't stay mad, and I was sure I needed to be mad. Whatever was coming—anger was due.

"My mom. She's, uh, moving? To, um . . ." You cleared your throat. "Arizona? Phoenix. With Jake? He got a really great job there at some big-time golf course? And, she, uh . . . Well, of course she wants me to, uh . . ."

"No," I said. As if it were up to me. But, no. Just no!

"She wants me to come."

"Mars."

"I know, I know!"

"You don't have to do this anymore! You said you *wouldn't*. You said you *couldn't*. And you're going to UW! This is your *home*." Sandrine's words popped out of my mouth. I mean, this was ridiculous. You couldn't possibly do this! Why would you even consider it?

"I can't explain. She needs me, Margaret. Around. I'm afraid that if I . . . I can't explain," you said again.

I got it, okay, okay. I understood about the family things that you can't explain. We'd experienced them that very night. Both of us had struggled with those things since day one. But this was *your life*. It was ours, us. It was your *dream*.

"No," I said.

"I get that you're upset. But it's not that far! And I've been looking into astronomy programs in Arizona . . ."

I looked at you, and . . . This is hurtful, I'm sorry, but you were a stranger right then. Like I had never belonged to you, and you had never belonged to me. You belonged to her, Janite. Your mother. There was a pull and a responsibility and a *commitment*, really, that I'd never be able to compete with, never. And I was suddenly so pissed. I'd been being all careful to say the right thing, and be the right thing, and do the right thing so you wouldn't leave and we wouldn't break up, and now that seemed ridiculous. My care did.

Maroon flag. I had my own, but I fought through it. We'd just sat in that living room, facing it together. But you couldn't fight through yours, you know. Flag on the ground, surrender.

"I can't believe this. I *cannot.*"

"Margaret."

"If you can't fight for yourself . . ."

"It's not that simple."

"If you can't fight for us, for your dream . . . 'A dream should be respected,' you said! What about that, huh?"

"I need to—"

"I'm done with this shit," I said. "Seriously." It had all been too much. That night of yelling, of Maurice's silence in the yelling, and now this. The ways we weren't free. The ways our lives would always be burdened by what we came with.

"Margaret, come *on* . . ." you pleaded.

"I mean it. I'm done." I didn't know if I meant it. My heart was breaking. I felt gross and ill and furious. I was swirling and spinning in *How could he?* I could've actually been sick, I was so disoriented.

"Okay," you said. "Okay, then."

It wasn't like the breakup with the leaf. I didn't have a feeling that we'd get back together. I was too mad to have any feeling other than mad. It's hard to know what's real in the mad. It's hard to know what's true, under all the noise and the roiling inside.

My arms were folded. I just kept shaking my head. We stood there in the street, our house lit with Christmas lights, silver reindeer looking on from our neighbors' yard, an inflatable Santa across the street. All of that cheer was over, you know. Christmas stuff after Christmas—it looked so sad, so effortful. I couldn't believe you would give up on yourself like this.

We stood there in silence for a few minutes. A standoff on my side, helplessness on yours. Frosty air in puffs from our exhales, but no words.

"I'm just going to go," you said finally.

And so I let you.

The next day, I didn't call or text. You didn't call or text, either. You were taking me at my word that I was done, I guess, but maybe I was still just mad. I couldn't tell.

I went over to Maurice's. Sandrine was at Trader Joe's. His place had gotten a lot tidier since Sandrine had moved in. His silverware each had their little compartment now, forks separated from spoons, from knives, and there was a cute towel with lemons on it hanging on the oven handle. They had a small tree still up, with white lights and sweet, funny ornaments that looked like sushi and snowmen, sharks and memories—*Baby's First Christmas*, with a photo of a newborn Sandrine.

"You're doing it," I said.

"I'm doing it."

"Leaving Papa Angelo's."

"Yup."

"Congratulations, Mo. That was brutal. But we have to do what we have to do, right? To look after ourselves. Even if it means going up against something big?"

"Or some*one*." Maurice was hunting around for our controllers and their cords, so I was talking to his butt. He pulled them out from a stylish basket. Usually, they were half in the couch cushions or under the coffee table, wherever we last left them.

"Or someone." I told him about you maybe moving. Probably moving. Would you really move?

"Aw, shit. I'm sorry. That's tough," Maurice said. "You okay?"

His kind eyes, his rumpled T-shirt with the faded red remembrance of ketchup—I almost started to cry. But I stayed in my anger. It felt more proactive than sadness. Like, maybe I could change things with fury in ways you never could with sorrow. Oh, God—maybe that's how my dad felt. "It's not what he wants. Not at all!"

"The poor kid," Maurice said. "It's gotta be tough. I know it's been a struggle all his life." I could tell that he and Sandrine had talked about it before. "Can you imagine? An only child? At least with Dad . . . His needs and wants and demands, the way we have to deal with his shit—it's spread around between us. One of us might get more of it during certain times, but we help each other carry it. Mars, it's just him. He's got to hold the whole thing. And I think it'd be so much harder, when the tyrant is fragile."

"Dad seems fragile to me sometimes." It seemed like a big thing to say. I thought for sure Maurice would disagree, but he only nodded. I wanted to explain, too, that my brothers and I carried it differently. I was a girl, and they were guys, but it all was too huge to describe.

"How would *that* be, though? When the powerful person uses weakness to control you instead of rage? Jesus." Maurice shook his head in sympathy.

It made me feel bad for you, and my own anger seemed shameful and wrong. I wanted to call you right then and apologize. Under the anger there was still so much love. *So* much. And belief, too. I could maybe talk you out of it. Me and Sandrine, and the rest of your family might. Maybe we could help you carry it somehow.

I didn't call you right then, though. I just played some Mario Kart with Maurice, zooming around in my little cartoon airplane.

I left before Sandrine got home. I wanted Maurice to be happy more than anything. But it might hurt, too, to see him and Sandrine so happy. To see her bring home their favorite cookies, their favorite cereal.

I almost called again that night. But I called Addison instead, and then Priya. They did their jobs as friends, agreeing with me, bolstering me. It was up to you to figure this out, they told me. To stand up. And if you couldn't . . . Well, this wasn't going to work anyway. I deserved better, they said. I tried to believe them, but I didn't really. It wasn't the *deserve* part I struggled with; it was the *better*. You were golden.

I believed it enough not to call you, though. Because, come on! *God, Mars!* I thought, again and again. I was punishing you, let's be honest. I still had that leaf from our last breakup. I took it from my bookshelf, held it by its only sturdy part, its stem. If I held it to the light then, I couldn't see the magic—the beautiful highway of veins that gave it life. It was opaque and about to crumble. It was a symbol, I thought. Something I wanted you to realize. How we were fragile, too. How easily we could be crushed to the point of goneness.

A new morning, an afternoon. The squeak of the ladder as my father took down the Christmas lights. I took a photo of him reaching for a blue bulb as if it were a distant star. Now, early evening. Dark already. No red and green and yellow and blue, only the stark white of the single porch light, only coldness. Dad went to work, and Mom and I ate leftover pasta. I mostly ate leftover pasta. I still didn't hear from you, and I still didn't call. It had been one whole day and one night, and now we were edging into another. I felt sick with sorrow and righteousness. Look what you were doing! I wanted to make you see. But the next day was New Year's Eve. We'd been excited about that. Kissing at midnight, a new year. I felt suddenly sick and anxious, full of self-doubt. I'd wait to discuss this with Winnifred Evans, with her socks and her sandals, her skirts, the definition of calm in that chair.

But then, all at once, I ditched any idea of waiting.

In a rush of fear and regret, I texted.

I'm sorry, I said. *I love you. Let's talk.*

It was 7:41. I've looked at that time stamp a million times.

You never answered.

Chapter Eighteen

"Good night, ladies and gentlemen.
Goodbye and see you next time."
–Indonesian greeting

I couldn't get to sleep that night. The silence from my phone was just too loud. I finally drifted off at, like, one, two a.m. When my phone started ringing and ringing, I was disoriented. It took me a minute to realize—Maurice's ringtone. I'd given him the song we'd heard in his truck that night, "Fast Car." So I kept hearing it—the line about having a fast car, and a ticket to anywhere.

Why, for the love of God, was Maurice calling me at . . . five-thirty in the morning?

"Mo, what?" I groaned into the phone.

"Margaret?"

His voice. His voice, okay? It was something awful. It was something beyond awful, I could tell.

He started to sob.

Oh my God. "What, Mo? What?"

"Mars. It's . . ."

"Mars what, Mo? Mars what?" I could feel hysteria rising.

"He's dead. He died. Last night."

"What? What are you saying?"

"Mars died last night, Margaret," he said again.

"What do you mean? He couldn't have died. I just saw him. Two days ago. This can't be."

"It is. He's gone, Margaret."

"No, Mo. No." I let out a wail, a horrible wail.

"It's true, honey."

The shock was . . . immense, hard to penetrate, but Maurice meant it, he did, this was what had happened. I started sobbing now. My body didn't even belong to me. It was doing grief on its own. "This just can't be. What happened? No, Mo. No. Please. I need to talk to him. I need to call him right now."

"Honey, honey, you can't call him." Maurice's voice was high and strained.

This was making no sense. This was not possible. It just wasn't. And then I had an awful thought. I mean, how did it happen? How? Please don't let it be my fault, I begged. "Did he . . . ? Did he . . . ?" I sobbed. I didn't think you would ever do something like that. You believed in the spirit, in the soul, in humanity, I don't know. It didn't seem like those two things could go together. I couldn't say the word. That word, it was too horrible. But, please, if you did this because of me . . .

"No, Margaret." Maurice knew what I was asking. "It was his heart."

"What? His heart?"

"His heart. Last night—"

"He's seventeen! It can't be his heart. His heart is fine. His heart is so good. This can't be." I was wailing. My mom was pushing open my door.

"Margaret?"

I waved my hand at her. Not now, not now.

"They think . . . it was something he had. Always. A heart issue."

"Maurice, no. No. Where is he? I just need to . . ." Talk to you. See you. We needed to sort this out.

But I couldn't talk to you or see you. This was the thing that would just not get through to my brain. It was impossible to believe. You were speeding away from me at thirty-eight thousand miles per hour, faster, even. I couldn't fathom it. It couldn't be true, but you were gone.

Chapter Nineteen

Silhouette of male and female: *Pictures of Earth*

It had happened at nine p.m. or so that night. This is what Sandrine told me after I made it to Maurice's place. *Told* is maybe the wrong word. She wailed the information into my shoulder as we held each other. I can't remember how I got to their place. My car, or maybe Mom drove me. The details fell away, same as those leaves on the huge maples on the UW campus, leaving the bare branches on trees that are still alive, though they don't look it.

Nine at night. You and your mom had eaten dinner kind of late, because you'd just gotten back from getting a haircut. Everything seemed normal. You did the dishes, and your mom started watching a movie. But then Janite heard a sound, a thump, a crash, falling, and there you were, in your room on the floor. The paramedics came, and they brought you to Harborview Emergency, but it was possible you were already gone by then.

Janite. I couldn't imagine her pain. You were her one and only. You were her everything. At that moment, she was with your aunt Gwen in North Bend, and Sandrine was leaving shortly to join them. She didn't invite me to come, and I didn't ask. They were your family, and I was . . . I wasn't sure. We'd broken up, sort of. Maybe we had, maybe not. I didn't know where I belonged, or if I belonged anywhere. It was so strange—if you were there, you'd say, and I'd say, that we were the most important people to each other, even if you did move to Arizona. We were crucial, we were the ones to each other, but not now. Now what we were was not family.

Nine o'clock. That whole night, while I was tumbling with thoughts about you moving to Phoenix, about you and your mom, and breaking up, you were having your last hours. And when I couldn't sleep, when I was tossing and turning, you were on the floor, and in an ambulance, and in a hospital, and I never even knew.

I sent you that text an hour and nineteen minutes before your heart stopped. Did you get it? Did you ever see that I was sorry, and that I loved you? God, please, please have read it! I *needed* to know. *Please.* Did the stress of our breakup contribute? Did I cause this? Was this my fault? God, I just needed to talk with you! I wanted to ask Sandrine if you'd told her about our breakup, but it wasn't the time. This was urgent, though. Like, the most essential thing. I desperately needed to tell you things I couldn't tell you anymore. That none of it mattered. That I was such a fool. So brave about breaking up, losing you, when you were still in this world. So righteous and cavalier, and it seemed so pointless. I needed to take it back. My words. I needed to do it over. My mind swirled and looped, and returned again to the start. Did you ever see that I was sorry and that I loved you? Love. That I love you. I couldn't stand that you might not have known that before you left. I needed, so very, very badly, to be sure you did.

Do you see how many times I used that word *need*? God, I already needed a word bigger than *need*—do you see? And we hadn't even gotten to the point yet where I had to *do* something about it. The something that would bring me here, right now.

Sandrine was searching for her keys. They were in her hand, but she couldn't find them. Things were chaotic. Maurice had to remind her that she was still in her pajama top, that she should bring a coat, and was she safe to drive? He was going to stay with me and take me home and meet her later. Did she need food? No one cared about food.

The sun had come up. I'd been there longer than I'd realized. Time shrank; time expanded. Time seemed like a weird thing that was impossible to understand. Sandrine left, and Maurice and I were at his place together.

"Did this really happen?" I asked him.

"It did. I'm so sorry, it did."

"Tell me what happened," I said. "He was eating dinner, and then *what*?" I wanted more details. Did you have your phone with you? Did you see my text? I wanted to know if you were okay. Okay in death, I mean. If you'd been in pain. Physical or emotional. If your heart, your emotional heart, not your actual heart, had been all right. At peace, I guess.

"She heard him fall."

"What else?"

"They took him to the hospital. But he was probably already gone."

I sobbed, my body racked. I bent over with the agony of it.

"It was my fault," I wailed. "I'd broken up with him. I think I did. I was mad, about him maybe moving. Did he tell Sandrine?"

"I didn't hear anything about that, Margaret. He never said, as far as I know. It wasn't your fault. It was his heart . . ."

Your heart. Didn't Maurice hear what I said? My body shook with something more violent than a gentle word like *sorrow*. More violent than a word like *grief*, even. And then I'd calm, and Maurice and I would sit silently together. He looked like a ghost, white-faced, his eyes vacant as he stared at a vague place on the wall. Then my mind would swirl, and then I needed to ask Maurice what happened again, and I would sob again, and then I'd calm again. How many times would I go through that cycle before it became real? Many. Many, many times.

Maurice took me home. I got in bed. My mother sat beside me and rubbed my back. I wanted this and didn't want it. It was a comfort and a distraction from the puzzle my mind was desperately trying to work out.

"Did he know I love him?" I asked her.

"Of course he did. Of course," she said, and rocked me.

It didn't seem like an *of course*. The idea that I could never be certain of that was intolerable, a life sentence. My body felt too heavy to move. It seemed possible that I might stay in bed forever.

I left only to pee, trudging to the bathroom, avoiding that wrecked creature in the mirror, slinking back to bed. Exhausting. And the idea of food, even the toast my mother brought, was revolting.

"Bella." There was Dad. I sort of sat up, and he held me, and the sobbing started anew. But then came this horrible sound. A deep, choking cry. My father, in tears. "He's just a kid," he said, or tried to. It seemed like a miracle, his grief over you, but I didn't care about the miracle. We didn't need it. We needed a different one altogether, a much larger and more impossible one. "It's going to be okay," he said again and again, but of course, it wasn't going to be, at least not entirely, and not for a long time.

George arrived, Arthur. Then Addy and Priya and Maddie. I felt like a washcloth, wrung out again and again and again, sobbing, rest, sobbing, rest. They sat with the lump that was me.

"It's my fault," I said to Addy.

"No, Margaret. No. It's no one's fault."

"It is. If I hadn't . . ."

"No. It's not true. Listen to me." She made me look at her. "This is not your fault or anyone else's."

Her words bounced off a shut door inside me that I was sure was permanent. It was. It was my fault.

After I ran to throw up, she brought me a cool, wet towel. How had she known to do this? My mom had given it to her. I couldn't see it then, but they, my family and friends, were each a thread, woven together, working together, creating a blanket to hold me. Or a parachute. Something strong and lifesaving as I plummeted.

Maurice—I had to talk to Maurice again. He was the one connected to Sandrine who was connected to Janite, your family, who might have more information. What information, though? Information, like this was a mistake. Information that would make this make sense. Finally, Maurice called me back.

"Have you heard anything?"

It was urgent—to know everything it was possible to know. It seemed like something could happen then; I'm not sure what. Something not this.

"Not really. Just, they think it was hypertrophic—"

"Wait. Let me write this down." I searched madly for a pen and wrote on the back of an AP Lit paper. "Hyper what?"

"Hypertrophic cardiomyopathy. A genetic disorder. Janite thinks maybe his dad had the same thing. No one knew. He never had any symptoms."

"His dad . . ." I'd forgotten about him. I'd forgotten about all the other people in your life besides Janite and Sandrine, Aunt Gwen and me. All the people who also had to hear this news came rushing in. Your relatives in New Mexico, your friends from California, but oh, God, Chester and Lily, Santiago, Norty, Ben, and Rainey. Your friends from work, from school. Your teachers and neighbors. Mrs. Fosmire, even.

Frank. I'd forgotten about Frank.

A sound escaped my throat. A cry of pain and disbelief. Unbelievable sorrow.

"His grandma was going to come. Fly here? But there's no real need. Janite . . . She doesn't want to have any kind of service. Aunt Gwen is trying to change her mind, telling her it's for other people, too, but she doesn't want to press right now, obviously."

A service? A funeral, oh my God. I couldn't imagine it. I had no idea what this would even look like. It made me think awful things, like you as a body. Like where you were now. Like where you would be.

"What about Frank?" I asked. Now I saw you, taking Frank's paw and dancing with him. Singing to him. *Keep on riding, riding, riding.* The "Frank and Jesse James" song that Frank was named for. My heart clutched. Frank had lost Jesse, and now you.

"We picked him up. He's here at Gwen's. Hey, I have to go," Maurice said. "I'll call when I can."

Maurice hung up. One by one, everyone left. George and Arthur, Addy and Priya and Maddie. I heard my sister-in-law, Maeve, downstairs at one point. My mom appeared and disappeared. It was one day and hundreds of days. A new world, one that existed for so many people, a world that I never had any clue about before. People went through this, people went through it every day, and how? Even Frank had. How did they survive it? So many people, every person who has ever loved. Dogs and elephants and crows and monkeys and giraffes and dolphins, every animal who has ever loved, too. I thought of the Earth held aloft by love, and I thought of the Earth still spinning in spite of sorrow.

"Bella, you need to eat," my dad said. He was holding a bowl, a napkin, a spoon. "This is the only thing I could get down after your grandma died."

"What is that?" It looked like food you gave prisoners. A smeary something. A cosmos in a bowl.

"Cream of Wheat."

"Gross, Dad."

It wasn't, though. It was kind of delicious. A soft nothingness, barely sweet. A food that could sneak up on you as food. I had a few bites, and then remembered that you couldn't eat. You wouldn't eat again. You ate a last food—I wondered what it was. I hoped so bad it was delicious. But more, it seemed wrong, to feed myself.

"I'm just going to sit here," Dad said, and he did. In the hard, straight chair by my desk. It was dark now, and he stayed in place, his big body a guardian there. I could hear my mother talking on the phone downstairs, too softly to hear. My parents were being parents, and now that made me choke up. "You want a light on?" he asked.

"Uh-uh."

"Okay. You try and get some rest." He was quiet. I was. He stayed for a long time in that hard chair, until he was convinced I was asleep, I think. He shut the door quietly behind him.

I was alone.

I felt more terrified and more alone than I ever had in my life. Death was a thing that really happened. The forever-gone of it was. I saw you again and again on my sidewalk, those white puffs from our exhales, our breath, your breathing, your alive breathing. I tried and tried to remember which shirt you were wearing, but it wouldn't come, and I couldn't ask you, and now every piece of history known to just us two would only be known, or not, by me. I hadn't forgotten your last words to me, though. *I'm just going to go.* They circled round my mind, taunting cruelly. Oh, they were vicious, and the ways I replayed them were cruel in a different way. *I'm just going to go*, you'd said. And I'd replied, *No, no, please don't.*

We can work this out. I love you. I love you forever. It was such a relief to imagine this. It actually gave me peace, until I remembered it wasn't real.

This is strange, but you seemed very close to me still. Were you? Because it felt like you were right there somehow. Just *around.* Nearby. Why you were gone and not gone—it was incomprehensible, and I felt furious, too. It was so wrong. You were so young.

It was New Year's Eve. I'd forgotten that until it somehow became midnight, and there was the explosion of fireworks, *crack-crack, boom!* A whistle and shriek and burnout that sounded like a comet, a falling rocket. I heard the silly tweets of horns from neighbors on their porch. In grief world there were no horns, but in regular world there were.

It was a cruel marker. A definite, noisy, attention-getting before and after, impossible to ignore. Last year, this year. Last year, you were alive, and this year, you weren't. I'd been shoved over it, unwillingly. Every year, I'd remember that marker.

I saw the flash of red from a firework, heard the *pop, pop, pop, boom!* The red flash looked like the light of an ambulance.

"Where are you?" I begged you for an answer to that, but it never came.

Chapter Twenty

"Greetings from a human being of the Earth.
Please contact."
–Gujarati greeting

"Bella, you have to." My dad's voice had gone from pleading to firm. He opened a window, and cold Earth air flowed in. It had become stuffy and stagnant in there.

"Can you close that?"

It had been nearly two weeks, and I'd barely gotten out of bed, in spite of the begging by both of my parents and my friends. I was missing school, so what. Only Maurice seemed to understand the need for this cocoon, possibly permanent. Sandrine was in one, also. We were each in our own, though. I hadn't seen her again since that night.

I tucked my chin into my flannel top to ward off the winter that was now marching through my window. I'd been wearing the same two sets of pajamas on grief rotation. Everyone had gone back to school after vacation, but I couldn't. I missed five days of school, then six, then seven. Addy brought my schoolwork to the house, but it just piled up, a mountain I didn't care about. My mouth felt thick, my hair lank. I was shivering, too cold, piled with blankets, then sweating, too hot, kicking them off. This was all a fever, and my body ached. It was so heavy. Didn't my father understand how heavy it was? How impossible it would be to drag around? I couldn't face winter, and what it had become.

"I'm not closing that," he said. "And I'm insisting that you get out of bed. You need to stand up, and walk, and move. One place, choose one place that's not bed."

I groaned.

"One place."

"Fine. Fine! Sandrine's," I said. Even I noticed it. I didn't say Maurice's. It was Sandrine I needed.

Her hair was greasy; so was mine. I wore pajama bottoms and a sweatshirt; she wore a pajama top and sweatpants. She looked like shit, and so did I, and we held each other like two crying magnets, while Maurice hunted for the Kleenex box.

"Sandrine." My eyes begged. I had to confess to her. I needed absolution. She knew what I'd done, I was pretty sure. Maurice was being too kind and gentle to admit it. "I'm so sorry. Please, please forgive me."

She scrunched her red, swollen eyes. "For what?"

Maybe you *hadn't* told her. "It was my fault. I broke up with him. Sort of. I wasn't sure if I did. But he was talking about moving, and he wanted to live here so bad, and . . . I got so mad, and we had a fight, and he said he was just going to go—"

"It wasn't your fault! That was such bullshit, him maybe moving to Phoenix. You had a fight, but he loved you. I seriously doubt—"

"I didn't hear from him. Or call him. Like, a whole day." How could I explain? I didn't need to be certain you loved me; I needed to be certain that you knew, without any doubt, that I loved you. That our goodbye, our permanent one, was what it should be.

"Margaret. You know how he was about arguing. He was probably giving you a little space before you talked. That whole moving thing—it was going to be impossible for him to tell her what he had to. He was working on it, but it was so hard! It wasn't your fault; it was *mine*. Mine! Right before he died, he called me, Margaret. He called and I told him I was just heading in the drive-through; could I call him later? Taco Time! Fucking Taco Time! What if he was telling me he wasn't feeling well? I could have saved him. It was *me*."

"No, Sandrine, no. It wasn't your fault."

Our eyes begged each other. We needed a forgiveness that only one person could give.

We needed an *answer*. My text to you, your call to Sandrine . . . Between us, we held a shared desperation.

We played out the familiar cycle: sob until exhaustion, quiet, repeat. In the quiet, Maurice started up Mario Kart and handed us controllers. He turned down the twinkly circus music, and we did not taunt each other or cheer in victory. We zoomed silently around in a pretend world, thankful for life on a different planet, even a cartoon one.

"No," I told my father.

"You're getting out of bed again. You're going to work. Today."

I took the covers down from my face. "Seriously?"

"Work. I mean it." His eyes looked almost mad. He'd gone from all that kindness to regular old Dad again. "One pizza. That's it. You can do one."

"I can't." I put the covers over my head. I couldn't, okay? Aside from the one trip to see Sandrine, I'd barely been downstairs. Maybe to get water in the middle of the night, because that's when I was awake. The moon out the window wrecked me, again and again.

"Goddamn it, Margaret! You're doing one fucking pizza. I don't want to hear any more."

I felt a familiar thin spiral of rage rise. I wanted to unleash it at him. I mean, really? He wanted me to deliver pizza right now? Rage would feel good. I was so pissed. Furious. He couldn't really be mad, could he? Was he that heartless? I sat up. His face was unshaven, his hair sporting more new strands of silver, and he was already in his Papa Angelo's sweatshirt, his daily winter uniform. He *was* mad. He actually was. His jaw had that tightness I knew so well; his eyes had that glare.

He was so frustrated with me. God! Just lying here, after—no. It struck me. Understanding hit. It wasn't me he was mad at. I realized it, all at once, that some people had anger and only anger—their sadness was anger, and their worry was anger, and their guilt was anger, and their shame was. They had all the feelings to choose from, and they picked anger, like I sometimes picked fear. Right then, his love was even anger. It wasn't okay. It didn't excuse it. He was responsible for it, and how it made people feel; I'm not saying otherwise. I just saw it, is all.

Plus, I was too exhausted to fight him. I groaned.

"It'll be good for you." He actually seemed to believe that pizza could cure most anything. That pizza could save you. Yeah, right. "Two o'clock. George will pick you up."

I didn't shower. I pulled on some soft sweatpants, a T-shirt, and my puffiest parka to shelter me from . . . everything, really. I pulled the hood up.

"Margaret?" Mom said, but I ignored her. She was in on this, I was sure.

The afternoon, being outside in it, was a shock. When I went to see Sandrine a few days ago, I saw nothing, but now I noticed that the neighbor's Santa was gone, and all the other decorations and lights, too. I shoved the thought away, how time had already moved forward. George sat in his old brown Subaru by the curb. Maybe Dad needed to give him a raise to replace it, but, too, George was the kind of guy who kept things. His best friends were from the sixth grade, and he'd had his favorite shirts forever. He tried to make his belongings last. He couldn't care less about material possessions, but he did care about our planet. His girlfriend, Cora, was the same way. Their little house was the kind that birds decided to make nests at. There was always a sweet circle of branches harboring tiny eggs in their flowerpots and trees and the eaves of their roof.

He leaned over the passenger seat and opened the door. "You look like shit," he said kindly. If it doesn't seem kind, you don't have brothers, probably. It was downright loving.

"Fuck off," I said. Which was all of the above and more. I was so grateful for him. For him and Arthur and Maurice. For Cora and Maeve and my nieces and nephew, for my whole family, but I couldn't think about that now. I'd lose it for sure.

George snapped off the music. He understood what music could do. I stared at all the crap in his console cubby. His Discover Pass, which gave you access to Washington parks; a phone cord; thermal gloves; a protein bar, and the wrapper of a protein bar.

He tossed me the gloves. It was true—it was freezing out there. I hadn't brought a hat or gloves, and my socks were the little ankle ones from summer, the first I'd grabbed. The gloves fit, like, well a glove. They were probably Cora's. We all expected them to be getting engaged any day now.

"Seat belt," he commanded.

We drove to Papa Angelo's. This seemed so cruel. I slumped down in my seat and waited for George to come back with our delivery. I made the mistake of looking out the window, and I saw Papa Angelo's, and the table you and I sat at when we went, and I saw the kitchen door that you popped out of that day, when you and Dad were in the kitchen. I spotted the back of Maurice's head, too. He'd gone back to work there for a while. The plans for the band were on hold, because Sandrine herself was on hold. You were like a brother to her, entwined in her songs, too, and her creative joy, her creative spark, had been snuffed out by grief and guilt. I got it, you know. I couldn't even listen to music, let alone make it. But right then, the sight of Maurice led to thoughts of Sandrine, and those led to you, of course. Our meeting on the mountain, dancing as she sang at the concerts, the way she'd ruffle your hair, and you'd swat her hand. Oh, God.

I wished there were only those beautiful-but-painful memories. Instead, there they were, shoving in again, all ugly and cruel. The unanswered questions of my text and Sandrine's phone call. The awful possibility that you had left without being sure of my love. Was this what they meant by needing *closure*? What a silly and insubstantial word. It sounded as quiet as the back cover of a book shutting, when the absence of it was a tormenting, taunting noise that never stopped.

George was back, quick. He tossed me the padded, insulated delivery bag. It warmed my lap. My fingers felt its edges, its thickness. "Just one?"

"Just one," George said.

I hoped it wasn't a setup of some kind. Like bringing me to the dock or something to see Janite. I hadn't spoken with her. She hadn't reached out to me, either, though she probably wasn't reaching out at all. I was mad at her, I guess. For all the ways her life had weighed on you. For planning to move, for not saving you.

But we headed out toward Gas Works Park and North Lake

Union. I caught sight of the lake and forced my eyes back toward George's car. I watched the map on the GPS, because I might accidentally see your dock, or the places we used to bring food for a picnic. That mini-mart, even. Where we stopped to grab some sodas. It was dangerous out here. Every corner was a precipice I might fall off, into some memory, terrible and perfect.

We pulled up to a marine supply store, and George idled at the curb. "Just some random stop?" I asked.

"Just some random stop," he confirmed.

I didn't usually come here, probably because my route was in the evening, so I didn't often go to businesses, just homes. I pulled the pizza from the bag. The Papa Angelo's menu was taped to the top. I saw the Sarafina, and my eyes pricked with tears. "Okay," I said.

"Hood," he reminded me.

I yanked my hood down. It was a rule. We didn't want to scare anyone, looking like some burglar. I hurried, because once the pizza was out of the bag, it got cold, fast. The door chimed as I entered. There were shelves of sailing stuff, and pieces and parts that I didn't recognize. Stuff that kept you afloat, I guess.

A young guy was behind the counter. "Hey! Nice!" he said when he saw me. He gave me a huge smile.

"One extra-large Arturo?"

"That's us. Skylar!" he called over his shoulder. "Pizza's here!"

I handed him the box. His eyes were super blue, happy. Lots of meat and cheese could do that. "Have a great day," I said.

"Thanks! Hey, wait. Here." He handed me one of their stickers.

It featured the outline of a sailboat. *Seas the day!* with *Moore Marine Supply* in tiny letters at the bottom.

I smiled my thanks. The door chimes marked my exit, and then I was back in George's Subaru. I shoved the sticker in my pocket.

"We done?"

"Yup. Good job."

George drove me back home. I remembered to hand him back Cora's gloves. My hands felt weirdly bare without them. Unprotected. I pretty much poured myself out of the car, hauled my body back up to my room, dumped my coat on the floor, and was back in my pajamas and bed in seconds.

But George honked his horn. Another time, another. Damn it. I had to get up again. I looked out my window.

He was just there, waving.

Okay, you people, okay. I waved back. The world was still there, like it or not.

The next day, we did two deliveries. A Maurizio to the bookstore across from Green Lake, and four Sarafinas to a little day care nearby. The Sarafina was becoming a kid favorite, with options to swap out the anchovies for other ingredients that were more child-friendly. In the bookstore, I was surrounded by the comforting, watery smell of crisp pulp, and the covers invited me to open them. At the day care, I spotted a lone, optimistic dandelion, oddly flowering in January, a tiny yellow sun in the grass. One of the kids must have been having a birthday. In the playroom, the little guy wore a hat and a paper lei, and another tiny little girl in a *Frozen* outfit ran to me, screeching, "Cheese peet-ZZA!"

"Four Sarafinas, no anchovies?" I said to the woman in the Sunbeam Day Care apron.

"Orange-pepper smile?" she asked.

I checked the order. "Orange-pepper smile," I confirmed.

If you could have seen this . . . I choked up. But George was beeping his horn for me to hurry.

On day three, three deliveries. I took a shower before I met George. He drove me to the Fred Hutchinson Cancer Research offices, where I brought two extra-large Romas. Across the street, Lake Union buzzed, busy even in winter. The Center for Wooden Boats was right over there, and my throat cinched tight seeing it. Chester had called and left a message saying that everyone was thinking about me, too, but I didn't call back. I wasn't sure I deserved those thoughts. I jogged back toward George's car. He was in a loading zone, so we had to rush even more. We delivered to an apartment, a door with a wooden welcome sign hanging from it, and a welcome mat that read, *Hi, I'm Mat.*

"Margherita for a Margaret?" the woman who answered said.

"Yep," I said. "That's my name, too," I told her.

We chatted for a second about all the ways people misspelled it, but I had to get going. We had an Arturo to get to our next place, a tiny Craftsman a few streets over. It was an old lady's house, and her television was blaring. She handed me a cookie on a napkin in thanks. I patted her dog's head as he stood on the porch.

Kids and old ladies, people at work, a dandelion, a party hat, a double welcome, a dog.

I'd been so silly, and my father knew this all along, I was sure. It wasn't the pizza that cured you, that saved you. It was the connection.

Chapter Twenty-One

The glug of a watercooler: *Sounds of Mars*

Connection–it was your word. Still, Mars, still . . . It was one thing to be forced into it, and something else entirely to connect to anyone or anything on my own. Because, no way. Almost literally, there was no way that I could see. Because I tried that, okay? With you. I did. I had gone down that road, tucking the protective force of my anxiety away, and look what happened. I'd been brave, I reached out, I stepped out of my comfort zone. I did all the things, looked straight at those maroon flags and went right ahead and loved you, loved you fully. There was a flag I hadn't even considered. Your heart, betraying both of us. So, no, thank you. Road closed. *I was right*, my anxiety taunted as it set up the barricade. *I told you. You should have listened.*

Even though I witnessed a glimmer of it during those deliveries—the world, you know, the people in it, the continuing, enduring life-force beauty of both—the glimmer felt so very small. Because a party hat, a cookie, a dog, a friendly chat—they were nothing against the anxiety roar that had now wrapped around my sorrow and guilt and love and need like a fire wall. I went back to school. Addy drove us in her new (old) Honda. She said she wanted to show it off, but I think she wanted to keep an eye on me. Liam drove his dad's former BMW, so her Honda with almost a hundred thousand miles and worn cloth seats was maybe less of a show and more just hers. Priya piled in the back. Maddie lived close to school and always walked, so it was just the three of us. It reminded me of the days before Liam and Maddie and you. When we were just us. We were never this quiet or careful, though. I could feel them holding me with love, but also unease. As if I were thin glass that might shatter at the slightest wrong touch.

That first week back, I felt like my mind and body were constantly walking in water, going the wrong way, pressing back against the force of the current. Trying to get through classes in a weird haze of unreality. My shock had turned to something else. Not an understanding, because who could understand this? Maybe a truth, *the* truth, that was beginning to grow roots, but only new and fragile ones, because the shock never seemed to be gone for good. I'd be doing something regular, unlocking my locker or checking my phone, and wham. I'd be struck by the fact that you were no longer in the world, and there simply was no explanation for this.

Where are you? I'd ask you for the hundredth time.

Ms. Denali, my AP Lit teacher, pulled me aside to tell me she was there if I ever needed to talk. She'd lost someone close to her very suddenly, too. I looked in her eyes after she said it, and she looked in mine. And it was like her eyes went back and back. They were full of stories, and I had no idea. I had never really seen her before, I realized, with her dark hair in that ponytail, the wisps around her face. In her flowered tunics with the black leggings, her hands absent any rings. I'd found someone who lived on my planet, anyway, and we recognized each other.

Mr. Chu, my AP Statistics teacher, also called me to stay behind after class. He told me I could have all the time I needed to finish my work. Grief is hard work, he said, let alone statistics. He said it like he knew. And I hadn't seen him, either, with his stylish haircut and large glasses, the smartwatch that showed he'd already exercised and exercised and exercised. I wondered if he needed those loops for a different purpose, one that never had an end point.

The people who showed up for me—it wasn't who I'd expected. When I saw Sujia again, I thought she'd be warm and comforting, but she seemed nervous and awkward with me.

"I'm sorry," she said. "About your boyfriend." She played with the tassel that hung from her backpack. "How are you doing?"

"Okay," I said. I mean, how did she think I was doing?

"He'd want you to be happy," she said.

I folded my eyebrows down. She'd never met you. And you'd want me to be whatever I needed to be.

Mrs. Swanson, our DECA advisor, stopped me in the hall. "Margaret! I heard about your friend. I'm so sorry."

"Thanks," I said. I wasn't sure how to answer this. *Thanks* sounded wrong.

"I know how you feel," she said, but when I looked in her eyes, they didn't go back and back. They stopped, right where I was looking. "But I hope you can remember, he's in a better place."

I kind of wanted to kick her. This made me so mad, even though she was trying to be nice. It sounded so smug and sure. She couldn't know such a thing; no one could. And I wanted you in this place. We needed you here. This was a pretty fucking best place, thanks.

But then, at lunch, Severin Gyles's friend Ramone came up to me. Ever since that kiss, Severin had been ignoring me as if he didn't know who I was, as if he'd never had his tongue in my mouth. Maybe he didn't know who I was. Yet there was Ramone, holding his lunch tray as I held mine, before we sat down.

"I just wanted to say . . . Me and my family, we've all been thinking about you and your boyfriend and your families." Ramone—he'd never really talked to me before. I had no idea what his family was like, or where he even lived. Yet there were these people, you know, who had me and you and all of us in their thoughts. "It's just fucked. It's seriously fucked."

My eyes pricked with tears, as if eyes recognize truth even before the rest of you does. "It is," I managed to say.

He moved down the table to eat with his friends, and I moved to our end. I saw him down there, plucking the pickle from his cheeseburger, as you would on an ordinary day. Oh, God, right then, his understanding made me want to set down my anxiety and just *trust*. It made me want to . . . Okay, okay, *connect*. I couldn't, though. I'm sorry, I couldn't. But what he'd said had mattered.

At the end of the day, I was exhausted. It had been a grief video game, dodging, weaving, hiding, plodding through a maze where snipers waited. I had the day off, because this was enough, making it through to the bell. Addy dropped me at Maurice's.

"I'll check on you later," she said. She'd been sending texts throughout the days. Sometimes just an emoji—a whale, an ice cream cone.

Maurice was at work, but Sandrine was there. She opened the door, wearing pajama pants and a T-shirt stained with something purple. Grape juice, maybe. You loved grape juice, and we always gave you shit about it, because it was gross, and no one else liked it.

"Grape?" I pointed.

She shut her eyes so she wouldn't cry. It was grape juice, all right. It took her a few seconds, but she opened them again. "Mario Kart?"

"Sure."

The cords were in a jumble, not wrapped up all neat like before, and there was a cup of coffee on the table that looked like it had grown cold, the milk settled in a cosmic swirl on top. The couch cushions were bunched up like she'd been there awhile.

I was Baby Rosalina, as per usual, and she was Bowser, Arthur's old favorite. I didn't ask her about the record deal, what was happening and when, or maybe even if. Or how Janite was doing, or your aunt, or your friends. And I didn't talk to her about what still weighed on me most. I wanted to. I wanted to keep talking and talking about it, about breaking up with you, sort of. If we had or hadn't. If you'd gotten that last text. If I'd hurt you enough for your heart to break. If this was my fault, because it felt like it. No matter what anyone said, it did. If you were going to be gone like this, if I had no choice in the matter, the thing I needed, so badly needed, was for you to know I was sorry and that I loved you. Love you, always.

At one point, Sandrine said, "I missed his call because I was at Taco Time." I could see it, how that weighed on her most, how she wanted to keep talking and talking about that. And I understood something else—that nothing I said then would fix it, her certainty that she'd done something to harm you.

Sandrine and I were there together, in that place of deep need and the unfinished business of love. I realized it: We were haunted. Not by you (I wish), but by ourselves, what we hadn't done. By those unanswered questions, too. What could we do now? Was there even a *what* that existed? There had to be a way! How do you send love to someone who is no longer here? How do you resolve a mystery that only one missing person can explain? It was you we needed to connect with, and that was impossible.

I held her hand.

"God," she said. "He used to hide my phone just to annoy me, all the time, and I'd get so pissed at him. He'd do that high, piercing shriek-laugh, and I'd want to whack him. Now I'd give anything for him to be here hiding my phone."

I didn't answer. We just zoomed around in that cartoon land, not even racing or playing the game, circling as if we were lost.

"I told him to *go*," I said to Winnifred Evans. I'd told her this many times now, too. She was the one person who allowed me to repeat it again and again. "I was angry at him. I told him to go, and he did."

I was trying and trying to give her all the evidence that this was my fault, but she just sat calmly in her leather swivel chair.

"You've heard of the stages of grief? Denial, anger, bargaining, depression, acceptance?"

I nodded. Sure, I had. Health class, junior year. They just seemed like words. It was all that and more, all the time, all at once.

"I'm convinced there should be another one," Winnifred Evans said. "Guilt."

I scrunched my nose. I doubted this particular guilt was universal. This guilt was actually guilty, a hundred percent.

"I'm going to guess, Margaret, that every person in his life is feeling some version of that. Guilty and responsible. Full of regret. Worried they hadn't been good enough, hadn't done right by their beloved Mars. A hundred instances of *If only I'd . . .*"

"I just need him to know I love him." My whole self wrenched. "Do you think he knew?"

"I have no doubt you showed him that while he was here." Well, I had doubt. "And I think it's an ongoing longing after a death, to somehow convey our love. To continue to do that."

"But *how* do you?"

"Hmm," she said, as she always did when she was taking something in. "People have been struggling with *that* one forever. The Taj Mahal, way back in sixteen hundred something? That young woman recently, with her late father's record collection?" I shrugged. I hadn't heard about it. "He left her his albums. *Ten thousand* of them. She began to play them online, to about half a million listeners now."

I didn't have ten thousand of your records to play. I didn't even have one record. I stared at my fingernails. I wondered if those weird ridges meant I had some heart condition I didn't know about. Lately, in my chest, I'd felt the actual beating of it. Too fast, maybe. Fluttering. A squeezing that meant something was badly wrong.

Just thinking about that squeezing made it hard to breathe. "I feel like I'm drowning," I said.

"The wave comes in, but it goes back out again, remember?"

It's what she always said about anxiety in general. "But this wave is huge. And I'm lost out here at sea! It's too much."

"The waves won't always be this huge," she said. She was wearing her glasses, which made it hard to see her eyes. I wanted to see if they went on and on, or if they just stopped. I guess I wanted to know if I could trust what she was telling me, because right now I didn't believe her.

"Have you been through this?" I asked. She rarely talked about herself. She always steered my questions back toward me. But sometimes I needed to know that she wasn't bigger and more, but that we were the same.

"Anyone who's lived awhile has experienced loss. Been on that sea, right? The sea of grief? But your voyage is uniquely yours. And your lost voyager was one of a kind, too."

I started to cry. Sob. Again, again. I remembered this fact I'd read once: That we have an ocean inside us. That, same as the Earth, we are 70 percent salt water.

Winnifred Evans just sat with me as my body experienced this unbearable pain. She handed me the tissue box. I wondered how many times she'd handed over that box or one like it. Before you left us, I never thought much about grief, how much a part of our lives it is. Everyone's life. *That* should have been on the Golden Record. So much of what made us most *us* couldn't be on it, could it? I was struck again and again by that. Loss and love—it couldn't be truly captured in photos or even in music.

I left Winnifred Evans's office, but I couldn't leave the building yet. I lingered in the waiting room, sat in the chair I'd been in that first time we met. No one else was in there. I looked over at your chair until you appeared, slouching down, wearing those jeans and your yellow sweatshirt. I saw your black curls springing every direction. The smile that went all the way to your eyes, without a doubt.

And then I saw you walking to the watercooler. The sag of your jeans on your butt. The tumbling cups, reaching for the one that had rolled under the love seat. The watercooler sending up its big, burping bubble.

Glug, you'd said, and I smiled, even now.

Your voyage is uniquely yours. And your lost voyager was one of a kind, too.

Voyage.

Voyager.

Maybe that's why I did it. The girl with her dad's albums, too—her with my same need, plus that word, *record*. The hollow fact that I didn't even have one record of yours, of *you*. It wasn't a plan, not yet. It was barely even an idea. If I'd known what it would lead to, I'd have been shocked. I probably wouldn't have done it. But I got out my phone. I covered the lens, because I only wanted the sound.

I put a little cup on the tray of the watercooler. I pressed the red record button, and pulled the lever.

Glug.

It wasn't the first thing you said to me, but it was the first time I heard you laugh.

Chapter Twenty-Two

Sarafina pizza in open box, with original anchovy smile,
photo by Margaret Vittorio: *Pictures of Mars*
"Keep Me in Your Heart" by Warren Zevon: *Music of Mars*

"Are you going to be okay doing this?" Mom asked.

It was a Friday night. For the first time in weeks, I was doing my regular shift, alone. I realized something: I had barely been alone since those horrific early hours I learned about you. My people were keeping me tethered to Earth, even if I couldn't see the cords.

"I think so," I said. "Yes."

"I'm here. I'm a phone call away."

I realized something else. She was. She had been. I felt her there. More than I ever had, maybe in my whole life. My eyes traveled to the books on our end table, right out in the open. *Eating Disorder Recovery. More Than a Body. Returning to Myself: Life Beyond ED.*

She saw me seeing. "I've been going to a counselor."

I wanted to cry. I was relieved, but also . . . hesitant. Not believing entirely. She'd gone before, and it hadn't lasted. Moving the food around her plate, the restricting, the exercise, the *disappearing*—it started up again. "I'm glad," I said.

"So much time has been wasted." I made a face. I mean, it wasn't forced on her or anything. Maybe it sounds cold, but you lose your warmth after so many years out in the cold yourself. "*I've* wasted so much time. Of my own. Of yours, and the boys'."

I didn't say anything. I waited for her to veer off into self-pity or blame. Blaming my dad, mostly, for his lack of attention and care. Self-pity for all the stress of being perfect, the perfect wife and mother and member of her community. This is what we'd heard before, after actually fearing for her life and after years of her denials.

"I'm going to be late," I said.

She came over to me. I was wearing my parka, but her hug was hard enough for me to feel the puffy fabric squish, to feel her pressing my actual body.

In some ways, I wanted to punish her and not press back. But I didn't. I hugged her. She was there, and I was there, too. She was right, about all the wasted time. You couldn't get it back. There weren't too many things that were very important, truly important, when it came right down to it. Maybe it was trite to say. Simplistic, too. But why, then, did we need to be reminded of it all the time? Why were we constantly forgetting that who we loved was all that mattered?

I hadn't even driven myself anywhere since that night. The people who loved me worried I was too distracted and distraught, not capable of focusing on the details of moving a vehicle. They were right, you know. Even right then, my car seemed like an old and distant friend, someone I was once close to but had mostly forgotten. It began to rain, and I had to search for the wipers, flicking my turn signal on accidentally.

I was one tiny person in the dark on a tiny planet in a large, endless universe. I passed other tiny people in their cars, too. On their bikes, at stoplights, their minds full of worry over that nasty thing someone just said or did, or what they were having for dinner, or what grade they got, or what grade they'd better get, or else. So many tiny people with tiny worries, too often forgetting about the largest stuff all around them.

I remembered Lily telling me this one night on Tiger Mountain: If you blasted off, zoomed two hundred miles from Earth, the distance from Seattle to Salem, Oregon, you could see our landmasses, our glittering lights. Just past the moon, we looked like the moon ourselves, and past the planets, we looked like a star. Nine billion miles from home, our planet went dark. We were so tiny, we were invisible. From that distance, it looks like we aren't even here, like we don't exist. But we are here, and we do exist. From out there, though, it would take belief to think so.

I pulled into the delivery parking for Papa Angelo's. The building was aglow, bright and bustling, our own starlight. I could see Maurice in there, and my father at the counter, lights within lights. God, how I wanted to talk to you about this, this Papa Angelo's star. I so badly wanted to tell you about Mom, about everything that was happening now. I wanted to tell you about flicking on my turn signal instead of my wipers. I needed to talk to you about missing you.

I walked through the front door to a familiar call. "Bella!" my dad said. "Get your butt in there! People are waiting for their hot pizza!" A couple at a table smiled, and so did the mom and dad sitting with their small children. It was a show, so I saluted. Maurice lifted a hand in greeting over by the pickup counter, and I lifted mine back. George was in the kitchen with the cooks.

"You're ready," George said, and pointed to my first small stack of padded bags for the night. I'd be back for more, and back again. A full shift, tomorrow night, too.

People were waiting. And how hot a pizza was and how right we got their orders were important to the tiny people on the tiny planet, and important to us, as well. I was supposed to hurry.

But on that long metal kitchen counter, I saw the circles of dough being prepared, the sausage eyes, the mushroom noses, arugula hair, the anchovy/orange-pepper/pepperoni smiles. There were two, three, four of them, all smiling at me.

I hadn't taken a photo since you left. The happiness I felt about photography, my fragile new dream of maybe studying it that I'd shared with only you—who cared anymore, you know? But I got out my phone and opened the camera. I still didn't have a plan yet, a plan that would lead to *this*, us here, right now. I just wanted to *show* you.

Click, and there they were. What you created, existing. Just pizzas, but never say that to my dad, or any of us.

The first photo, Mars. If we'd sat and planned it out, we might have chosen something different, but there it was, a row of your smiling Sarafinas. I looked down at my phone, and the image made me so freaking sad, but I couldn't help but smile back, too.

My father had popped his head through the kitchen door, and I could see part of Maurice, peering through the open area of the pickup counter. They didn't say anything about dawdling or getting my ass in gear, though, none of the shit all of them usually gave me. They didn't say a word.

It was another thing not on the Golden Record. Silence, you know. The many types of silence, but loving silence most of all.

I drove home at the end of my shift. I'd made it. I'd dragged myself through the current, and I'd gotten to the other side.

It seemed wrong, that normal night. To have one. To have those moments where I forgot entirely that you were gone. I couldn't say that other word yet, the one that started with a *d*. But the point is, I'd been busy. I hadn't thought of you for a few stretches of time. The guilt crawled into my stomach and chest, squeezed my heart.

Which is probably why I played that song. I'd stayed away from music, same as Sandrine, even though music was her life. *Because* music was her life. It wasn't my life, but I understood the danger of it. In general—how crucial it was, how connected to our humanity and our emotions, something a person felt whether they even understood the words or not, just like we felt "El Cascabel." But specifically, too. How music was so present in our time together, from that first moment I saw you at the houseboat.

It was punishment, probably, for letting you leave my mind, but it was longing, too. Oh, it was so cruel, how that longing would never ever be met.

I played it. "Keep Me in Your Heart." That tender, crushing ballad.

I bent in half. Racked with sobs, wrecked. The tiny people on the tiny planet were also doing this, mourning losses so loud, they were powerful, violent storms. Blazes, impossible and forever. God, I was so clueless. I'd never even realized it. How had I not? I was in love, and I heard it as a beautiful romantic song about a loved person on your mind. But it was a song about death. Our song was.

Did *you* know that?

Could you hear me playing it now? Could you feel my loss and my longing? We knew how far light traveled, but we had no idea how far love did.

Chapter Twenty-Three

Carl Sagan in a frame, photo by Margaret Vittorio:
Pictures of Mars
Tiny *Despicable Me* Minion, photo by Margaret Vittorio:
Pictures of Mars

It was a day I'd been dreading, February fourteenth, Valentine's Day. It had always seemed silly in so many ways—the forced declarations, the pink, the foil hearts of chocolates that tasted like their boxes. But it didn't seem silly that year. It seemed immensely heartbreaking. A loud, lacy celebration of romance turned inside out to its opposite, a sorrowful hole of love-loss.

And I hadn't fully realized *that*, either, the way there would be so many days on the calendar to dread, even fear. Valentine's Day, Mother's Day, graduation, Christmas, the anniversary. Another new year. I never noticed how many anniversaries a calendar held. All the markings of how we matter to each other. Beautiful when someone is alive, just cruel when not.

Oh, God. Your birthday. In the hierarchy of dread, it suddenly zoomed to the top spot. That would be the worst one, wouldn't it?

The day that marked the beautiful, promising beginning of you? You were turning eighteen in May. It was confusing. Did you still turn eighteen, even though you'd never turn eighteen? What would it mean when I was twenty and then thirty and forty, and you were still seventeen? I would change, but you wouldn't, and neither would my feelings for you. I'd have experiences, and you wouldn't. I would graduate, and go to college, and maybe get married one day, and you wouldn't. I would get lines on my face, and my hair would turn gray, and yours never would, and I'd still love you, seventeen. I had no idea how to understand a real human being frozen in time. Part of me would remain frozen in that time with you, seventeen, too. That was the only solution I could think of.

Valentine's Day was a Sunday, and I stayed in bed, tormenting myself for the millionth time about that text and its unsolvable mystery, with my constant regret of breaking up, sort of, maybe not. I couldn't tell you how much I loved you on a day I was supposed to, on a day where it was easy, when flowers could say it, or a hand-drawn card, or a frosted cookie. God, I needed to tell you! I needed to know that we were still together, connected, even now. I needed this so badly. I would *have* to find a way, like the young woman and her dad's records. I could do something like that! I *would* do something like that, I vowed, as my anxiety laughed. *Haha. Right.*

I also wondered how Janite was doing on this Valentine's Day. She held your history of red construction-paper hearts and glue and glitter, but I was too much of a coward to reach out. Even thinking about it—my panic rose. I couldn't face how destroyed she must be, and I couldn't imagine my guilty self even talking to her. I wondered how Frank was doing, too. I missed him.

I started to text Sandrine that day, just to . . . I don't know. Be together with her, our two guilty selves with our love and the unknowable things that tormented us. But it seemed so wrong, a text. Making a phone call to anyone but you had always been confusingly stressful for me, as you know, but now, with the fire wall . . . Well, my devastation was overwhelming on its own, so Sandrine's might tip me over.

Calling her required an epic pregame pep talk with my inner coach. *Come on! Stop thinking about only yourself, you ungenerous scaredy-ass butthead.* My inner coach was a meanie.

"Hey," I said. "It's me."

"Hey," she said. She knew better than to ask how I was doing, and so did I.

"I'm not sure what to say, but I just wanted to—" I was interrupted by . . . barking? Lots of barking. "Is that *Frank*?"

"A doorbell just rang on TV."

"Is he staying with you?"

I knew what she was going to say before she said it. "He's ours now. Mars's VW is mine now, too. Aunt Janite's moving. To Phoenix."

"Still?"

"She's been struggling, bad. She was taking sedatives after he died, but my mom got rid of them. She's got a . . . history?"

"I remember."

"She said she has to get out of here. She's leaving next week."

Next week? Already? I felt a messy rush of panic. If she was gone, you'd really be gone. Somehow, while Janite lived in your houseboat, you were still here. And if she left, so would my chance for . . . A goodbye? Closure? Forgiveness?

An answer, my worst, most selfish voice said.

Because if anyone knew whether you'd gotten my text or not, it would be her, there with you that night. Janite might have the information that would give me some peace, or no peace, but a resolution, at least. One week, and that chance would be gone.

A rush of urgency filled me. But the thought of seeing your mom filled me with dread. How could I face her? I'd harmed your heart, and maybe broken it for real. And I'd witness her grief. She was the woman who loved you every day of your life, and even before. Who gave birth to you, and changed your diapers, and struggled to feed and house you and her; who watched you leave for kindergarten, and admired your school pictures, and, and, and . . . All the way up to that last dinner the two of you had together. She knew what it was, what you ate. She watched you eat it.

How could I even go to her with my own need? My loss felt so small and unearned compared to hers. I'd loved you for such a short time. We were together in ways only we could be, but this seemed so inconsequential compared to sharing every day, to sharing generations of DNA. I didn't understand, you know, what I had a right to, in terms of sorrow and devastation. Janite's loss was bigger, so mine felt like nothing in comparison. It was embarrassing, unworthy, as if it hadn't met the requirements of some impossible-to-understand ranking.

I remembered Sujia's close friend Emily, who was with us one day when Sujia asked if I was doing okay. *Wait.* How *long did you know him?* Emily had said, in that high-pitched way that conveyed a disbelief, a doubt, suspicion, even. She was doing a mental calculation, indicating that the time we'd been together equaled zero on the allowable sadness scale. She didn't know me or you or us together; she wasn't there in the forest that day, hadn't danced to the Golden Record, or watched as you made the infinity symbol in the air, and loss didn't follow the neat rules of an equation. There is no calculus for what we are to each other, no number to apply to meaning or feeling or experience. It was in my body, and was true and real because it was there. It occurred to me then: We did the same thing about love. We said you couldn't feel it, it wasn't real, depending on our own judgments, when what did we know? How did we have any clue about another person's heart? Tell me that.

"Wow," I said. "Maurice didn't mention it. About Frank."

"It just happened. Aunt Janite, uh, came by last night, driving the VW. Bringing his crate and stuff. The dude, what's his name. Jake. He's allergic to dogs."

I wanted to say, *WHAT? She just dumped him on you?* but instead, I just said, "Oh."

"Come here, boo-boo," Sandrine said. "What are you doing, huh?" I thought she was talking to me at first. "That's you, Frank. That's not another dog; that's you. He's looking at himself in the long mirror, like he can't understand who he is. Totally baffled." I could hear Sandrine smile. "Come here, boy." Now I heard him climb up, and her warding him off. He was licking her face; I was sure of it. Remember how wild he got, the moment he was allowed on your lap? "Ouch, ouch, your toenails! Oh, God, his tongue went in my mouth!"

"Oh, yuck, Frank," I said. But I was envious, and I could hear how glad Sandrine was to have him. Frank's little warm body, and his funny chin whiskers, and his soulful eyes—it was something she could do for you, and it was another way to be close to you. I didn't have many ways, aside from Sandrine herself. Every now and then, I thought about joining the astronomy meetup, just to see Chester and Lily and all the people who meant something to you, but that would mean climbing the mountain on my own, the real one *and* the anxiety one. Suddenly, I understood why people had funerals, even though your mom didn't want one. All the connections without calculations—they had a place to be together, to say, *We have all loved, and will continue to love*.

"I've got to go. I have to deal with this beast," Sandrine said.

We said goodbye. But I felt for Frank. I felt *like* Frank—looking at himself in the mirror, sure that he was someone else. Wondering, no doubt, who he was, and how he got here.

One more week! Seven more days!

It was a last-chance thrum, and already, it was relentless.

Six more days, five. Four, three, two, one, like the blastoff of a rocket.

But I couldn't do it. And then Janite was gone.

Of course, it was inevitable—I got a delivery to your dock. I almost asked one of the other drivers to swap. But when I checked the order again, I didn't.

Mrs. Fosmire. An Arturo, medium.

Just there in the parking lot, before I even got out of my car, my heart was beating hard. I felt sick. You were everywhere—standing at the entrance, running out to meet me, kissing me goodbye, getting the mail, hauling your and your mom's groceries down the dock in the big handcart.

I wanted to be there, you know, so bad. To *see* you. But, equally, I didn't. Who knows what I wanted. At least your mom wasn't there. I felt a distinct relief about that. Thank you, anxiety, for helping me avoid it, even if it meant that I was still stuck in the ruthless void of unanswered questions.

We were a week past Janite's move. I was scared to see your house empty. Or, maybe worse, to see someone else living there. I looked away from your house as I walked past it. I averted my eyes. It was another thing I just couldn't do, because my body was suddenly a hundred doors, shutting in a panic. I felt you there, urging me to look, but I fought you. I'm sorry. It was weird, how close you seemed sometimes. It was like you were right there with me, and I'd say, *I'm so sorry. I love you. Mars, Mars! Where are you?* These were the things I needed you to know, and the thing I needed to know.

I rang Mrs. Fosmire's doorbell. I could avert my eyes all I wanted, but there was the end of the dock where we swam, and the lake, and the boats, and our city, and our state, and our world, and you were everywhere.

At first, I only saw Mrs. Fosmire's scowling face through the mesh of the screen door, and then she opened it. She seemed as cranky and pissed as ever, her face hard and resentful of all that life had brought her. I'd never been so glad to see anyone in all my life.

She took that box and gave it a gentle Frisbee toss, and then she reached her arms out to me, because I was suddenly crying.

She let out an impressive stream of *fuck*s. They sounded rough and right when she linked them to other words like *unfair* and *wrong* and *horrible*. They sounded impassioned and heartfelt when she linked them to words like *special* and *loved* and *one of a kind*.

She didn't cry, but when I stopped, I could see that her eyes were watery. I saw something else, too—that her eyes went on and on, that she was familiar with this particular planet, the one that was new to me, but that we were both on.

How many times had you told me that connection could save you? Standing there with Mrs. Fosmire, I actually felt ever so briefly that I might survive this.

"You come and see me anytime," she said.

I was thankful that Mrs. Fosmire's was the last delivery of the day. I was a mess, and suddenly exhausted. That dock—it might as well have been the aisle of a church, the way it seemed that the walk back down it, back to my car, would be a last walk, a march from my old self to a new one that seemed too far away to even see. The walk was something to face, and I could do it, okay? Mrs. Fosmire was there, and I could.

Good luck with that, my anxiety said.

I peeked at your houseboat, a few floats away. It looked unchanged—the tiny cottage with the shingles worn and fading from sun and time. There was the blue door, and Janite had left the flowerpot on the porch, and she'd left the set of table and chairs, where you and I sat all the time, eating food and looking all lovey at each other as music poured from the open windows. Maybe it belonged to the people who rented out the house and would be there for the next renters. Other people would sit in those spots, unaware of who'd been there before. Those windows were all shut tight, though. They were always open when we sat out there.

I inched closer. All right, I would look! It would be my last chance, because I was going to tell Maurice and George that this place was off-limits from here on out. This was a goodbye. The only one I'd get.

I cupped my hands around my eyes, peered in the living room window. And then I pulled back in shock.

Oh, shit! Shit!

It was full of boxes, stuff packed, but not entirely. A chaos of objects here and there—crumpled newspaper, a marker with a cap off, the barely legible scrawl of *Kitchen*, *Living Room* on the cardboard containers. A sheet was thrown over the couch. I recognized it. I'd lain in that sheet. The way objects had a history was unnerving. I'd always thought so. A trip to Goodwill always left me feeling weird and haunted. All those possessions sitting silently with their stories and secrets.

She was still here, oh my God!

Oh, no. No! She saw me! *Fuckfuckfuck!* She was in the kitchen, holding one of those giant tape dispensers, pointing it absently forward like a flashlight in the dark. It was winter, but she was in denim shorts and a T-shirt. I recognized that shirt, too. It was your

Arcade Fire one, with the drum set and instruments ablaze. I understood it—why she'd want to wear something of yours. But then, wait, I realized . . . Maybe it was *hers*, and *you'd* been the one to borrow it. This is how connected you'd been, mother and child, in ways I couldn't really understand. I was a child, but not a mother.

I wanted to run, but she hurried to the door and opened it before my feet could move.

"Margaret! Thank God!" she said. Now her arms were around me. It seemed inexplicable, after what I'd done to you. She was clutching me to herself and crying now, and I didn't sob as I had with Mrs. Fosmire. I was in shock and suddenly overwhelmed. I couldn't breathe, and, thankfully, she let me go, and I tried to balance myself again. There was something about her that always made me feel like that. That I couldn't get air.

"Janite, I'm . . ." What? Sorry, so sorry. So very sorry, enough that I'll never forgive myself.

"I was hoping to see you before I left. Things have just been . . ." She swirled her arm in circles. "I was supposed to go last week, but it's been one thing after another. The truck got delayed, and then Jake said we couldn't sign the new lease until the end of the month, and then I lost my phone, and—it's just been too much. Come in! Please."

She held my hand, something she'd never done before, and pulled me inside. It was a tornado of stuff, a tornado of memories, too. Janite dropped to the couch covered in that sheet, exhausted. She dropped her head in her hands, too weighty to even carry, and then I saw her shoulders move up and down, and she began to howl. "Why, why, why?"

In some ways, it was the only question. The only one without an answer somewhere, too. Where and what and who, you could always count on. Why, though, that was a whole other story. *Why* was skittish and unreliable and stubbornly withholding.

I sat beside her on your sheet. Our sheet. It was all too much. I put my arms around your mom, and found myself rocking her. I didn't know what else to do.

But then she gathered herself. She shook her head, and a shiver went through her, like some exorcism in those movies I refused to watch. In some ways, I did understand this; it was familiar, the way the pain came in racking waves and then left you empty and stunned. "How can he be gone?" Her eyes pleaded. "I am gutted. I am a wreck. I'm barely alive myself."

I couldn't speak. I could tell my role was to be the strong one, so I didn't dare. I only shook my head. It was all I could do and still hold it together. From there, I could see those boxes labeled with the black marker. *Bathroom. J's room.* But two sat next to each other. *Mars. Living.*

"You meant so much to him," she said. What was ours was ours, so she likely had no real idea. *Meant so much* was not love, the way we felt it, real and deep. The way it was interrupted now, without a natural conclusion, leaving it in some strange limbo like Voyager itself, built to last five years but still going on and on. But Janite didn't say what I feared she would; she didn't speak to the ways I hurt you. It gave me hope, you know. If you didn't tell her we broke up, maybe we hadn't. Maybe we were still together.

"He meant so much to me," I managed to say. My words

sounded like the tiny squeak of a hamster wheel, spinning without a destination.

"Maybe you'd like something of his."

"Oh, I couldn't . . ." I could. Yes, yes, please. I wanted it all, I wanted everything, ten thousand records. I had that dried leaf, and the silver bracelet you'd given me, but I was afraid to wear it. I might lose it, like I lost you. I didn't trust myself with it.

"Go ahead." She waved her arm toward your room. "I can't go in there. Sandrine's been helping, and I try, but . . . Go on."

"Okay," I said. "Thank you."

She eyed the padded pizza warmer over my shoulder. "Don't take anything without asking."

She'd never known who I was, that was for sure. I wished she'd gotten the chance to, Mars. I really do.

It was like willingly walking into a tidal wave. You might have died right there on that floor. I didn't know for sure. Through your doorway, my whole body clutched, like a faulty engine shutting down. I willed myself to hold it together, seeing your room in such an unusual disarray, seeing the room in general, without you in it. I imagined you collapsed there, and over there, too. For the millionth time, I couldn't understand where you were now.

The bed was still in place, stripped of its sheets and cover, just a bare mattress. Boxes were strewn around in there, too. Only one or two had reached the point of being taped up and labeled; the others spilled clothes and school papers and books. The most prominent thing in your room, your Voyager poster, had been taken down, but it was now lying on the floor, the universe upside down and at my feet, only the pinholes remaining in the wall where it had hung. That Golden Record replica that Sandrine had given you was gone; there was now just a nail hole, minus the nail. Your shelves were still up, and an attempt had been made to pack them, but the task had been abandoned. I could see your astronomy volumes in an open box, but the shells and rocks, that laminated ticket to the Santa Cruz Boardwalk, the Sky Glider card from your friend, Ella, your baby photo with your mom, and all the others of your California friends were still there. But you know what broke my heart? The most? Carl Sagan's photo in the frame. It was on your nightstand, and Carl was still gazing in the direction of your bed, now just a blue satiny mattress with a sagging you-imprint in the center.

Carl—it was like he was speaking to me. You were; everyone and everything was. Ms. Costa, and the photographs with meaning, too, because I realized I was looking at both ten thousand records and a single one.

I removed my phone from my pocket. I opened the camera and took a photo of that Voyager poster. Next I took photos of photos, the ones you treasured, of your friends, and baby you and your mom. I snapped a shot of that Santa Cruz Boardwalk ticket key chain, and the Sky Gliders card. The shells and the rocks and everything else on your shelves. And, of course, Carl Sagan in the frame. Right then, it was all just for me. What was coming was still in the unknowable future. I was just trying to hold on to you, to keep you, to show what had mattered.

Your mom said I could have something. I moved to the box of your shirts. You always see this in a movie, the person smelling the missing loved one's shirt, but that's what I did. I actually did that very same thing, with the shirt on the top of the pile, a blue flannel one. I remember you in it once or twice, and I held it to my face. I closed my eyes. I inhaled until I couldn't smell you anymore.

"Margaret?" Janite's voice called out in suspicion. We were already past the romantic hand-holding portion of our relationship. She stood in the doorway, her eyebrows folded down. I wished I could love her like you had, Mars. We could have had an ongoing connection to you together, then, but this would never, could never, happen. Not when we were some weird, hard-to-understand rivals.

"I'm here." Not entirely true. It was all so surreal.

We looked at each other, her in the doorway, me by that box. I needed to apologize to her. I badly wanted to be forgiven for the wrongdoing I carried, but I couldn't speak.

"Is that what you want?"

I was still holding your shirt. I just stared at her, drowning.

She rubbed its sleeve. "I guess you can have it."

"Oh! Thank you." I almost wished I could look through that box, though. I maybe would have chosen your yellow sweatshirt, the one you wore when we first met, or your favorite T-shirt with the retro rocket blasting skyward, or the heather-blue one from our time in the forest. I couldn't bear the thought of your clothes staying jammed and meaningless in that box, or worse, disappearing somewhere, into the great sea of used clothes, looking like just another T-shirt when none of them were. These thoughts, you know, they could build to a panic if I wasn't careful.

"Great," Janite said. The way she leaned in that door with her arms folded, I understood that we were done.

"Wait."

It was here, the moment. My chance to ask her if you had gotten that text. If you knew, before you left, without a doubt, that I loved you. I looked in her eyes as she stood there. And I saw that they did not go on and on. They stopped at a blaze of pain.

Oh, God. It wasn't possible right then, okay? To connect, to take that chance to ask. There was just no way. We were a fire wall and a wall of fire. I moved my eyes to Carl's then, seeking comfort.

"You want *that*?"

She misunderstood my gaze. She saw longing, which was so true. But yes, yes! I wanted it so bad, Carl in the frame. His comfort that was your comfort. I wanted his help, even. And with that thought, right there, this idea, this *plan*, began to form. "If it's okay. If you don't mind."

She waved her hand, *whatever*. I picked up the frame and held it close. How well did she know you, if she didn't understand the importance of that photo to you? I'm sorry I even asked that. It's petty. I really am sorry.

She held her fingers to her necklace, rubbed an amethyst crystal hanging on a chain. "Did I tell you?"

I shook my head. She hadn't told me anything, so it was a safe answer.

"The clock in my room. It stopped at nine-fifteen. Like, months ago. But that's *right* when he died. The exact same time."

"Wow. That's unbelievable," I said. Maybe unbelievable, literally. No one was with you. Who could be sure of the exact minute? Could I blame her, though? I wasn't any different. Everything seemed like a sign. When the sun was out, you were sending a message, and when the moon shined down, you were. When I once saw a comet, for sure. It was right over our house, and I thanked you.

I needed a sign. You were so quiet.

A phone began to ring. Muffled. It was coming from that box of clothes. Of course, maybe *that* was a sign, a call from your box of clothes just as I had the thought about your silence.

"My phone! There it is! I've been looking everywhere!" Janite flung the clothes from the box. One after the other, your flannel shirts were in the air, and then there it was, the T-shirt with the rocket. God, I wanted it. I wanted every single one. I wanted the shoes and the socks, even the worn-out flip-flop that now lay on the floor.

Janite held the phone up victoriously. "I've got to get this. It's Jake."

"Thank you," I said, holding up the blue flannel and the frame. She waved me off again.

I made my way through the disarray of the living room. I'd never be in that place again, and I gave it a final look, and that's when I saw the urn on the mantel. I'd never seen an urn that held ashes before, but I instantly understood what it was. Gray stone, with a lid. It looked large and heavy, but not large or heavy enough to hold you, my Mars. I couldn't understand it, that jar. It made no sense to me, what became of you.

I closed the door behind me. *Goodbye*, I said, *goodbye*. But this wasn't where you were.

It's where you had been, but you'd been everywhere. You'd been in the houseboat, and on the dock I was now walking on, and you'd been in my arms, and your breath had been in the air, and your feet on the Earth, and your eyes on that sky.

Your eyes had met *those* eyes, every night before you closed them. The eyes of that dude in the turtleneck, Carl Sagan, Mr. Rogers of the cosmos. Those compassionate eyes that would now meet mine every night before I closed them.

I could see it, even in the photo, how Carl Sagan's eyes went on and on.

You are special, I said to the photo, and the dock, and my arms, and the air, and the Earth, and the sky, everywhere you once were.

Chapter Twenty-Four

Dog barking: *Sounds of Mars*
"Frank and Jesse James" by Warren Zevon: *Music of Mars*
Rain, thunder, lightning: *Sounds of Mars*
Leaf, photo by Margaret Vittorio: *Pictures of Mars*
"Baby, You Got Me" by Solar Flare: *Music of Mars*

"There she is!" Addison cupped her hand around her mouth. "Go, Maddie!"

"I can't look." Priya hid her eyes on my shoulder. She got more nervous for Maddie than Maddie got during soccer, too. Last year, when Maddie had a two-second part in *The Matchmaker*, Priya was so nervous, her hands gripped the railings of the theater's woven red seats, and I could see her mouth move, urging the correct lines into Maddie's mouth.

I'd gone with them to the track meet, dragged reluctantly around my wall. Addison had pleaded, and then stooped to making me feel guilty. *We never see you. Do you still love me?* She did it on purpose, and it worked. I jammed my hands in my pockets. Somehow, I'd transitioned from sobbing every minute to this, moving around in this thick, anxious underworld, a slow, dark place where I forgot about things like clouds and sun. A place that seemed even more perilous than ever. Was Maddie's shoe untied? She could fall. She could hit her head on that sharp ledge thingy by the track right there. What were they thinking, allowing a ledge like that? How dangerous.

It was incredible, the way your insides could control the outside, what the world even seemed like or actually was. I'd forgotten about a lot of things: sky, trees, planets, little children. I hadn't babysat my nieces and nephew for months. Baby Millie had started to walk, and I hadn't even seen it. The idea of playing dinos or running around and shrieking or hiding with Millie behind a curtain so Maya and Max could seek us, everything we used to do, seemed as impossible as flying.

"She's next," I said.

I squinched my eyes, and fine, okay! Her shoes were totally tied. She wasn't going to die right that moment, but my chest was getting that weird flutter again, so maybe I would. I'd been trying to fight off these thoughts, that alarming squeezing in my chest, too. Trying to stay present, to ask myself, *Is it happening now?* as Winnifred Evans suggested, but the minute Maddie's feet started to speed toward the high-jump pit, the protective walls crumbled, and there *you* were, running toward it, with your skinny legs. *Look at these babies. I never made it over the bar once.*

Maddie didn't make it over, either. The bar clattered down, and so did she.

"Ouch," Addy said.

"Just tell me if she's okay," Priya said.

When you land on that thing on your back . . . Fuck, that hurts.

"She's getting up. You can look," Addy said.

Priya and I both opened our eyes. "Way to go, Maddie!" we yelled.

Priya flashed her two thumbs up, and Maddie flashed one back. "That takes guts, you know?" Priya was so proud. They were good to each other. Kind. A spiral of guilt and shame, an indefinable yuck, filled me. The slime trail of self-hatred, for sure.

I'm just going to go. I replayed it again and again in my mind.

I didn't mean it, I shouted after you. *I didn't! I'm so sorry.*

Going out in the world—it was just dangerous. There were punishments everywhere, the things that might sink you. How long would it be this way? Forever, it seemed. My small, narrow life of school and Papa Angelo's was perilous enough, but anything more opened me to things like the high jump. Things like a couple in love, who would never do to each other what I had to you.

"Most inspirational," I said, and Addy and Priya smiled. They didn't realize I wasn't even there.

The place I could go: Maurice and Sandrine's apartment. It was always a shock, seeing your VW parked on the street in front. My brain and body would have a moment of forgetting, and would shoot me an ordinary lift of happiness that you were over at Maurice and Sandrine's. That I would see you.

I'd head over after school, if I wasn't working. Just to hang out, even if they weren't there. If they were, Sandrine and I would play Mario Kart as Maurice made dinner. We shared that Taco Time guilt and that maybe-breakup guilt with each other, confessed our terrible crimes again and again and heard them again and again, like two repentant prisoners sharing the same cell, sentenced for life, needing one piece of nonexistent evidence, just one, needing it so badly, to free us. But more than that, even, we just shared you, Sandrine and me. You were alive between us. That framed Golden Record that was in your room now hung next to Sandrine's side of the bed, just as Carl Sagan's compassionate eyes stared me to sleep on the nightstand next to mine.

"Come on, Frank!" I said. "What is going on? You're never this quiet." He sat like a proper gentleman and stared at me. Okay, what I was asking him to do was strange, I admit it. How could he begin to understand what was required of him? I tried again. I rang the doorbell, and then pressed record on my phone.

More staring.

Sandrine pulled into the driveway. She hauled her body up the sidewalk to the porch, a plastic grocery bag hanging off one arm.

It was a bag of boulders, by the look of it. And she was wearing a hoodie made of the heaviest metals, shoes of cement. Sandrine and I also shared the skyless, thick underworld. She was wandering there, too, as lost as I was. Solar Flare hadn't done a gig since last December, and that recording deal from Sub Pop still sat unsigned. It was April. In grief time, this was seconds. In recording-contract time, it was years. I'd heard Maurice talking on the phone to Dre, who was losing patience out of anxiety and a need to pay his rent.

Sandrine hadn't gone to the astronomy meetups, either. Chester had broken the news to them all, but Sandrine couldn't bear to even take their calls. That group, those nights on the mountain, looking in the direction of Voyager—it was more you than anything else.

"What are you two doing?" she asked. Frank jumped up on her knees. He was probably relieved to be saved from this confusing experience. Not meeting a person's expectations can be so distressing.

"Trying to get him to bark."

"Huh."

"It's for a . . ." It was the first time I said it aloud. "Project." I blushed. It sounded silly.

"Oh, all right. Let me put the ice cream away, and I'll help. It's easy."

I unloaded the milk and the bananas. There was a lot of ice cream. A lot. More than you'd ever imagine for two people, but I wasn't judging. *Whatever gets you through* was my new motto.

"Okay, ready?"

"Just a sec." I cued up my phone. One finger hovered over the video button; the other covered the lens. Sound only.

"Frank!" Sandrine made her voice all excited. "Squirrel!"

He raced to the front window, barking his head off. He was practically frothing, and a line of hair stood up in a ridge along his back.

"Wow, thanks," I said after I'd gotten it. I felt bad for Frank at the false alarm, but he didn't seem to care. Anything to liven up his day, I guess. I mean, the highlight was normally brown crunchy stuff twice a day, so . . .

"He freaks out whenever he sees one or hears the word. I can't blame him, honestly."

"Squirrels in hair. Total nightmare. Plus, that *eek, eek* sound they make." I shivered.

"You never know what they're going to do. Tiny mind like that? You know what I read once? In the UK somewhere, two squirrels boarded a train and started to attack rush-hour commuters. They refused to leave."

"The commuters or the squirrels?"

"The squirrels, the evil motherfuckers! They had to cancel the train service. I remember that they used the word *pandemonium*."

"Oh my God. Frank, you're a hero."

"What project?" Sandrine handed me an A&W and plunked on the couch with hers. When you're sad, vegetables just won't do the trick. They just won't. Name one time broccoli cheered a person up.

"Um . . ." I wasn't sure how to explain. My face flushed again. How did I get myself here, to the point of sharing this with her? I wanted to blame Frank. If he'd barked on command, we wouldn't be here, or here yet. I was suddenly extremely nervous. My project had been this quiet thing, between me and you only. But even in its silence, I could feel it growing, becoming very important to me. Becoming essential, let's be honest. Essential enough to reveal.

"You can tell me," Sandrine said. Her open expression, her own creativity, our mutual love for you, and guilt over you, and unanswered questions about you . . . I *could* tell her. She was safe, and I loved her, and, of anyone, she would understand, but I was starting to sweat, actually sweat, and I felt a terror that made me wonder how she did it, wrote honest things and then shared those honest things, up on a stage. This was me and her in her living room. "It, um, has to do with him, okay? Just to warn you."

"Okay. Thanks for warning me. All right. Spill it."

I opened the album on my phone. I hadn't named it. It was just called *Album*. I turned the screen toward her. I thumbed through the photos. The pizza, the poster, the key chain. Rocks and shells. Carl Sagan. The photo of the leaf I took the other night before it crumbled and was lost.

At first, her eyes filled, but then she blinked and took my phone from me. She scrolled again, narrowing her eyes in appraisal. "Those are really good," she said.

I snorted.

"Margaret. They are."

"You're kidding."

"Not at all. They're *really* good."

"I took that photography elective? And then I got out of Graphic Design so I could take Advanced Photography."

"I mean, yeah, I remember. But it's more than something technical. Like, more than skill in taking the photo. It's not just a pizza, you know? Or a shell. Or a photo of a photo. You *feel* something when you look at them."

"Maybe *you* just do."

"I don't mean it like that. I mean, each photo *speaks*. Margaret. They speak like art speaks."

"No way." I was blushing so hard, I swear to God.

"Yes way."

I took my phone back. I tried to view the photos the way she had, but all I could see was my own feeling about them, my own feelings *in* them. I tried to tell her this.

"That's exactly my point. That's art. That's when art has impact. That's when art *connects*. You are connecting. You should do something with these."

I shrugged, but I felt so pleased. That someone as talented as Sandrine felt that way about what I'd made, yeah. But even more, I was pleased that I had done it. The thing that was so important to you. I made an outreach. I connected. Even if it was just to Sandrine in her living room.

"But, wait. Why do you need the barking?" she asked.

Oh, God. I felt anxious and uncertain all over again. I would wreck it now, maybe. This wasn't art, I was pretty sure. Still, I chanced it. That was another one of your things, the chancing, the *you never know*. Okay, okay. She might think this was completely ridiculous, but fine.

I played her the glug. I played the rain and thunder I recorded the other night, rain and thunder that reminded me of another night, the one on Tiger Mountain, prom night, when I arrived with Maurice and there you were, like a miracle.

"I hear rain and thunder, but the other one . . . No clue."

I realized I was holding my breath. "It was, uh, one of the noises from the day we met?"

How *could* she have a clue? I was suddenly embarrassed. This had maybe been a bad idea, to show her what I'd been doing. It was private. It was small. Meaningless, or, at least, it had meaning only to me. "Is it a belch? Don't tell me. The first thing he said to you was *buuuuurp*."

"A watercooler. In the doctors' office. Remember? I saw him there the first time."

I worried she would laugh. Instead, she looked at me with an expression that was hard to read. A quizzical astonishment plus compassion. "Margaret," she said. "You're making a Golden Record. For *your* voyager."

She understood. I knew she would, and she had. My chest was squeezing again, but not from fear. From emotion, from some sort of relief that felt a tiny bit like hope.

She made me show Maurice the photos when he got home.

"Wow." He rubbed the nonexistent whiskers on his chin, the way he did when he was surprised.

"See?" Sandrine said.

"These are really good."

"Told you." Sandrine was pleased with herself. And this is hard to describe, too. But I felt a little bit of her old energy. Just talking about this, I could see that her own creative spark was still there, trying to shine.

"That pizza box . . . I don't understand how, but it makes me want to cry."

"But you have the story already. About Mars and the Sarafina."

"Even if I didn't, it would. That shell, too. The photos of the photos. Huh." He couldn't believe it. He looked at me like I was new.

I did that scoffing in the back of my throat, the *ckkk* kind that sounded like Frank about to hack up some gross thing he ate. (When you heard it, you'd rush him outside, and then he'd sometimes stare up at you, like, *Why am I here?*)

"Seriously, MG. You should do something with these."

"Margaret, yes. You *have* to get these out there."

"Out there? I have no idea what that even means." My voice was starting to sound panicky. I shouldn't have said anything. I shouldn't have told them. Making art, if that's what this was, was one thing. It was me and you and it, no one else. Telling Sandrine and Maurice was another step, still okay. *Out there*, though, was . . . out there, my God. That took a whole other something.

"It means you offer it," Sandrine said. "What came from inside. It's one of the most beautiful, powerful, most magical tricks in the world. People feel it, and then they give that back to you, and you give it back again, in this incredible . . ." She finished her own sentence by making a figure eight with her finger. Oh, Mars, she was making an infinity symbol. Were you sending me a sign right then and there, through Sandrine? God, I was going to have to listen, wasn't I? Well, look. I'm here right now.

Maurice tilted his chin down and stared at Sandrine, scrunching his face.

"What?" Sandrine folded her arms. We all knew what. "Stop. You're better off working for your dad! How do you actually see this going, anyway? We make a record? We succeed in a business that's basically impossible to succeed in?"

"The most beautiful, powerful, most magical tricks in the world . . ." Maurice said.

"Yeah, Sandrine! God! You *have* to offer *yours* again," I said. She didn't, of course, and neither did I, but I remembered, how could I not, the way her voice made me feel. The way her voice made all of us feel.

"She said, from the safety and comfort of her brother's couch with the soy-sauce stain on it," Sandrine said.

"I always wondered what that was. I feared worse," I said.

"Let's just get pizza and forget it," Sandrine said.

I put my phone in my pocket.

"Real artists are the ones who fight lethargy," Maurice said. "Who put stuff out there not just *in spite of* what's going on in their lives and the world, but *because of* what's going on in their lives and the world. Honest stuff, because if it's honest, it's felt. And if it's felt, it has meaning. That's what you always say, S. And if I see or eat one more pizza this week, I'm going to scream my head off. If we order, we're getting Thai."

"You're bossing us around like a true misogynist," Sandrine said. Maurice couldn't be a misogynist if he tried. A miracle, after our dad. Some people seemed to become their most difficult parent, and others their opposite. "Fine, Thai."

"Fine," I agreed.

"Just one gig, S. One," Maurice urged. "And if you don't feel it anymore, okay. If you don't want to be who you are anymore, all right. You can be someone else. But right now, I'm looking at three people who are just locking their talent behind a door."

"Three?" I grinned.

"Have you seen Frank's paintings?"

Sandrine smiled, and I laughed, and we loved Maurice so much. We loved each other so much. We loved Frank so much, even if his only paintings were wet paw prints on the rug.

"Margaret," Sandrine said solemnly. "I will if you will."

"Will what?" I truly didn't know. She was putting us both on the same line, and this made no sense to me.

"Offer it, Jesus! Put your project out there. Seriously. I hate seeing talent go to waste."

Now I really saw the glimmering of the old Sandrine. Her drive. Her passion. I wished it weren't directed at me, though. I should have known that if she liked my photos, she would push me forward. Maybe I did know, but . . . Not right this minute! "I wouldn't even know *how*."

"Just take a step forward. Reach out. An account on Snapshot, even."

"Social media?" My voice was full of . . . Don't laugh, Mars. *Terror.* Oh my God! Sure, I scrolled through other people's stuff on Snapshot, but I was never brave enough to post on social media myself, as you knew. "And it's him, though. Us. I mean, how would your family feel about that? I don't want to, like, *claim* him in some public way! How would Janite feel?"

"That's not claiming him. It's honoring him. And he didn't belong to anyone. He belonged to himself." Sandrine stuck her hand out toward me to shake. To make a deal. "I'll do *one* show." She was so stubborn. No wonder she was already successful. And she was going to be a great mentor to a lot of people one day, too.

"Fine, I'll try to put it out there somehow," I said, hedging my bets. Regret was pouring in. Fear was. *Somehow* could mean anything, right? I could maybe fulfill my end of the bargain without truly fulfilling my end of the bargain.

Sandrine's hand was in mine. I squeezed that hand with its chipping green polish on her fingernails, the remaining bits of color from December. We shook, made a pact. It was like jumping off a cliff, or stepping, together, out of the murky underworld. But she had done it for me, I knew. And I had done it for her.

That night, after Thai food and Mario Kart, Sandrine walked outside with me as I headed to my car. We stood together under the moon, with the triangle of pizza grinning at us.

"The record you're making . . ." she said. "It's a love letter."

My throat tightened with emotion. My eyes filled with tears. She was right, I understood.

She touched the tip of her Crocs to my Converse, toes to toes, same as you used to. "How's he going to get it if you don't send it?" she said.

That night, in bed, in my room, I reached for my phone. I scrolled through those photos. I listened to the rainstorm, and the thunder, the glug, and Frank the dog, barking.

Next I scrolled through Snapshot. Oh, jeez, no. Intimidation joined the roar of anxiety, and I closed it.

I couldn't do that, but I could do this: With Carl Sagan looking on, I backspaced over *Album*. The cursor blinked, waiting for a new name.

My Voyager, I typed.

Chapter Twenty-Five

Engraved silver bracelet, photo by Margaret Vittorio: *Pictures of Mars*

Blue shirt, photo by Margaret Vittorio: *Pictures of Mars*

VW, photo by Margaret Vittorio: *Pictures of Mars*

Dandelion, the underdog of flowers, photo by Margaret Vittorio: *Pictures of Mars*

"This is for you, Mars." –Greeting from Sandrine Laurent

"Infinity," performed by Solar Flare: *Music of Mars*

Not long after, one Thursday night, I dropped my car keys on the kitchen counter. The house was dark, aside from the living-room light Mom always left on for me. Dad was still at Papa Angelo's closing up, but Mom had already gone to bed. It was only ten, but I didn't usually work this late on a weeknight. We were just back to school after spring break, only months before graduation, and we were getting hit hard with homework. I hadn't even had time for my project the last few weeks; at least, that's what I told myself. I'd tried to take a photo of your blue flannel shirt, moving it from my chair to my bed, and even various places outside, but it wasn't working. I mean, I was thinking about how other people would see the shirt if they saw it, rather than the shirt itself. Rather than you, and what the shirt meant, and so I deleted all of them. My project felt frozen. Too large and too small at the same time. The vow I made with Sandrine, to share my project, had shoved it behind the fire wall with me. Maybe this was what writer's block was like, only it was photo block. Blue-flannel photo block.

That night, I hurried upstairs. The day had been the kind I appreciated most since you left, head down, classes, delivery, delivery, delivery, a pile of diverting homework, five paragraphs on a symbol in *Macbeth*, plus fifteen dialectical journal entries for Acts I through III. I opened my laptop and got to work. I'd chosen the snake, and was writing about how *Macbeth* looked *like an innocent flower* but really was a serpent underneath, when I stopped suddenly.

My bracelet. I always put it on when I came home. I never wore it outside. If anything happened to it, I'd be devastated. I got up to find it, but to tell you the truth, the panic was already there. It overtook me the second I didn't see it on my wrist. It wasn't in the little dish I kept it in, either, beside my bed next to Carl Sagan. Had I worn it to sleep? I flung my pillow aside, shook out my covers. Nothing. I yanked them off, looked underneath the bed, crawled on my hands and knees to search the floor. Nothing! My dresser, the desk, my pockets—I flew around the room in horror. I ran downstairs and checked the kitchen, the living room, under the couch. The front step, the back porch, the bathroom, the drawers. My room again, the covers, the dish, nowhere, nowhere! Oh my God! No, no, no! I was so careless. It was gone, and it was my fault. Everyone, my small everyone, my family, my friends—they thought I was so responsible, so nice, so caring, God! I was awful. I was so awful. I was reckless. I wrecked, and was wrecked. I started to cry.

"Margaret?" It was Mom. She knelt beside me, where I was kneeling on the floor. We could have been two people in a church, praying.

"It's gone," I said—no, I wailed. "My bracelet. I lost it."

"Oh, honey . . ." She put her arms around me. I would never, could never tell her this—her body needed to be her own without remarks—but she felt more substantial to me, wearing her regular old terry-cloth robe as she held me. She felt sturdier. She was trying to be sturdier for me, and she was.

"What have I done? How could I?"

"Let me look," she said. "Okay?" I nodded. I stayed there on the floor, on my praying knees.

She moved around my room carefully. Lifting, looking. "Margaret," she said. She held up the bracelet. "It's right here."

"Where was it?" I was flooded with relief, but even as I looked at it, I wasn't convinced.

"It was right by your keyboard, under your papers." She handed it to me. I put it on. I twisted it on my wrist, so very grateful for the cool, smooth feel of it there again. "Margaret? This is probably because—"

"No," I interrupted her. I didn't want her to say it. I was avoiding knowing what day it was. I avoided the calendar, even as I looked at the calendar. I tried not to see the specific dates. But Winnifred

Evans had warned me that the body remembered, the mind did. That they had a calendar of their own. This might happen, years later, even. The body kept track of the anniversaries, with the dedication of those distant relatives who still sent Christmas cards.

I reached for my phone. Typed in the question, just as I had the day we met. Who was I kidding. My body already had this information, my mind did. It was not just any day of that week. It was Thursday of National Depression and Anxiety Awareness Week. An anniversary of us.

Later, when I was alone once more, I held the silver band to my cheek, and then to my lips. It might be unnerving, the way objects had a history, but it was comforting, too. Crucial, even.

"I thought it was every day," I whispered to you.

I placed that bracelet so carefully in the spot where I thought I'd lost it but hadn't. I took a photo of it, and it was easy.

And then, another night, *that* night, a few *more* weeks later, Maurice was pacing. Sandrine wasn't there yet. He and Dre and their new sound guy, Xavier, had gotten to Neumos early to set up, but now they were backstage. Dre and Xavier were sitting on the ancient, dirty couch back there, verbally dueling over the worst candy ever. Dre tried to say those red wax lips, but Xavier said it didn't count if you couldn't really eat it. His vote was Good & Plenty, until Dre said Necco Wafers, the brown, and they both folded toward agreement. Maurice wasn't thinking about candy. He kept texting Sandrine, who wasn't answering.

"Is she coming?" It was the worst thing to ask when he was already worried about it. I was backstage myself because Maurice had asked me to take some photos for their website and Snapshot, promotional stuff they thought they better get going on now that they'd signed with Sub Pop. I'd felt more like a real photographer when I was a toddler, carrying around that toy camera shaped like a fox that sang out, *Say Cheese!* when you pressed his nose. Basically, I was walking around with my phone, and I doubted they'd want images of Maurice panicking and a round of affectionate shoving as Dre and Xavier remembered some white nougat thing with jelly blotches that Brach's made when they were kids.

I'd been taking photos for my project again, though. I'd gotten through my blue-flannel panic and had added images to the file. But I still hadn't fulfilled my part of the vow. Tonight, Sandrine was fulfilling hers.

"I have no idea if she's coming," Maurice muttered, but barely. "I never should have let her try to do this today, of all days." His jaw was clenched so tight, I could see the outline of his cheekbones.

"But that's *why* she wanted today," I said. I didn't need to tell him this, though.

The Neumos guy appeared, and he and Maurice had a brief, tense conversation. Just as the manager returned to the front-of-house, Sandrine rushed through the side door, followed by her mom, your aunt Gwen.

"Hey, so sorry, everyone!" Sandrine said.

"Are you okay?" Maurice went to her, took the handbag that had slid down her arm. "I was worried." *Today, of all days.* The warm-up band started to play. It was almost hard to hear him.

"Oh, my car . . . No idea what was going on. Wouldn't start. Ugh!" Sandrine was wearing her black jeans and her navy-blue T-shirt with the yellow comet, but there were signs of a struggle. An internal one. Her hair, which she hadn't gotten cut in months, was pulled back in a ponytail, but wisps had escaped, and her face looked blotchy from crying. Aunt Gwen raised her hand to me in greeting, but she was quiet. Well, talking was getting difficult; the guitars and bass of that other band were rocking the building, but Aunt Gwen was subdued. The car thing—Sandrine didn't meet Maurice's eyes when she said it.

"So glad you made it, S, God." Maurice took her hands in his, but then he refocused. He moved toward Dre, and they huddled over the set list.

"Your car?" I said to Sandrine. My chest ached.

She shrugged. Leaned in close. "This is a rough one. I maybe just needed my mom."

I got choked up. It *was* a rough one. But, too, what she said about her mom . . . It was so beautiful, you know. So simple and wonderful, and I wasn't sure I'd ever experienced that, the need and the need met, both at the same time, in a way that seemed entirely natural. Aunt Gwen was at the food table, ripping open a honey packet with her teeth, squeezing it into a cup of hot water the way Sandrine liked. Maybe lately I had felt it. More so.

Aunt Gwen handed Sandrine her cup. "You're gonna *blaze*," she told her. "So bright, you'll be seen from . . . everywhere."

They looked at each other, and I could see them sharing years of memories, as if they'd just passed a hundred snapshots between them. One of a kid with candles in his cake for sure. And, oh, you were a cute little kid. I've seen the pictures now. Sandrine put her palms to her eyes so she wouldn't cry.

"Let's go out front, huh?" Aunt Gwen said to me. We'd be Sandrine's tiny audience, the ones she could see and trust in, her loving support amidst all the strangers. That place was packed.

We edged our way in there, found a spot near the stage where Sandrine wouldn't miss us. It was hard to pay attention to the other band. I was getting nervous, really nervous, for Sandrine. For Maurice, too, all of Solar Flare, but Sandrine mostly. It made me think of Priya and Maddie, the way you could hold the people you love right in the center of your chest. Anxiety, well, okay, it wasn't just a personal tormentor. It was sometimes an expression of how deeply you cared, how essential someone was to you.

The crowd applauded, and there were a few whistles, and then there was Xavier, plugging mysterious cords into mysterious places. I had no idea about any of that. I could feel the anticipation in the crowd, the restlessness of waiting plus readiness, on the verge of too ready.

And then Maurice took his seat behind the drums, and Dre stood and walked toward the keyboard, as the audience clapped and yelled. But when Sandrine appeared, they went wild. Shrieks, whistles, a hooting yell of *We love you, Sandrine!*

She smiled. They quieted down. Maurice held his drumsticks on his lap. Dre took a step away from the keyboard. I took out my phone, got it ready. Sandrine stood in front of the microphone, then gripped it with one hand. She shut her eyes briefly.

I pressed the red record button.

"This is for you, Mars," she said, and began to sing "Infinity."

Her voice . . . Tears just flowed down my face. I wasn't sure I was even breathing. I wasn't sure when exactly we linked arms, either, Aunt Gwen and me. Her face was aglow as she watched her daughter, more history, more, hers and her sister's, too, their babies, grown, gone, still here, her daughter holding this crowd in the palm of her hand as she sang to one beloved boy on the day he was born.

Your birthday, Mars. Your fucking eighteenth birthday, you cherished, loved light.

The audience was so still, but my eye was caught, a flash of recognition in my peripheral vision, and I saw him, Chester. Chester! Chester was there, too? And wait, wait! He was with *Lily*. Lily was at Neumos? Lily was at Neumos! A giddiness rose in me, emotion and joy, Lily in that all-ages club, and then it rose again, because I saw Norty there, as well, up way too late. Santiago was holding him up so he could see, and Ben, and Rainey, everyone—they were all in the front where Sandrine would spot them; they were all her tiny audience, the ones Sandrine could see and trust in, her loving support amidst the strangers. Their faces were tipped up to Sandrine, and Chester's face was streaming with tears, and Ben was wiping his eyes. Wait—Bao and Amelia were also there, I saw, on Chester's other side. Mars's friends from the Center for Wooden Boats.

And I saw you, of course. You were there, looking in my eyes as we danced. You were there, and you were in your bed, and in the forest, and swimming in the lake, and at my house, and looking through your telescope, up toward the brightest star in the Ophiuchus constellation, the spot where Voyager was still speeding away from us at thirty-eight thousand miles per hour.

You were on the mountain. *You're home now*, Sandrine was telling you.

The song ended. The crowd was silent for one brief moment, and then, well, there's no other way to put it—they lost their shit. She had offered it, what had come from inside her, and they felt it, and were giving it back to her.

The astronomy meetup group, plus friends, were pushing their way through the crowd, and we were pushing our way to them. "My God, she's incredible!" Lily said, Chester said, Santiago said, everyone said. We hugged, all of us; I even hugged Bao and Amelia, who I didn't know very well. Lily was wearing a T-shirt that said *The Doors*, which must have been some old rock band, and I could imagine her in front of her closet, deciding on it, you know, pushing aside her flannel and quick-dry hiking pants, because what did you wear to an all-ages club, and Ben was blowing his nose from crying, and Amelia's mascara had gone a bit raccoon-eyes from the same.

It was beautiful, you know, so beautiful, because you hadn't had a funeral, but maybe this was it. A funeral and birthday, a celebration of a life. Something had been released, not you, never you, but maybe a sorrow that had gotten lodged, and might have lodged permanently. It shifted, ever so slightly. Sandrine had done it, sending her love out there like that.

The band moved on to their next song, "Seeing You, Seeing Me," and then Maurice's "Speed of Light," and then "Radio Signals." We danced our butts off, getting smooshed by the crowd around us, Ben dancing with Lily, Rainey dancing with Aunt Gwen, me dancing with Chester and then Santiago and Bao, and everyone dancing with everyone, a total Mars-love extravaganza, until they did their last number, "Greetings in Fifty-Five Languages."

We straggled to the parking lot to wait for Sandrine and Maurice and Dre and Xavier to appear. When they exited out the stage door, we all cheered.

"I haven't stayed out this late in thirty years," Lily said. She didn't look in the least bit tired. Her blue eyes were jazzed, alight.

"Me neither, in at least twenty," Chester said.

"I've *never* been out this late," Amelia said.

What was time, anyway, in all this love? You were eighteen today, and would never be eighteen; you were forever years old. Voyager was supposed to last five years, and it was still going on and on after fifty. The Golden Record could survive for billions. On this night, looking up there at those stars, looking right there, at the people around me, love could outlast them both, I was sure.

Going out in the world—yeah, it was just dangerous. There were punishments everywhere, the things that might sink you. But there were offerings everywhere, too, the things that might save you.

It was late, so late. I'd reached the point Amelia had, where I had never been up this late before. I was wired, electric. It was hard to come down from all the emotion, from being overcome with connection, to you, to each other.

I was so wired that I hadn't even taken my coat off yet. I held my phone and turned down the volume so I could barely hear it, not wanting to wake my mother or father. I played the glug, and the rain, and Frank barking. I played, *This is for you, Mars.*

Sandrine had been so brave, with her art and what was inside her. She gave you her love, in spite of her guilt, and questions, and grief. I put my hand in my pocket, and my fingers detected something unfamiliar. I pulled it out. It had been jammed in there with some old Kleenex and a crumpled candy wrapper, that sticker the guy in the marine supply shop had given me.

Seas the day!

I smiled like it was a sign. One from you, even. But maybe even more, it was connection doing its magical work again, a small kindness, an outreach, and you could never know necessarily what one of those might mean to someone, how rightly timed they could be.

Okay, then! Okay, I would do just that—seize the day, connect, be inspired by Sandrine and her art and her love. I would spread it, you know. I'd be part of the grand scheme of loving, and moving us all forward when it so often seemed impossible.

I would send you my love letter. In spite of my guilt and the awful mystery of not knowing, I would.

I opened my photo album of connection, and then I made a

new profile on Snapshot. Social media, God, how it scared me, the word *social* right there. But I seized and was brave, and I called it *My Voyager*, a Golden Record for a golden human being we'd lost. It felt like leaping, because, all at once, I did it. *Post.* The sounds, and the photos. You, me, us. It didn't matter if anyone saw it. It was my offering.

"This is for you, Mars," I said, too.

Chapter Twenty-Six

Birdhouse in an evergreen tree, photo by Margaret Vittorio: *Pictures of Mars*

Statue of Belief in Nathdwara, Rajasthan, India: *Pictures of Mars*

Mount Si, photo by Margaret Vittorio: *Pictures of Mars*

Circular dent in kitchen wall, photo by Margaret Vittorio: *Pictures of Mars*

"Oh, jeez, I screwed up. Let me try again," Aunt Gwen said.

We were in her kitchen in North Bend. Just me and your aunt Gwen. I'd never driven that far from home before on my own. Oh, man—my anxiety was shouting. I had to brave I-5, and then I-90, that scary merging part near Factoria, and finally the stretch of freeway where the speed limit went up to seventy before I could finally take the exit to your aunt's house. But I did it—I made it. I was there. I'd have to drive home again, too, but the return seemed like nothing compared to the setting out.

The thing was, the *problem* was, your record would have to

be more than you and me. Way more, because you were, your life was. And your record would have to have, *deserved* to have, the same hundred and sixteen photos, twenty-seven songs, and fifty-five greetings as the Golden Record you loved so much. I didn't know how I was going to do it. I didn't know if I could do it. But I knew I *needed* to do it. Badly. So, fine. I would drive out there past the fire wall and see Aunt Gwen.

"Okay, no problem," I said.

"Are you sure you want me to do this?"

"Very. I mean, if you'd rather choose something else . . ."

"No. It's great. I'm just such a shit singer. Sandrine must have gotten her talent from the other side of her family." Your uncle Bernard was a sweetie. It seemed like a miracle, how they were divorced a jillion years ago, but how he lived right nearby, in Issaquah, everyone friendly enough that I'd even met him with you those few times.

"It's not the quality, it's the . . . *The*."

"Got it." I couldn't believe she understood what I meant, but she did. Well, she was already following my page, so she likely *more* than understood already. I was worried about what your family would think about my project, but your aunt loved it. She liked every photo I posted, and each video of only sound. And so had a few of your friends, Rainey and Ben. Sandrine's, too—people from North Bend you both knew. My brothers weren't much for social media, but Cora and Maeve were there. It was wild, but your page had actual followers.

It was more than *I* deserved, that's for sure. There wasn't a photo of what I'd done to you.

Aunt Gwen took a big breath, ready for her performance.

"Hey, wait! Is that a deer in your yard?"

"Probably." She seemed unimpressed.

I moved to the sliding door to look. "He's eating one of your bushes."

"She." Aunt Gwen stood beside me now.

"She's beautiful. Look at her. Deer are the top of nature's quiet list, don't you think? No, wait. Snow."

"Quietly destroying my last rosebush."

"Deer eating roses is like an illustration in a fairy tale. It's a nature wonderland out here. That is the chubbiest robin I've ever seen." On the way in, I'd also seen two rabbits on their front lawn. And to our far right was the looming, majestic Mount Si, which just kept on being a mountain, no matter what. It seemed like the worst thing and the best thing, the way life kept going forward.

"Do you know who made that birdhouse?" she asked.

"I think I do now. It's pretty smeary." I smiled.

"It was the first time he came to live with us. We got one for him and one for Sandrine. You basically hammered the sides together? But then he researched which colors would be best. Green, brown, gray—camouflage, to keep the birds safe. They love it. They pretty much ignore *that* one." She pointed. Whoa—it was painted in flashy rainbow hues.

I laughed. "That's got to be Sandrine's. It's totally her."

"And his was . . . totally *theirs*? The birds', I mean. He was good at seeing people and animals."

"There's so much I didn't know about him." I pictured a little you with your black curls, concentrating hard on making that camouflage. "And will never know. But I can really see why he wanted to live out here after college."

"He said that?" She looked so pleased.

"He thought Mount Si was like this big guardian. Watching over you guys in every season. Like this statue in India of this Hindu god? He's got his leg crossed, so it's sort of the same shape as Mount Si?" I got my phone. Typed in the search bar. Pulled up the image of the enormous Hindu god Shiva, smiling serenely toward the sky. You loved it.

"The *Statue of Belief*," Aunt Gwen said. "Huh. It *is* the same shape as Mount Si. I guess there was a lot that *I* didn't know, either."

"Sometimes . . ." I wasn't sure how to explain this. It was a confession. It wasn't *the* confession, the big one, the one that weighed on me daily, all day, the new skin of guilt I'd grown over the old one, but just something I kept thinking about.

"What?"

"We were just getting started. I worry that I'll never really know all the bad stuff about him, either." Aunt Gwen waited. She put her hands in her jeans pockets and just looked at me with her kind green eyes with the wrinkles at the corners, eyes that gave me a glimpse of what Sandrine would look like when she was older. "I mean, he'll always be so good and so perfect, a good and perfect no one else will ever be able to live up to, because we weren't together long enough to see all the bad and real stuff."

"Like the way he gave too much to people sometimes? And could go on and on about the stuff that interested him to the point of head-throbbing-ness?"

"I already did see that." I smiled again. I loved this; I loved talking about you. At school, this never happened. We talked about what wild and over-the-top way someone got asked to prom, or graduation ticket logistics, or about the most unfair final that was coming, an oral report entirely in French based on *Les Misérables*, but I never got to talk about you. Still, it was also unnerving, the way we were talking. What if you retreated into . . . *fondness*? That's not a word I even usually use, but it was accurate, an old, cozy description that belonged in an attic. Describing stuff you used to like but couldn't remember all that well.

"Okay. How about the way he'd get so involved in one thing, he'd forget the other thing he'd be doing? So many burned baked items, and water faucets left on, and forgotten sports equipment. Or the way he'd fart as loud as possible to gross us out?"

"Didn't know." I chuckled. I guess you could keep learning about a person, even when they were gone. You could still keep talking to them, too. Like now. Like this.

"While eating."

"Ooh. Ouch."

"Or the way he'd lean back in the kitchen chair, even though I told him not to a hundred times? And of course, he did fall once. Look at that wall right there. It's still got the indent to prove it." I glanced over. Sure enough, it was there. A slight hollow in the plaster, where the back rung of the chair had landed. "And . . . I'd give anything to see him do that again."

We both stood there for a while, watching that robin trying to get big twigs into a little door. She kept at it and at it.

"Shall we?" Aunt Gwen asked finally.

"Let's do it."

"No one's going to see me, right? My roots are growing out something terrible." She ran a finger down the highway of her hair part. She looked beautiful to me, honestly.

"Just sound," I said. "Ready?"

She nodded. I pressed the red record button.

"'Husky fever!'" she sang. "'I think it's going around, and around, and around!'"

I wasn't sure the photo of Mount Si was all that great. I took, like, twenty of them that day, after I left Aunt Gwen's house. I stared up at that sheer rock, hoping it would guard me, too, even if I didn't live in its shadow. The Statue of Belief.

All twenty—they looked kind of the same. And certainly, they weren't any more stunning than the hundreds of photos of the mountain other people took, professional photographers took. They looked average, if you asked me. But a week or so later, I did what I'd been doing lately. I got up my courage, and then I closed my eyes as Sandrine had before she sang. I sent it to you first. And then, as if leaping, I pressed post.

It was such a shock, every time. Nearly fifty people liked it. More followers were trickling in, and it was inexplicable, and nerve-racking, yet somehow okay, because they were your followers to me. I guess it was what Sandrine had said, that when you give honest stuff, it's felt. And if it's felt, it has meaning.

Sandrine shared that photo, and so did Maeve. And then *a lot* of followers appeared, people who were strangers, even, more new fans of Sandrine's since the band started playing again. Maeve's mom group, too, and fans of Papa Angelo's. A classmate of yours from California. People who just saw my hashtags and who loved Voyager and the Golden Record. People who were grieving, who had somehow found me, grieving.

I had offered, and it was coming back to me, just like Sandrine had said. Each comment was a little present. *We miss Mars so bad*, and *I think of him every day*, and *This is a beautiful tribute to your friend*, and *Thank you for this. I lost a loved one, too.* On the photo of the Sarafina, someone wrote: *Couldn't get through a Friday night without one of these for the kid*, heart emoji, pizza emoji. Your Voyager poster—*The Grand Tour and Beyond* . . . It had somehow been discovered by sixty-five people and counting. *Love it! I did a report on that when I was a kid*, a guy about my dad's age wrote. Man, there must have been a lot of those reports in those days.

My photo of that dent in the wall a week after the Mount Si one—it looked like nothing. If you didn't know better, you might think it was a smeary image from a satellite, a faraway crater on a distant planet. But it got ninety-five likes. Connect, connect, connect, and it was okay. I was okay. Okay, and a little less alone. I can't believe I'm saying that.

This makes my heart ache, said LittleByrd466. *I know someone at NASA. You should blast this up to space for real*, said Roketguy2027. Heart emoji, crying emoji, heart emoji, heart emoji, wrote Aunt Gwen, and Chester, and Mars's baseball coach, Hal Jericho, and someone named CosmicRayS32, who'd been showing up regularly.

My brother used to do that. I miss him so bad, wrote MaiseyDayseee. *We have that exact same hole.*

"If you'd stop giggling, we could get this," Bao said.

"I'm sorry, I'm sorry! I'm nervous." Amelia pulled her T-shirt over her nose to half hide and sober up. She popped out again. "Bao! Remember when—"

"I was just thinking it." Now Bao was giggling.

I put my phone down. "What, you guys?" I barely knew Amelia and Bao. Driving over there, my stomach was a knot of nerves, but here I was. Oh, Mars. I *liked* being here with them.

"One time, Mars—"

"Oh, jeez." Bao was losing it.

"He took this couple out. For a test, and—" Amelia snort-snickers.

"The boat starts to totally heel! Like, bad! And Mars starts giggling, you know, the way he did when *he'd* get nervous?"

I did know. I wasn't going to tell them about that time with the condom, though. How you kept on giggling, even when you finally got the thing on. I thought you were back into our serious kissing when you laughed right in my mouth.

"The boat was—" Amelia waggled her hand.

"I've never seen one look like it was *actually* going over, I swear. And you could hear his high-pitched cackling coming over the water, and he was kind of hunched, and—"

"How'd they even make it back in?" Amelia shook her head.

"And when they did?" Bao continued. "The test wasn't finished.

The couple asked for a new instructor. Chester went with them. He wasn't exactly pleased."

"He wasn't exactly pissed, either, though," Amelia said. "Look at him. Big softy."

We stood at the end of the Center for Wooden Boats dock and took in the wide view of the lake with its Richard Scarry–like busyness: boats and canoes, kayaks and seaplanes. Looking back toward the shingled shed and the center's main building, we could see Chester on his knees beside *Pelican*, dunking a big sponge into a bucket and mopping the bottom.

"I never heard that story," I said. "He didn't tell me."

"Would you tell anyone that? He was probably embarrassed," Bao said.

Sucks to be gone, Mars. I was learning all your secrets. (Sorry.)

"Okay. I got the giggles out. Let's do this." Amelia wiggled her shoulders and stood straight.

Bao nodded. "Go."

I pushed the record button.

"Sending you huge love from the southernmost point of Lake Union to wherever you are now," they said in unison.

"Perfect," I said.

I clapped my hands over my ears as a seaplane landed. From where we stood, I could see Mrs. Fosmire's houseboat, marking the end of your dock. She belonged on the record, too, but I didn't think I could go back there. I was doing lots of things I didn't think I could, but still. George had even made sure to reroute my deliveries to avoid it. I'd said goodbye that day. I could revisit all these people and all these memories, but laying eyes on that house again was too much.

We passed Chester on the way back up. "Someone spilled a latte." He rolled his eyes but didn't really look mad. He wrung out the sponge. "Winston, the new kid, is coming in at ten," he told Bao, and she nodded. Your replacement. Ouch. Necessary, now that the center was getting busy again. Chester shook his head, as if trying to dislodge something unpleasant. "Ack," he said, at the wrongness, all wrongness. "Hey, Margaret . . . When are you bringing that up the mountain?" He nodded his chin toward my phone. "A bunch of astronomers want in. Or on."

"Soon!"

"You said that last time I asked."

He was right—it was the exact response I'd given to his comment on the post of Aunt Gwen's Husky song. *I know a group of folks who got things to say on your Golden Record*, he wrote. *Soon!* I'd answered, adding a heart emoji as a shield.

The only thing worse than going back to that dock was going up to that mountain. How to explain it? I'd seen everyone that night at Neumos, but standing on that mountain looking up at the night sky was different. I couldn't get any closer to you than that. That was your church.

I was scared, you know. To face you like that. I'd be looking up toward those sparkling stars for forgiveness, for answers, but I just might get only an endless, dark nothingness.

"It's the real church," Chester said, reading my mind.

I had to drive right by the houseboat docks when I went home from South Lake Union. They circled the lake; there was no avoiding them. I averted my eyes past your dock, but then I reached the stop sign. It was one of those times when your body has a different plan than your mind does. I was suddenly turning around in a condo parking lot. What was I doing? No, the only question again: *Why?*

It was a negotiation, I suppose. Guilt was a hungry bonfire, and I fed it the last log so I wouldn't have to burn the furniture. I didn't want to go up that mountain, so I went to see Mrs. Fosmire instead.

I walked with some determination right past your houseboat, snuck a peek. Someone else had moved in, I could tell. The same old welcome mat was still there, but there were new curtains in the kitchen window. A cat sat on top of our table outside. I suddenly felt like I had swallowed something too large, and it had lodged in my body, only I couldn't tell where—my throat, my chest, my stomach. Your home had moved on, you know.

God, I hoped Mrs. Fosmire was there, because I didn't want to do this again. I felt the now-familiar creeping shame—about myself, about the project itself—maybe because I could practically see your mom walking right out of that houseboat as she had so many times, coming toward you and me with her eyes fixed on you. All those likes and comments and connections—they belonged to her, not me. Especially after what I did to you.

Thank goodness, here came Mrs. Fosmire's footsteps stomping toward the door after I rang. She was ready to tell someone off. Couldn't they see the *Residents only* sign at the dock entrance? The doorknob rattled aggressively, but then her whole body relaxed when she saw me. How exhausting it must have been to be on guard like that all the time. "Margaret! What a surprise! God, don't look at my hair. I look like shit." She patted it with a resigned generosity, like you would an ugly old dog you were fond of. But she didn't look like shit. Her crabby old face was such a comfort.

"This is going to sound really strange," I said. "And I'm not sure if you've heard of this?" The words sputtered out: Voyager and the Golden Record and you, my project. It all sounded like rusty water out of an unused faucet—I wasn't sure I was making sense. The cat and the curtains had thrown me.

"What's strange about that? It's just your love, trying to find a new place to go. And of course I've heard of it! I did a report on Voyager in the eighth grade. Didn't your dad do one, too?"

"Mars told you?"

"Oh, we talked about a lot of things when he'd come over to borrow my kayak. Northwest birds, gardening . . ." Mrs. Fosmire had some beautiful, overflowing planters on her deck. "He came out to look at the supermoon one night, which was sitting practically right up on the Space Needle like it was balanced there. We got chatting about eclipses, how his mom made a viewer out of a Frosted Flakes box."

"She did?"

"Mm-hmm. And Voyager, of course. Jesus Christ, he loved that. I told him I watched it take off when I was twelve. All kids were space enthusiasts back then. My brother? He even became an actual rocket scientist. His boy, Austin, is working on the Vulcan Centaur."

"Wow," I said. I had no idea what the Vulcan Centaur was, but

I was still stuck on that image of your mom, cutting and taping that box to show you magic.

"I think about Mars a hundred times a day. Especially when I see his bulbs popping up now. See those there?" She gestured down the dock to the planter box on your float. I hadn't even noticed. It was packed full of the coolest, oddest flowers. Dandelion-like puffs, but big, really big, and purple. I wanted to pat one.

"What are those?"

"Alliums. He liked mine from last year, so I gave him some bulbs. Look how well his did. He was going to be a great gardener."

It took a few tries, but we finally got something recorded.

"Greetings from an old broad on planet Earth. I fucking miss you, kid."

As I walked past your houseboat again, something odd happened. My heart didn't clutch as much as fill. I hoped the people who lived there didn't see me, but I took a photo of the houseboat. I took photos of your alliums, another thing I hadn't known about you. I took one of our table, too, just ours again, since the cat had run off. The welcome mat. I even hurried back to the end of the dock and took the view of the lake from there. The swim ladder, my own feet dangling in the water as I sat on the edge. You and you and you. The last time I was here—it hadn't been goodbye after all.

Chapter Twenty-Seven

"Husky Fever," sung by Gwen Laurent: *Music of Mars*

"Sending you huge love from the southernmost point of Lake Union to wherever you are now." –Greeting from Amelia Weintraub and Bao Zhang

"Greetings from an old broad on planet Earth. I fucking miss you, kid." –Greeting from Ilene Fosmire

Frosted Flakes box, photo by Margaret Vittorio: *Pictures of Mars*

The post of Mrs. Fosmire's greeting got nearly four hun-dred likes and comments. I couldn't believe it. I didn't know what was going on here, but something was. I thought it was because of Sandrine, mostly, how she shared stuff with her own large number of fans. But it wasn't just Sandrine. HarveyWanderer0077 shared it with the Voyager 1 and 2 fan club on Snapshot and other sites. *Remember OortCloud8?* he wrote. *To the stars, young dude!* What? When I looked it up online, there you were! You were part of the online Voyager fan club—of course you were! Your name: *Oort-Cloud8*. You commented on other people's posts, mostly, but I got to hear you say things, new things I hadn't seen before. *The wonder of it! Looking like a golf ball when you peel off the white!* you replied when someone posted Voyager's first images of Uranus, taken in 1986. *Gas giant—that's what my aunt calls me*, you wrote after someone else shared an article on the Jovian planets, Neptune, Uranus, Saturn, and Jupiter, the gas planets.

Another older neighbor from the dock, Mae Donnelly, shared Mrs. Fosmire's greeting with her bake club. *That's where I got the espresso brownie recipe!* she wrote. *That boy made them for me once. Incredible, but don't expect to sleep after you eat them, which you already know if you tried it.* Mrs. Fosmire's nephew Austin shared it on the Intuitive Machines page, the company building the next lunar explorers for NASA. *Your auntie is cool*, drLizEngr wrote. *That kid was cool, RIP*, wrote RashmonSCI2026.

A week later, *My Voyager* had over twelve hundred followers.

It was unnerving and astonishing, but I could do it. Those strangers were . . . *distant*, if that makes sense. It was easy, to press a little heart next to their comments.

But then a DM arrived. Of course one would. Why hadn't I foreseen this? The way the project would grow, would push me farther and farther beyond the fire wall? *Mars was my good friend, if you ever want to talk.*

It was Ella. She left her phone number.

Oh, God. My anxiety rushed around, trying to rapidly rebuild the barricade that had been slowly crumbling. I mean, your friends here, Aunt Gwen, the people I already sort of knew myself were one thing. But Ella was a stranger. A real, in-person one. Your stranger, but still!

Carl Sagan in his turtleneck gazed at me from his frame. His eyes were full of compassion and understanding. You'd told me about the obstacles he'd encountered making the record, the technological problems, and impossible debates, and public pressure, but his need to send a message of humanity and hope, a message that might never be heard, was larger than any of that. And my need to send my own message was larger, too.

Shit. It just was.

My fingers were suddenly pressing those numbers in the same way my car had turned around in that parking lot to see Mrs. Fosmire. A part of me made me, is all I can say. A part of me looked after my greater good, the way I ate the banana instead of the chips I really wanted.

And, Mars . . . Ella and I talked so long, I was almost late for work. The anxiety that had filled me loosened like a knot and became a new thing entirely, something *good.* Oh, God—I almost said, *You would have died*, but what I mean is, you wouldn't have believed it, and would have loved it. We laughed so hard at the story of your flip-flop dropping when you rode the Sky Glider, and how you spit right into Ella's dad's face when he was teaching you to swim. Before then, I guess you could only dog-paddle. You never told me you only recently learned to swim! I get it, but I would have understood. Imagining you with your chin up in the pool, your hands cupped and scooping water to stay afloat, my heart broke, and I loved you so big. We both kept saying, *Can you imagine how happy Mars would be if he saw us talking?*

I'd thought Ella was a maroon flag, but I was so wrong.

You wouldn't believe this, either (honestly, I barely did), but

I told her it was okay to share my phone number. Soon, I heard from your other friends in California, and one of your teachers, Mr. Ramirez, percussion ensemble (percussion ensemble?!), and the grocery-store lady from the market where you did the shopping for you and your mom, and your track coach, Shannon Unsler, who'd awarded you Most Inspirational. She told me the story about you coming in last, very last, all the teams, nearly every meet, practically throwing up after the four hundred meter. She was laughing about it, and then her voice got all wobbly with tears.

Ella wasn't a flag. She, and all of them—your coaches, your neighbors, your old friends, your family, your coworkers, the individuals you shared a joke with online—were something else, I was beginning to understand. I looked it up, information about tethers, the straps that keep the astronaut fixed to her spaceship so she doesn't fly off into some distant forever orbit all alone in the universe. Some sites said they were sixty feet in length, some said twenty-five, some said fifty-five, the exact number of greetings on the Golden Record. Once described by *Smithsonian Magazine* as "not a terribly exciting piece of equipment" in an article about astronaut essentials, they were also said to be made of nylon, or heat-resistant webbing, or simple rope. In photos, they look like the sort of nondescript strap that you yourself might have used to keep the shit in the truck when you and your mom were moving. Plain old tan or gray, with hooks on either end. It didn't look like enough, important enough, to keep that space traveler safe, but it was.

All of those people had kept you anchored to the ship, and now they were keeping me from spinning out into darkness, too.

The thing about nylon, or webbing, or rope—it looks like a

single entity, but it isn't. It's made of a bunch of strands, all woven together. That's what gives it its strength.

"I thought you were through with this shit!" my father shouted.

It might have been my imagination, but I swear, the water glass on my desk . . . It was like that scene in *Jurassic Park*, concentric circles forming, ripples from the footsteps of the monster approaching. Did you think he was gone from this story? Changed forever after getting a gut-punch of perspective after what happened to you? Nope, nope, nope. If a person allows his monster to stomp around like that, he'll never be gone. Believe me, you'll see him again, even if he's been lying low.

"How is this a surprise?" Maurice said. "I told you we signed the deal."

"You didn't say you were going to *quit*."

It was Monday, and I had the night off. Maurice told me he was going to come over to do the deed. Dad had him on the schedule into next spring. It was the beginning of June. They were supposed to start recording on Wednesday. He'd waited until the last possible moment, which was understandable, but, God.

They were in the kitchen. I heard the drawers opening and shutting. Pans rattling. I couldn't imagine one of them cooking right now, so maybe Mom was down there. I hoped so. Neither of them should've been holding a knife right then.

"I can't exactly spend weeks in the studio and then months

on tour, I can't *build a career*, while doing front-of-house for your business."

"Are you kidding me? Are you fucking kidding me? *My* business? This family's business? You think I built all this for myself? I did it for *you*."

"You did it for me. But you never asked me if this is what *I* want."

"What you *want*?" I heard the sizzle of oil in a pan. In moments, the heavenly scent of garlic wafted up. "Do you want to be able to pay your bills? Do you want to have enough money to raise a family? Do you want one shred of security? What do you think, you're going to be John Stewart?"

"*Rod* Stewart?" I had no clue who he was, but he must have been a really famous music guy. Even from upstairs, I could hear Maurice snort.

"No, smart-ass. *John* Stewart. Never heard of him? One-hit wonder, you know-it-all. 'People out there turning music into gold.' "

Okay, that was it. The smart-ass, the know-it-all . . . It didn't matter how brave you were going into a talk like that. He could pierce your armor, quick.

I shoved aside the last of my homework. There were two more weeks left of school. Prom was on Saturday, and in three weeks, we'd graduate. The shiny gown and that silly flat hat for the ceremony would be arriving any day now. I didn't even want to go, but Mom had insisted. Sitting in maroon satin with a tassel tickling my temple seemed absurd in regular times, and cruel when a chair was empty somewhere. It was a celebration of life moving forward, so what would the cheering feel like? That particular moving forward didn't matter to me, but this one did. Maurice's did.

What could I do but stand beside him? If that's all I had, I'd give it. I didn't look all that strong, in my old, ragged tank top and pj shorts. I tossed on your blue flannel. Over the past months I had learned one thing for sure: You were someone who showed up for people.

I was halfway down the stairs when I heard her: "You don't have to be an *any*-hit wonder, Maurice. As long as you're doing what you love," my mom said.

I stopped. It was shocking. A small moment, the smallest, up against him. Yet still, she'd used her voice. I felt a tiny curl of anger, too, I admit. A *finally!* But larger was the thrill of her standing up to him.

"Doing what you love? That's gonna keep your cupboards full of food?" my father said. "That's gonna pay your insurance?"

"Your happiness is the thing that matters, Maurice. Not our plan for your happiness." Mom's voice was quiet. But it didn't have to be loud. It didn't have to shake a water glass for us to know she meant it.

Now I was in the kitchen, too. Her strength gave me strength, the strand and the strand. I wished I'd always had a cord, her cord, but here we were now, and she was trying. "You'll work it out, Maurice," I said. "No matter what."

Maurice didn't even have a chance to respond. My father opened his mouth and then banged it closed, like an unhinged shutter during a storm, because we were interrupted by the *ding-dong, ding-dong, ding-dong* of our doorbell, the noisy, unignorable arrival of Arthur and gang.

"Hello, Vittorios!" Arthur shouted as Maya, Max, and Millie ran inside, with the galloping feet and shoves of baby goats racing toward their pen. Max spotted me and jumped straight up into my arms.

"Hey, Bunny," I said.

"I saw you yestaday!" Well, he saw me a week or so ago, but every day was yesterday to him, and to me, too, to be honest. He took my cheeks in his hands and kissed me hard on the mouth.

"So, we're here to celebrate the great news," Arthur said, and I realized it—it was a plan. That woman wearing the oven mitt decorated with teakettles had arranged this. "We're sure proud of you, Maurice."

"I brought a salad," Maeve said.

Now another voice joined the mix. "Is this where the party is?" George called as he came in with Cora behind him. He was wearing his Papa Angelo's T-shirt and was carrying a cake. He lifted the foil in a flourish for Maurice. I could see the icing from there, blue on chocolate, looped in letters that read, *Happy Retirement, Maurice*.

Maurice laughed. "Thanks, asshole."

"Fuck you, dude."

It meant: *I love you*, and *I love you, too*.

My father—he'd gotten quiet. A-bucket-of-water-on-a-fire quiet. The doorbell rang again. A subdued one ring, a person who would wait on the other side of the door rather than barge in like my noisy brothers.

“Can you get that?” Mom asked. Was that a . . . *lasagna* coming out of the oven? A giant, family-sized pan, burbling sauce, melty cheese, heaven? Well, Dad could make pizzas, but Mom could make everything.

I opened the front door. There was Sandrine, in her Solar Flare T-shirt, and next to her was Dre, in his. New merch from the shop now on their website. “Your mom asked us to come over for dinner. Is Maurice . . . ?”

“Alive and well,” I said. “SWAT team save?”

“Sarah team save.” Sandrine smiled. My mom . . . I guess it was step one, reaching out. It took courage to do that.

“Come on, everyone! George, would you get the extra chair in the living room?” Mom asked. I’d be the one to sit on that—the chair that put me an inch or two lower than was right for the table, chin too close to the plate. It was my designated spot, and I wanted it, and the teasing that went along with it, the pointing and calling me Mini M.

When we were all seated, after Arthur trotted back to the kitchen to get the Parmesan and returned again, and then Max got up to pee and ran back fast, no sound of the toilet flushing, Sandrine lifted her glass. “I just want to thank the entire Vittorio family—Angelo, Sarah, Arthur, George, Margaret . . .”

“Maya,” Maya reminded. The five fingers of her left hand now sported little olive hats.

“*Maya*. For your support. We couldn’t do this without you.”

“Well, yeah, you could, but we’re here,” Arthur said.

I looked down the table at my father, seated with Cora on one side of him and Baby Millie on the other. The fire had not only gone out; it had stopped sizzling. It was just the idea of a fire now, what was left, the *never mind* of stuff singed but not destroyed. He closed his eyes for a second, rubbed one with his fingertips. It was defeat or exhaustion or maybe a prayer.

"To Solar Flare," Mom said, and lifted her glass. She was at the head of the table. She'd always been there, but I hadn't noticed before. She might not have, either.

"Do the cheers, Grandpa," Max said to Papa Angelo, and he lifted his, too.

Maurice was blinking hard. His wineglass was still in the air, even after we—his nylon, his webbing, his rope—clinked our glasses and drank.

Chapter Twenty-Eight

"You were singular." –Greeting from Ella Ortiz

"You're still the most inspirational." –Greeting from Coach Shannon Unsler

"Keep the beat going, Mars, wherever you are." –Greeting from Hugo Ramirez

"I hope they've got maple bars in heaven." –Greeting from Gail McPherson, Red Apple Market

"Can we have music?" I asked Maurice. We were in his truck, and this time I knew where we were going. It was a beautiful night, and the lake had those golden sparkles they did at that time of year and at that hour, as if the world's fairy godmother had waved her wand over all of us.

It was a perfect evening for prom. I wondered what it would have been like, for Mars and me to have gone like we'd planned. It was the same wondering as always, but fancier.

Come on, Margaret. Come with us! Addy had begged. *You can be my date! We can all be each other's dates.*

What about Ramone? I lifted one eyebrow, or tried to. I probably lifted them both, to be honest.

No! she protested, like *Yes!* Like *I wish!* She'd broken up with Liam, who started going out with Zoe Zhan, like, the next day. Over the last few weeks, Ramone had migrated to our end of the table. He'd offer Addy his Cool Ranch Doritos, and she'd toss him some grapes, trying to get them in his mouth. I think he was worried about choking on one, because he kept missing on purpose. Ramone worked hard at looking not-anxious, which is something an anxious person like me notices straight off. He glanced at the clock on his phone a lot, even though a bell rang when lunch was over. He couldn't trust the bell, so I knew he was one of us, the mass of people who were silently sure that something was about to go terribly wrong. *I hear you, Ramone*, I said silently. After you and your heart, I kept my eye on Ramone and those grapes, too, and tried to remember how a person did the Heimlich.

Ramone was a serious upgrade from Liam.

He asked you what color your dress was? Maddie reminded her, as if she'd forget.

He's getting a tie to match, I bet you ten bucks, I said. Addy was driving us home, and she'd gotten so flustered, she'd missed my street.

Seriously, Margaret. You should come, Priya said.

But I didn't want to go to prom. There was only one place I had to be. I don't say *wanted to be*, because even at the thought of it, dread would drop down in my chest like a curtain, The End. *Had to be*, though? Yes. *Needed* to be. Anniversaries were the overambitious employee who brought doughnuts for everyone, and worked overtime, and did his job beyond compare, but who was quietly plotting with the boss behind your back. Manipulating all the pieces into position with a warm smile and hidden cruelty. Boom, one day on the calendar and you were on your knees. Forced to face what you'd been managing to hold at bay.

That guilt, you know. It hadn't gone anywhere. I could send you a message of love, could try and try to do that, but what I did to you still slithered viciously around, teaming up with that unanswered text.

"Some song in particular?" Maurice asked.

"Nope. Just random shuffle?" It was silly, but that's how you might speak to me, I always hoped. Well, I hoped you would speak to me in hundreds of ways—bird formations, weather, a dream, luck. But music would be the most likely. For the first few months, I couldn't listen to music at all, but now I did as often as possible, just waiting for you to send me a message back. I'd wish and wish that "Infinity," or "Keep Me in Your Heart," or "El Cascabel," or so many others would play the minute I turned my engine on, a sign. When they didn't, when it was just some random song I'd downloaded long ago, I'd fast-forward. The *next* song would be you speaking to me. Or the fifth one would. Or the tenth.

"Sure." Maurice pushed play. Drumbeat, then the song began. *Let me ride on the wall of death—*

"Oh my God." I'd never heard *that* song before. It sure wasn't one of ours, unless it was meant to be one of mine.

"Jeez, sorry." Maurice quickly advanced to the next. *Tear off your own head*, a guy sang. Not ours, but harmless.

"One year." My voice wobbled.

Maurice guided us to safer territory. "Man, MG. Twenty-two hundred followers, the last time I looked?"

"It's so wild. I don't get it."

"*I* get it. Anyone who lost someone would get it."

"Not Janite. Still no Janite."

"You can't expect that. She's going through her own . . ." What would be the right word for it? Maurice put his turn signal on. He looked in his mirror and looked again, changing lanes like an old man. I understood. I did it, too. I had those moments where I was scared that I might be next. Newly aware of how quick it could all be gone.

"Hell."

"Right. Her own hell. Can you imagine?"

I shook my head. I couldn't.

"Your page . . . It's not about her, anyway, though, right? Or even . . . you? It's about him. And now it's also about all of them. The other people with the praying hands and the crying emojis and the hearts."

"Rainbows, clouds, planets, stars, rockets, and one panda."

"Emoji humanity."

"Hey, a new song title?"

"Waaay too hard to sing." Maurice turned down the music. "MG? We wanted to ask you . . ."

"We? Is this a wedding thing?"

"Wedding thing? No! It's a *photographer* thing. We were wondering if you might come to the studio and take some photos while we're recording. We'll be there for a couple of weeks, after you're done with school."

"Really?"

"Really. What do you think?"

"If Dad'll let me get off work."

"Are you going to stay at Papa Angelo's forever?"

I used to think so, but now I wasn't so sure. I shrugged.

"Mom will send in the cavalry if he gives you any trouble." Maurice grinned.

"Mom two-point-oh." I smiled, too. "Maurice? Sandrine's going to be here tonight, right?"

"I told you, after she helps Gwen change her oil and gets some dinner, she's heading over. She's probably there already."

It felt important for this night, prom night, to be as similar to the last one as possible. Of all people in all places—we were both there on that mountain. I had some silly idea that if I replayed that night as closely as possible, maybe fate and meaning would back me up as I faced you up there, in that place where you were most you.

Maurice took the exit. Already the plan was slipping, because I was familiar with that exit now. I knew exactly where we were going as we turned off on that gravel road, as Maurice's tires crunched, the nose of his truck slanting upward.

He pulled into the little circular parking area. I spotted Sandrine's car, your VW, and recognized Chester's and Lily's. Rainey's and Ben's, as well, though maybe Santiago got a new CR-V, an unfamiliar one with a car seat in the back that was parked next to Lily's Jeep.

Maurice turned his engine off. "Hey, MG? Before we go up? I haven't, uh, had my turn. With the, you know . . ."

I smiled. He felt shy, I could see. Shy about speaking up, about being a part of my project.

"Funny you should ask." I waggled my phone. I'd been waiting for a good moment.

"I'm not sure what I should say, though. It seems so important, like it should be a big grand summation, and I don't have a big grand summation."

"No way. It's just—being there. Showing up. You should hear the greetings on the actual record. They're basically, 'Hi, from me to you.' "

"Okay."

"We're doing it?"

"Sure."

"Go," I said, and pressed record. He laughed and snorted and messed up the first few times, and then he was done. We sat in silence for a while, thinking of what might have been.

"Ready?" Maurice said finally.

I was scared, you know, so scared. To see you up there. To really *face* you. To tell you how deeply sorry I was, where you could maybe really hear me. I closed my eyes. Rubbed one with my fingertips. God, it was the same thing Dad did when he was defeated. But I wasn't him, I reminded myself. I could apologize. I could ask for forgiveness.

"Hey," Maurice said. "These people love you. And you love them."

The plan slipped some more. Maurice was right. I'd go up that mountain and see family. Your family.

Oh, it was as creepy as ever, walking down that trail in the dark where bobcats maybe hunched with glowing eyes, but no tigers.

I heard their voices.

On the other side of that trail, there were still a bunch of people and their telescopes, though, all sizes, all different ages of people. But a dog ran to me this time, thrilled to see his people.

"Hey, Frank." I scruffed his head.

Sandrine waved. She still had a cute nose piercing, and torn denim shorts, and hair that looked like she took some scissors to it, and the warmest smile you could imagine, and my brother Maurice was still giddy.

"Seeing anything?" he said, just as he had.

But Sandrine's shirt sported an oil stain, and she poked his chest and then mine. "Seeing you, and you."

"I got Saturn," Chester said. We knew each other well enough that he didn't even say hi. "Where's your recorder? I know exactly what I'm going to say."

"Recorder," Rainey snorted.

"She brought her fax machine, too," Ben joked.

"Snarky young 'uns," Lily said. She had a new neon-yellow North Face jacket and striped socks.

I looked toward the spot where you'd been standing, gazing at the dark section of sky that held a magnificent secret, a living truth beyond our ability to see it, but Norty was there instead. He was a year older, and Santiago had gotten him his own telescope. He wasn't looking in it, though. Instead, he sat on the ground, flicking a pocket flashlight on and off.

Chester went first, and then Ben, and Rainey, Santiago, and Norty, each walking with me to the edge of the woods, where I captured their greeting and the voices of the others in the background, plus crickets, plus rustles in the underbrush, plus Norty asking for a snack.

Lily was last. I could pretty much guess what she'd say, and I wasn't wrong. *How* she said it, though—as if it were just to you. Staring hard into the vast black, up toward the sparkling unknown. As if you could actually hear.

This night hadn't been like the other one at all. Everything had changed, and yet it was all still universe-huge, a gift. I was still surrounded by people who didn't forget to look up. And I was trying to do that, as well. Trying so hard. Even with only my own eyes, the stars were astonishing, a glow-in-the-dark mural of magic, a sparkling carpet sky, but still, where were you, you know? Where could I find you, so you could forgive me? So I could make sure we were okay? Maybe I was going to work hard at this puzzle my whole life long and never have an answer.

"You all right? You need some water?" Lily asked. "Or food? Or a chair?" She pointed down to what was left of a fallen tree.

I couldn't tell her what was weighing on me so heavily. I just couldn't let it go, how I'd let *you* go. I couldn't confess how I'd let you down, broken your heart, actually broken it. It was too terrible. What would she think of me? What would they all think of me? I doubted they'd love me anymore. Sandrine still did, but she carried her own weight of wrongdoing. That Taco Time call, the way she might have saved you, she was sure.

"I just really miss him," I told Lily. That was maybe the simplest truth in all this. I missed you. I just missed your voice being a voice and your eyes being eyes and your whole self being you. "I keep looking for signs in everything. Like tonight. I just wish there were some way I knew for sure we were still connected, you know."

"Up there, you see so many signs." Her old blue eyes squinched at the stars.

"You do?"

"Oh, for sure. Ophiuchus, the direction he always had his telescope focused on? The constellation where Voyager is now? The guy with the snake?"

"Yeah?"

She sat down on that log, and I sat beside her. "He's the god of health and healing. And that snake he holds—some say it represents the Ouroboros, another snake that winds itself in an endless loop." She swirled her fingers in a figure eight, just like you used to do. Like I used to do, too. "It's a symbol that shows up in every ancient culture, and it—"

"Infinity," I said. "It was . . ." Too personal. Too important to Mars and me to explain.

"Infinity, right! A symbol of the everlasting. Those loops are *everywhere* in space. The Milky Way galaxy. The sun's path, viewed from above. The Hubble telescope took images of MyCn18, the Hourglass Nebula, and it looks just like one. You want signs . . ." She lifted her chin upward.

"It's . . ." I wasn't sure how to explain it, or if I should even try. "Like, hard to know whether I even deserve signs. Or if it's my place to even do this." I held up my phone, indicating my project. "I mean, we were together such a short time."

"You were. So short."

Man, that hurt me, but it was true. "Did it even matter? Love for so short a time coming from, like, small me?"

"*So* small," she agreed.

I knit my eyebrows together, went silent.

"Don't you think it's strange," she asked, "how people think it's the huge, long, loud things that matter? We're sitting here surrounded by the immense universe, so in that way, I get it. But the small . . . The small is where things get even more interesting. Look here." She stomped one sneakered foot on the ground. "Our Earth. This rotating beast that seems so enormous to us? So small! Absolutely minuscule! In that universe out there, we are less than a dot. Our sun and all our planets are about as wide as an atom, in terms of the universe. We are unseen, we're so small. And then there's this mountain we're on right now, smaller yet, and you and me right now, us together, even smaller yet. On this Earth, we're an unseen dot on another unseen dot. This log—invisible. My hand"—she reached for mine—"in yours. Infinitesimal. My eyes, yours. These words I just spoke, *my*, *yours*, *us*, *together*, tiny, tiny, tiny. The molecules inside us, in the breath I'm using to say these words, vanished. Nonexistent. Poof! Our time here—your time with Mars, with me, tonight, on this log . . . In the grand timeline of human existence, in the long, forever history of the cosmos . . . Nothing. And yet, and yet . . ."

She paused. She held me there with her eyes, but there was no way I was going anywhere. She had me riveted in place, forgetting about the hour and the cold that was beginning to creep into my fingers and toes. No wonder she had a reputation as an amazing professor. No wonder she'd captivated you.

"Well, let me interrupt myself and say that this is not one of those hideous lectures of someone claiming something awful about God's will," she said. "Or how Mars dying was meant to be, because *no*. If God exists, and he created this"—she holds her hands out, indicating the up, the down, the everything—"then he is indeed loving. Too loving to take a beautiful kid like that from us, I'm convinced."

"Yeah," I said. Yeah to all of that.

"What I *am* saying is that an unseen chemical connects with another unseen chemical, and there is a reaction. Or there's the *smallest* connection like this . . ." She holds up our clasped hands. "Or this . . ." She circles her arm, indicating all of us together on the mountain. "And there is a reaction. There's a change, the smallest, tiniest, invisible change, even, and that creates another change, and another, and all those tiniest shifts gather with all the other tiniest shifts, the most brief, indiscernible connections. And then . . . something moves. It becomes something else that moves something else!" She windmills an arm, releasing an ectoplasmic glow of neon yellow from her sleeve, which lingers in the black of night before disappearing. "The connections—they go on and on. Him here, you loving him, us loving his, him loving us, it altered things. It will have never not happened. He will have never not been."

My throat got too tight to speak. I squeezed her hand. Her skin was old and soft. It had seen some things.

"Everything is a chain, and a chain reaction." She winds two fingers around each other like a cord, like a rope. A tether. "Wait! Mars and I talked about this before! Have you seen the images of the chain reaction that is DNA?"

"They're amazing," I said. "It's hard to believe that's *in* us."

"In us. *Is* us. And do you know what it looks like?" I did. I remembered the pictures of it, and understood where she was going with this. I hadn't even realized it before. "A figure eight connected to figure eight connected to figure eight. Infinite mattering. Isn't it wild, how we can't see some of the most essential things that exist?"

I was feeling it right then, the connection, the chain reaction, the way this tiny, invisible, and brief moment had changed me. Like that first night, but different. Everything seemed unimaginable but possible. And then Chester called out.

"Where the hell are you guys? You better not have been eaten by a tiger."

"We're here!" Lily called, waving her glow-arms. Her tiny glow-arms, next to tiny me, on this small, small log that was once a minuscule tree, on an invisible dot of a planet.

"We're right here," I called, too.

We were. I was. Loss wanted to take me with it, but I was still here.

Before we headed back down the dark trail, Sandrine found it for me, Ophiuchus.

"Dark patch of sky," she said.

"Dark patch of sky," I agreed.

"Do you know the thing I keep forgetting but try to remember? We can't see Voyager, but it's looking back at us."

And then Rainey appeared by Sandrine's side.

"Hey." She seemed hesitant. I realized that it was maybe more than the reluctance an average person might feel walking up to two grieving people on an important mountain under a somber and too-meaningful night sky.

"Hey, Rainey," Sandrine and I said at the same time.

"I, uh . . . I never told you guys . . ." Rainey trailed off, like she wasn't sure we'd want to know whatever it was she was going to say. But if it had to do with you, and it seemed like it was about to, we wanted. We wanted it all. Everything.

"Never told us what?" Sandrine said.

"It's awkward. I feel a little funny about it, and I wasn't sure if I should share it, and then I thought, I should just . . . I think, um . . . I was maybe the last person to talk to him. Or, communicate with him."

"You were?" It felt like every dial in my body had suddenly been turned up. "What did he say?"

"It wasn't much. It wasn't anything. Something silly. It wasn't like him at all. I mean, sometimes he'd send me some astronomy article, but never anything like this."

"What, what?" I asked.

"It seems wrong that this is the last thing, and maybe that's why I didn't mention it. Because he was embarrassed. And he wanted a . . . female perspective. He said he tried to call you . . ."

She looked toward Sandrine, and now every dial in *her* body had been turned up. "He *did* try. But I . . ." Sandrine's voice was high, squeezed as if she'd forced it through the narrowest opening. She couldn't say it. "You know *why* he called?"

"Well, yeah. He'd gotten his hair cut."

"He'd gotten his *hair cut*?" We knew that. But that's *why* you called? Sandrine's pitch went up another notch. It was hope and confusion. A haircut? She hadn't even dreamed of that, I'm sure. A hundred other things, but not a haircut.

"He was so embarrassed about it! He thought it looked bad. He hoped it looked okay. He wanted my opinion. He was worried what *you* were going to think of it, Margaret."

"What *I* was going to think of it?" Now my voice was high and squeezed.

Rainey showed us the text. Sandrine read it aloud. " 'Be honest! Oh my God, I look like a pruned hedge! Or a hedge*hog*. Margaret loves my hair. What if she hates it?' "

Sandrine and I looked at each other. "The Taco Time call," I said.

"That's not a breakup," she said.

"Oh my God," I breathed.

"I told him he looked fantastic," Rainey said. She showed us the texts. *You look fantastic.* And then your reply: *Honestly?* And then Rainey again: *She's going to love it*, and then the tiny heart of your reaction.

Oh, Mars. Oh, oh, oh.

That was it. That was all. But it was the most immense all to both Sandrine and me.

"I want to see the picture," Sandrine said, and so Rainey found it and turned her phone so we could.

And, Mars! There you were. You were in your car. It must have been immediately after you left the salon. You must have been experiencing that post-bad-haircut panic we all have, in desperate need of reassurance that we haven't drastically wrecked ourselves. I could see a streetlight behind you, and the dome light of your VW above, two glowing moons. And your hair *did* look a bit like a pruned hedge, and it *did* look a bit like a hedgehog, the most beautiful hedgehog I'd ever seen. A bit uncertain, a bit worried, a bit goofy, and so very beloved.

"Rainey, oh my God. You have no idea what this means." Sandrine had started to cry. With relief, you know. With utter relief. You called her about your hair!

"Really?" Rainey said.

"Thank you, Rainey. Thank you for telling us." Now I started to cry, too. With relief, with a new hope, because we *hadn't* broken up, had we? You didn't think so.

We launched our bodies onto a surprised Rainey, group hug. What if she hadn't told us? What if she hadn't shoved aside her second thoughts and taken this maybe-risky chance to share? We all hold the pieces to one puzzle, don't we? Your haircut, Mars. Your bad haircut was such a fucking gift.

We lifted Rainey right off her feet. She still had her phone in her hand, and so you, that photo of you with your funny flat hair and sweet, vulnerable eyes, bobbed and lit in the night around us. You shined, we all did, tiny, tiny, so very small and momentous, under the spectacle of the universe, the starry blanket deserving our awe and astonishment.

Thank you, Mars, I silently said toward that dark patch of sky. That's all it looked like, but just because something is invisible, it doesn't mean it isn't there.

I was hoping for rain, but that didn't happen. There was no storm. There was just a hedgehog haircut, and Chester giving me a giant bear hug as we all stood in the parking lot before we got in our cars, Santiago buckling Norty into his seat in the new CR-V.

"You should try to get that thing in a rocket," Chester said.

"My phone?" I was teasing him. I knew what he meant.

"Put it on a real record, and get it sent up." He loved this whole idea, the record of you, golden.

"I'm pretty sure *that* won't happen," I said. "I'm not exactly Carl Sagan."

"Are you kidding? There's been lots of stuff that's gone to space. Ben!" he shouted. "Tell her some strange shit that's gone to space. Eleanor Roosevelt's watch, or something?"

"Amelia Earhart's. Astronaut Shannon Walker wore it up. You're thinking of the hair samples of presidents that Enterprise is taking up," Ben called.

"Lots of musical instruments," Sandrine piped in. "Saxophone? Flutes, guitars, bagpipes . . ."

"A didgeridoo," Santiago added.

"Didgeridoo doo. Didgeripoo poo," Norty said. When is a poop joke not worthy of a chuckle, I ask you.

"Didn't Legos go up once?" Rainey asked.

"Legos and . . . Wait. You guys will love this." Ben pointedly looked at me and Maurice, who leaned against the back of his truck. "Pizza delivery."

"You're kidding me," Maurice said.

"What? No way," I said.

"I think it was Pizza Hut? In 2000-something. They filmed the guy eating it. A Russian cosmonaut. If I remember right, they even got the logo painted onto the ship." Ben unzipped his backpack, retrieved his windbreaker, and put it on.

"We've got to tell Dad he's thinking too small with those baseball caps," I told Maurice.

"Seriously, though. You've got to get that thing up there," Chester said.

"Hello, NASA? This is Margaret," I joked. My project wasn't even a thing. It was just stuff on a phone.

"Can you even imagine?" Sandrine said. "That was his real dream, ever since he was a kid. To blast off into space." I remembered. Also, this: *A dream should be respected.*

"A Buzz Lightyear toy . . ." Ben was still thinking.

"Don't you know anyone, Lil?"

"That was a million years ago. Everyone's dead. Cool idea, though, Chesty."

"Ooh, ooh," he said, doing his best gorilla. I wished I'd recorded that. "Well, you *have* to put it on a record, at least."

It seemed pretty much impossible, Mars. But tell that to Carl Sagan. And after that night, after a second miracle on Tiger Mountain, tell that to Margaret Vittorio.

"Hey, is that rain?" Sandrine said. "I felt a splotch on my head."

"Let's get out of here," Maurice said.

Chapter Twenty-Nine

"My brother . . ." –Greeting from Maurice Vittorio

"Greetings from this planet of water, earth, and sky, to you in the infinite cosmos. Love you, buddy." –Greeting from Chester Gibson

"From the tiny blue marble in the Orion Arm, all honor and respect, dude." –Greeting from Ben Woods

"Hello and love from this earthling to a human being who was one in a billion in an expanding universe." –Greeting from Rainey McDougal

"Miss you, buddy. I know you're out there." –Greeting from Santiago Abril

"Miss you, buddy. I know you're in here." –Greeting from Norty Abril

"On to the Oort, my cherished friend!" –Greeting from Dr. Lily Salzman

Guy with the most handsome haircut ever, photo by Mars Zevon Rivers: *Pictures of Mars*

You weren't sure if you were even going to go to your graduation ceremony, remember? You were still deciding, anyway. Since you'd been going to Seattle Central College and had only spent a year at North Bend High, you kept saying it seemed silly to go, and things like caps and gowns and yearbooks were expensive. You were saving for UW, and all the stuff you'd need when you moved out and into the dorms, your solid plan until your mom and Arizona. You still had a lot to decide. You had a lifetime of decisions ahead of you, plus mistakes, plus successes, plus regular old days of TV shows and getting the flu and the plunge of cold when you swam in the lake, let alone things like babies that had your eyes, or a home. But I saw you at my ceremony anyway. I imagined you walking up there and shaking with one hand and getting the diploma with the other. I imagined it the whole time, except for the moments when Addy was up there, and Priya, and Maddie, and when I was.

I saw you at the party my family threw, too, even though I told them I didn't want one. I saw you scooping Mom's amazing potato salad onto your plate, and chatting with Arthur by the grill as he kept careful watch on the hot dogs. Addy was showing you her new red Chucks, and Priya was telling you about when she first learned to dive at the pool in Kirkland, her fingertips joined in a point in the air to demonstrate. I saw you playing badminton on the back lawn, me and you and Maya and Max on one side, Maurice and Sandrine and Millie on the other, Millie swinging her racket around dangerously. Without you, we lost. Maurice could get surprisingly competitive at sports. I saw your mom with us, too.

Invited and feeling a bit awkward until Mom showed her the small, round piece of lapis lazuli she kept in her pocket lately—a reminder of inner vision and self-awareness.

It was going to be like this, I guess. The daily jabs—from a slice of bacon cooked just right (we agreed: crunchy, not floppy), to your same nose on other people, to songs, always songs. And then the huge pummeling on big life moments like graduations. Like starting college. And college graduations, and weddings, probably. Births, deaths, planetary alignments. Those eclipses that happen once in eons, those moons.

The Snapshot numbers ticked up and up and up. It was hard to believe that so many strangers wanted to see a photo of a leaf or listen to Lily saying, *On to the Oort!* But it was more than those things individually, I was beginning to understand, just as the Golden Record itself was more than the individual voices or the songs or the diagrams of the human body, the photos of traffic or birds in flight. All those things spoke to the largest things you couldn't see and couldn't put on a record. You couldn't put love on that record, the complications of it, the enduring nature of it, and you couldn't put hope on it, either, or struggle, or sorrow, or confusion, or the glorious lift of insight. You couldn't put the frustration of that traffic, and the wonder of those birds in flight. You could show the dolphins leaping and the sound of dogs barking, but not the way dolphins name each other and remember each other, even after years of separation, and you can't show the way a dog will put his chin on your knee when you're sad. You could record the sound of a kiss and a laugh, but not how that kiss and that laugh made you feel alive. I could show the photographs of your friends, but not how their steadiness got you through the worst times. The most profound things couldn't be seen: the hope, the fear, the struggle, the survival. The joy and the grief. The love and the loss, most of all. Why couldn't we have one but not the other? We just couldn't, and both were what it really meant to be a human in the world.

I could include a photo of Mom and Dad dancing on the Marymoor Park grass to Solar Flare, the opening act to Panorama City at the summer concert series, but it wouldn't capture Maurice's joy and pride and relief that I swear I could feel as I watched him on that stage. I could also record the conversation that Sandrine and I had had that day at Bear Creek Studio, but it would never show the way pieces were falling into place, as if the finished picture were making us, rather than the other way around.

"You're so cute. Look at you," I told Sandrine.

She stuck her tongue out at me. Bear Creek Studio was in a converted barn in Woodinville, and, wow, what a setting for photos. The barn itself was beautiful, with its deep-toned wood, and there was a pond, and a wide, picturesque lawn, and a tree house, even, for writing or editing or recording vocals.

That's where Sandrine and I were right then: on the deck of the tree house with its gnarled wood railings. I'd just taken some shots of her in her jeans and T-shirt, barefoot, as she sat in that black chair in the corner, next to the curved, rough-hewn wall that looked like bark. The more I got to know her, the more I understood why

Maurice was head over heels for her. We both were. I hoped we could have her forever.

"You should ask Everett," she said then.

Everett was the young sound engineer. He was fluffy-bearded and unnervingly quiet, with intense, dark eyes that zeroed in hard as he listened. He only became animated when he was speaking another language containing words like *Avid HDX* and *Neumann-U-*something, *Teletronix* and *Trident* and *Phoenix*. Code words. Space words. *Crowley and Tripp Naked Eye*—cool telescope words.

"Ask Everett what?"

Sandrine tipped her chin at me, as if to say, *Come on, Margaret.*

Of course, I knew what she was talking about. We'd been discussing it a lot, after Chester's *You have to!* that night, after the miracle on the mountain. And I'd been thinking about it endlessly, nonstop. Without an actual record, the project seemed like a new hole of unfinished business. A longing, unfulfilled. Once I reached a hundred and sixteen photos and twenty-seven songs and fifty-five greetings, I'd need to stop. But then what? It would be an ending, and neither Sandrine nor I wanted that.

"The record," I said.

"I can't stop thinking about records!" Sandrine said. "And not just because we're recording an album. The word itself . . . Referring to the physical object, yeah, but also *the record*, the story written down. Did you know that when Sagan was making the Golden Record, he realized that 1977 was the hundredth anniversary of Edison inventing the phonograph? But, also, 1977 was the year that Peter Goldmark, the dude who created the LP, died suddenly in a terrible car crash. The symmetry, you know?"

"Wow. That's wild. I feel like you have a new song coming on."

"Maybe, sure. Probably. But, Margaret, we *need* an actual record. We need the object itself."

"We do," I agreed.

"There's got to be a way."

"*No one's* going to be able to do it. I've looked it up a hundred times, I told you. The greetings and the music, yeah. But the images were, like, binary numbers that corresponded to pixels? I think it's impossible."

"But what if Everett knows? He could be *right here* with the information we need, same as Rainey was."

I groaned. She was right; he might be the one to ask, if he weren't so intimidating. Everett, who had the reputation of being exceptionally good at what he did. Everett, with his silent but penetrating talent. I had beaten down my anxiety again and again over this, over you, but it took every chance it could to roar back.

"Ask."

"He's always so . . . busy," I said. Busy, singularly focused, locked away on the other side of that glass and tucked into the enormous L of that control panel, which had so many switches and dials, it looked like command central to our rocket ship. If you were there, Mars, you'd get Everett talking about his grandmother and his favorite Mexican restaurant, and how he fell in love with his first turntable. Connections mattered to me now, so much, they did. But they were still difficult. Starting one up on my own, you know. Each person was a world, something large and somewhat overwhelming to navigate.

"Come on." Sandrine grabbed my hand and pulled.

"I'm coming, I'm coming." The tree house stairs were circular and steep. She was going to make me break my ankle. Did they really need me there to take photos for the Solar Flare site? I doubted it. Not all day, every day, for sure, but I think Sandrine liked having me around. Needed me around, maybe, the same way I needed her. We held you between us, like those parents who swing a child by each hand, only our loved one wasn't here.

We found Everett in the kitchen, slicing a mango. The band was taking a break. The Sub Pop guys had just left, and Xavier was up in the lounge, messing around on his phone. Maurice and Dre were sitting under the umbrella table outside, drinking the Sanpellegrinos with the lemons on them, our favorites.

"Hey, Everett," Sandrine said.

I became automatically nervous, really nervous. Silent, intense people like Everett *really* made me uneasy. Like, you're busting into the closed, quiet museum of their mind, and the guards are on their way. You need to grab the artwork, and quick.

"Mm-hmm," he said. His cheek was full of mango.

"I'm not even sure how to ask this, but can you record both sound and images on an LP?"

He chewed. His gaze went hazy as he hunted in the jammed file drawers of his vast knowledge. "Well, you could store sequenced or encoded data on vinyl. A video of the images. The resolution would be shit, but analog video encoded on vinyl—they did it on gramophone records in the 1920s—Phonovision." He grinned.

"Awesome name," Sandrine said. She said it all offhand and casual, right? But she was making excited *See? See!* eyes at me.

"And then, in the late seventies, early eighties, CED . . ." I'm going to admit right here that he went on to explain how it worked in detail that just made *my* eyes glaze. "Just a sec." He typed into his phone. "Some of these dudes just fucking love their ancient tech, you know? And, uh . . . Hang on."

We hung on. As we did, I ventured forward. I risked it, you know. Connection. I told him about my project now, too.

"Oh, yeah?" He looked up. As I mentioned, he didn't say a lot, but when he did, you listened. Sandrine sure did when he was in that booth and they were on the other side of the glass. "Cool. I did a project on Voyager when I was kid. A diorama, cardboard and sugar cubes." I smiled. We'd had lots of school reports, but this was our first diorama. "Okay, okay. Found it. Some people in Vienna sell the old VinylVision records? You need a turntable and a TV and a converter box to play them."

"Playing it isn't even the most important part, is it? Otherwise, we could just do a video. The thing is, we just want the actual record." I'd never said it out loud like that to anyone but Sandrine. But even I could hear it, the determined will behind the word *want*.

And then, just as Lily had said, a small shift gathered with another. "Whoa, wait!" Everett said. "Looks like you can send them an image, and they'll send you the *sound file*. Results may vary. Haha—it actually says that. But if we can get those files, I know a place that does custom lathe-cut vinyl records."

We. Another we joining the thousands on my site who were on board for this particular voyage. "That sounds really expensive," I said.

"I'm thinking, crowdsource?" Sandrine was always one step ahead.

"A hundred bucks," Everett said.

"That's *all*?" Sandrine's eyes popped. "Can you send me the link?"

Zoop, zoop went the texts, like aliens communicating. In seconds Sandrine was scrolling the site as I looked over her shoulder.

We both spotted it. "Custom colors!" she said.

We stared at each other. Do you see what I mean? We could have recorded that entire conversation, but you'd never be able to catch what we both felt inside right then, at the same moment. Her eyes began to water, and then mine did. That shining bit of humanity that is hope, though—it was completely invisible, completely silent, even if it was the loudest thing in the room.

We knew which color, of course. We didn't have to say it: gold.

Chapter Thirty

Diagram of infinity symbol, carved into fifteenth-century stone: *Pictures of Mars*

First known representation of the Ouroboros on a shrine of the sarcophagus of Tutankhamun: *Pictures of Mars*

Ophiuchus: *Pictures of Mars*

Diagram of DNA: *Pictures of Mars*

Hands making infinity symbol, photo by Margaret Vittorio: *Pictures of Mars*

One thing about a family business: The family and the business sit as close as me and my brothers when we're all around the dinner table. Or as close as salt and pepper. They go together sometimes, sure. But other times, they're best kept separate.

The point is, I asked George first, not my father.

"You want *more* hours?" he asked. "Not less, for school?" Around us, there was the slam and banging of pans, and the *whick, whick, whick* of chopping knives, and a call of *hot, hot, coming through!* But Dad was up front, BSing with the customers, doing what he liked best.

"More, for, like, a year?"

"Huh," George said. "But UW in the fall?"

"*Next* fall."

George let out a low whistle. "You haven't told him yet." Him, meaning our father, of course.

"I need some time, George. I'm not ready. And the band's going to be recording into November, at least. Sandrine wants me around to take photos."

"And that's what you want to do?" It sounds like a romantic comedy featuring a pizza place, but George seriously had flour on his cheeks.

"That, and study photography next fall. I want to get better before they go on tour after the album releases in a year."

"Awesome. You and Maurice, you got the creative genes. Me and Arthur got the pizza genes. And, hey. More hours, easy! Do you need some backup when you break the news? Family dinner?"

"Nah. I got it." He didn't look too sure, but I wanted to face this myself. "Hey, George? I have a question. Speaking of, you know, the pizza genes? The *that's what you want to do* . . . Is this what *you* want to do?" I gestured around. Papa Angelo's, the whole salt and pepper, together always.

He smiled. "I know it's hard to believe, but yeah. I always have. Me and Arthur both. It's in our blood. Well, it's in *all* our blood, but we got some strange passion for it, too, I guess? Dad, he likes the people. But Arthur and I, we like the pizza. We like making it. We like making it really, really good."

"It's in your blood *and* your heart," I said.

He patted his apron. The triangle of pizza right there on his chest. He grinned, shrugged. "If my clothes didn't smell like marinara, cold cheese, and charred crust, I wouldn't recognize myself," he said.

"God damn it, Margaret! NO!" My father slammed his fork on the table. In terms of objects to slam, it was pretty mild. It made a loud *tink*.

"It's just for a year," I said.

"And then a year becomes another year? What then? What about all you worked for? You'll skip college over my dead body."

"I think a year sounds like a great idea—" Mom said, tried to say, before she was interrupted.

"How many pictures does that band need? What the hell is *that* about? Hanging around them doing this—" He pretends to snap photos with an imaginary phone.

"I'm building a portfolio. And I want to study photography next fall."

"Study *what*?"

I practiced this with Addy and Priya, and especially with Winifred Evans. Speaking my truth. Staying grounded in it, in his storm, or anyone else's. Risking it. Saying the thing, because you didn't know what was possible when you did. You could make new friends, or find a new career, or experience a hedgehog-haircut miracle.

"Photography. I love it. I just love it."

"And you're really good at it," Mom said. Oh my God, she *meant* it. It sounded like she maybe even believed in me.

"If I learn and get good at it, and take some great shots on the Solar Flare tour, who knows what it might lead to." *A dream should be respected.*

"*Tour?* Absolutely not." My father shook his head. I told myself it looked more like Frank than anything else, that time Sandrine had to put drops in his ears. "A tour is no place for a young girl."

"A young woman—"

"Sex, drugs, who knows what goes on." He interrupted Mom again. "You think I'm gonna let you do that?"

Mom's face was turning red. "First, you don't get to let—"

"It's not even *safe*," he said. "The creeps around the music scene? All those sleazy guys looking for girls?"

"ANGELO VITTORIO!" Mom slammed both of her palms on the table, hard. This was no *tink* of a fork. "*Stop* interrupting me. And stop interrupting Margaret." You wouldn't have believed it, Mars. She was furious! I'd never seen her like that, her face so red, her eyes blazing. Jeez. Where had *that* been? Maybe she'd been afraid of it herself, you know, because *man*. It was a little stressful, honestly. I hoped someday she might find a middle ground, you know, between saying nothing and this anger, but it was a start, I thought. It's hard to explain, but I could *see* it starting.

Well, my father could, too, because he went silent.

Whoa, the land in front of me was entirely unknown, but I kept my voice firm, just like I'd practiced with Winnifred Evans. "This is my plan. For my own life."

"Margaret? You don't need your father's, or *anyone's*, permission to do what's right for your own self." Her voice was firm, too, now. Maybe she'd also been practicing.

The man in question pressed the back of his spoon into his mashed potatoes, making a lake.

I stepped even further into the unknown land. My mom was beside me, so I could. "Dad. You actually take away my power and agency when you do all that *big man protecting the purity of the girl* shit," I told him.

"God, I wish I'd said that, Margaret," Mom said. I felt bad for all the regret in her words, but I was also glad for it.

"I didn't mean—I, uh, I . . . mean . . ." he stammered.

"It is," I said. "Mean." And more, so much more. Domineering and controlling, but he had shut up. I didn't entirely understand what had happened, but I could see one thing. Here it was again: a shift making another shift.

And, wow—yet another one was happening now.

"I'm sorry," he said.

I couldn't keep up with all the comments and messages. *Love is forever!* said finneyl89. *RIP Walt Drucker, Voyager Fan Dad*, wrote dannydruck89. *Beautiful tribute!* wrote Ready21Greta, and on and on . . . Five thousand, ten, thirty-five thousand . . . Inexplicably, the followers of *My Voyager* grew and grew over the summer. Grief groups shared. Solar Flare fans shared. After Panorama City shared, the numbers jumped to fifty-two thousand.

I didn't even understand a number like that. I was afraid of that number, my God. But my love for you—I don't know. Somehow it was larger than the fear. I was learning this about anxiety, Mars. It was a lot like grief. It was persistent. It came and it went and then it came back again. It was never gone, and likely never will be. And it wasn't some evil outside force to fight against; it was an understandable part of me that I had to work with. One thing I could do was let the love be louder. Let the belief be louder.

Photo of Dr. Quentin Baleaf's waiting room

Photo of a photo: dolphins leaping

Photo of grass mat of porch reading *elco*

Photo of a milkshake straw

Photo of University of Washington Planetarium

Photo of a text: *I miss you so much I can't stand it.*

Photo of *Pelican*

Photo of Tiger Mountain

Photo of a mossy glade surrounded by ferns and huckleberries

Greeting from Adelaide O'Riley, neighbor: *Greetings from the folks on the dock to wherever you are, son.*

Greeting from Yves Leroux Lo, water taxi driver: *Hey, Grom! Hope you're hanging loose, dude.*

Music of Mars: "Frank and Jesse James" by Warren Zevon

Sounds of Mars: The splash of a girl jumping in a lake

Sounds of Mars: Bell tower with recorded chimes

Sounds of Mars: The flap of a sail

And on, and on. Music, sounds. A hundred and sixteen photos, beginning with the one of Janite holding baby you, twenty-seven songs, and fifty-four greetings.

There was one left. It was the middle of September, and it was starting to get dark earlier and earlier. The leaves were suddenly orange again, and the air smelled like the sun leaving. I opened my window so I could inhale the night and look at the sky. Carl, snug in his turtleneck, looked on calmly from his frame.

I put on your blue flannel shirt. I pressed record.

After I got the sound files of all the photos from the company in Vienna, Everett helped me add them to the files of the music, the sounds, and the greetings. Sandrine and me, we'd made the artwork for the label, a copy of the real Golden Record, with the starburst and the squiggles, and the symbol that would always look like infinity to me.

We sent it off to the place that custom-made the lathe-cut vinyl records.

We waited.

While we did, on a whim, on a chance to connect, to make a small shift or a big haircut miracle, I gathered up all the photos and sounds and sent them to the email address Sandrine had given me.

You never know, I thought. It was important to say the thing, whatever it was. Just, Janite might like to have them, too.

Chapter Thirty-One

"That quote you loved from the Carl Sagan article—how, somewhere, something incredible was waiting to be known? You were my something incredible, you were my known, you were my voyager. I love you, Mars, and I miss you so much, I can't stand it."

—Greeting from Margaret Vittorio

Three weeks later, I watched the tracking of my package as it moved from Chicago to Seattle. The day it was expected to arrive, I got all nervous. I didn't even tell Sandrine or Maurice that it was coming. It felt huge. I maybe needed a moment alone with it first.

With it? With *them*. There were two Golden Records, one on Voyager 1, and one on Voyager 2, and when I opened the box, there they both were. They were not made of copper and covered in gold plating, and they would not be affixed to the outside of a space probe, but they were there in my hands. Your Golden Records.

That night, I drove over to Maurice and Sandrine's. Before going up their steps, I rested my hand on the curved top of your old VW, and then I gripped the driver's-side door handle, then placed my hand on the hood.

"What?" Sandrine said. Her beautiful face was full of surprise. "You made one for *me*?"

"There were two," I reminded her.

We held them up. Their edges touched, two circles.

A figure eight.

At home, alone in my room once again under the wise and compassionate gaze of Carl, I set the record on my windowsill, the black night beyond.

I took a photo. *It's finished*, I typed. I added an emoji, the gray infinity symbol.

My last post. It was over. At that thought, my stomach wrenched. I held your record to my chest, and I sobbed, and then I was quiet, my sorrow doing its own figure eight.

I pressed *share*. That word could have been another one, a favorite word of yours. It could have been *connect*.

She didn't call, and we didn't see each other again or even speak, but a few days later, she was there. JaniteGooligan. It was a new account, and your mom was following only one page. The notifications went on and on. JaniteGooligan liked your post. JaniteGooligan liked your post. JaniteGooligan liked your post. JaniteGooligan liked your post. The shirt, the houseboat, the welcome mat. The leaf, the sounds, the everything.

She'd left only one comment. One beautiful heart on that photo of her holding baby you.

It was enough, you know. Her heart there, with mine.

As we headed into winter, my dread grew. October, November, Halloween. Thanksgiving, December first, then second, then third—we were getting closer, you know, to the worst day. It felt like a march, the heavy, horrible boots of soldiers, bringing devastation. It was the most ominous cloud, descending. I tried not to look at the calendar. I avoided dates. Every time one snuck in, I counted. How many until. How many were left. It was not just the anniversary (just), the way it would brutally smack and pummel, but it was the change into a new year, a year where you wouldn't be, wouldn't have been living in at all, any day of it, or day before it.

It had been a bad idea, maybe, to take a gap year. To just be at the studio with the band, and delivering pizzas, and hanging out with Addy and Priya and Maddie when they weren't in class. It wasn't enough, distracting enough. I'd open the *My Voyager* page and look at the images. I would play the sounds. I would see and feel everyone there, all the human beings who had experienced this part of human beingness. It made me feel less alone, but that hole was there and there and there, and I missed taking those photos. I missed the project, and the way it kept you with me.

I had worked most of that Sunday, a frigid, frigid day, wearing my fingerless gloves as I drove to Green Lake and Lake Union and Westlake, to all the people who greeted me with anticipation, reaching their hands out for a warm box. It was eight or so when I headed back to Papa Angelo's, done for the night.

The golden glow of the store looked snug and welcoming when

I arrived, but I felt so sad, you know, the kind of sad that would hit hard at moments, a sad that seemed like it would go on and on. I didn't go in yet. I sat in the car, and I took out my phone. God, it was cold! I was going to open Snapshot. I wanted to just see your shirt, or your shells, or *Pelican*. Just something. I wanted to hear the glug, which would bring back your laugh, and the way you'd crawled on that floor, gathering the cups. I wanted to hear a song that would bring back your dancing—on the crowded floor of Neumos, or on the grass in the evening at a summer concert, or in your living room, barefoot. Doing your signature move, the little shimmy plus the occasional finger snap for flair.

Oh, Mars.

Right on my screen, I saw the notification that indicated a message had arrived. There used to be many, many every day, but since I'd stopped posting, they'd gone down to a trickle. That night, there was just the red dot with a number one inside.

I tapped the icon, hit the message squiggle. And then, in the small circle, I saw the profile photo of a woman next to a rocket. Abby Oliveras.

I read the message.

Hi, Margaret! I'm one of the astronauts on the crew of an upcoming Artemis launch, NASA's new lunar exploration program, which will reestablish a human presence on the moon for the first time since 1972. My mission isn't scheduled to launch for several years, but I heard about your project and am very moved. We're not going as far as Voyager, but if you're interested, let's talk about bringing your Golden Record into space.

Was this real? It couldn't be real, could it? I looked up *Abby*

Oliveras, and there she was, in her orange space suit with the American flag on the sleeve, looking out at us with compassionate brown eyes and a warm smile.

I clicked her profile, and there she was again, the American flag behind her, a verified account.

My heart beat hard. My breath came out in little puffs as I sat outside Papa Angelo's. My hands shook as I typed. *I would be so interested. Thank you so much!*

I pressed send, and then panicked. Two *so*s! I sounded childish. I sounded juvenile. I *was* juvenile, okay! Oh my God, I couldn't believe it. I looked at the message again to see if I'd imagined it.

A response. A response already! *Wonderful. Let's talk.* Her phone number! Her actual phone number!

I let out a little *ah!* A gasp. My throat tightened with tears.

This was Lily's doing, I was sure of it.

I called Sandrine.

"OH MY GOD!" I shrieked.

"Are you all right?" She'd been answering her phone this way since you left us, even when someone wasn't screaming into it.

I told her. "It was Lily. I'm sure it was Lily!"

"Margaret! We're all on the mountain tonight. You've got to come and tell everyone! We're in the parking lot right now, about to head up. Maurice is here. Say hi, Maurice."

"Hi, Maurice," Maurice said. He sounded far away, but he wasn't. On this Earth, in the giant universe, he was right here.

"Wait," I realized. "Why are you there tonight?" It was a Sunday. They usually met on Saturday nights.

"It's the tenth, Margaret. Geminids," she said.

"Oh my God. I've got to go. I'll be right there."

"Jesus Christ, drive safely. It's so cold tonight. The roads—"

But I was already rushing inside Papa Angelo's. There was time for anxiety later. There was always time for anxiety, but not right now.

It was harder going up that trail carrying a bunch of pizzas, that's for sure. When I arrived, they were surprised to see me, and even more surprised to see three extra-large Sarafinas.

"Hot damn," Chester said.

"The pizza is smiling," Norty said.

"It sure is, and so am I," I said. I breathed into my hands. It was freezing up there.

"What are we celebrating?" Lily said.

"December tenth," Ben said. It was enough, actually, but there was more.

"As if you don't know," I said to Lily.

But she scrunched up her old face, baffled. "What?"

"The *thing* you did," I told Lily.

"Tell them, tell them!" Sandrine said.

"Tell us," Rainey said, her cheeks full of cheese and arugula and orange pepper.

"Lily, come on. Abby Oliveras? You told her about the record? You told ASTRONAUT ABBY OLIVERAS about our Golden Record and she wants to BRING IT UP TO SPACE?"

"Oh my God, Margaret! Wow. How *wonderful.* I swear, I had nothing to do with it," Lily said. "I wish I *had*. But this was all you."

And it was, sort of. Not all me, though. Me and you. Me and you and everyone on the record. Me and you and everyone on the record, plus CosmicRayS32, who was Evan Dellario, an engineer on Artemis. His dad did a report on Voyager when he was a kid, and it sparked a love of space that he shared with his son, which brought Evan to NASA, which brought him to my page, which then went to Abby Oliveras, which brought her to me on that cold, cold night.

It was another miracle of connection, maybe, or fate, or a sign, or the universe speaking. Or maybe just a tiny shift causing another tiny shift. New links joining other links, elements combining with elements. Carl Sagan and his whole team, with a dream and a hope of connecting to life on other planets, connecting to generations of children on this one, my father and Mrs. Fosmire, Everett the sound guy and his diorama, Evan Dellario and his dad, *you*. All the little kids and big ones, looking up at the stars and imagining what was possible.

And right then, as I stood on that mountain with a frozen nose and pizza breath, I got it. I finally got it.

I understood the Golden Record, and why it meant so much to you. It wasn't the record itself exactly, was it? It wasn't the sounds, or the images, or the attempt to describe what it was like to be a human on Earth. The fact that it was made at all—*that's* what mattered. The wild, beautiful idea of it, the outreach, the pure and improbable *hope* of that record said more about us than anything on it. It revealed the most essential things about us human beings. Our goodwill, for sure, yeah. But even more, our deep desire for connection. Our against-all-odds and everlasting *faith* that there is more out there, that there are mysteries worth believing in, even if you can't see them.

A shift, and then another, and another, and now here I am, ending one of the longest letters that ever was. Hurrying, because I want to finish this, I *need* to finish this, before I pack it into my bag along with your Golden Record. This record of the record, it's going with it. It's my *Murmurs of Earth*, the accounting of how *our* record was made.

I won't let that bag out of my sight on my way to Orlando, that's for sure. I'm a nervous wreck, and working hard to let the love be louder, because it's anxiety-provoking, to say the least, to carry something so precious. And to meet the person who will carry it in her actual arms as she boards that ship. To look into her actual warm, brown, compassionate eyes. To hand it over.

I have to finish this, is the point. But one thing is very clear by now. I'll never stop talking to you. I'll never stop hoping that you can hear. There are mysteries worth believing in, even if you can't see them.

And, you, Mars . . . You'll never stop talking to me, either. You have been, all along. Your whole life has been speaking to me.

This letter will already be with the record, golden and imperfect, an object in space joining other unlikely objects in space, Legos and guitars, dinosaur bones, a gorilla suit, and that pizza, of course. So, in these pages, I can't tell you what's going to happen. I'll be taking photos, though, and writing it all down, most definitely. Recording for the record what happens in this briefest of moments in the longest span of time.

But I can imagine it, because I understand how we got here: A man puts on a turtleneck and contemplates connection. Two people stand naked, holding hands; someone records a heartbeat, and a laugh, and a dog barking, a rainstorm; an engineer designs a piece of a rocket that connects to another piece. A record says, *Here I am, here we were*, to anyone who might find it. You can't even see these pieces, or even the spacecraft in the cosmos that carry them. You can't hear the laugh or the dog or the rainstorm on this tiny blue dot, but something has happened that matters. A shift, and then another: A song leads to a kiss, and a kiss to more, to DNA merging with DNA, to a baby, to tiny fingers that will one day become a young man's hand reaching for a young woman's hand, as they play a song that leads to another kiss. A circle and then another circle, a shift and another shift. Someone receives a recipe for espresso brownies, handwritten on notebook paper, and something shifts; someone gives a bulb to someone else to plant, and something shifts. Someone says, *Don't fall off that chair*, and someone says, *Here was that chair, here was that fall.* A record says, *Here I am, here we were*, to anyone who might find it.

And in a few days' time, that tiny, tiny record will be carried aboard that ship, as a tiny, tiny girl watches, anxious while trying to be brave, to be open. Elsewhere on that tiny, tiny planet, a tiny singer on a tiny stage sings a small song, silent from space, but here on Earth, hundreds of tiny feet tap, and somewhere else, a minuscule woman watches her minuscule television while holding a microscopic photo of a cherished son, and elsewhere, other tiny friends and loved ones gather around their little TVs like it's 1977, and elsewhere still, a tiny man makes a tiny pizza, and another sails a tiny boat, and an old woman looks into a tiny telescope on a tiny mountain.

They are invisible, but they are there, no doubt about it. That girl—she puts her tiny hands over her tiny ears now, because there it goes. The blast is enormous; it is so, so loud, but it's a blip, a bleep, a whisper. As that rocket rises, as it disappears, she sends her love straight up, up and outward, and she will go on and on loving, as that record spins, too, as *those* records spin, in parts of space that she can only imagine. Those Golden Records, about a golden boy, and a golden humanity, on a tiny spinning world. We connect, we bind. We're ropes, coils, strands, figure eights. On this invisible spinning dot, we are the tiniest human beings giving the biggest something we can, not an object you can see and hear, but a force you can only feel, a force that moves and shifts, that creates a chain of change, that matters. Something large, large, large—love. Love plus love plus love. Invisible, ongoing.

Lasting a billion years, Mars, my voyager. Lasting a billion years, at least.

Acknowledgments

Forever love and thanks to Michael Bourret, my incredible agent, who somehow manages to be exceptional at what he does, and kind, too. Huge gratitude, as well, to everyone at Random House Children's Books/Labyrinth Road—especially my editor, Liesa Abrams, who leads with such immense passion and heart, along with Mallory Loehr, Emily Shapiro, Rebecca Vitkus, Clare Perret, Ray Shappell, Liz Dresner, Cathy Bobak, Gabriella Murdoch, and Sarah Lawrenson, the RHCB marketing group, the school and library team (with special gratitude to Adrienne Waintraub, Katie Halata, Michelle Campbell, and Erica Trotta), our sales force, and the production and supply chain.

Love always, dear family: Evie Caletti, Paul Caletti, Jan Caletti, and Sue Rath. John Yurich, my husband: I love you beyond words. Thanks for being your exact you. And to my shining, funny, loving, and oh-so-precious clan of my kids and their kids—Sam and Nick and Erin and Pat and Myla and Charlie and Theo and Riley and Olly—thank you for being the joy and the light. I love you, infinity.